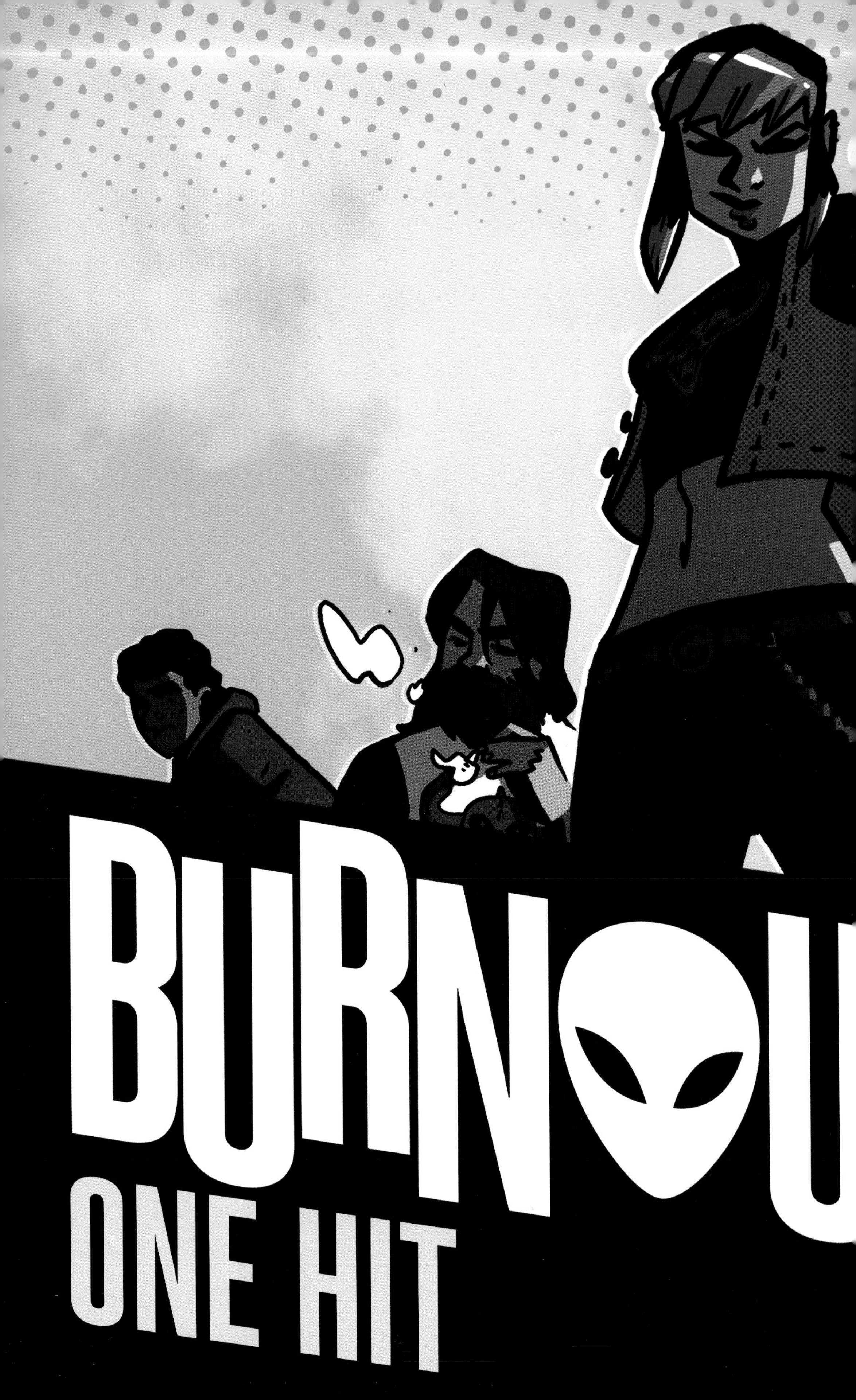
BURNOU
ONE HIT

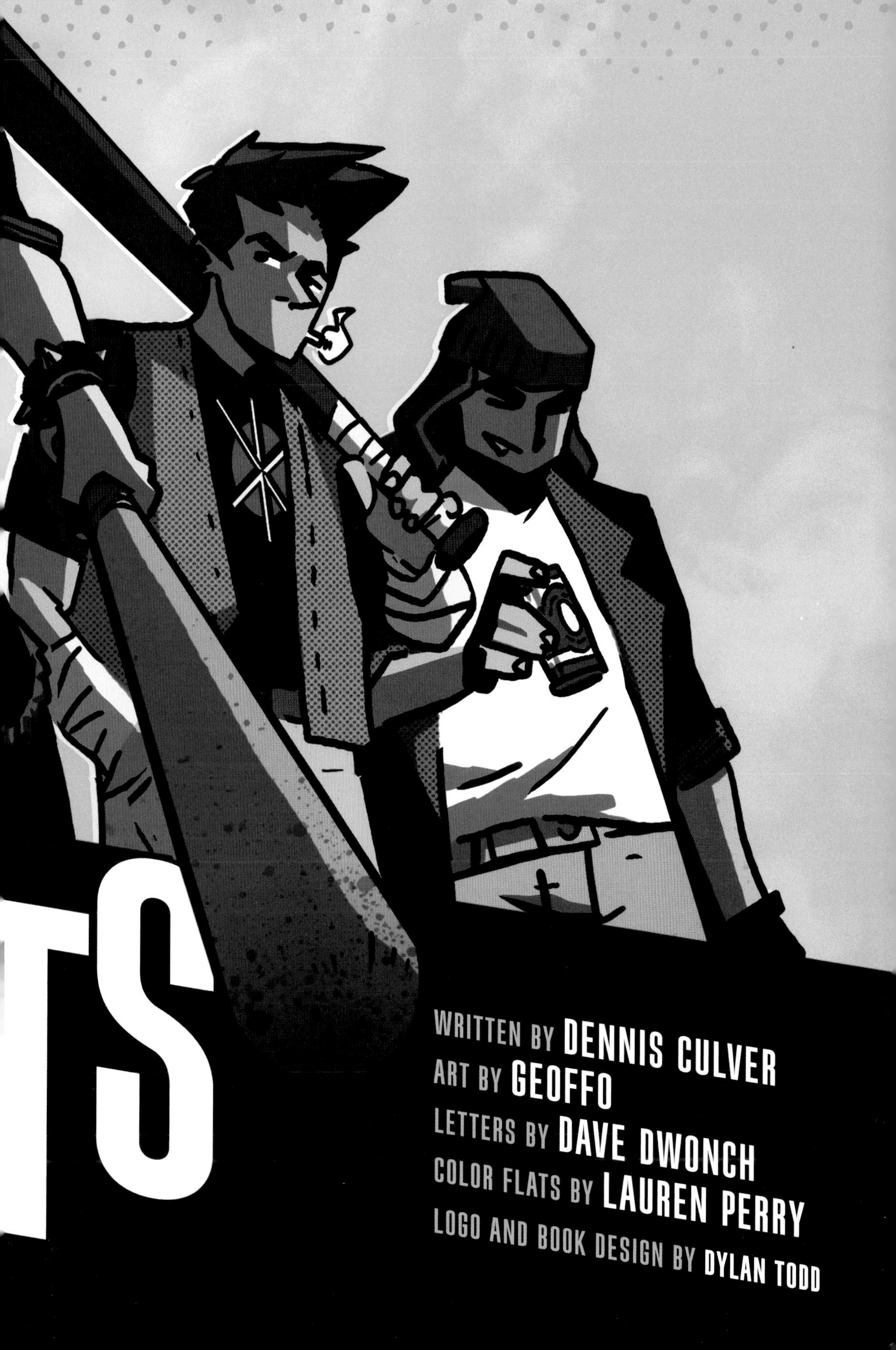
TS

WRITTEN BY **DENNIS CULVER**
ART BY **GEOFFO**
LETTERS BY **DAVE DWONCH**
COLOR FLATS BY **LAUREN PERRY**
LOGO AND BOOK DESIGN BY **DYLAN TODD**

IMAGE COMICS, INC.

ROBERT KIRKMAN chief operating officer

ERIK LARSEN chief financial officer

TODD McFARLANE president

MARC SILVESTRI chief executive officer

JIM VALENTINO vice president

ERIC STEPHENSON publisher / chief creative officer

COREY HART director of sales

JEFF BOISON director of publishing planning & book trade sales

CHRIS ROSS director of digital sales

JEFF STANG director of specialty sales

KAT SALAZAR director of pr & marketing

DREW GILL art director

HEATHER DOORNINK production director

NICOLE LAPALME controller

IMAGECOMICS.COM

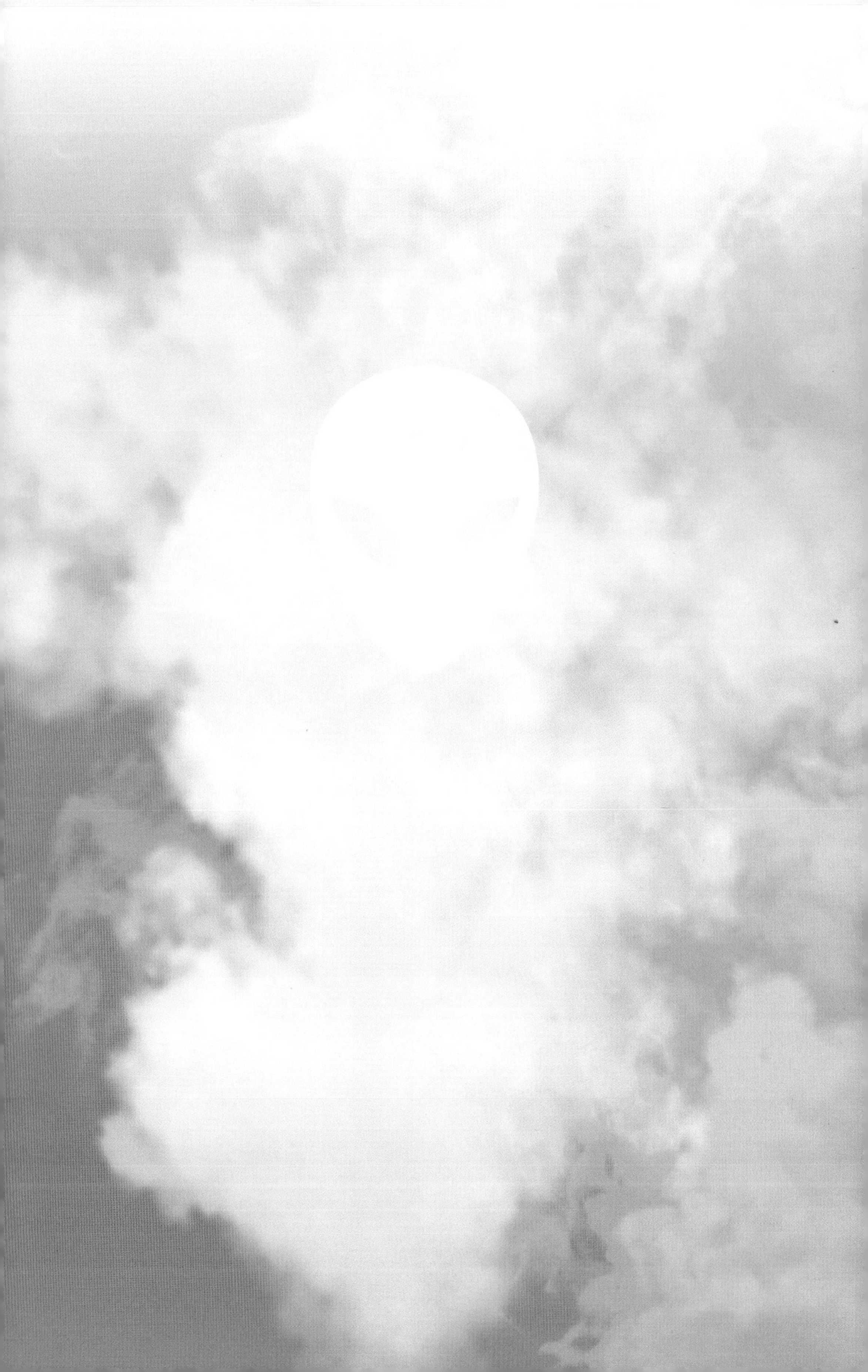

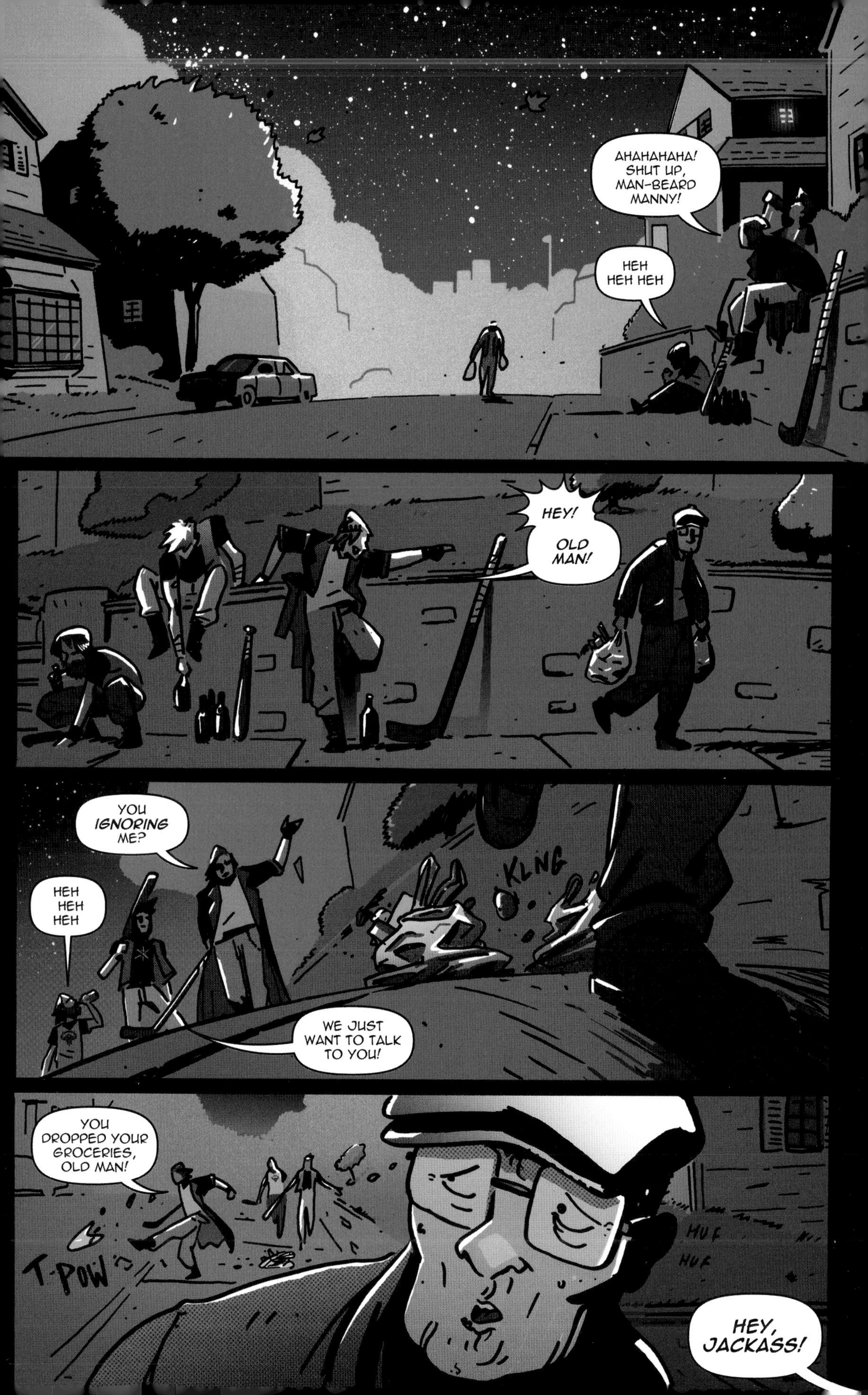
AHAHAHAHA! SHUT UP, MAN-BEARD MANNY!
HEH HEH HEH
HEY!
OLD MAN!
YOU IGNORING ME?
HEH HEH HEH
KLNG
WE JUST WANT TO TALK TO YOU!
YOU DROPPED YOUR GROCERIES, OLD MAN!
T-POW
HUF
HUF
HEY, JACKASS!

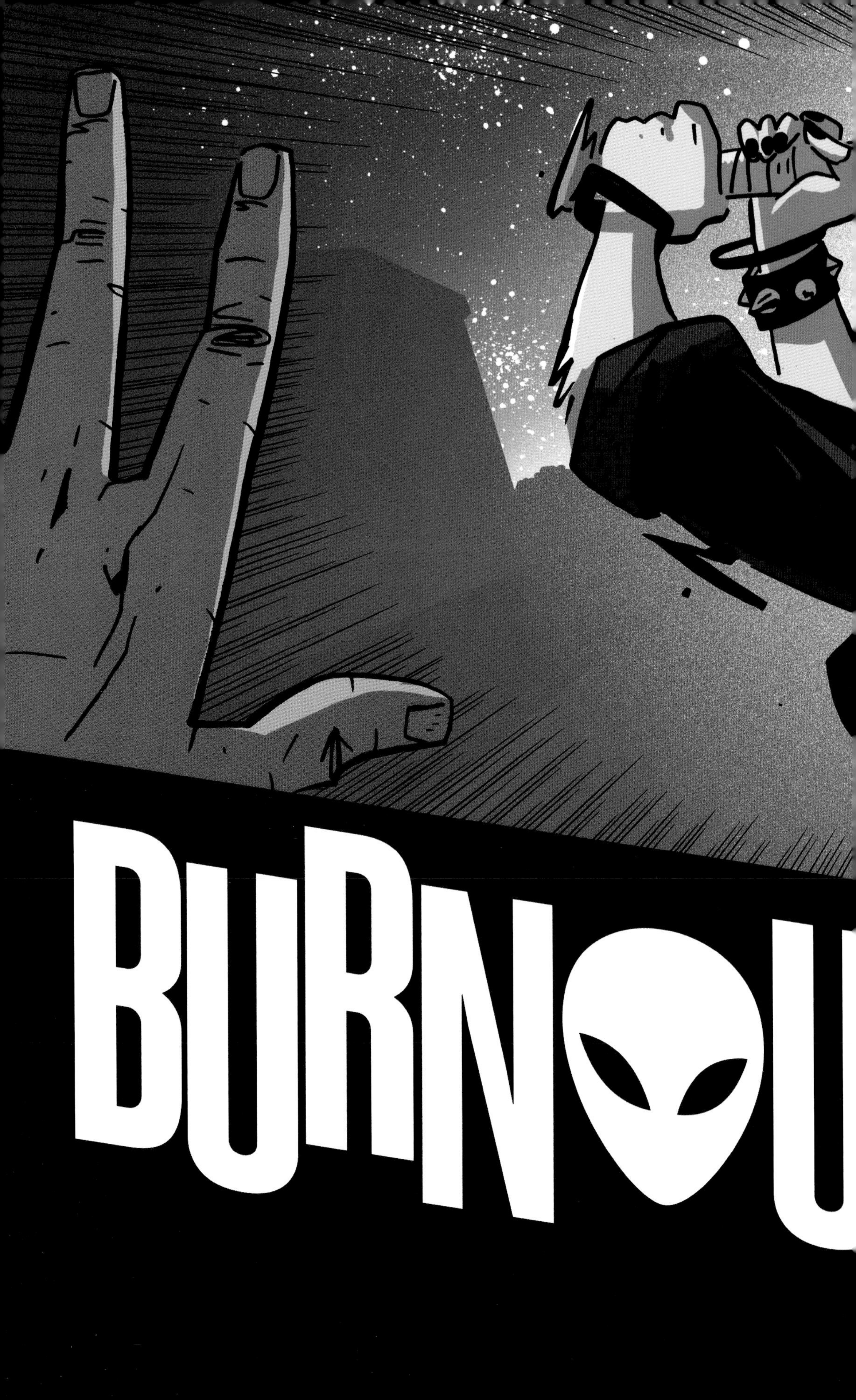
BURN

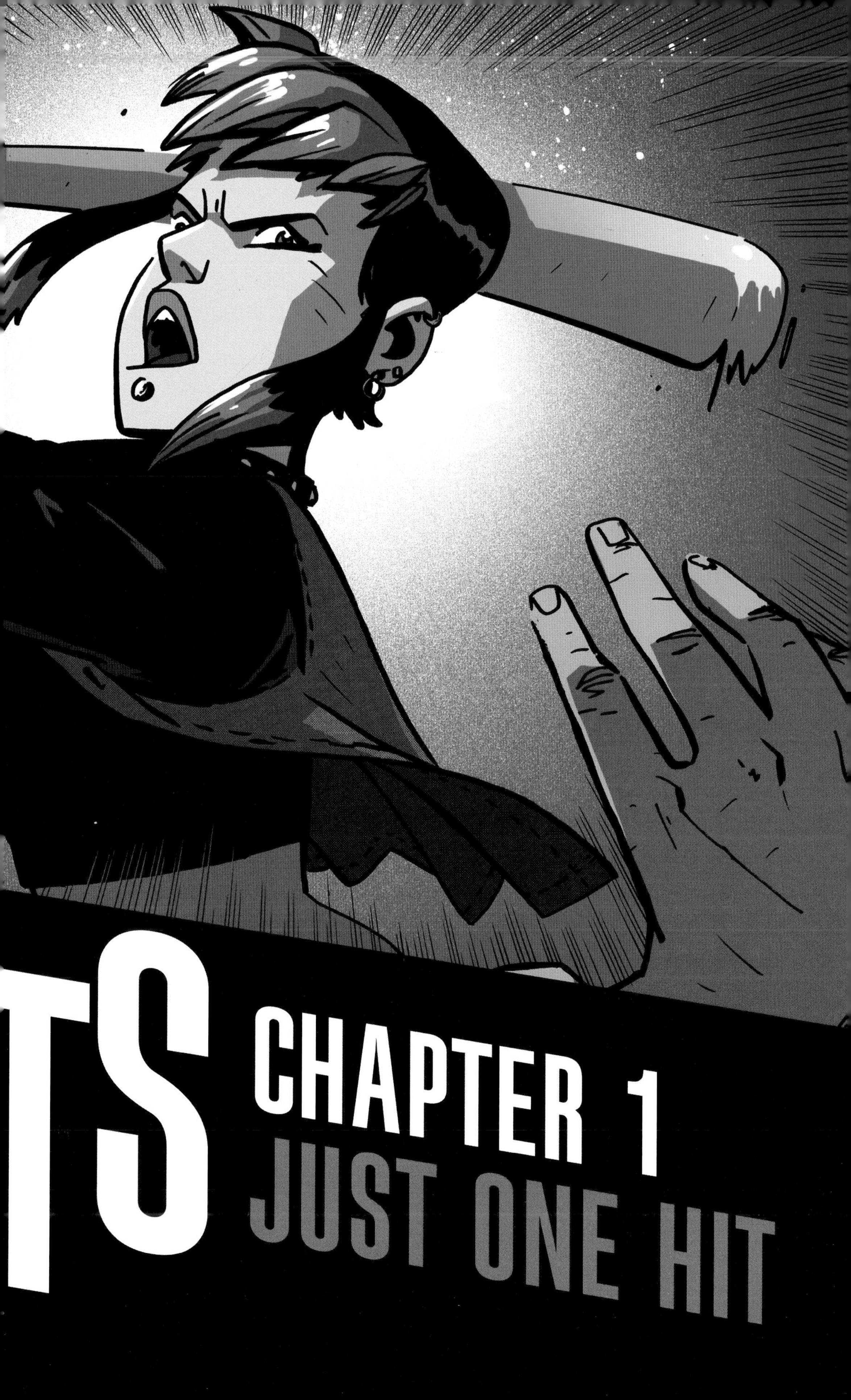

TS

CHAPTER 1
JUST ONE HIT

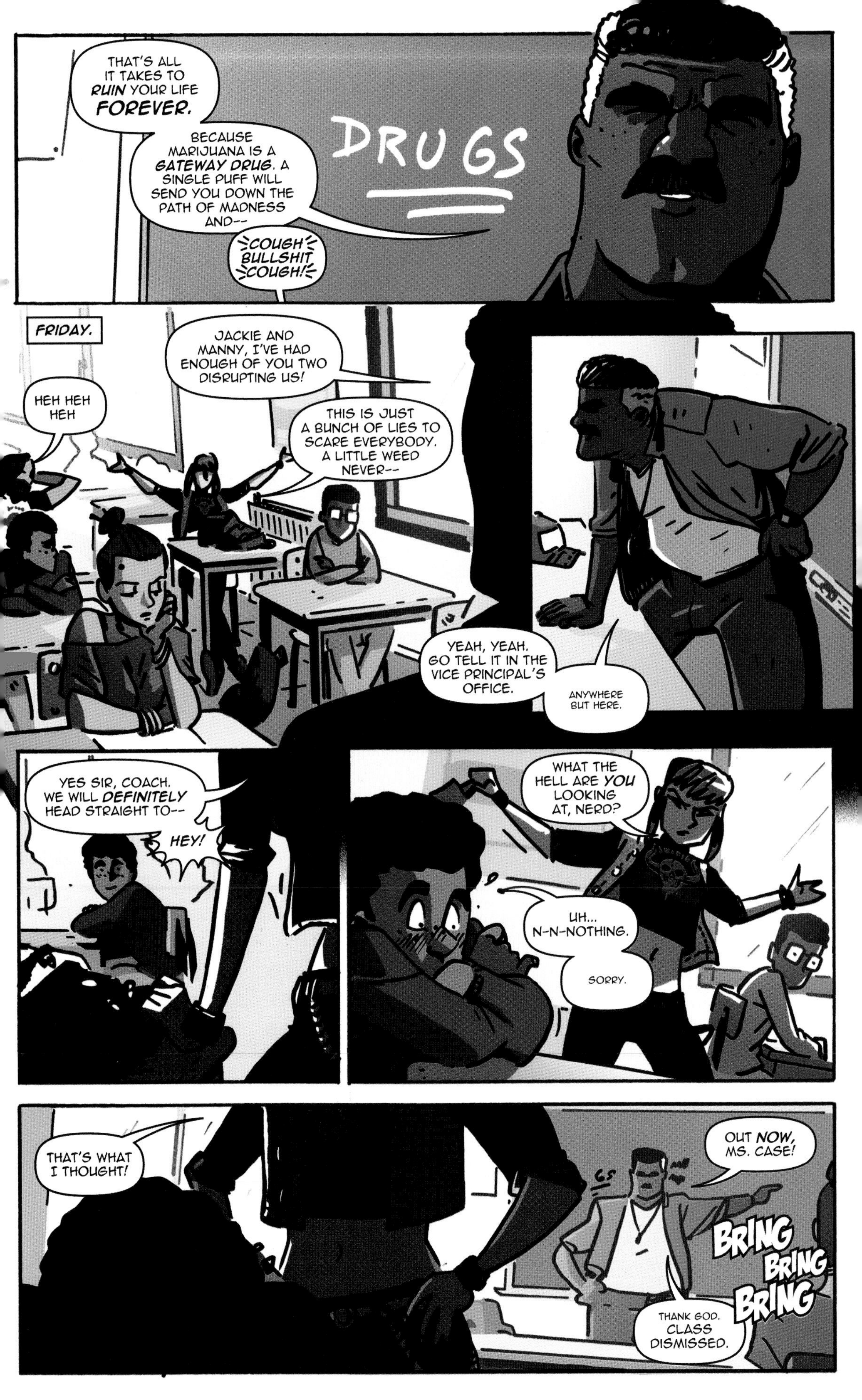
THAT'S ALL IT TAKES TO RUIN YOUR LIFE FOREVER.
BECAUSE MARIJUANA IS A GATEWAY DRUG. A SINGLE PUFF WILL SEND YOU DOWN THE PATH OF MADNESS AND--
DRUGS
COUGH BULLSHIT COUGH!
FRIDAY.
JACKIE AND MANNY, I'VE HAD ENOUGH OF YOU TWO DISRUPTING US!
HEH HEH HEH
THIS IS JUST A BUNCH OF LIES TO SCARE EVERYBODY. A LITTLE WEED NEVER--
YEAH, YEAH. GO TELL IT IN THE VICE PRINCIPAL'S OFFICE.
ANYWHERE BUT HERE.
YES SIR, COACH. WE WILL DEFINITELY HEAD STRAIGHT TO--
HEY!
WHAT THE HELL ARE YOU LOOKING AT, NERD?
UH... N-N-NOTHING.
SORRY.
THAT'S WHAT I THOUGHT!
OUT NOW, MS. CASE!
BRING BRING BRING
THANK GOD. CLASS DISMISSED.

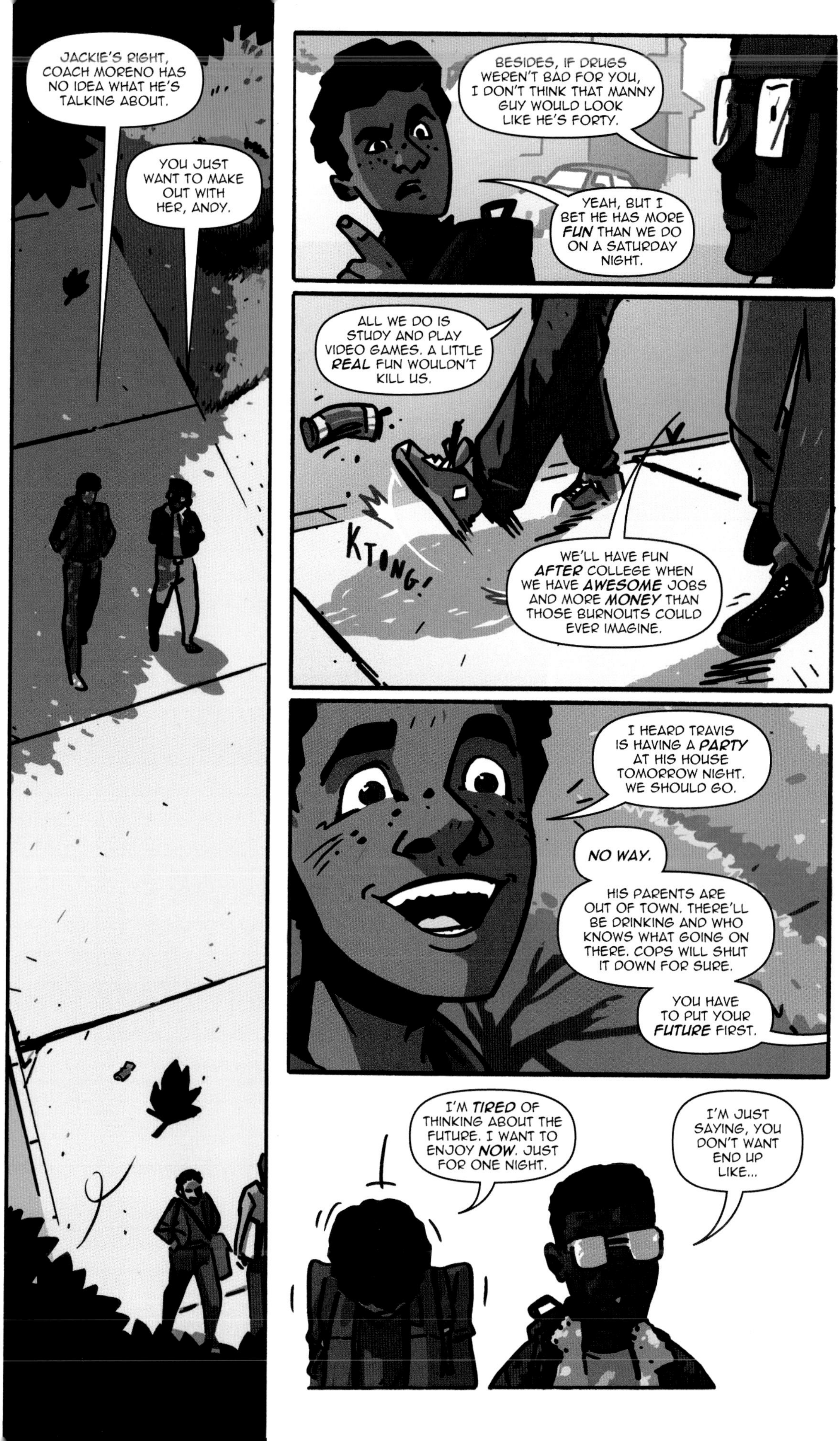
JACKIE'S RIGHT, COACH MORENO HAS NO IDEA WHAT HE'S TALKING ABOUT.
YOU JUST WANT TO MAKE OUT WITH HER, ANDY.
BESIDES, IF DRUGS WEREN'T BAD FOR YOU, I DON'T THINK THAT MANNY GUY WOULD LOOK LIKE HE'S FORTY.
YEAH, BUT I BET HE HAS MORE FUN THAN WE DO ON A SATURDAY NIGHT.
ALL WE DO IS STUDY AND PLAY VIDEO GAMES. A LITTLE REAL FUN WOULDN'T KILL US.
KTONG!
WE'LL HAVE FUN AFTER COLLEGE WHEN WE HAVE AWESOME JOBS AND MORE MONEY THAN THOSE BURNOUTS COULD EVER IMAGINE.
I HEARD TRAVIS IS HAVING A PARTY AT HIS HOUSE TOMORROW NIGHT. WE SHOULD GO.
NO WAY.
HIS PARENTS ARE OUT OF TOWN. THERE'LL BE DRINKING AND WHO KNOWS WHAT GOING ON THERE. COPS WILL SHUT IT DOWN FOR SURE.
YOU HAVE TO PUT YOUR FUTURE FIRST.
I'M TIRED OF THINKING ABOUT THE FUTURE. I WANT TO ENJOY NOW. JUST FOR ONE NIGHT.
I'M JUST SAYING, YOU DON'T WANT END UP LIKE...

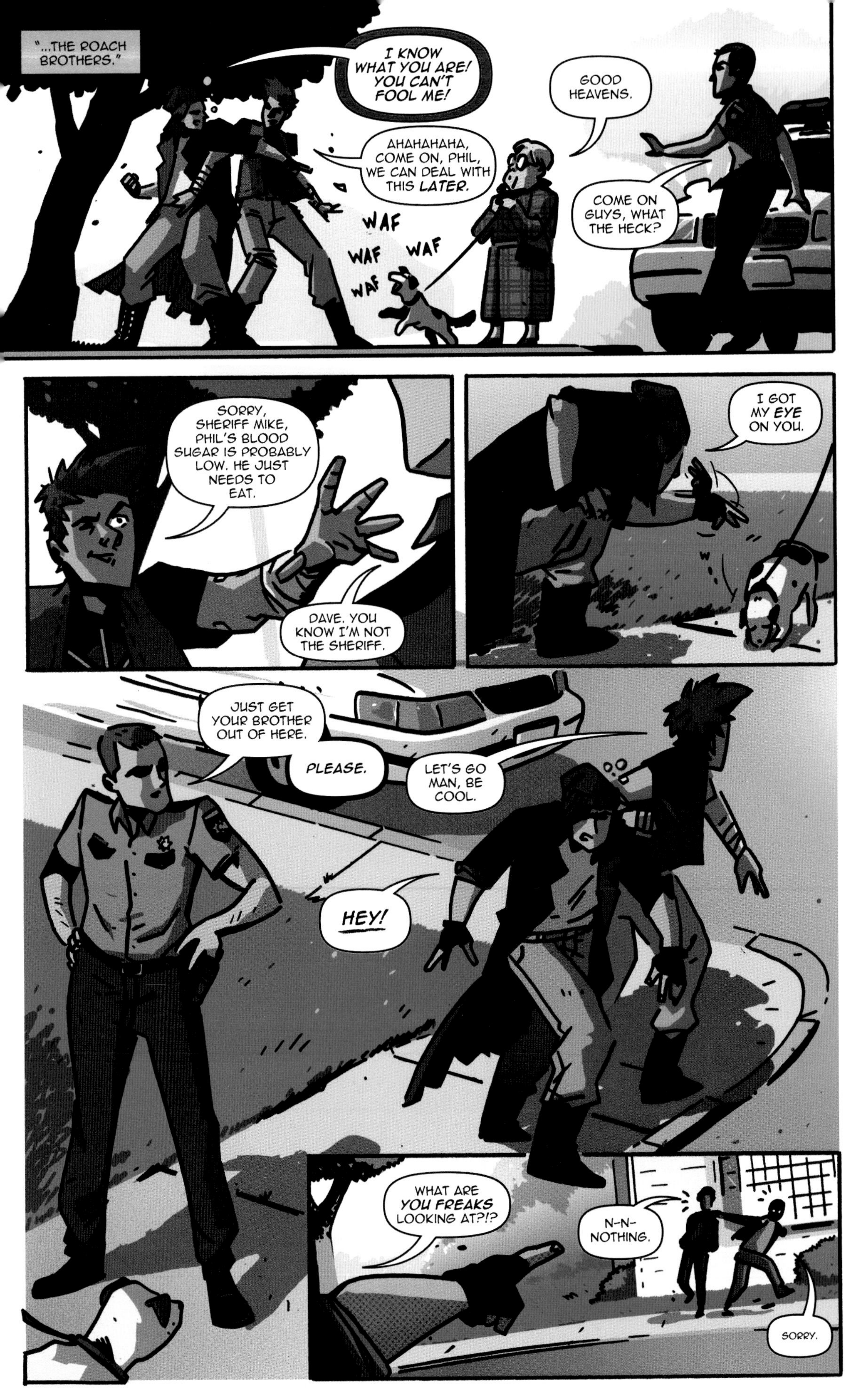
"...THE ROACH BROTHERS."
I KNOW WHAT YOU ARE! YOU CAN'T FOOL ME!
GOOD HEAVENS.
AHAHAHAHA, COME ON, PHIL, WE CAN DEAL WITH THIS LATER.
WAF
WAF
WAF
WAF
COME ON GUYS, WHAT THE HECK?
SORRY, SHERIFF MIKE, PHIL'S BLOOD SUGAR IS PROBABLY LOW. HE JUST NEEDS TO EAT.
DAVE. YOU KNOW I'M NOT THE SHERIFF.
I GOT MY EYE ON YOU.
JUST GET YOUR BROTHER OUT OF HERE.
PLEASE.
LET'S GO MAN, BE COOL.
HEY!
WHAT ARE YOU FREAKS LOOKING AT?!?
N-N-NOTHING.
SORRY.

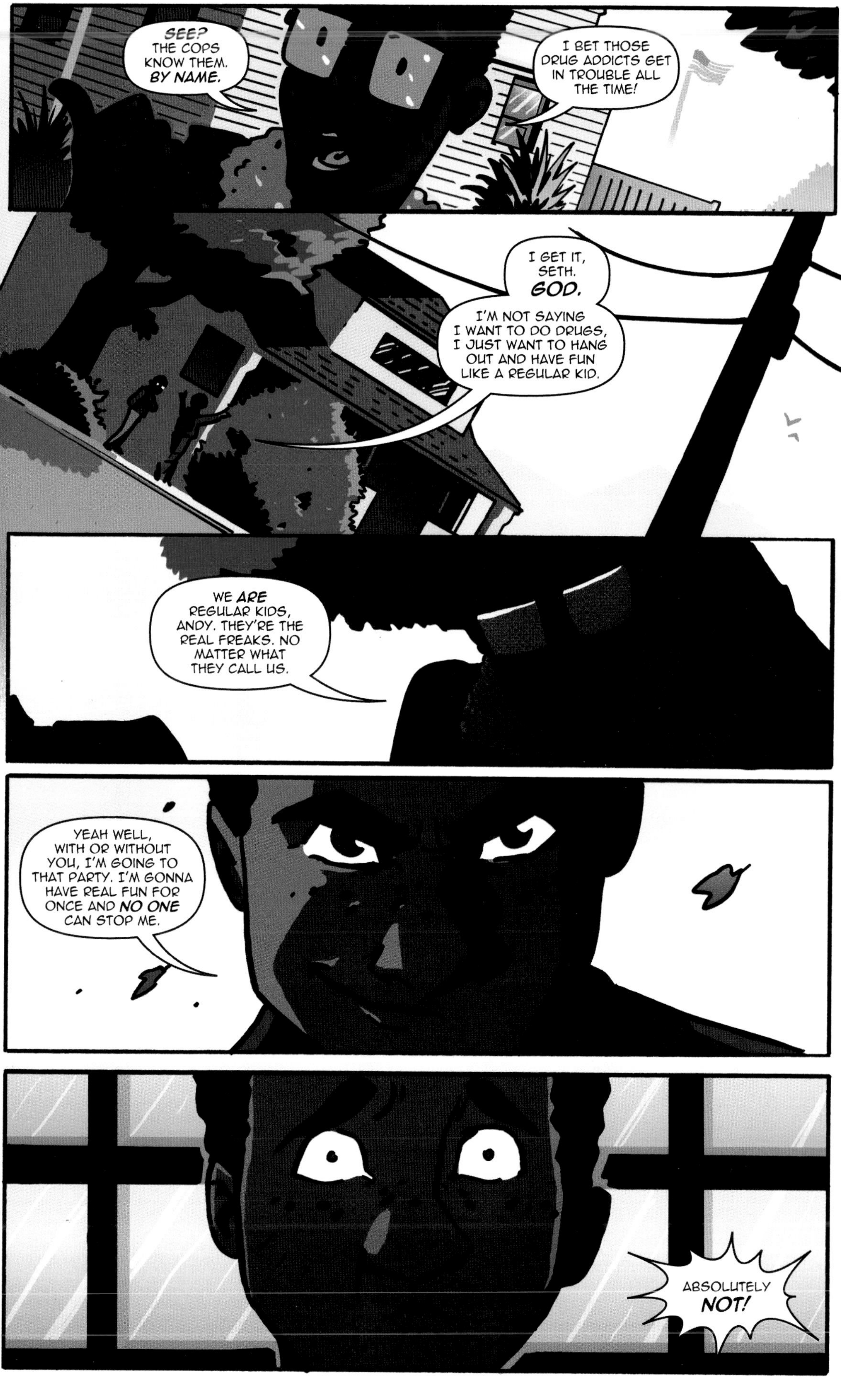
SEE? THE COPS KNOW THEM. BY NAME.
I BET THOSE DRUG ADDICTS GET IN TROUBLE ALL THE TIME!
I GET IT, SETH. GOD.
I'M NOT SAYING I WANT TO DO DRUGS, I JUST WANT TO HANG OUT AND HAVE FUN LIKE A REGULAR KID.
WE ARE REGULAR KIDS, ANDY. THEY'RE THE REAL FREAKS. NO MATTER WHAT THEY CALL US.
YEAH WELL, WITH OR WITHOUT YOU, I'M GOING TO THAT PARTY. I'M GONNA HAVE REAL FUN FOR ONCE AND NO ONE CAN STOP ME.
ABSOLUTELY NOT!

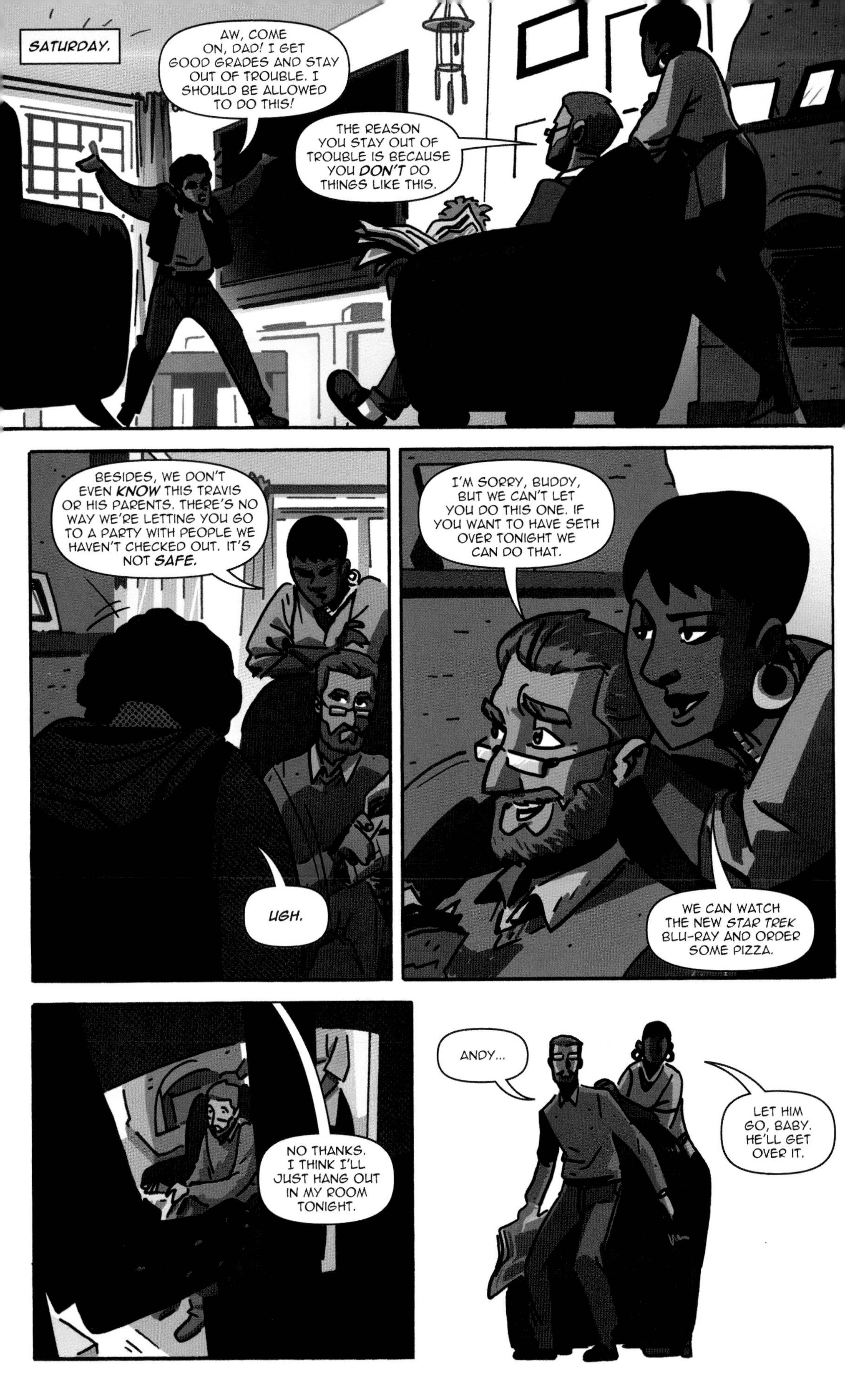
SATURDAY.
AW, COME ON, DAD! I GET GOOD GRADES AND STAY OUT OF TROUBLE. I SHOULD BE ALLOWED TO DO THIS!
THE REASON YOU STAY OUT OF TROUBLE IS BECAUSE YOU *DON'T* DO THINGS LIKE THIS.
BESIDES, WE DON'T EVEN *KNOW* THIS TRAVIS OR HIS PARENTS. THERE'S NO WAY WE'RE LETTING YOU GO TO A PARTY WITH PEOPLE WE HAVEN'T CHECKED OUT. IT'S NOT *SAFE.*
UGH.
I'M SORRY, BUDDY, BUT WE CAN'T LET YOU DO THIS ONE. IF YOU WANT TO HAVE SETH OVER TONIGHT WE CAN DO THAT.
WE CAN WATCH THE NEW *STAR TREK* BLU-RAY AND ORDER SOME PIZZA.
NO THANKS. I THINK I'LL JUST HANG OUT IN MY ROOM TONIGHT.
ANDY...
LET HIM GO, BABY. HE'LL GET OVER IT.

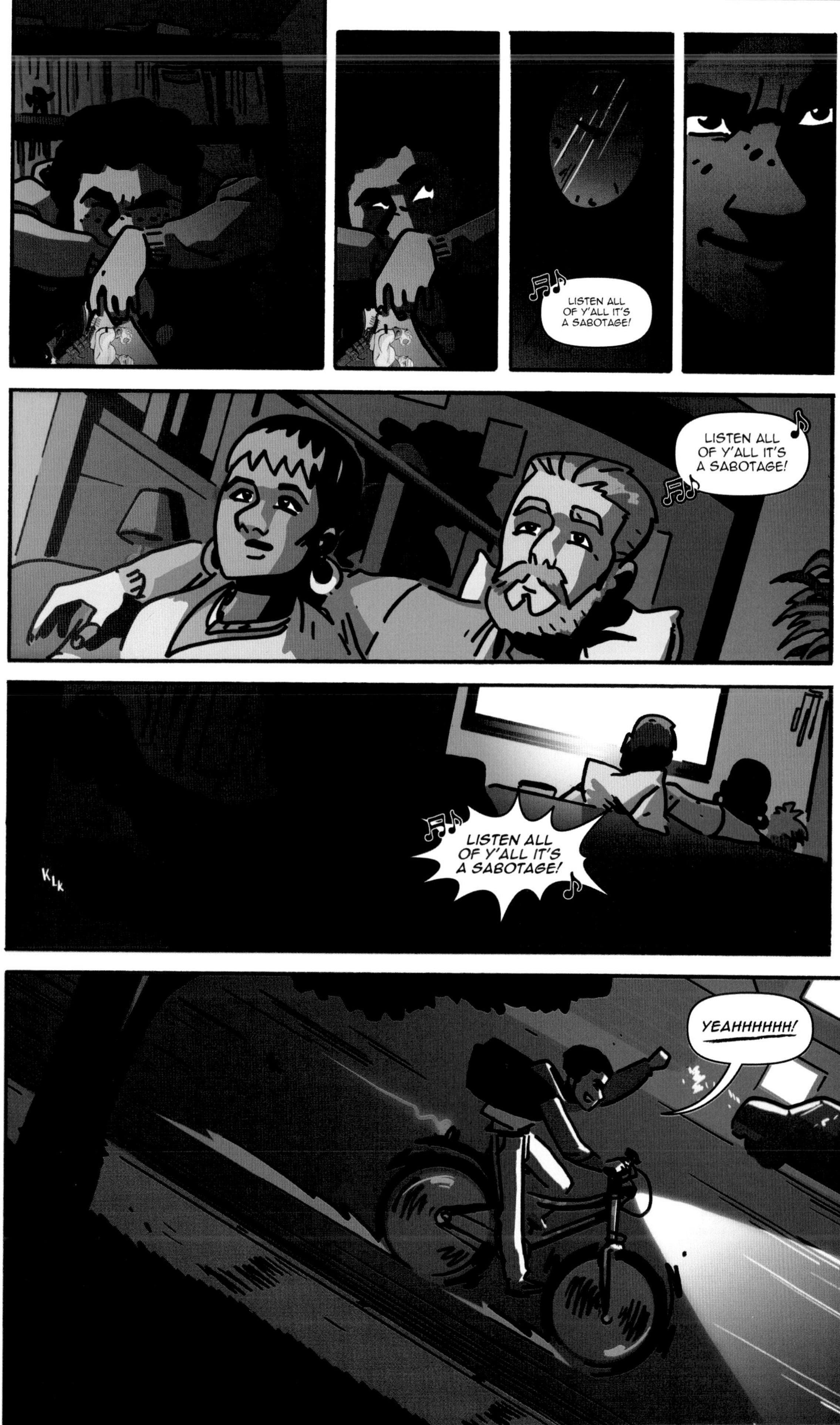
LISTEN ALL OF Y'ALL IT'S A SABOTAGE!
LISTEN ALL OF Y'ALL IT'S A SABOTAGE!
KLK
LISTEN ALL OF Y'ALL IT'S A SABOTAGE!
YEAHHHHHH!

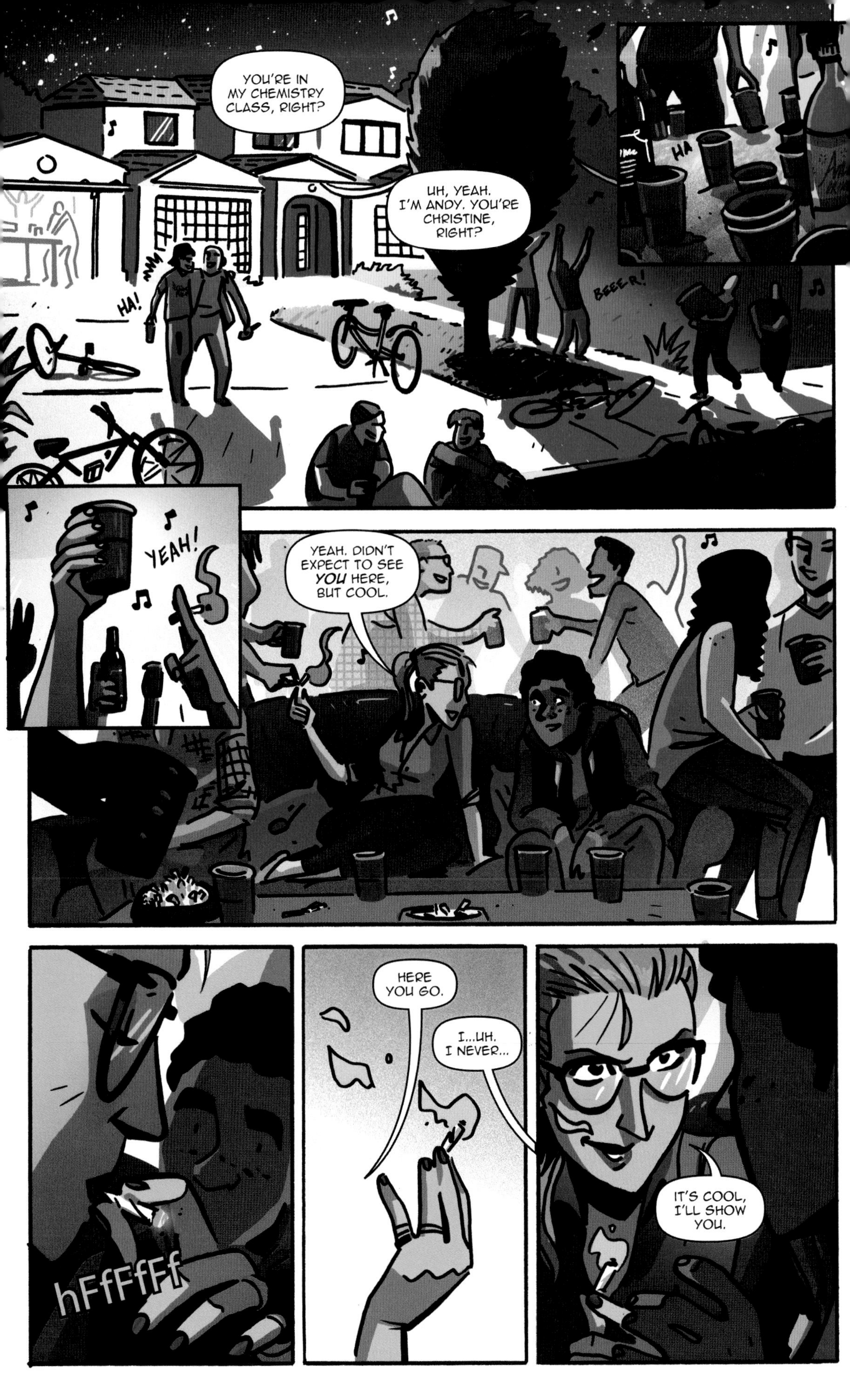
YOU'RE IN MY CHEMISTRY CLASS, RIGHT?
UH, YEAH. I'M ANDY. YOU'RE CHRISTINE, RIGHT?
HA!
BEEER!
HA
YEAH!
YEAH. DIDN'T EXPECT TO SEE *YOU* HERE, BUT COOL.
hFfFfFf
HERE YOU GO.
I...UH. I NEVER...
IT'S COOL, I'LL SHOW YOU.

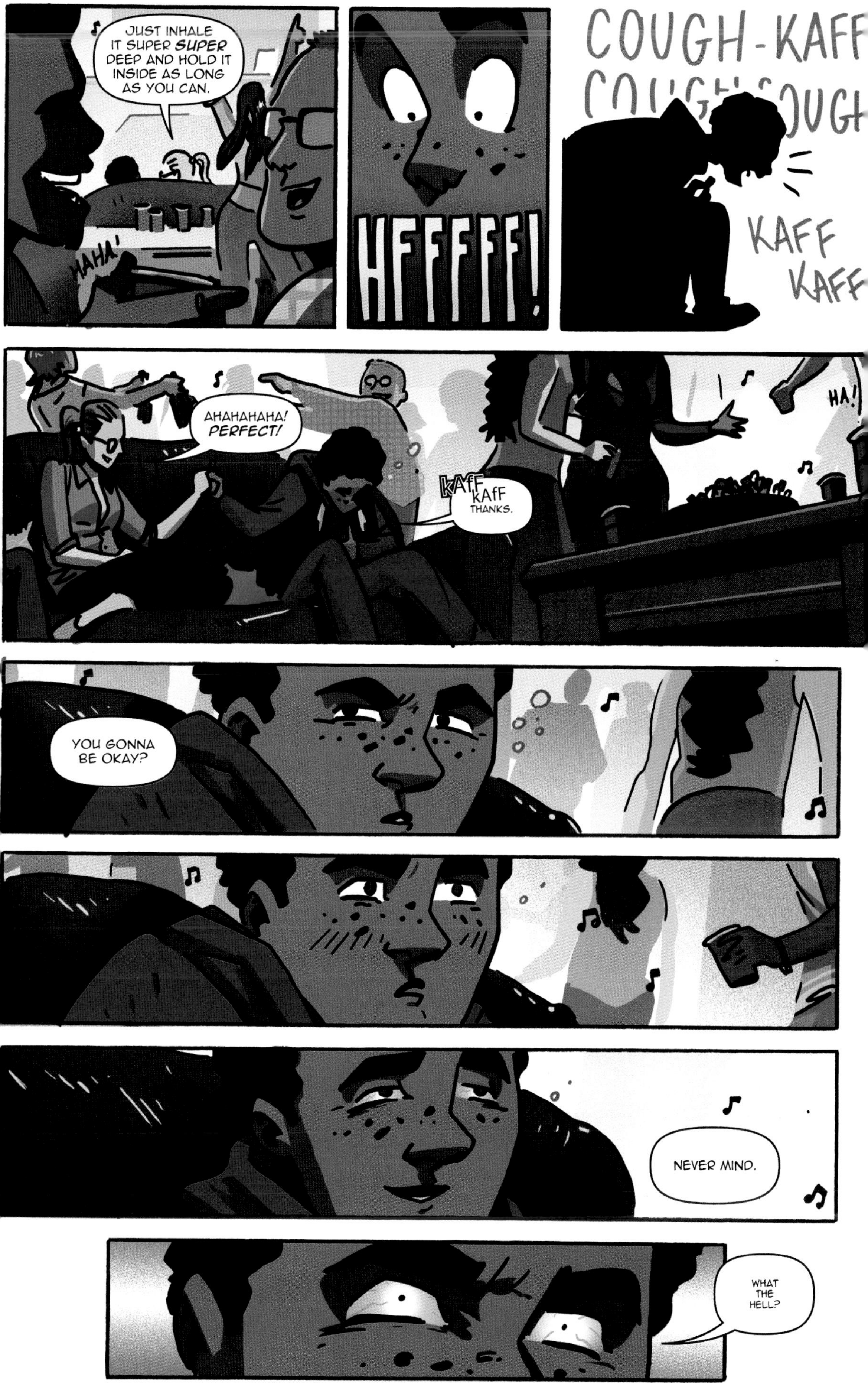

JUST INHALE IT SUPER **SUPER** DEEP AND HOLD IT INSIDE AS LONG AS YOU CAN.
HAHA!
HFFFFF!
COUGH-KAFF
KAFF KAFF
AHAHAHAHA! **PERFECT!**
HA!
KAFF KAFF THANKS.
YOU GONNA BE OKAY?
NEVER MIND.
WHAT THE HELL?

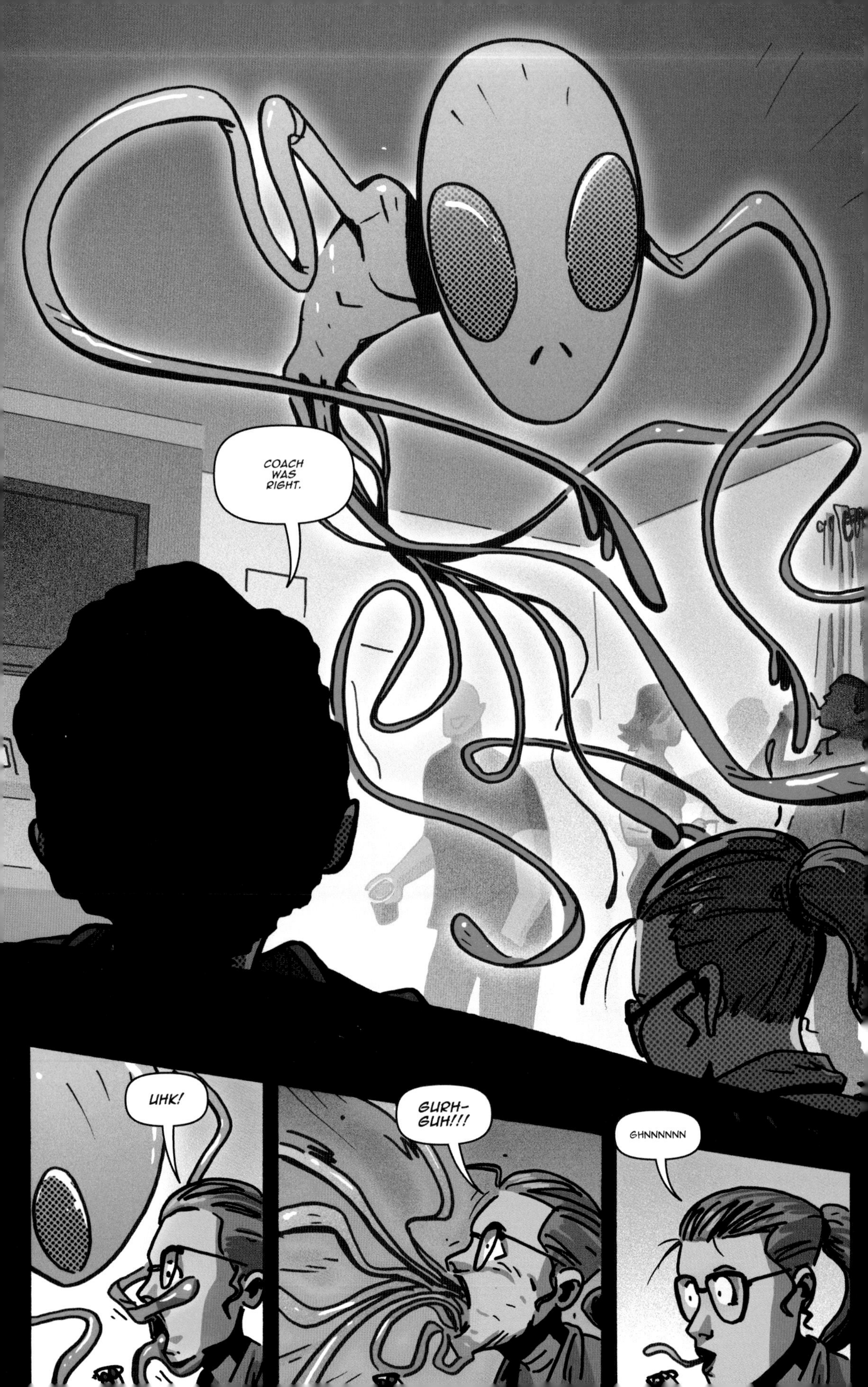
COACH WAS RIGHT.
UHK!
GURH-GUH!!!
GHNNNNNN

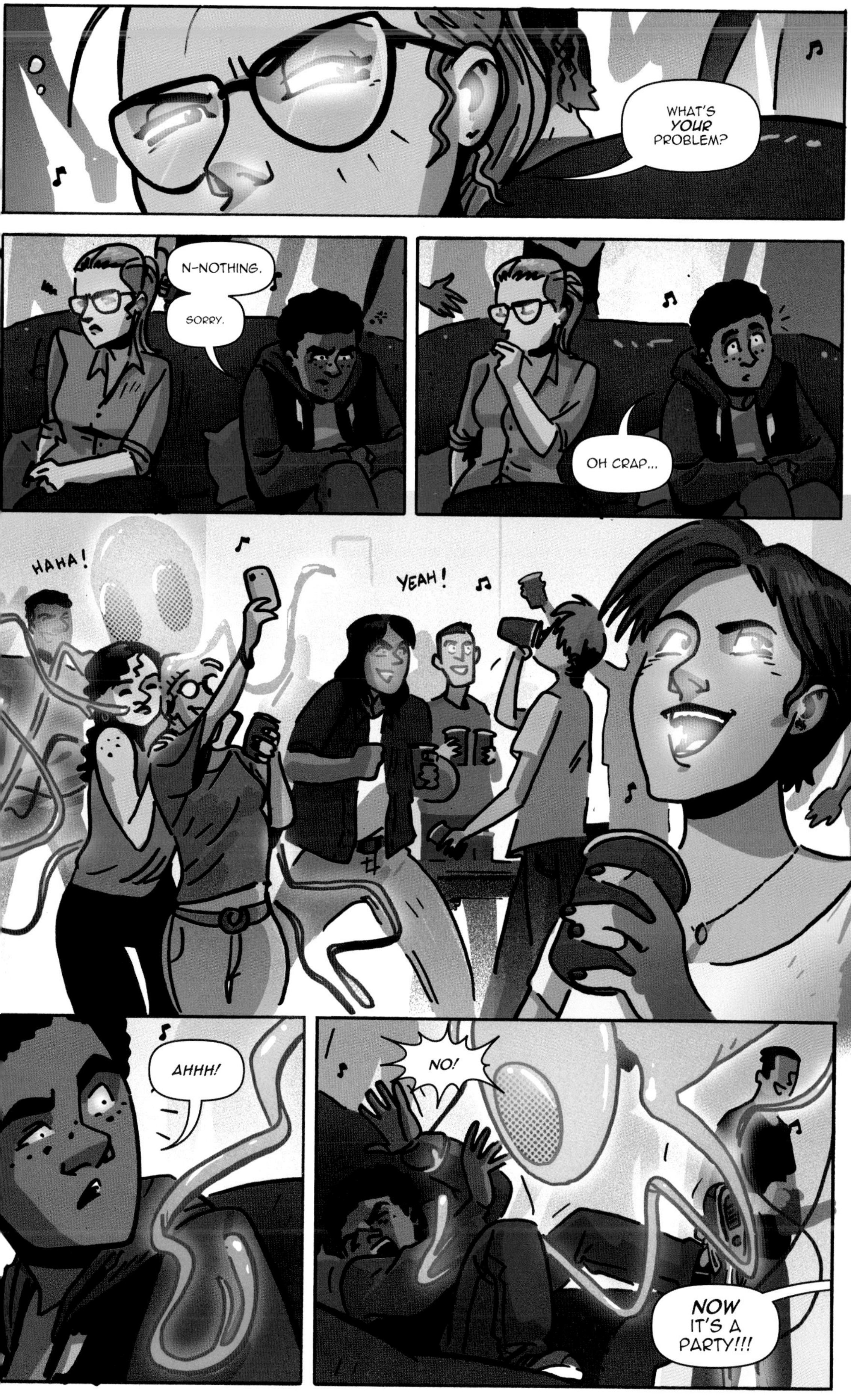
WHAT'S YOUR PROBLEM?
N-NOTHING.
SORRY.
OH CRAP...
HAHA!
YEAH!
AHHH!
NO!
NOW IT'S A PARTY!!!

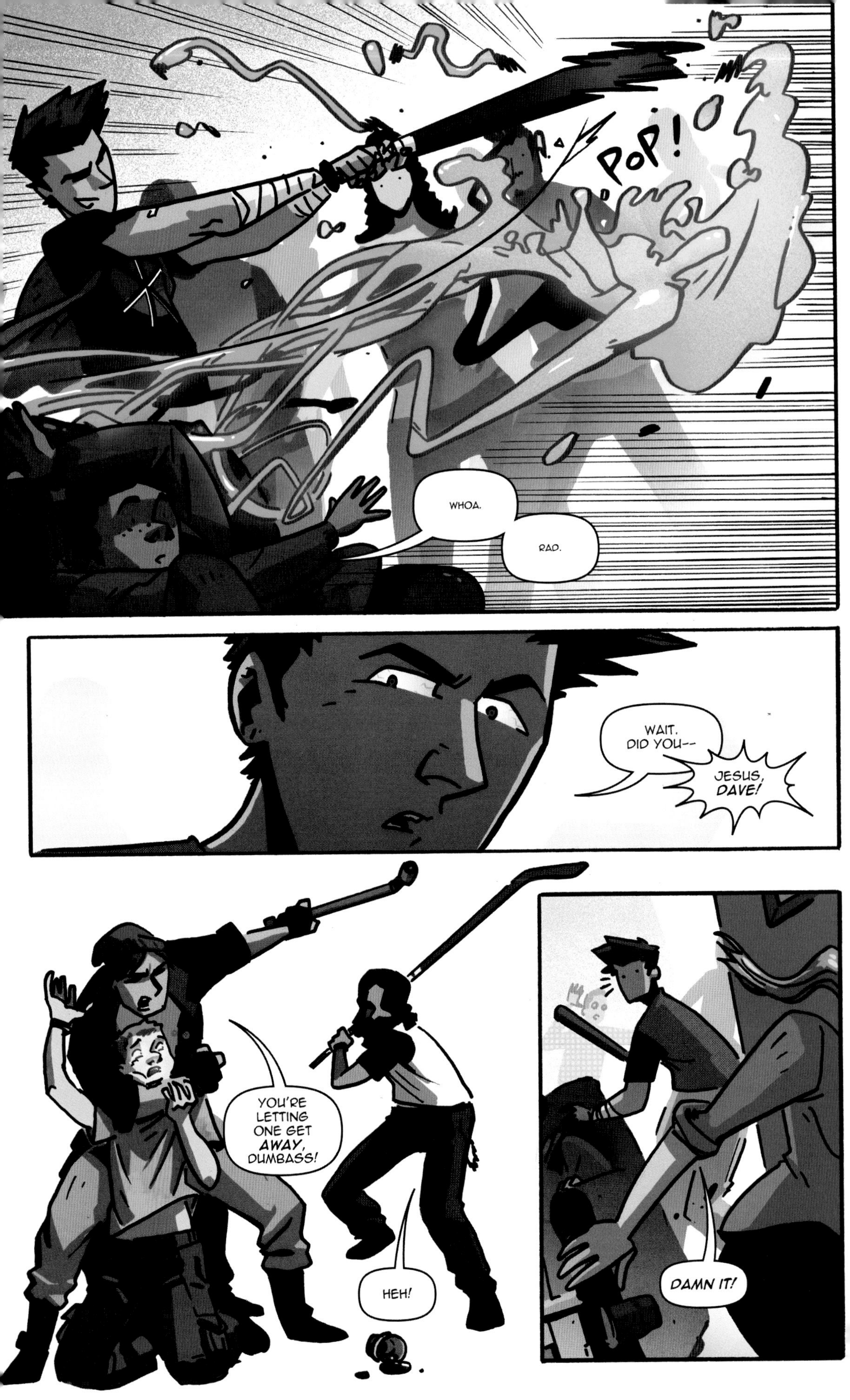
POP!
WHOA.
RAD.
WAIT. DID YOU--
JESUS, DAVE!
YOU'RE LETTING ONE GET AWAY, DUMBASS!
HEH!
DAMN IT!

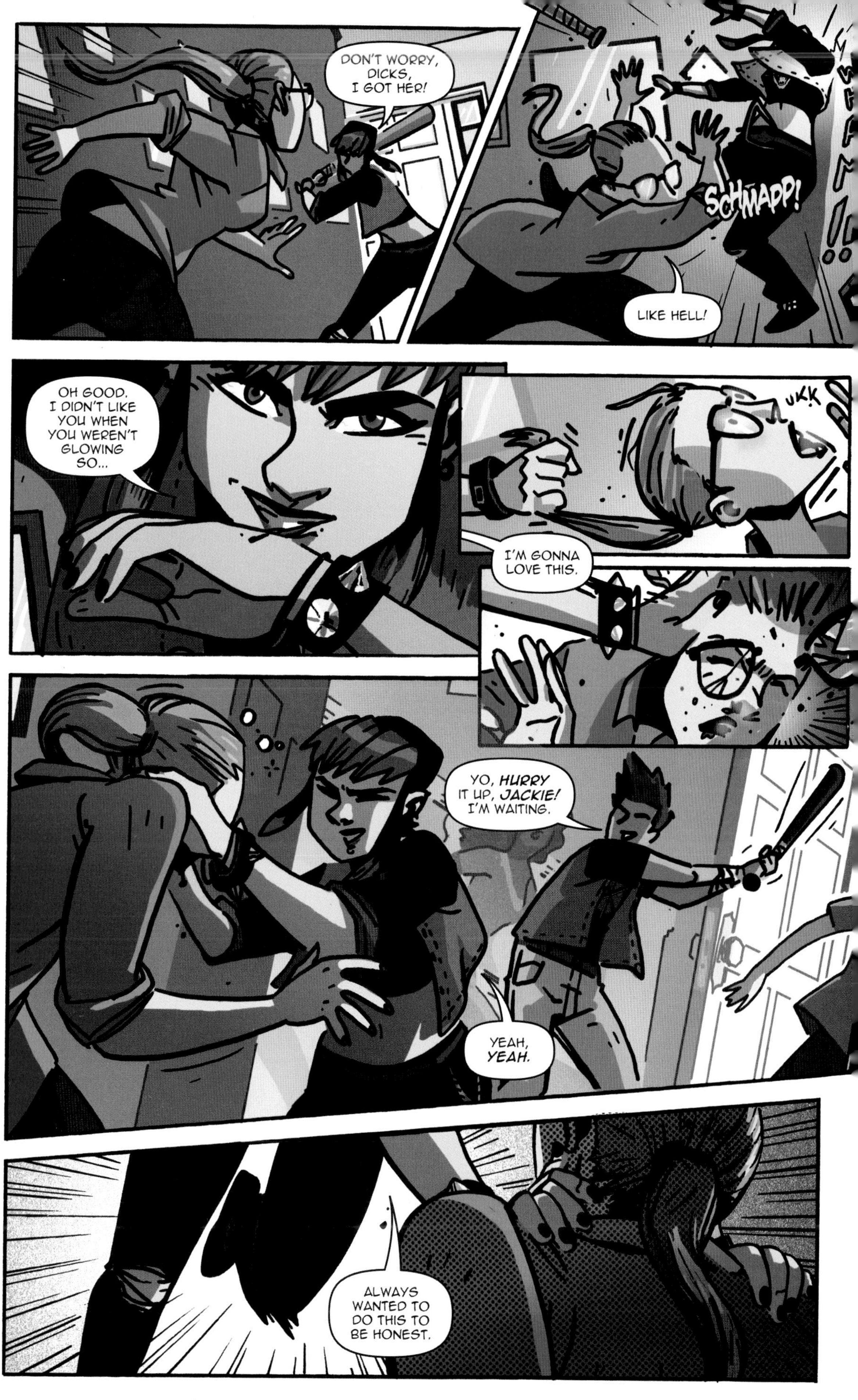

DON'T WORRY, DICKS, I GOT HER!
SCHMAPP!
LIKE HELL!
OH GOOD. I DIDN'T LIKE YOU WHEN YOU WEREN'T GLOWING SO...
UKK
I'M GONNA LOVE THIS.
YO, **HURRY** IT UP, **JACKIE!** I'M WAITING.
YEAH, **YEAH.**
ALWAYS WANTED TO DO THIS TO BE HONEST.

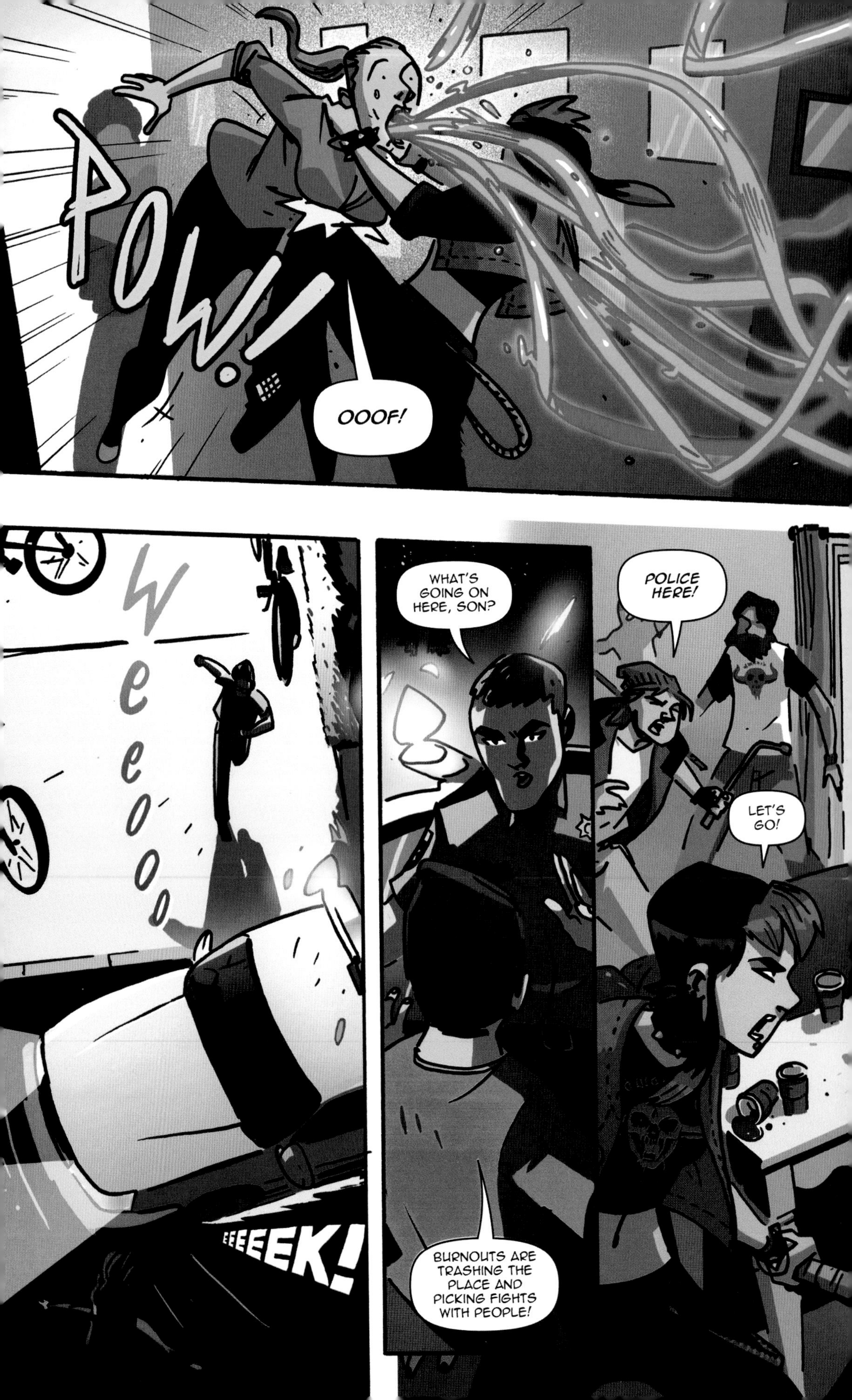
POW!
OOOF!
Weeeooo
EEEEK!
WHAT'S GOING ON HERE, SON?
BURNOUTS ARE TRASHING THE PLACE AND PICKING FIGHTS WITH PEOPLE!
POLICE HERE!
LET'S GO!

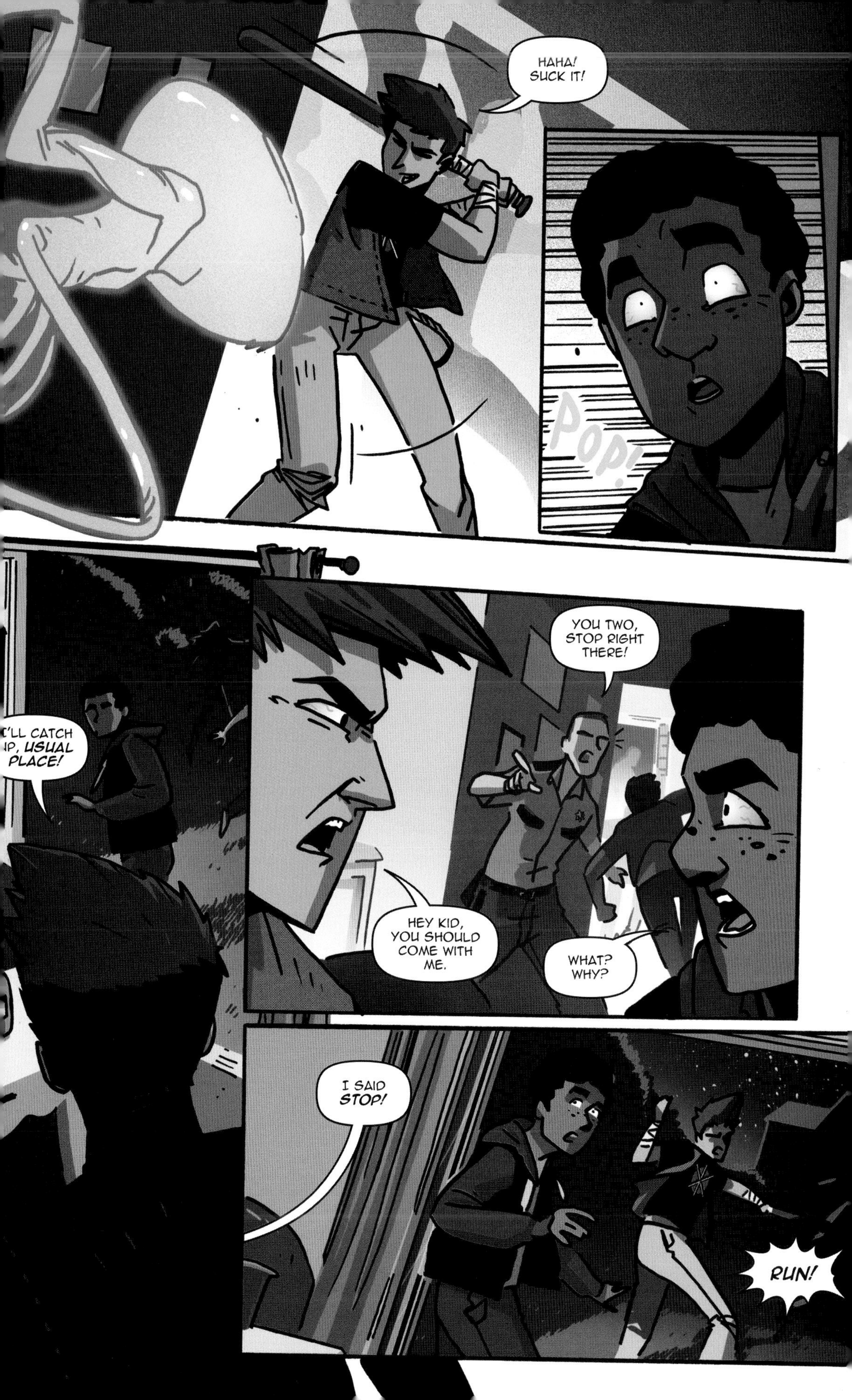
HAHA! SUCK IT!
POP!
'LL CATCH P, USUAL PLACE!
YOU TWO, STOP RIGHT THERE!
HEY KID, YOU SHOULD COME WITH ME.
WHAT? WHY?
I SAID STOP!
RUN!

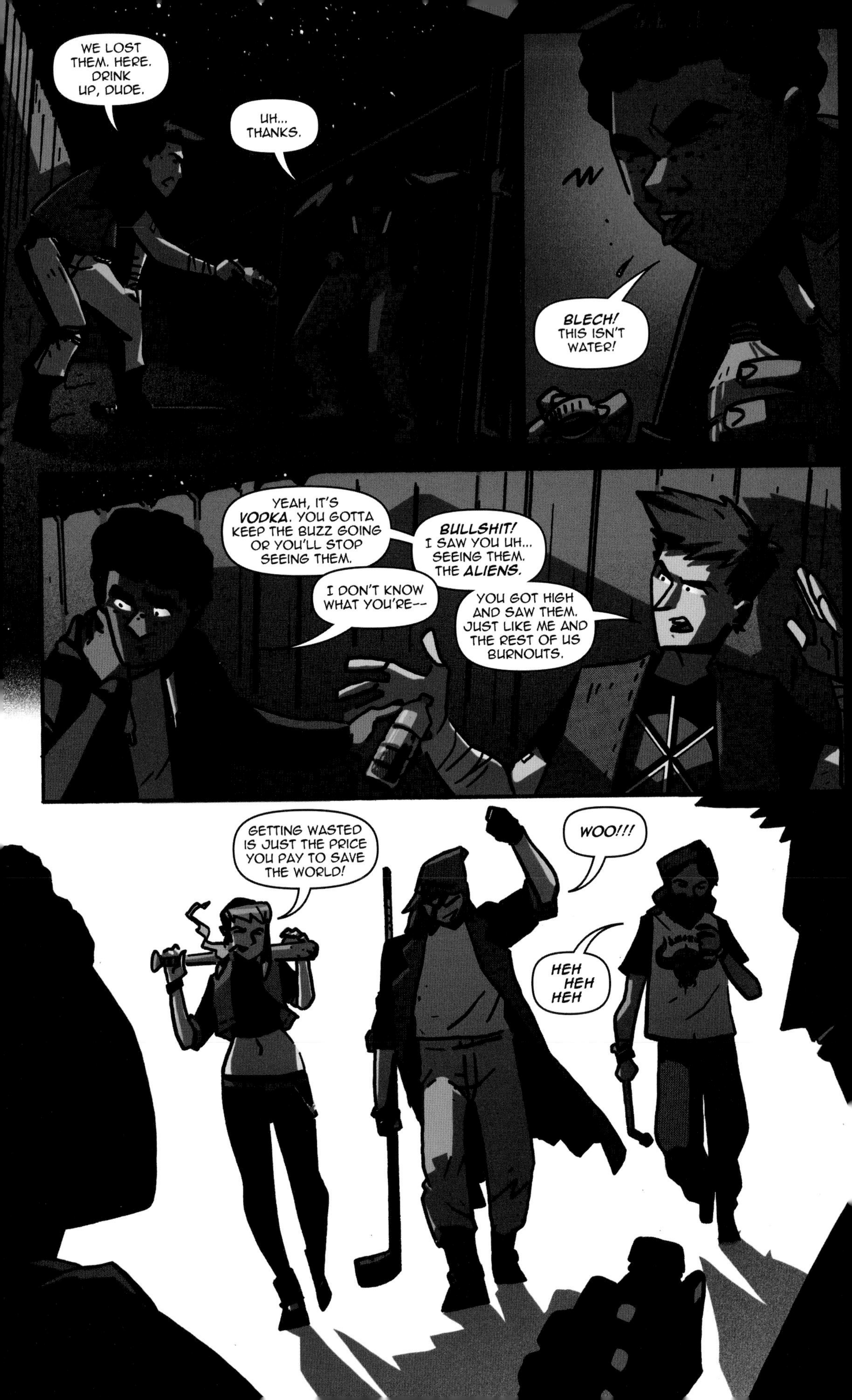
WE LOST THEM. HERE. DRINK UP, DUDE.
UH... THANKS.
BLECH! THIS ISN'T WATER!
YEAH, IT'S VODKA. YOU GOTTA KEEP THE BUZZ GOING OR YOU'LL STOP SEEING THEM.
BULLSHIT! I SAW YOU UH... SEEING THEM. THE ALIENS.
I DON'T KNOW WHAT YOU'RE--
YOU GOT HIGH AND SAW THEM. JUST LIKE ME AND THE REST OF US BURNOUTS.
GETTING WASTED IS JUST THE PRICE YOU PAY TO SAVE THE WORLD!
WOO!!!
HEH HEH HEH

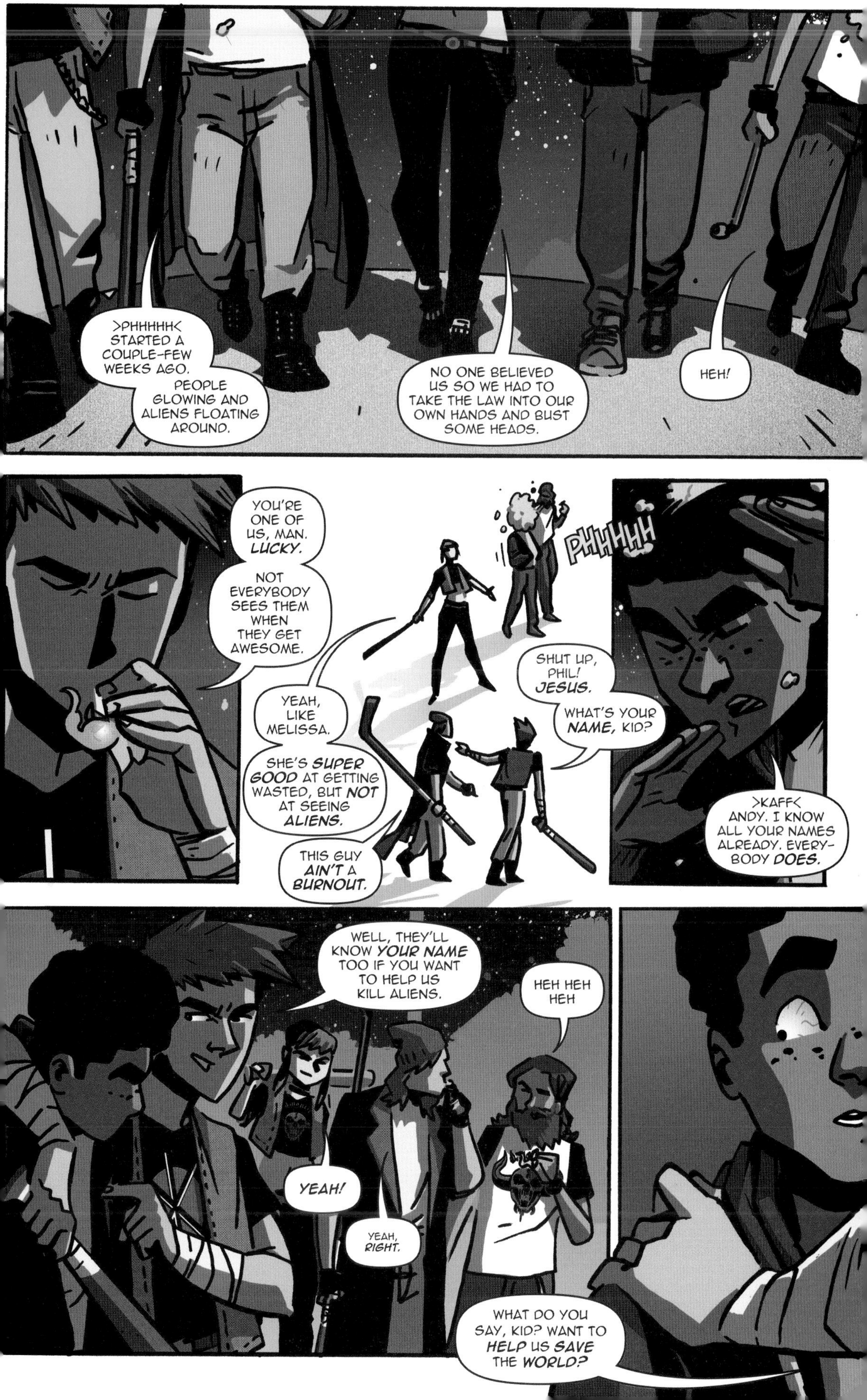
>PHHHHH< STARTED A COUPLE-FEW WEEKS AGO.
PEOPLE GLOWING AND ALIENS FLOATING AROUND.
NO ONE BELIEVED US SO WE HAD TO TAKE THE LAW INTO OUR OWN HANDS AND BUST SOME HEADS.
HEH!
YOU'RE ONE OF US, MAN. LUCKY.
NOT EVERYBODY SEES THEM WHEN THEY GET AWESOME.
PHHHHH
YEAH, LIKE MELISSA.
SHE'S SUPER GOOD AT GETTING WASTED, BUT NOT AT SEEING ALIENS.
THIS GUY AIN'T A BURNOUT.
SHUT UP, PHIL! JESUS.
WHAT'S YOUR NAME, KID?
>KAFF< ANDY. I KNOW ALL YOUR NAMES ALREADY. EVERY-BODY DOES.
WELL, THEY'LL KNOW YOUR NAME TOO IF YOU WANT TO HELP US KILL ALIENS.
HEH HEH HEH
YEAH!
YEAH, RIGHT.
WHAT DO YOU SAY, KID? WANT TO HELP US SAVE THE WORLD?

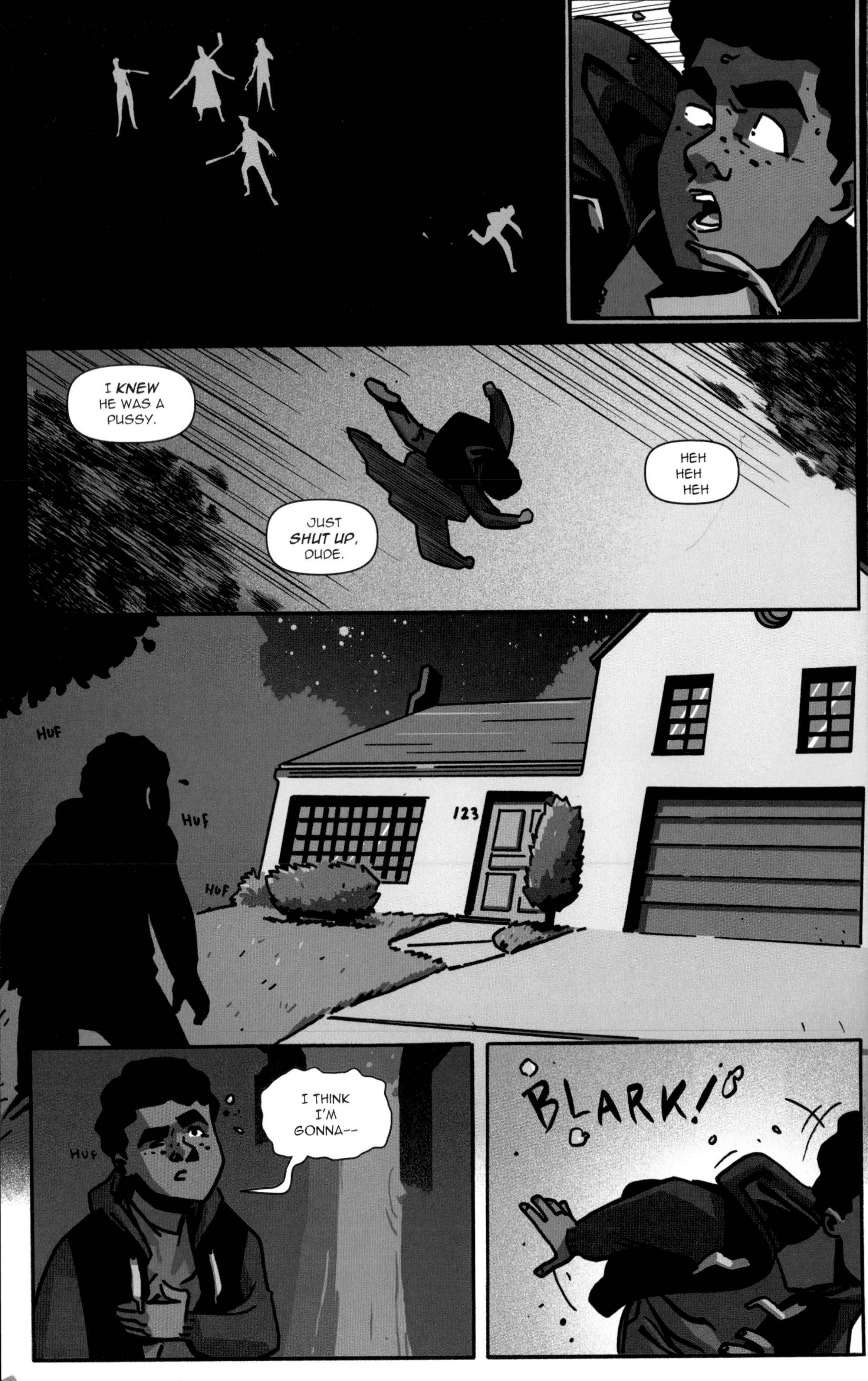
I KNEW HE WAS A PUSSY.
JUST SHUT UP, DUDE.
HEH HEH HEH
HUF
HUF
HUF
123
HUF
I THINK I'M GONNA--
BLARK!

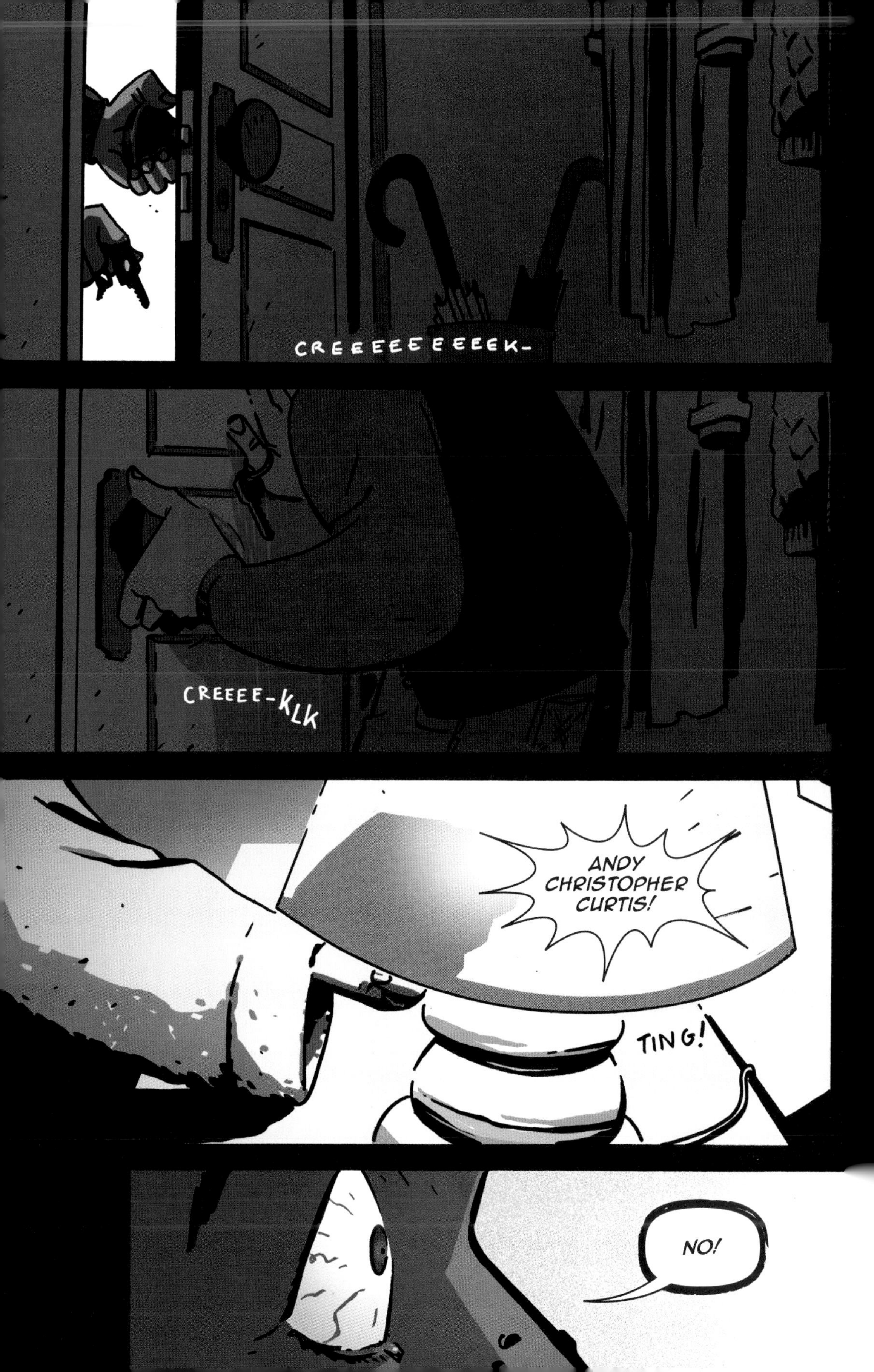
CREEEEEEEEEK-
CREEEE-KLK
ANDY CHRISTOPHER CURTIS!
TING!
NO!

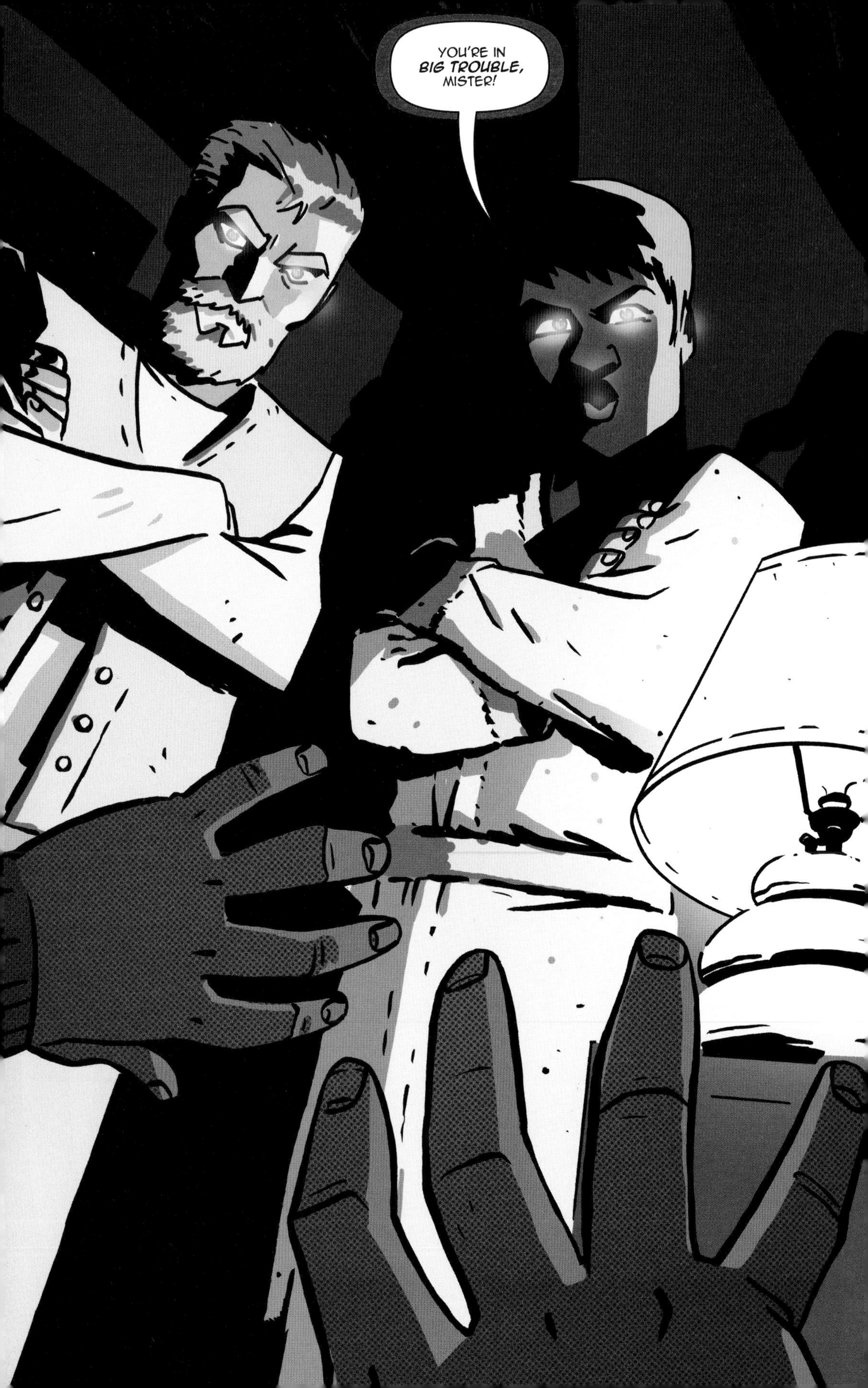
YOU'RE IN *BIG TROUBLE,* MISTER!

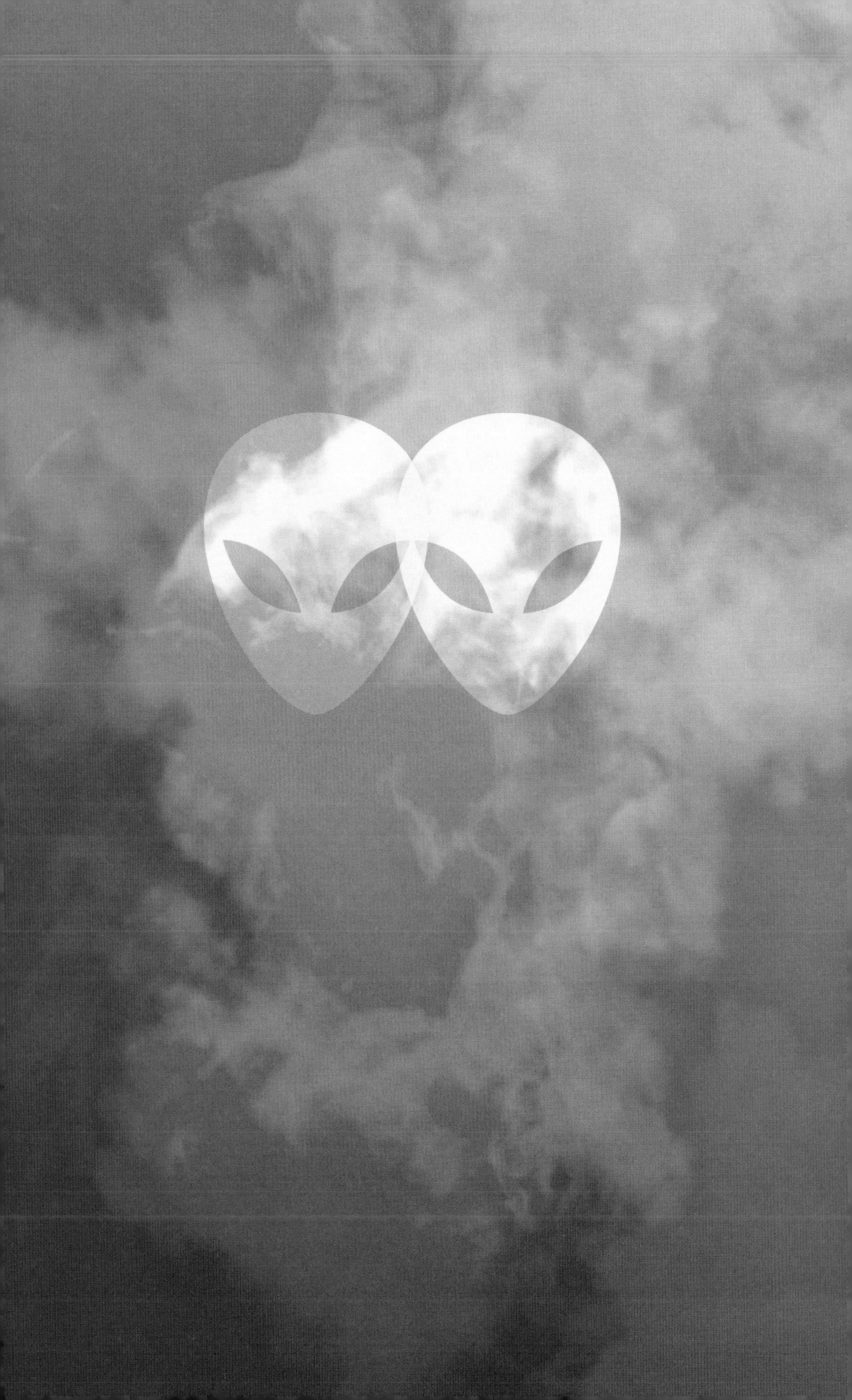

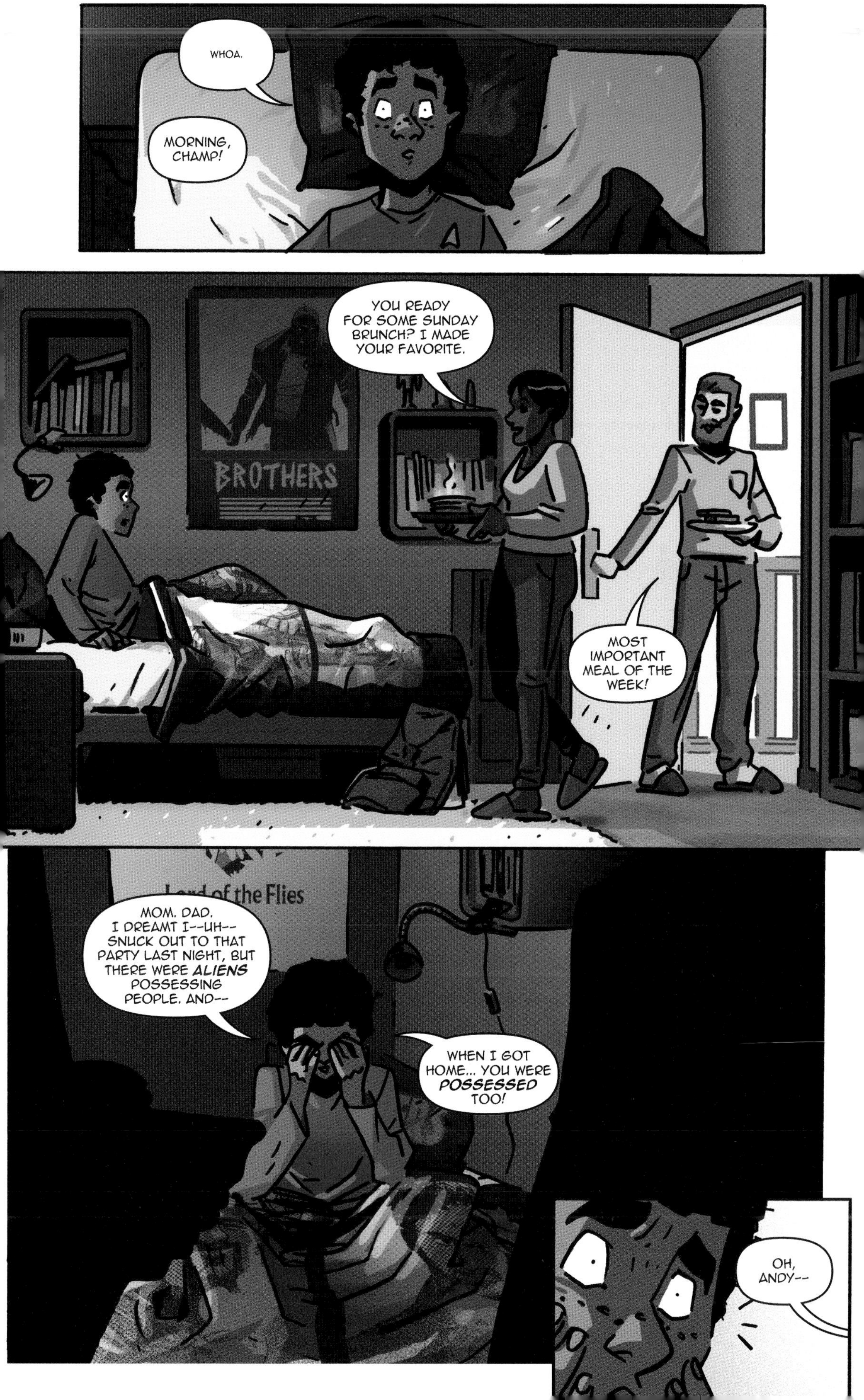
WHOA.
MORNING, CHAMP!
YOU READY FOR SOME SUNDAY BRUNCH? I MADE YOUR FAVORITE.
BROTHERS
MOST IMPORTANT MEAL OF THE WEEK!
Lord of the Flies
MOM. DAD. I DREAMT I--UH-- SNUCK OUT TO THAT PARTY LAST NIGHT, BUT THERE WERE ALIENS POSSESSING PEOPLE. AND--
WHEN I GOT HOME... YOU WERE POSSESSED TOO!
OH, ANDY--

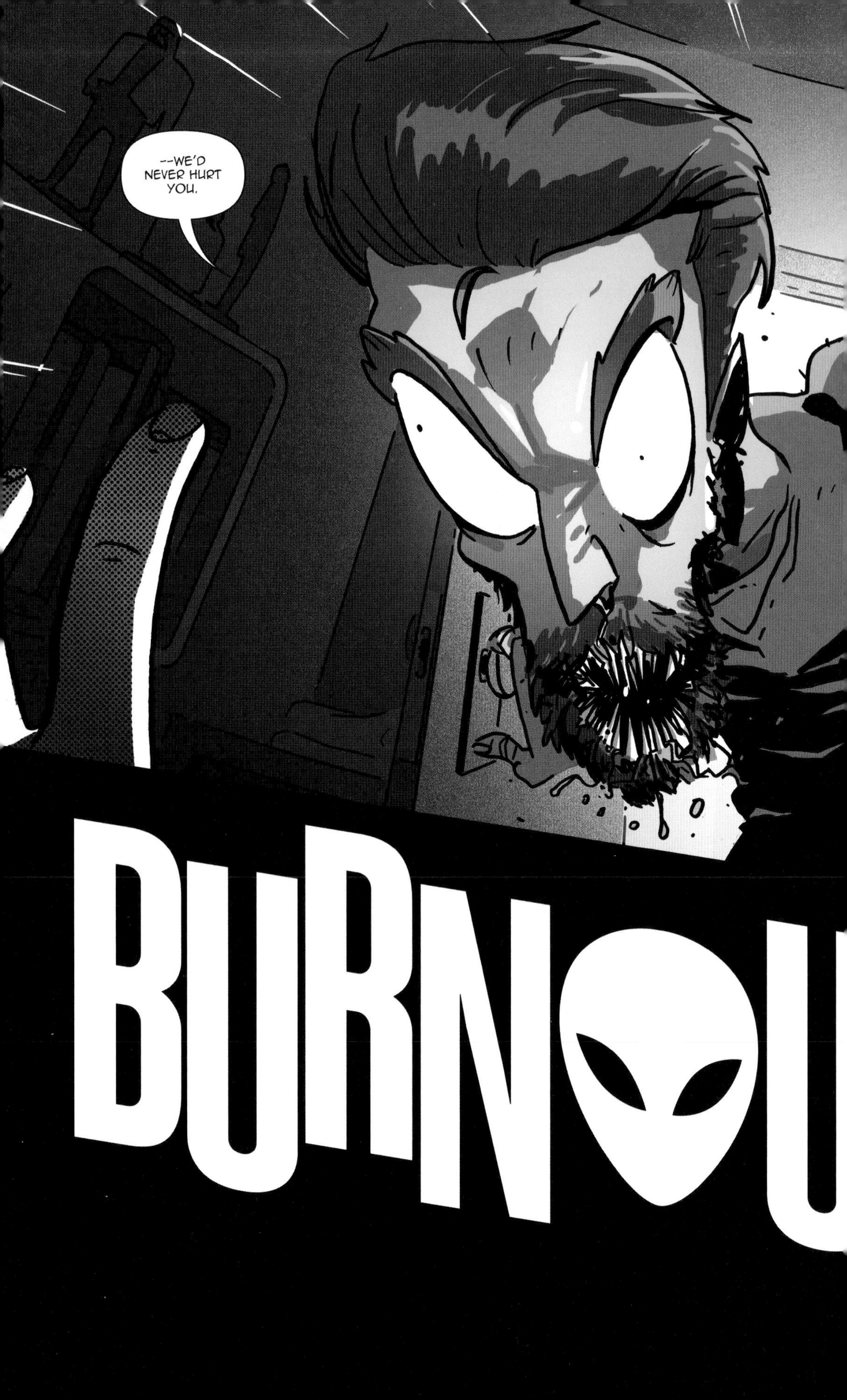
--WE'D NEVER HURT YOU.
BURNOU

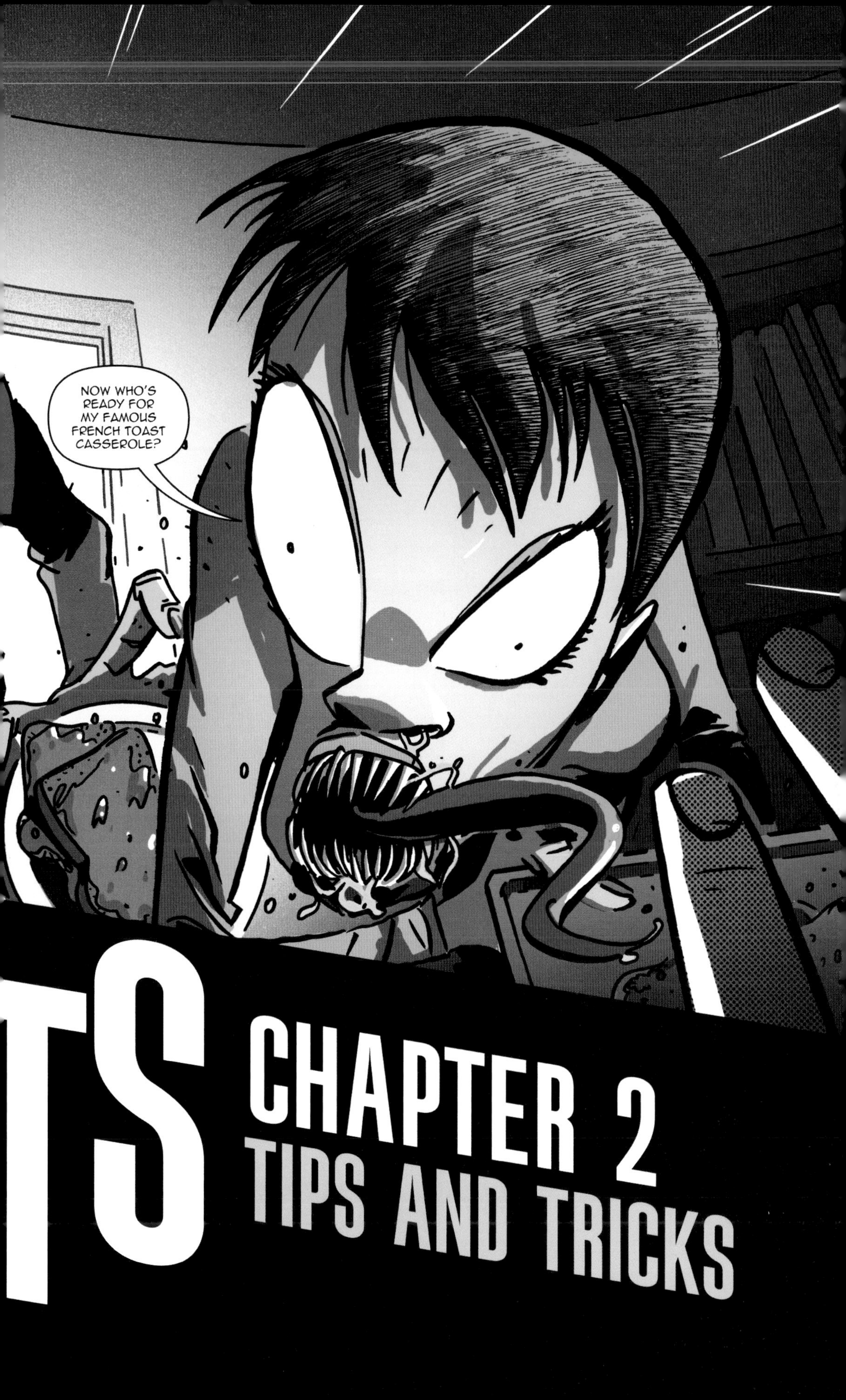
NOW WHO'S READY FOR MY FAMOUS FRENCH TOAST CASSEROLE?

TS

CHAPTER 2
TIPS AND TRICKS

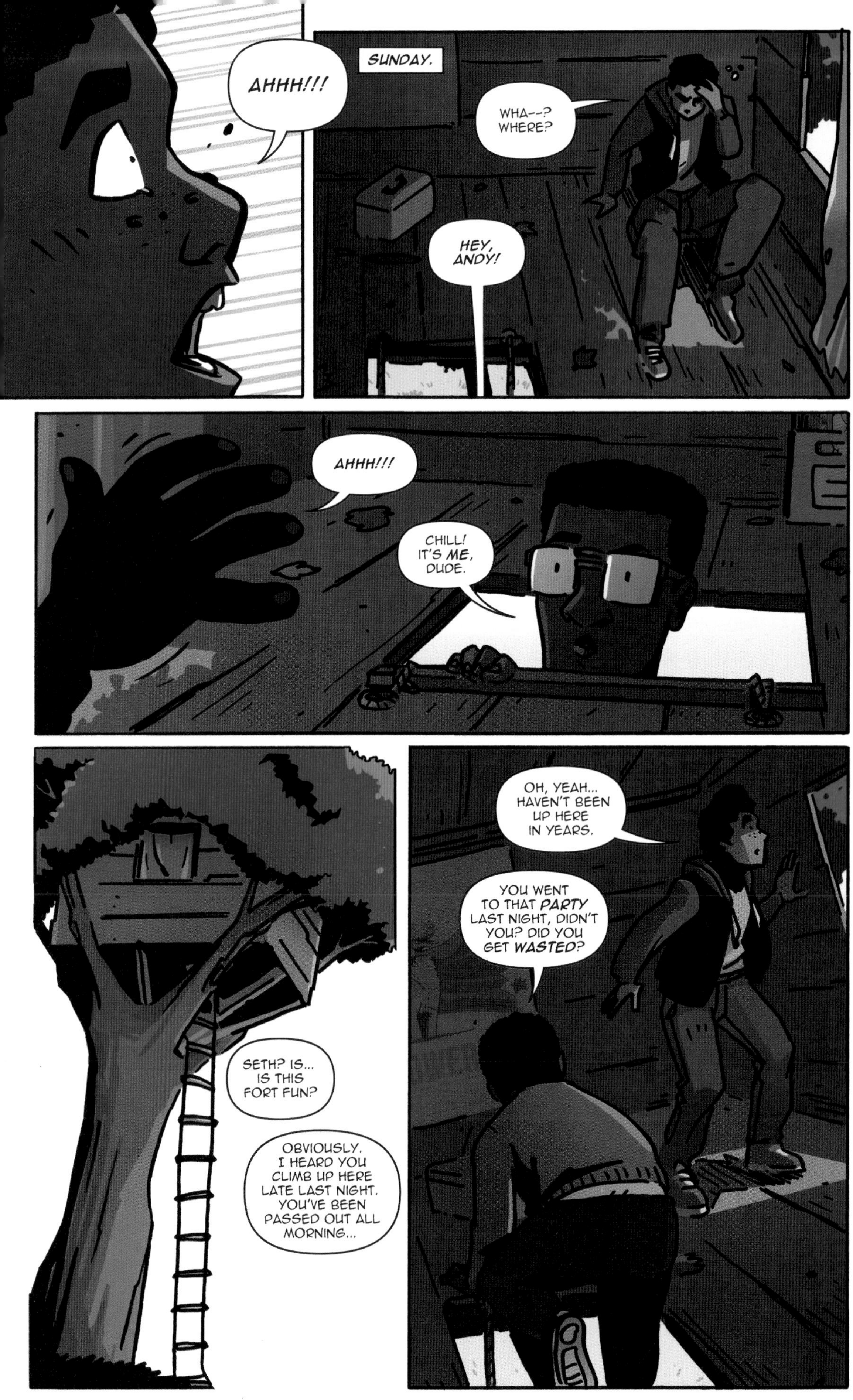
AHHH!!!
SUNDAY.
WHA--? WHERE?
HEY, ANDY!
AHHH!!!
CHILL! IT'S ME, DUDE.
SETH? IS... IS THIS FORT FUN?
OBVIOUSLY. I HEARD YOU CLIMB UP HERE LATE LAST NIGHT. YOU'VE BEEN PASSED OUT ALL MORNING...
OH, YEAH... HAVEN'T BEEN UP HERE IN YEARS.
YOU WENT TO THAT PARTY LAST NIGHT, DIDN'T YOU? DID YOU GET WASTED?

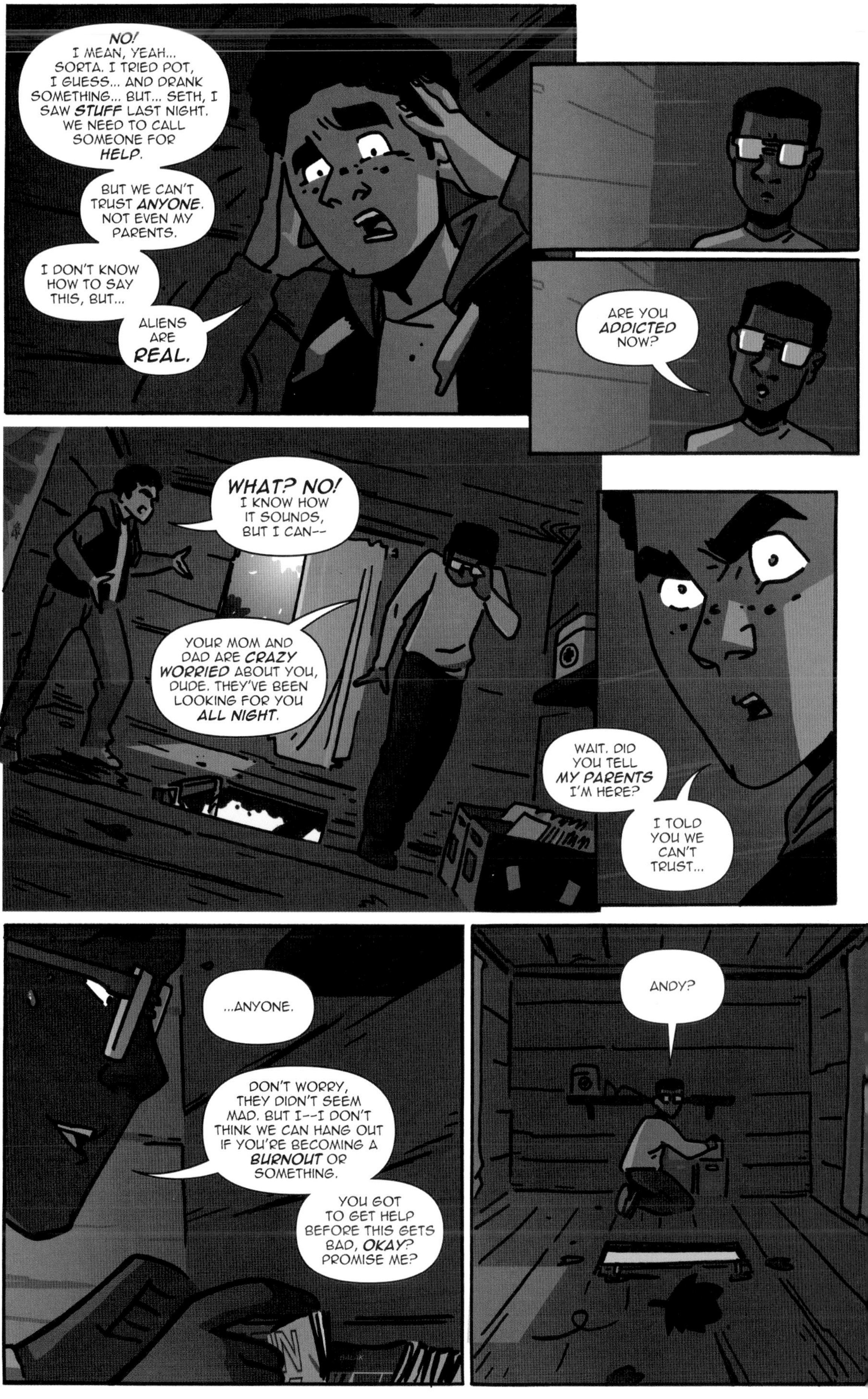
NO! I MEAN, YEAH... SORTA. I TRIED POT, I GUESS... AND DRANK SOMETHING... BUT... SETH, I SAW STUFF LAST NIGHT. WE NEED TO CALL SOMEONE FOR HELP.
BUT WE CAN'T TRUST ANYONE. NOT EVEN MY PARENTS.
I DON'T KNOW HOW TO SAY THIS, BUT...
ALIENS ARE REAL.
ARE YOU ADDICTED NOW?
WHAT? NO! I KNOW HOW IT SOUNDS, BUT I CAN--
YOUR MOM AND DAD ARE CRAZY WORRIED ABOUT YOU, DUDE. THEY'VE BEEN LOOKING FOR YOU ALL NIGHT.
WAIT. DID YOU TELL MY PARENTS I'M HERE?
I TOLD YOU WE CAN'T TRUST...
...ANYONE.
DON'T WORRY, THEY DIDN'T SEEM MAD. BUT I--I DON'T THINK WE CAN HANG OUT IF YOU'RE BECOMING A BURNOUT OR SOMETHING.
YOU GOT TO GET HELP BEFORE THIS GETS BAD, OKAY? PROMISE ME?
ANDY?

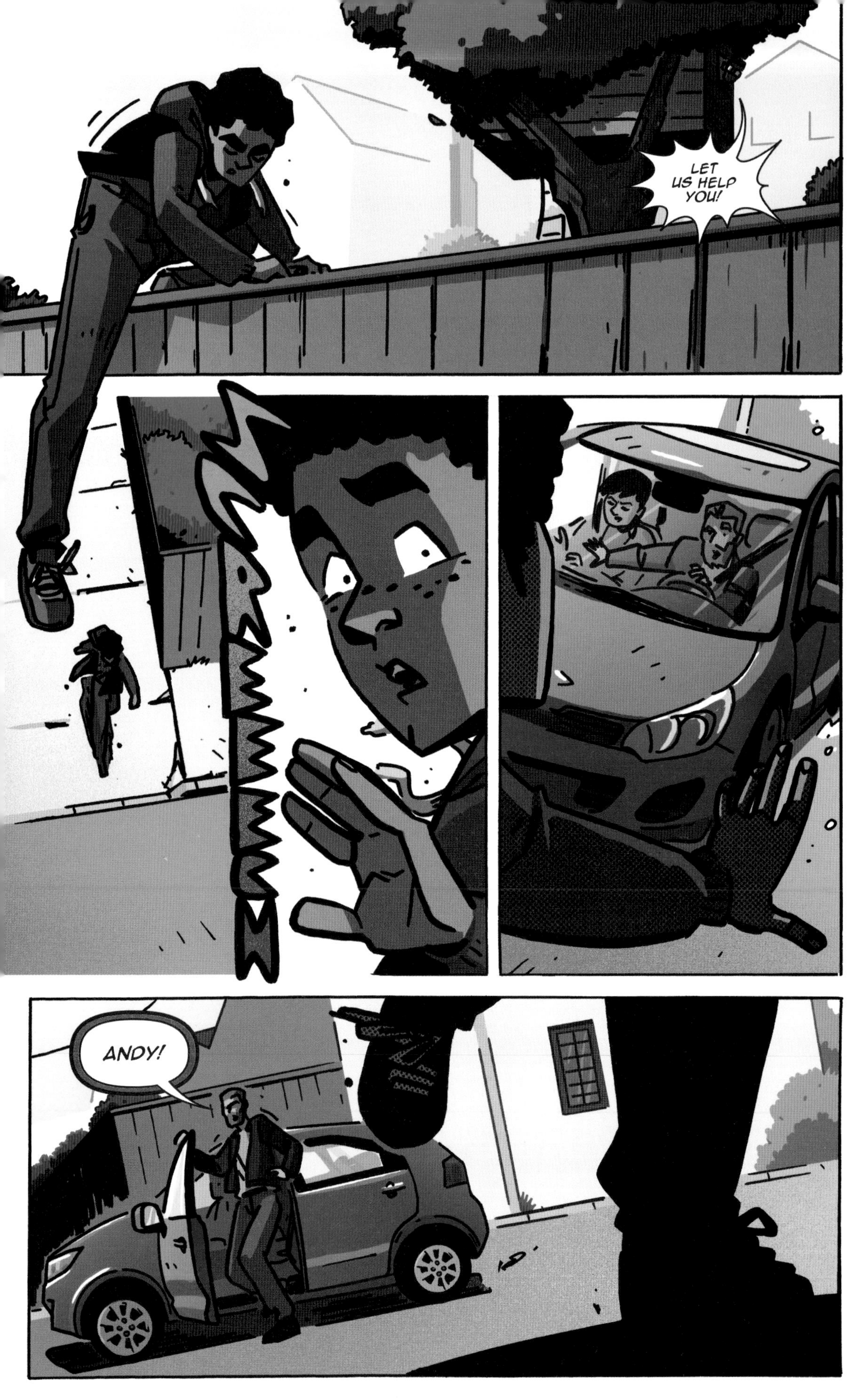
LET US HELP YOU!
ANDY!

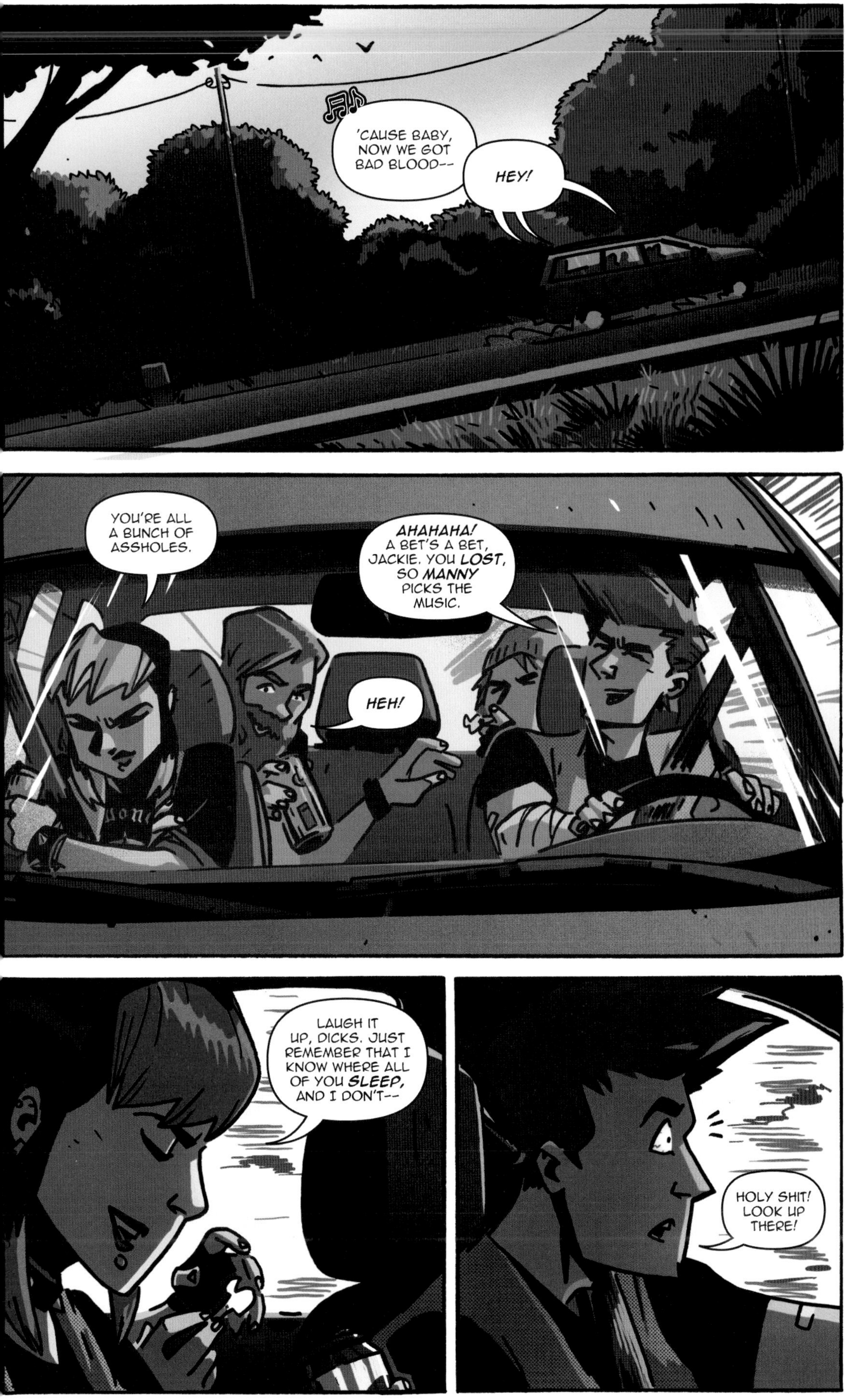
'CAUSE BABY, NOW WE GOT BAD BLOOD--
HEY!
YOU'RE ALL A BUNCH OF ASSHOLES.
AHAHAHA! A BET'S A BET, JACKIE. YOU LOST, SO MANNY PICKS THE MUSIC.
HEH!
LAUGH IT UP, DICKS. JUST REMEMBER THAT I KNOW WHERE ALL OF YOU SLEEP, AND I DON'T--
HOLY SHIT! LOOK UP THERE!

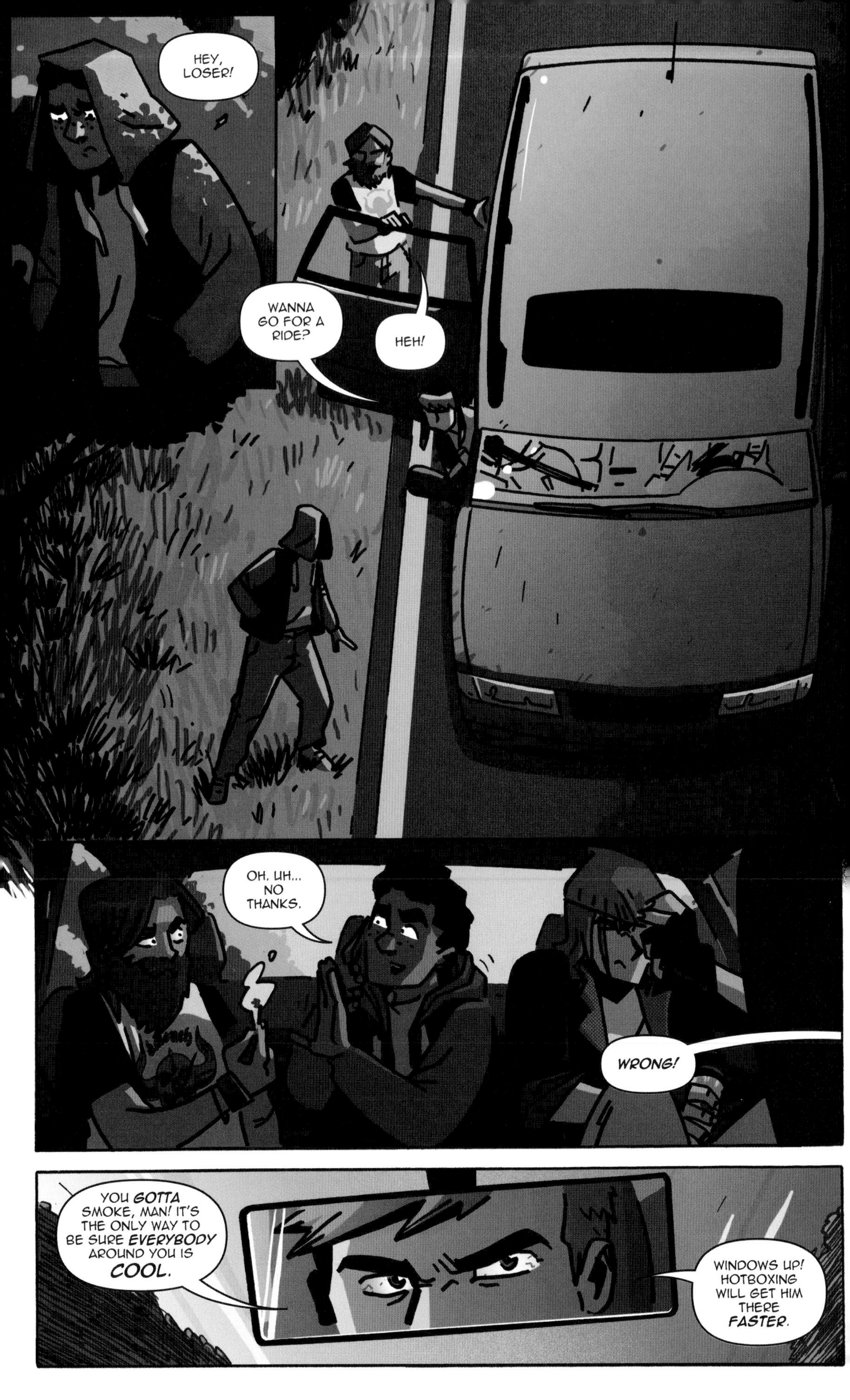
HEY, LOSER!
WANNA GO FOR A RIDE?
HEH!
OH, UH... NO THANKS.
WRONG!
YOU GOTTA SMOKE, MAN! IT'S THE ONLY WAY TO BE SURE EVERYBODY AROUND YOU IS COOL.
WINDOWS UP! HOTBOXING WILL GET HIM THERE FASTER.

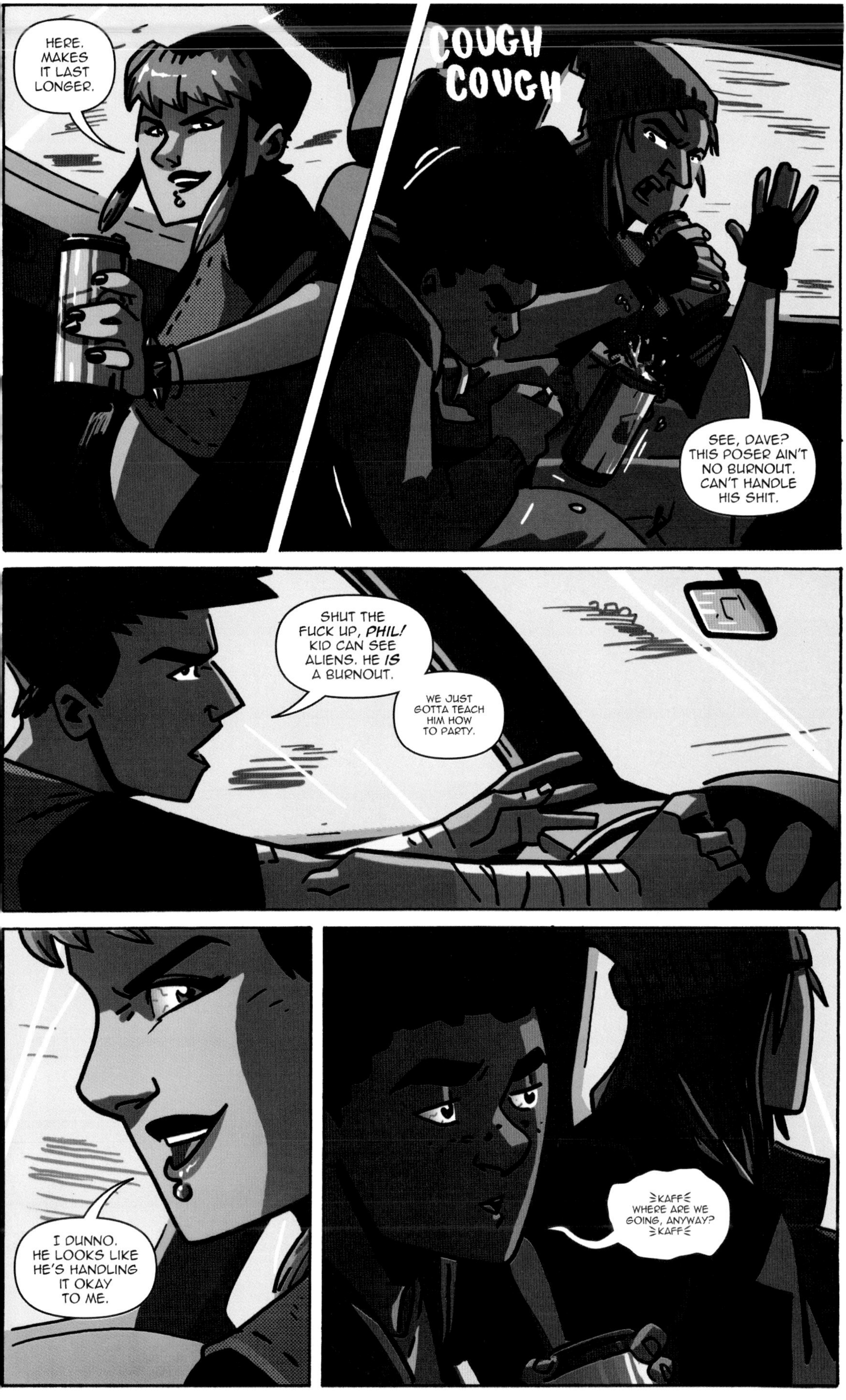
HERE. MAKES IT LAST LONGER.
COUGH COUGH
SEE, DAVE? THIS POSER AIN'T NO BURNOUT. CAN'T HANDLE HIS SHIT.
SHUT THE FUCK UP, PHIL! KID CAN SEE ALIENS. HE IS A BURNOUT.
WE JUST GOTTA TEACH HIM HOW TO PARTY.
I DUNNO. HE LOOKS LIKE HE'S HANDLING IT OKAY TO ME.
KAFF WHERE ARE WE GOING, ANYWAY? KAFF

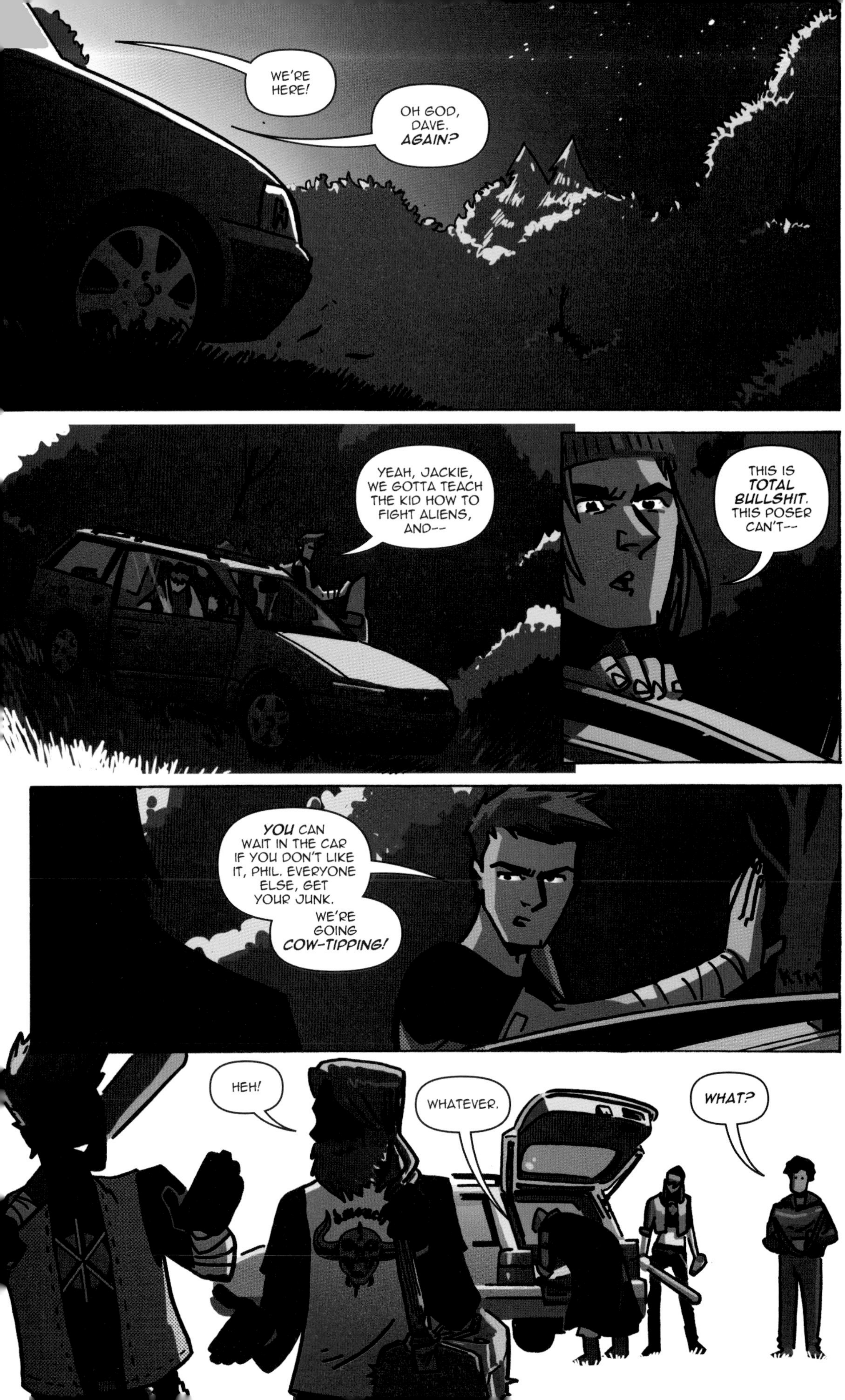
WE'RE HERE!
OH GOD, DAVE. AGAIN?
YEAH, JACKIE, WE GOTTA TEACH THE KID HOW TO FIGHT ALIENS, AND--
THIS IS TOTAL BULLSHIT. THIS POSER CAN'T--
YOU CAN WAIT IN THE CAR IF YOU DON'T LIKE IT, PHIL. EVERYONE ELSE, GET YOUR JUNK.
WE'RE GOING COW-TIPPING!
KTM
HEH!
WHATEVER.
WHAT?

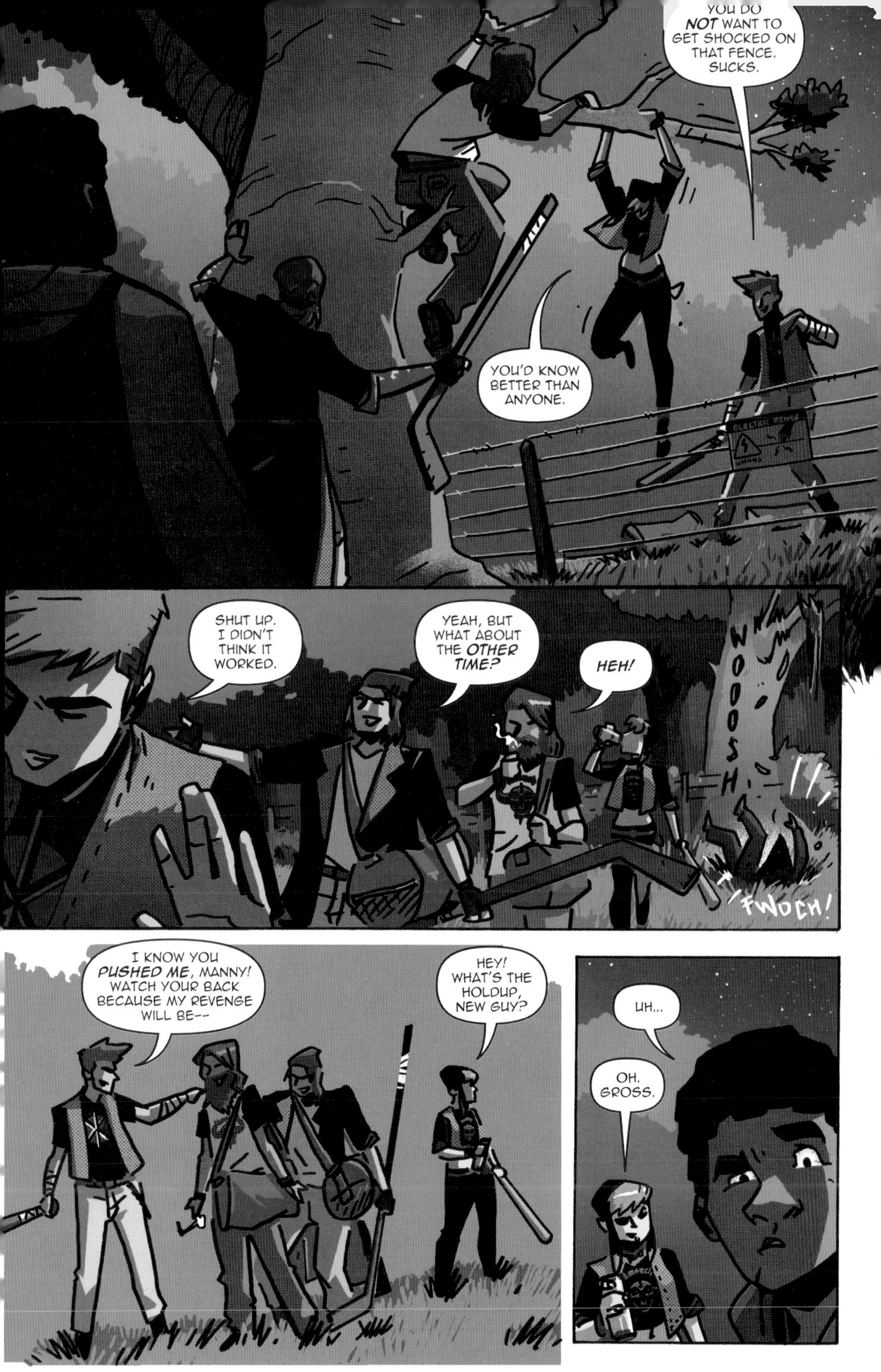

YOU DO *NOT* WANT TO GET SHOCKED ON THAT FENCE. SUCKS.
YOU'D KNOW BETTER THAN ANYONE.
SHUT UP. I DIDN'T THINK IT WORKED.
YEAH, BUT WHAT ABOUT THE *OTHER TIME?*
HEH!
WOOOOSH
FWOCH!
I KNOW YOU *PUSHED ME*, MANNY! WATCH YOUR BACK BECAUSE MY REVENGE WILL BE--
HEY! WHAT'S THE HOLDUP, NEW GUY?
UH...
OH. GROSS.

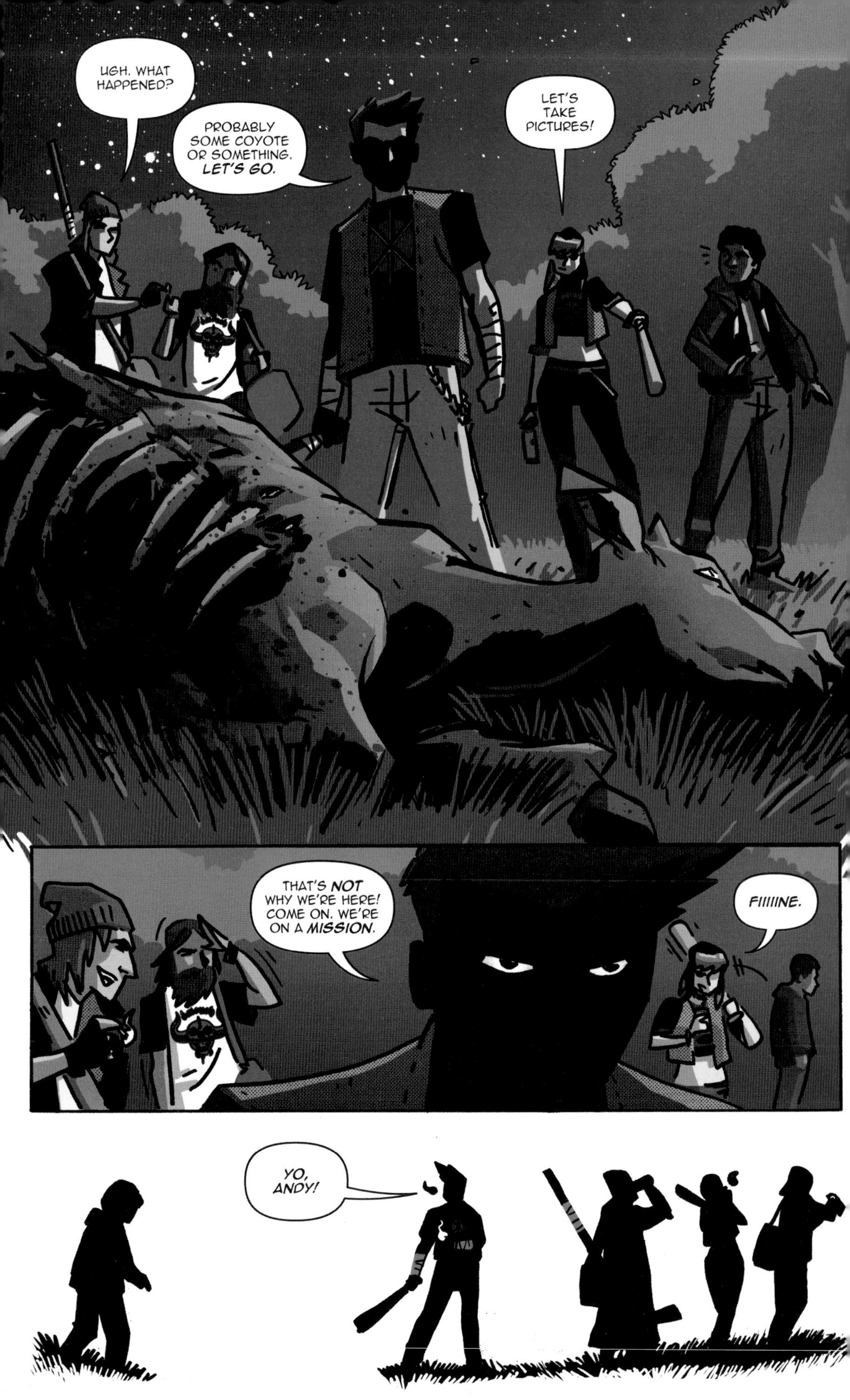
UGH. WHAT HAPPENED?
PROBABLY SOME COYOTE OR SOMETHING. LET'S GO.
LET'S TAKE PICTURES!
THAT'S NOT WHY WE'RE HERE! COME ON. WE'RE ON A MISSION.
FIIIIINE.
YO, ANDY!

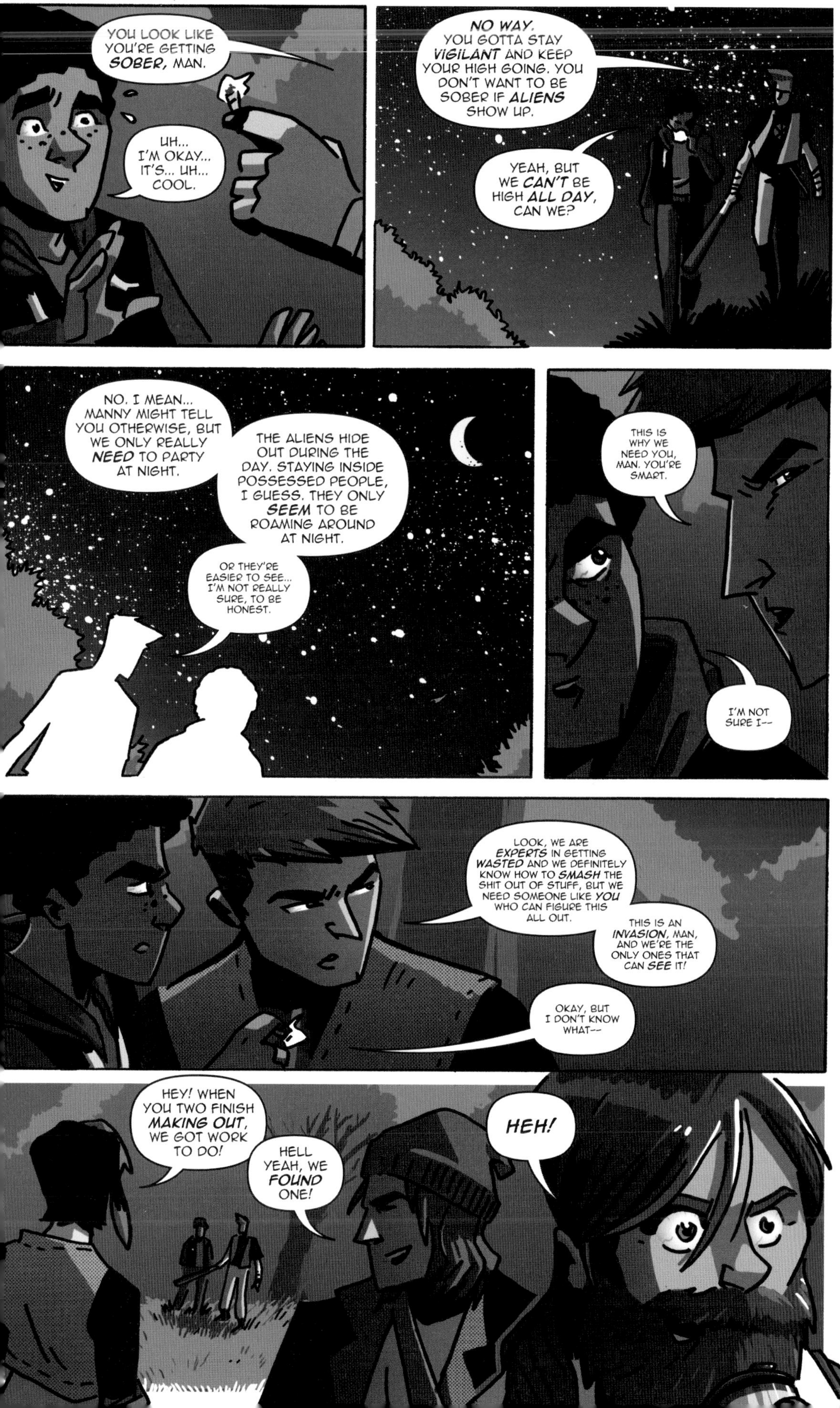

YOU LOOK LIKE YOU'RE GETTING SOBER, MAN.
UH... I'M OKAY... IT'S... UH... COOL.
NO WAY. YOU GOTTA STAY VIGILANT AND KEEP YOUR HIGH GOING. YOU DON'T WANT TO BE SOBER IF ALIENS SHOW UP.
YEAH, BUT WE CAN'T BE HIGH ALL DAY, CAN WE?
NO. I MEAN... MANNY MIGHT TELL YOU OTHERWISE, BUT WE ONLY REALLY NEED TO PARTY AT NIGHT.
THE ALIENS HIDE OUT DURING THE DAY. STAYING INSIDE POSSESSED PEOPLE, I GUESS. THEY ONLY SEEM TO BE ROAMING AROUND AT NIGHT.
OR THEY'RE EASIER TO SEE... I'M NOT REALLY SURE, TO BE HONEST.
THIS IS WHY WE NEED YOU, MAN. YOU'RE SMART.
I'M NOT SURE I--
LOOK, WE ARE EXPERTS IN GETTING WASTED AND WE DEFINITELY KNOW HOW TO SMASH THE SHIT OUT OF STUFF, BUT WE NEED SOMEONE LIKE YOU WHO CAN FIGURE THIS ALL OUT.
THIS IS AN INVASION, MAN, AND WE'RE THE ONLY ONES THAT CAN SEE IT!
OKAY, BUT I DON'T KNOW WHAT--
HEY! WHEN YOU TWO FINISH MAKING OUT, WE GOT WORK TO DO!
HELL YEAH, WE FOUND ONE!
HEH!

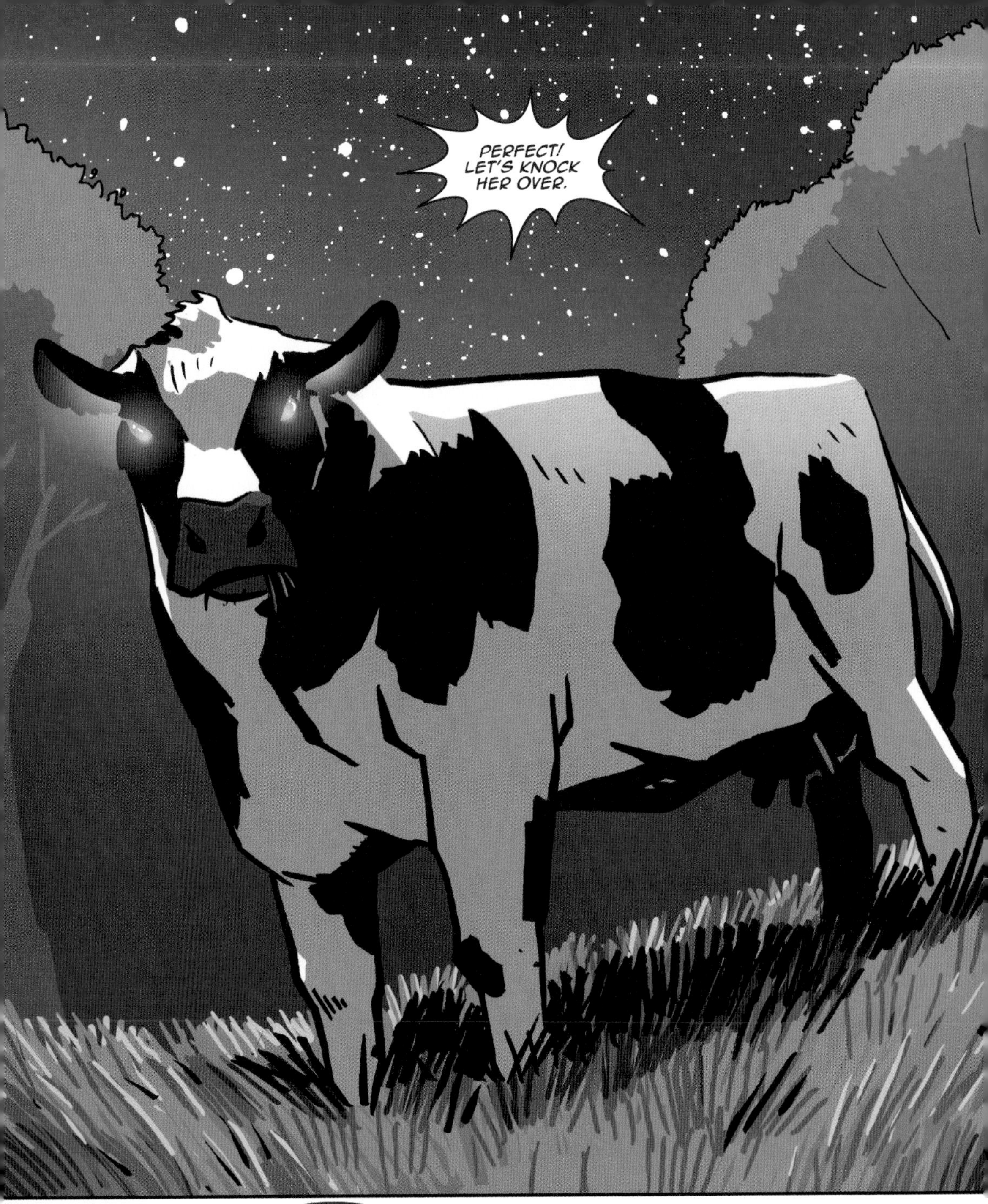
PERFECT! LET'S KNOCK HER OVER.

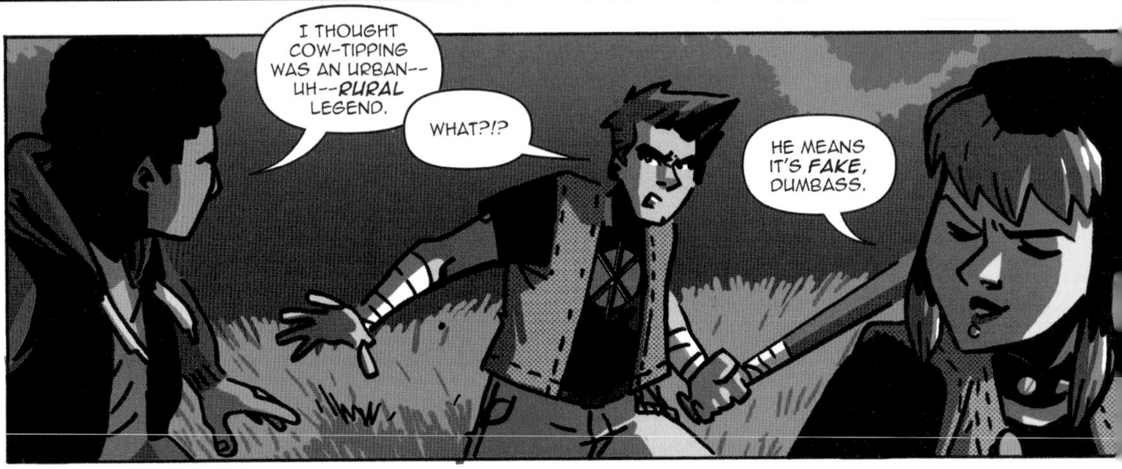
I THOUGHT COW-TIPPING WAS AN URBAN-- UH--*RURAL* LEGEND.
WHAT?!?
HE MEANS IT'S *FAKE*, DUMBASS.

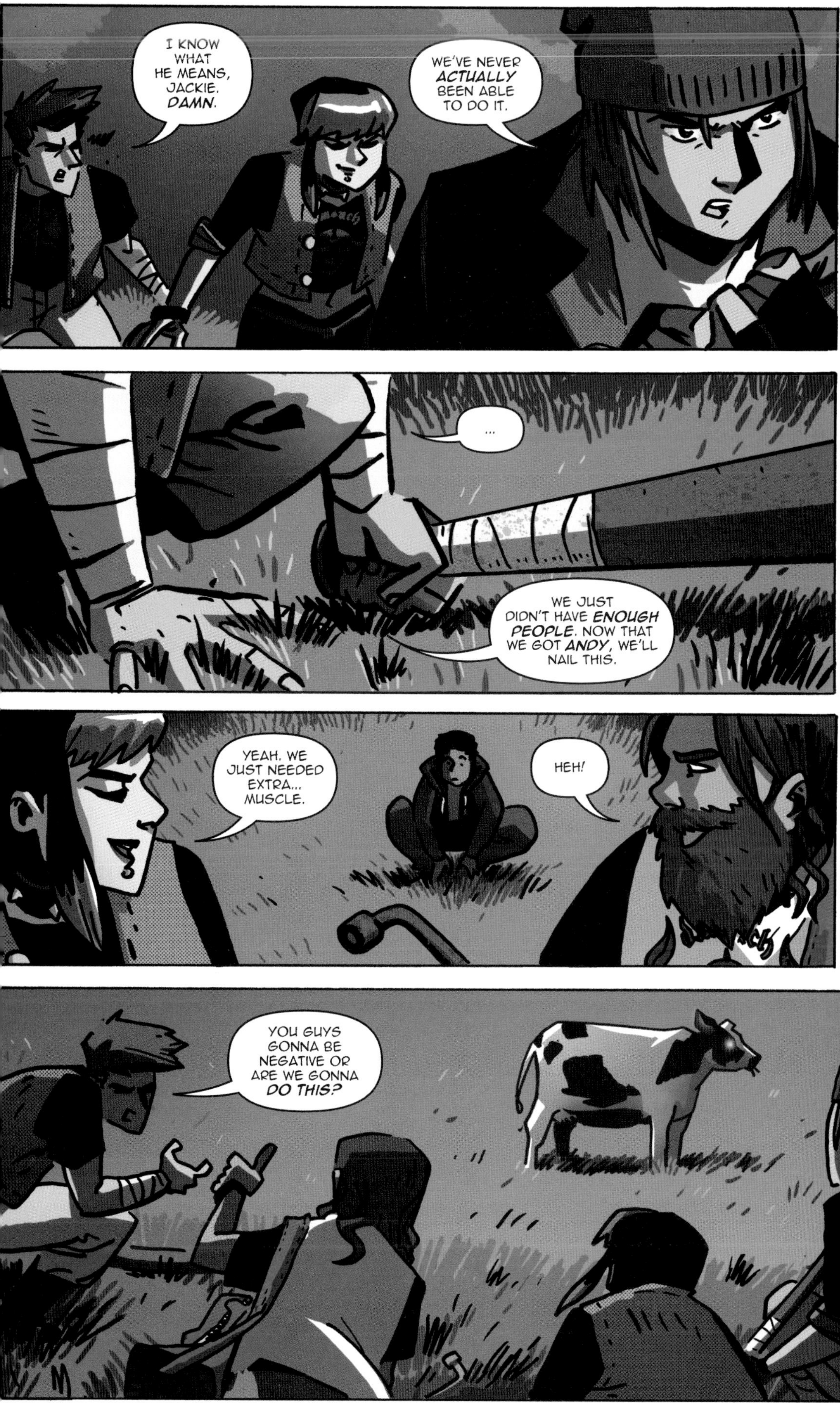
I KNOW WHAT HE MEANS, JACKIE. DAMN.
WE'VE NEVER ACTUALLY BEEN ABLE TO DO IT.
...
WE JUST DIDN'T HAVE ENOUGH PEOPLE. NOW THAT WE GOT ANDY, WE'LL NAIL THIS.
YEAH. WE JUST NEEDED EXTRA... MUSCLE.
HEH!
YOU GUYS GONNA BE NEGATIVE OR ARE WE GONNA DO THIS?

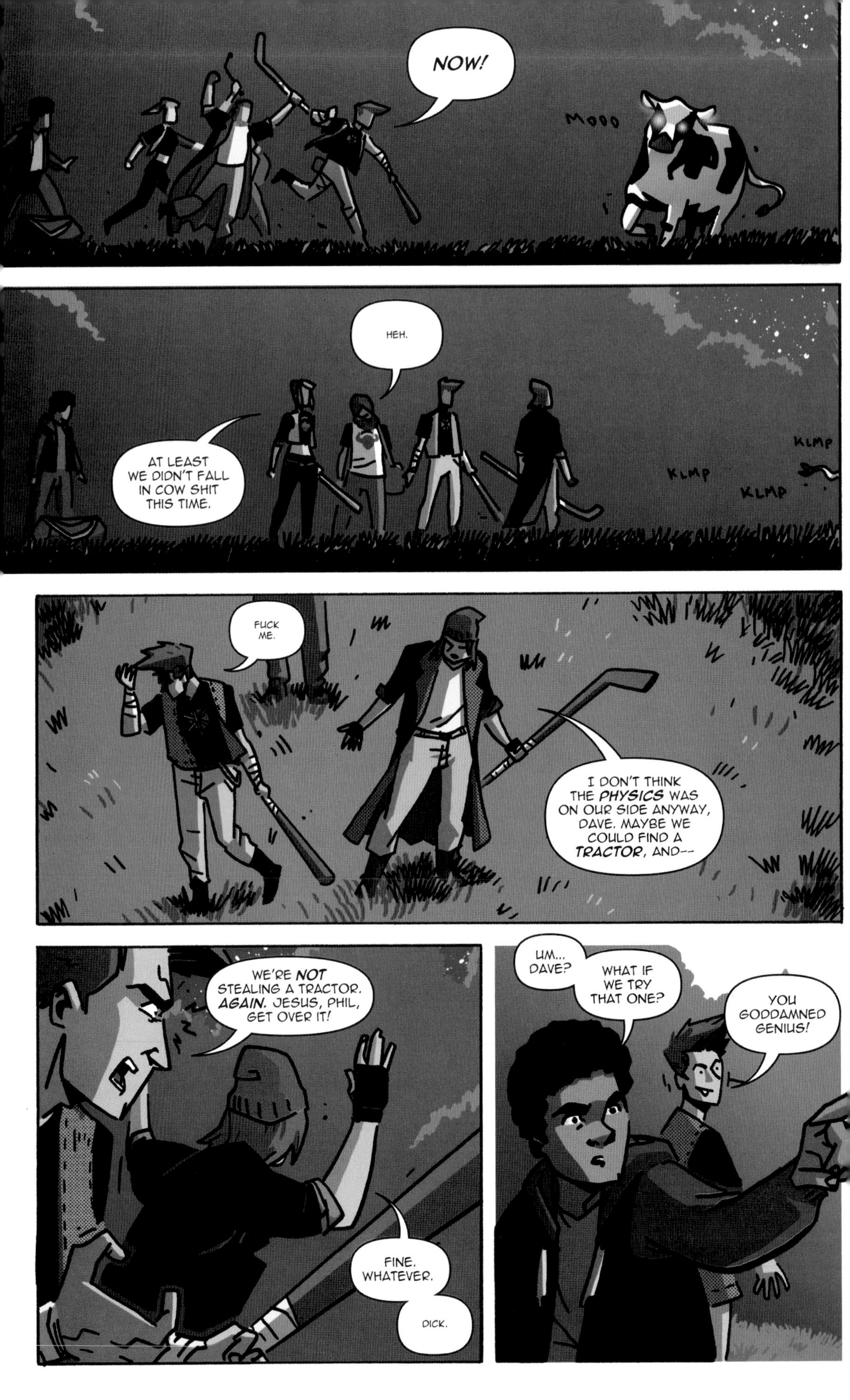
NOW!
MOOO
HEH.
AT LEAST WE DIDN'T FALL IN COW SHIT THIS TIME.
KLMP
KLMP
KLMP
FUCK ME.
I DON'T THINK THE PHYSICS WAS ON OUR SIDE ANYWAY, DAVE. MAYBE WE COULD FIND A TRACTOR, AND--
WE'RE NOT STEALING A TRACTOR. AGAIN. JESUS, PHIL, GET OVER IT!
FINE. WHATEVER.
DICK.
UM... DAVE?
WHAT IF WE TRY THAT ONE?
YOU GODDAMNED GENIUS!

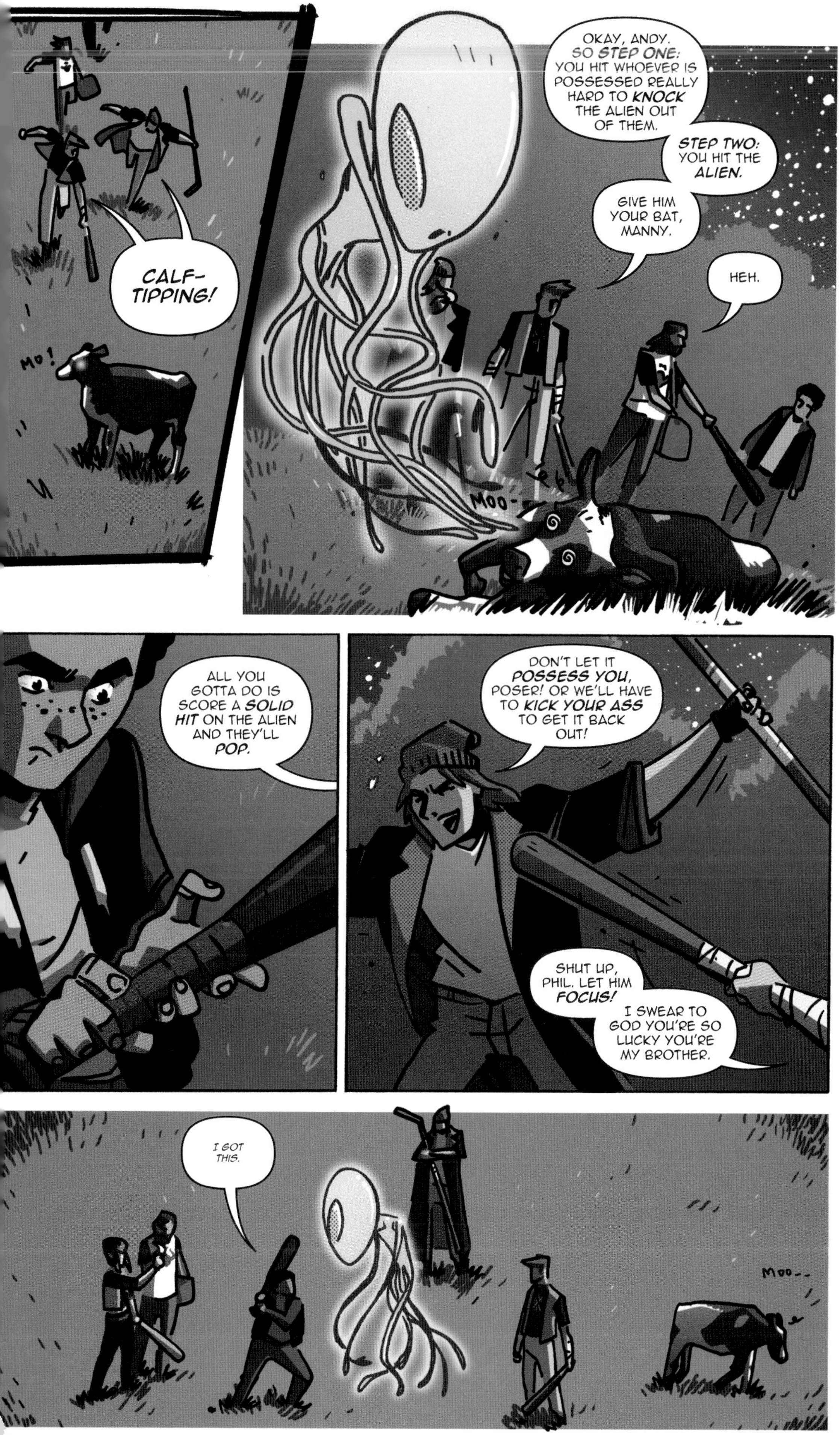

CALF-TIPPING!
MO!
OKAY, ANDY. SO STEP ONE: YOU HIT WHOEVER IS POSSESSED REALLY HARD TO KNOCK THE ALIEN OUT OF THEM.
STEP TWO: YOU HIT THE ALIEN.
GIVE HIM YOUR BAT, MANNY.
HEH.
MOO-
ALL YOU GOTTA DO IS SCORE A SOLID HIT ON THE ALIEN AND THEY'LL POP.
DON'T LET IT POSSESS YOU, POSER! OR WE'LL HAVE TO KICK YOUR ASS TO GET IT BACK OUT!
SHUT UP, PHIL. LET HIM FOCUS!
I SWEAR TO GOD YOU'RE SO LUCKY YOU'RE MY BROTHER.
I GOT THIS.
MOO--

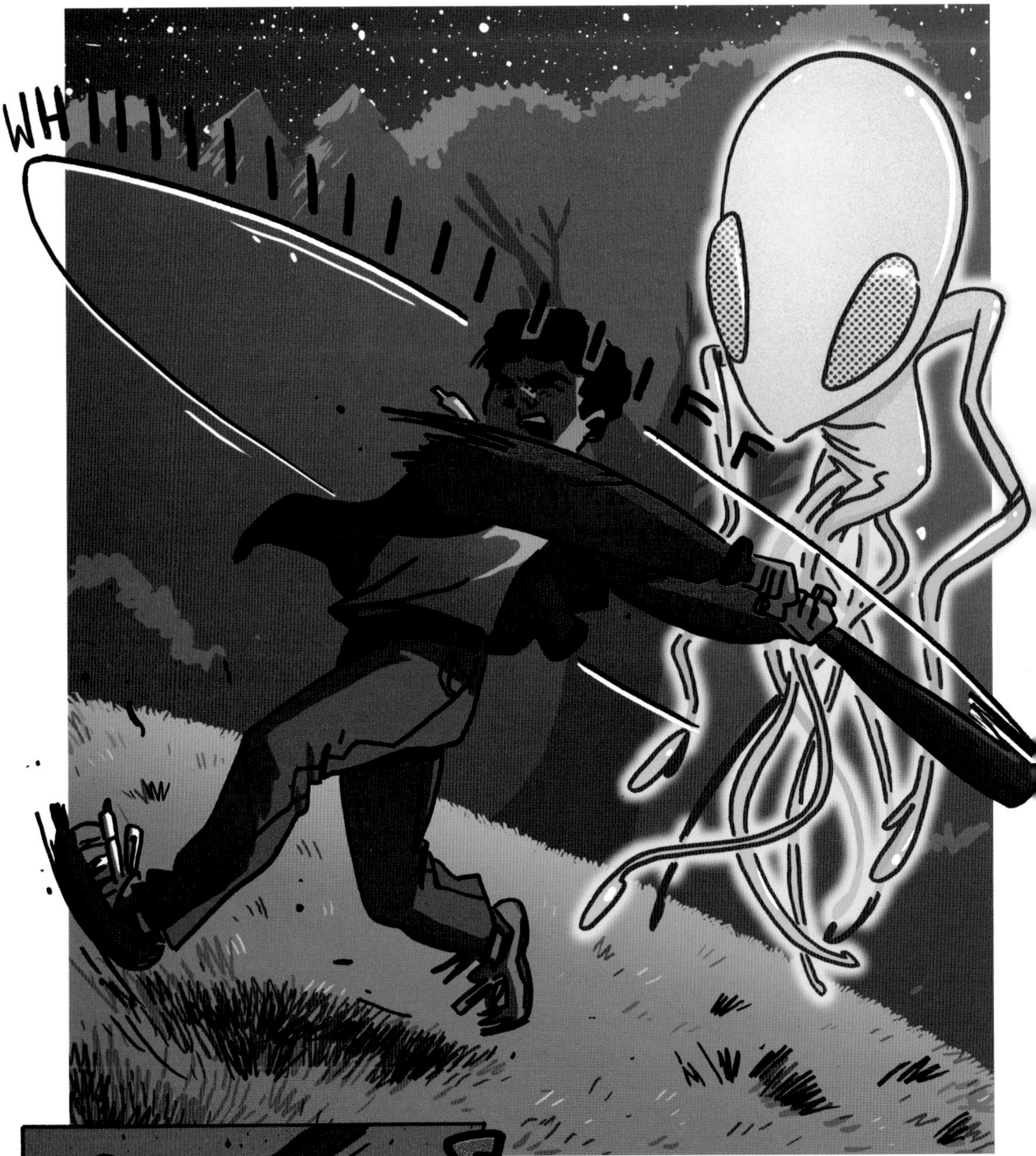
WHIIIIIIIIIIIIIIFF

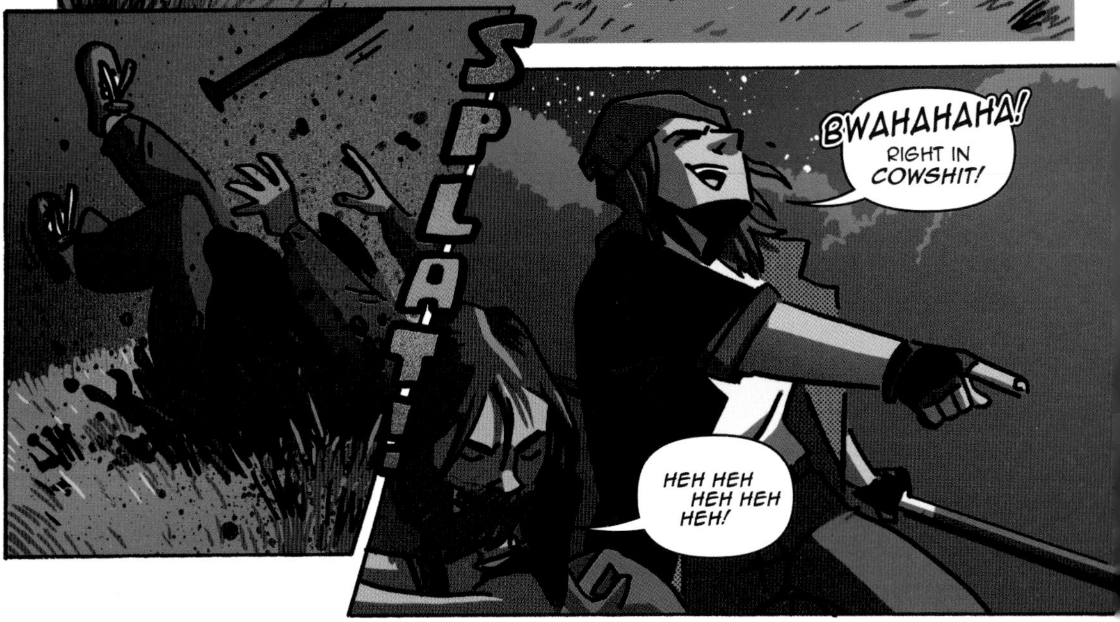
SPLAT!
BWAHAHAHA! RIGHT IN COWSHIT!
HEH HEH HEH HEH HEH!

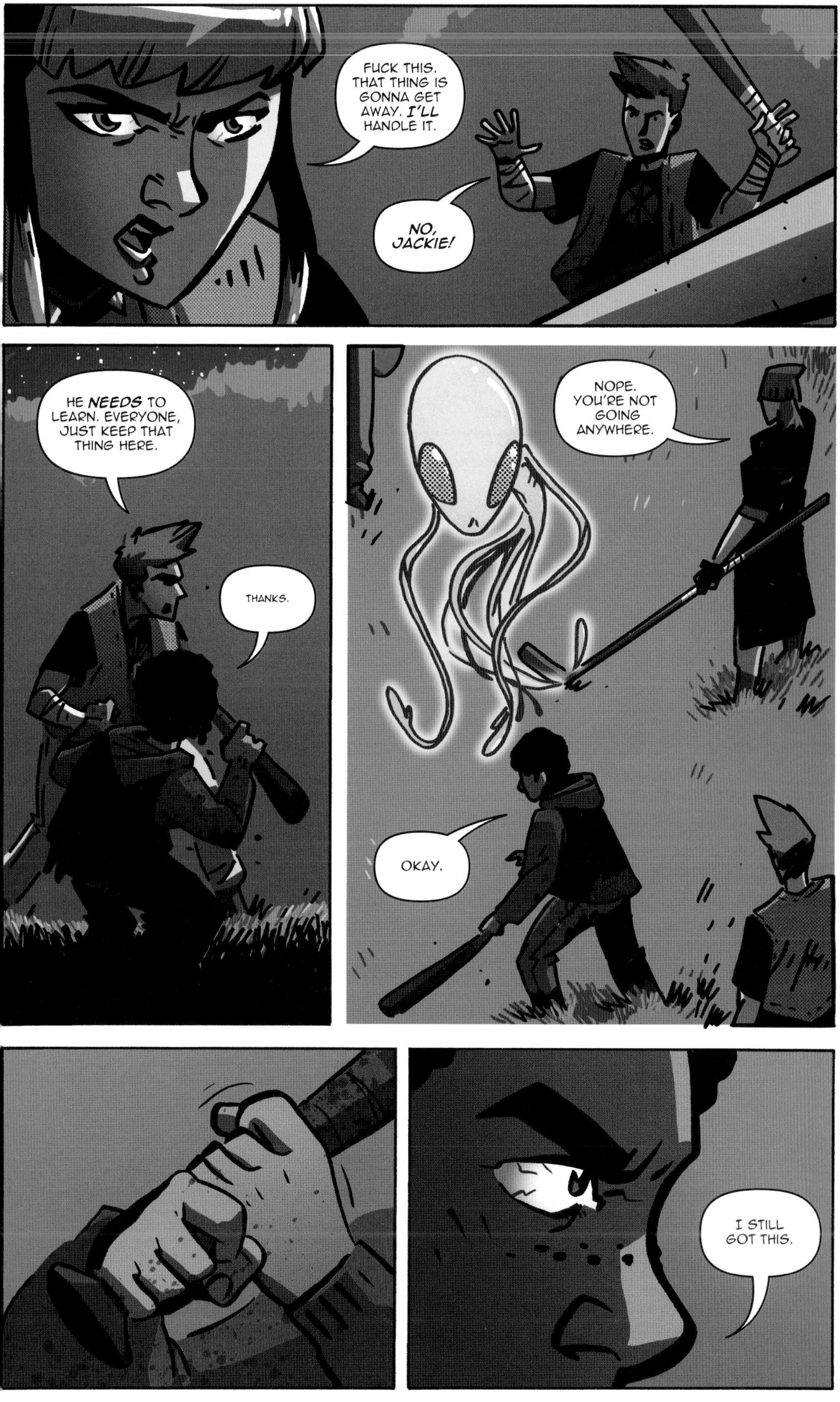
FUCK THIS. THAT THING IS GONNA GET AWAY. *I'LL* HANDLE IT.
NO, JACKIE!
HE **NEEDS** TO LEARN. EVERYONE, JUST KEEP THAT THING HERE.
THANKS.
NOPE. YOU'RE NOT GOING ANYWHERE.
OKAY.
I STILL GOT THIS.

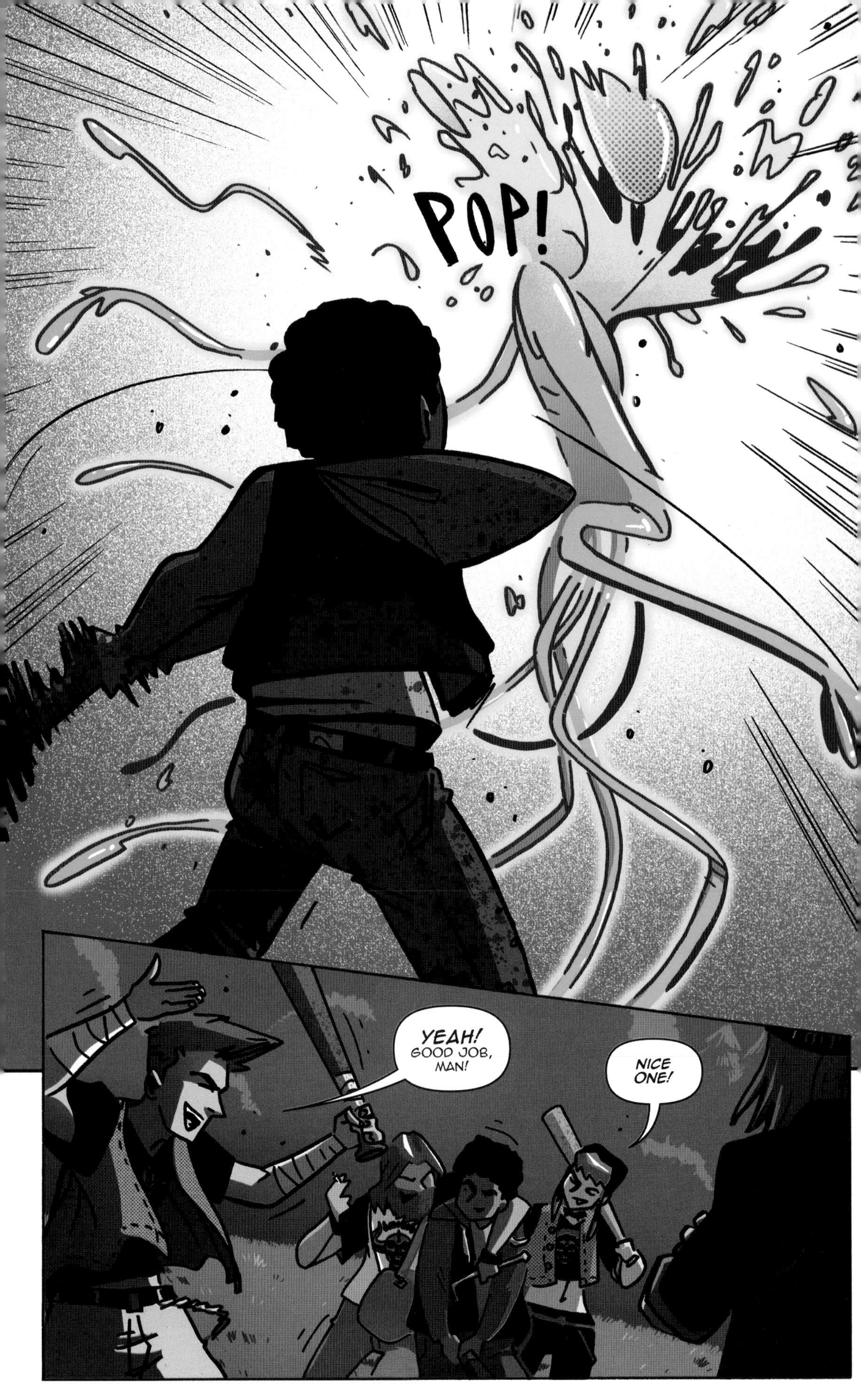
POP!
YEAH! GOOD JOB, MAN!
NICE ONE!

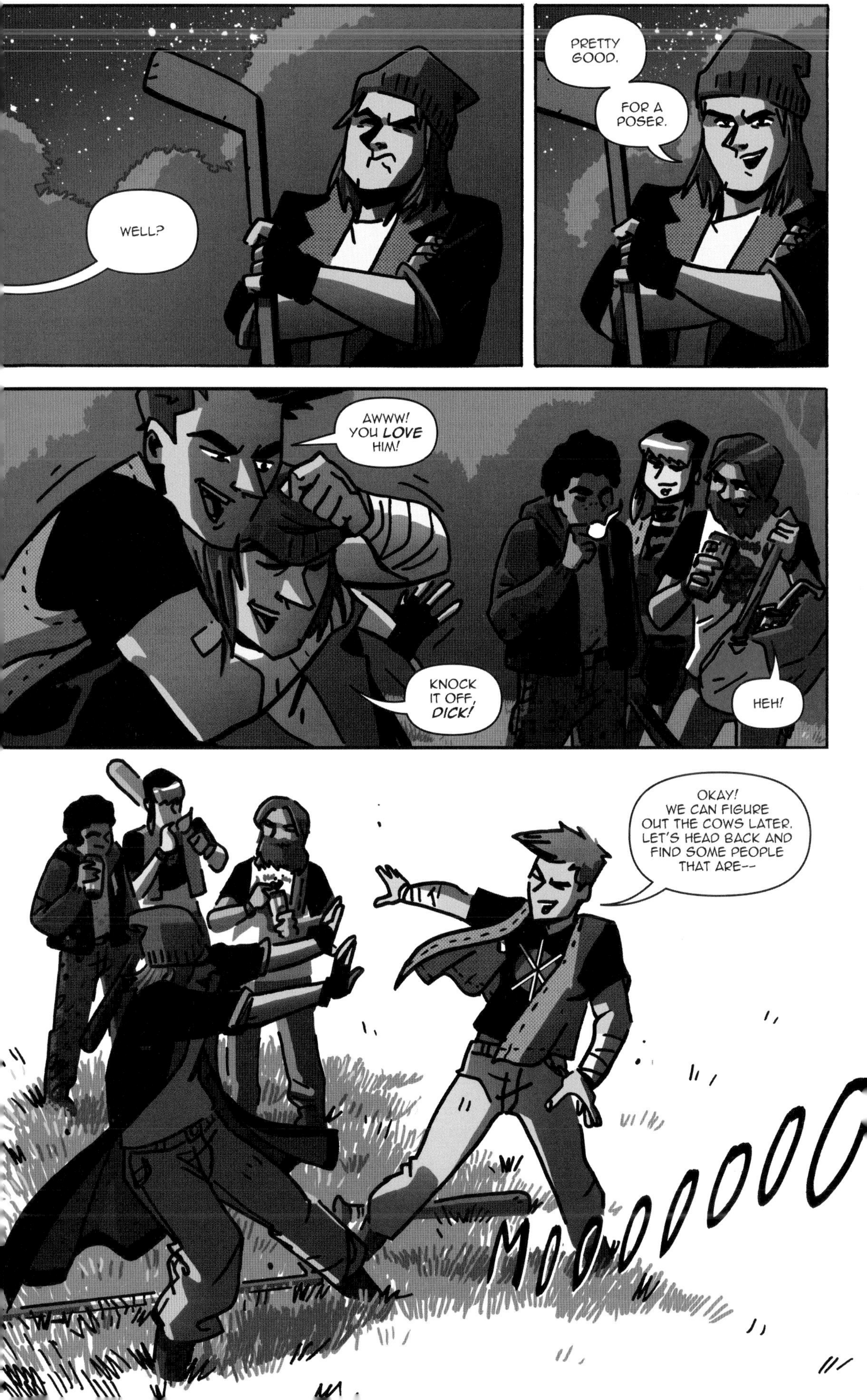
WELL?
PRETTY GOOD.
FOR A POSER.
AWWW! YOU *LOVE* HIM!
KNOCK IT OFF, *DICK!*
HEH!
OKAY! WE CAN FIGURE OUT THE COWS LATER. LET'S HEAD BACK AND FIND SOME PEOPLE THAT ARE--
MOOOOOOOO

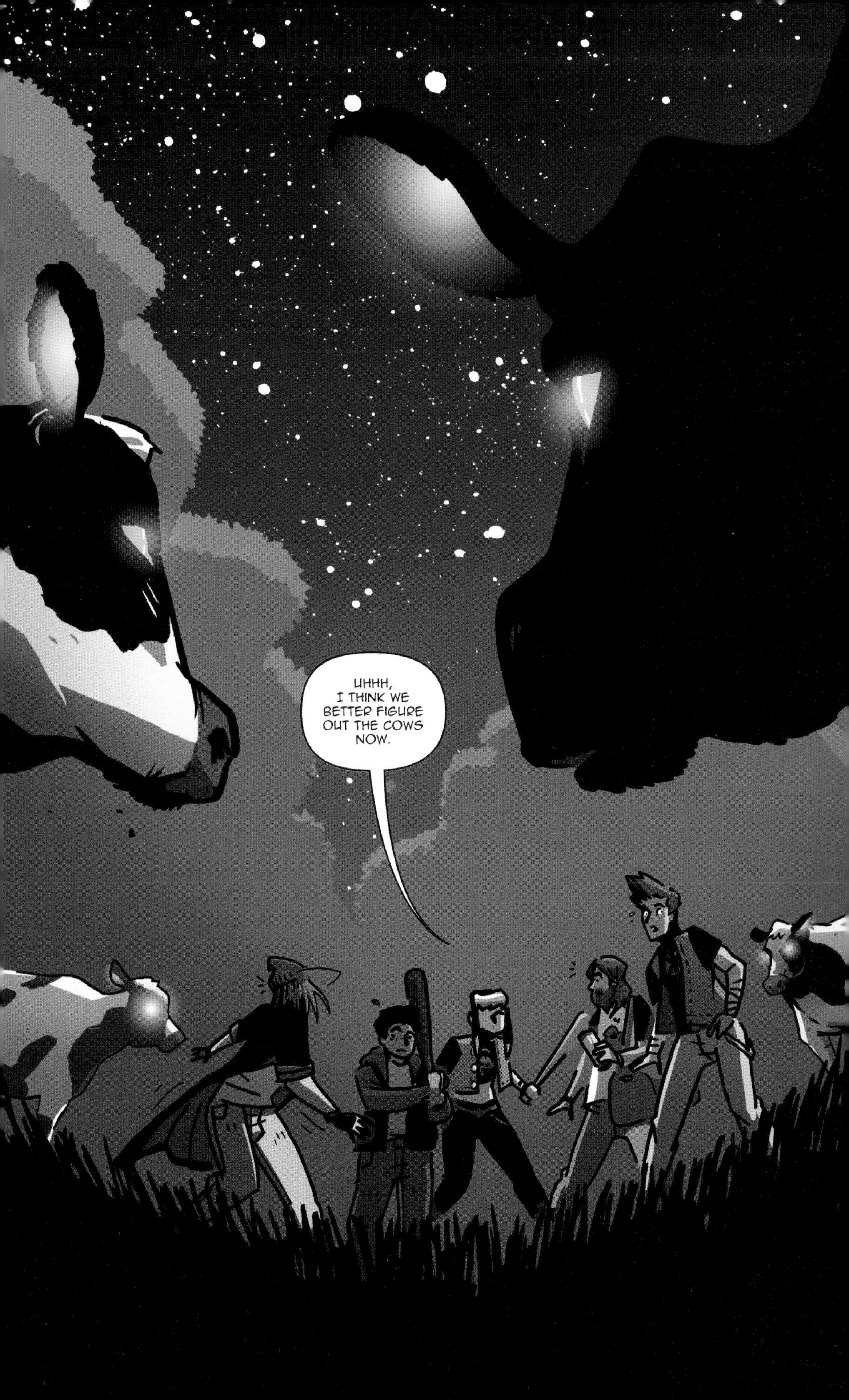
UHHH, I THINK WE BETTER FIGURE OUT THE COWS NOW.

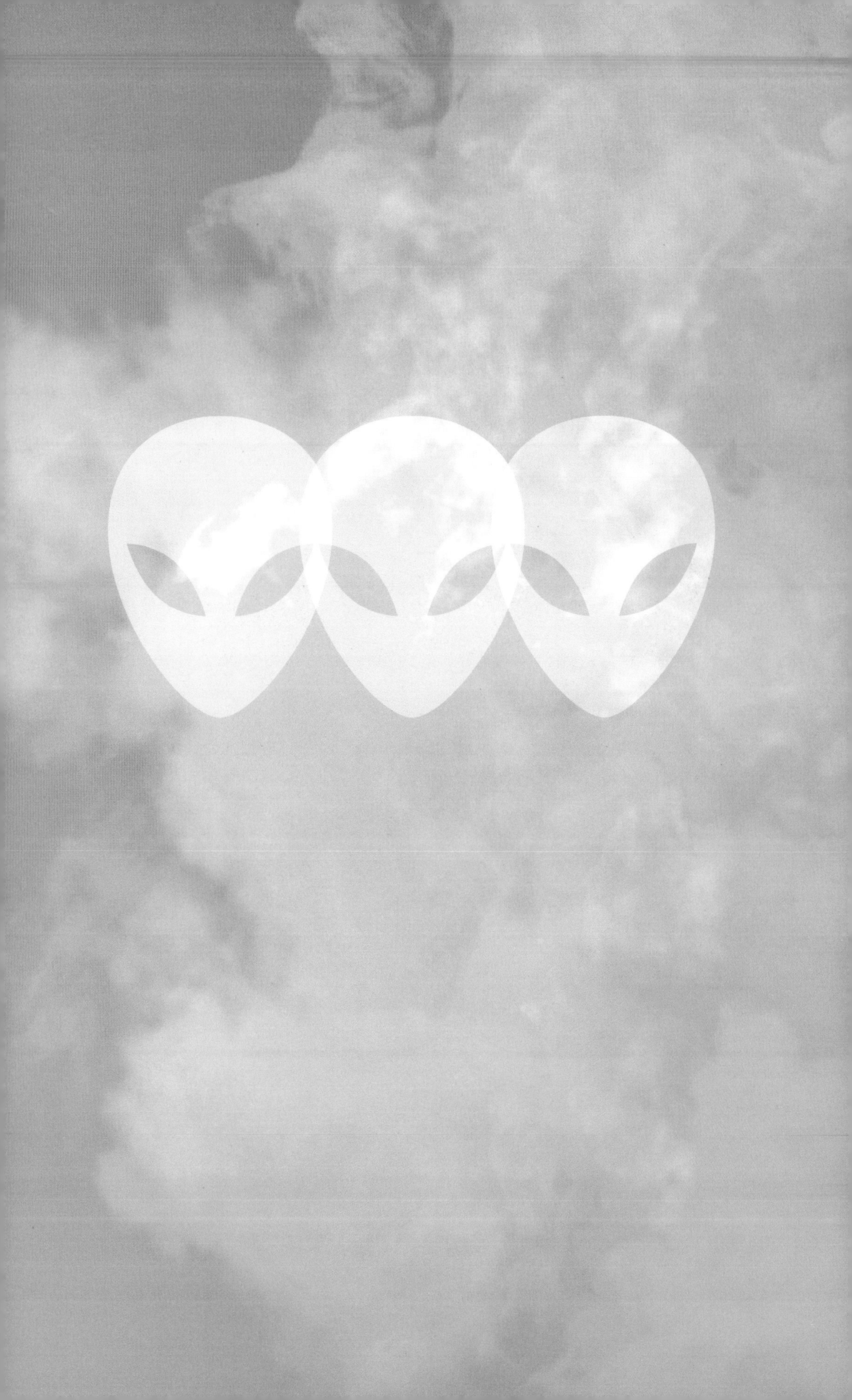

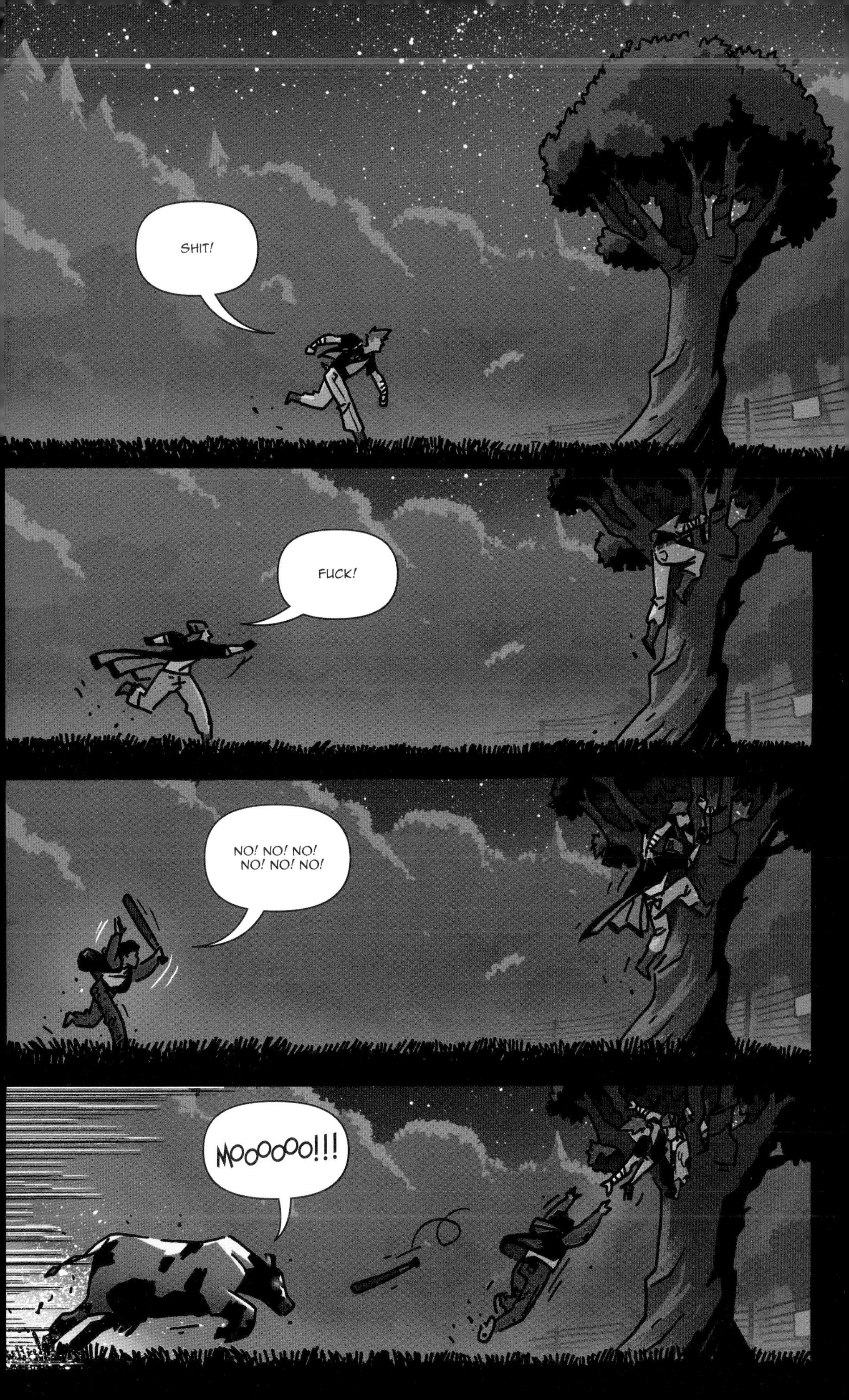
SHIT!
FUCK!
NO! NO! NO! NO! NO! NO!
MOOOOOO!!!

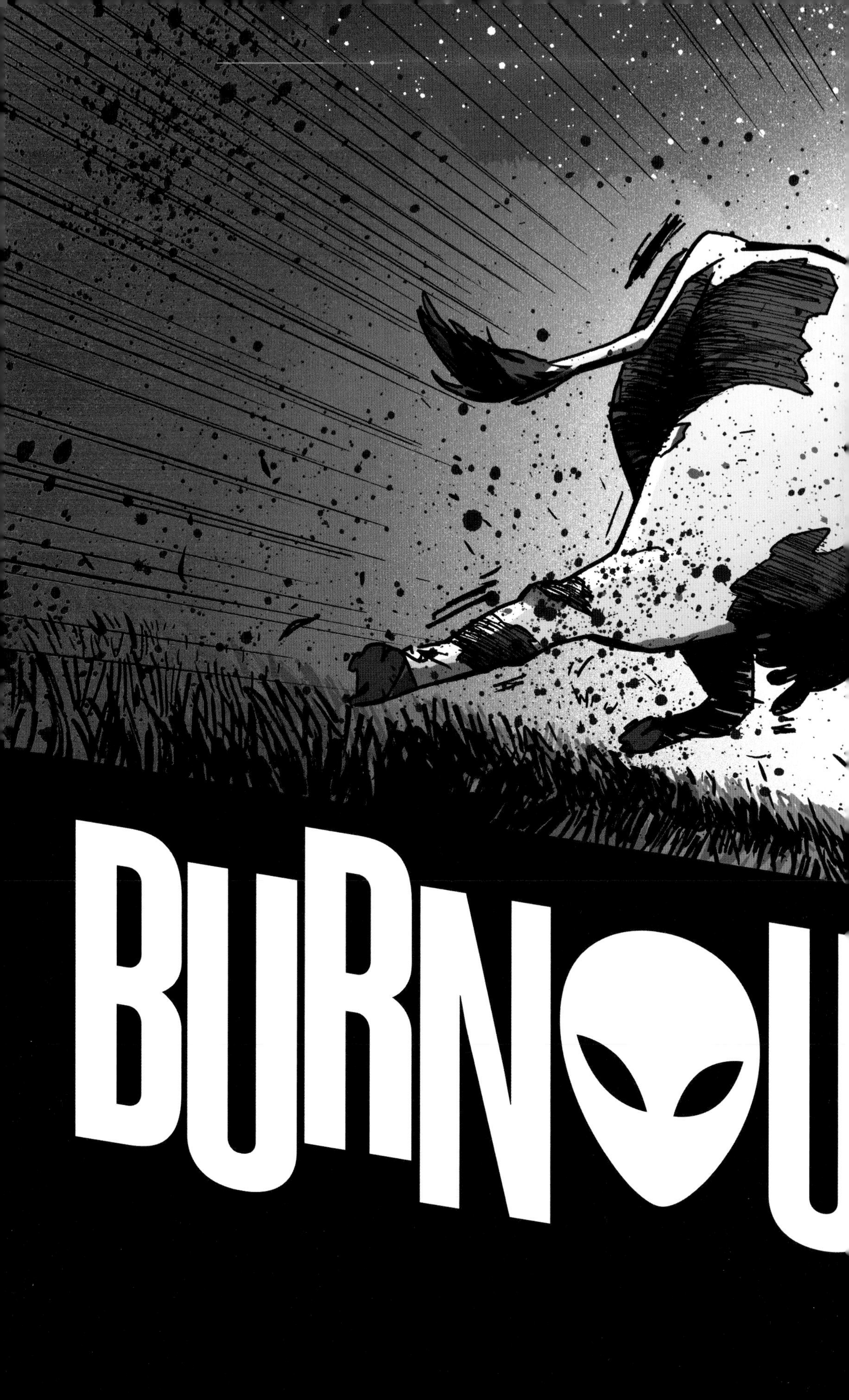
BURNOU

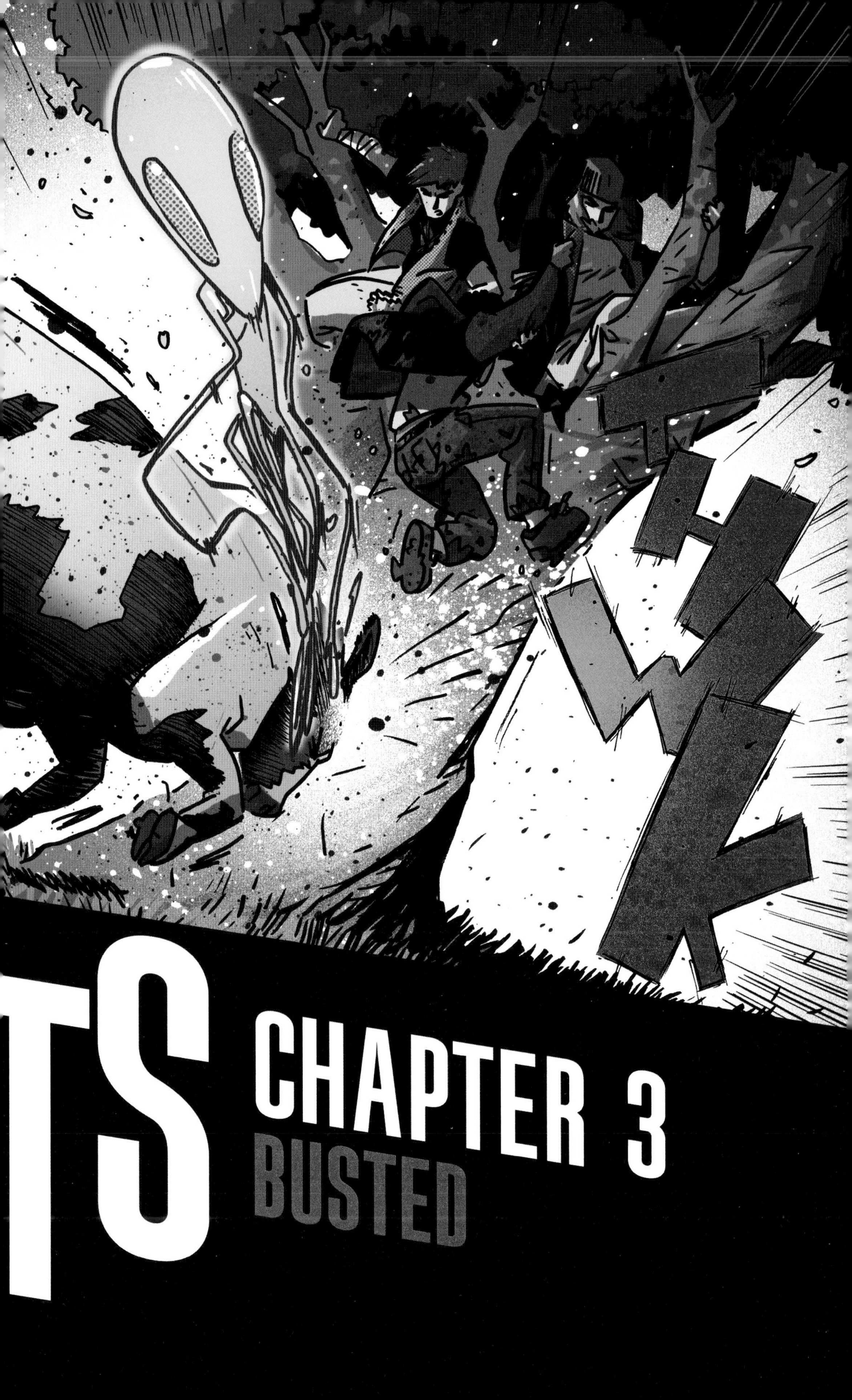
THWK

TS

CHAPTER 3
BUSTED

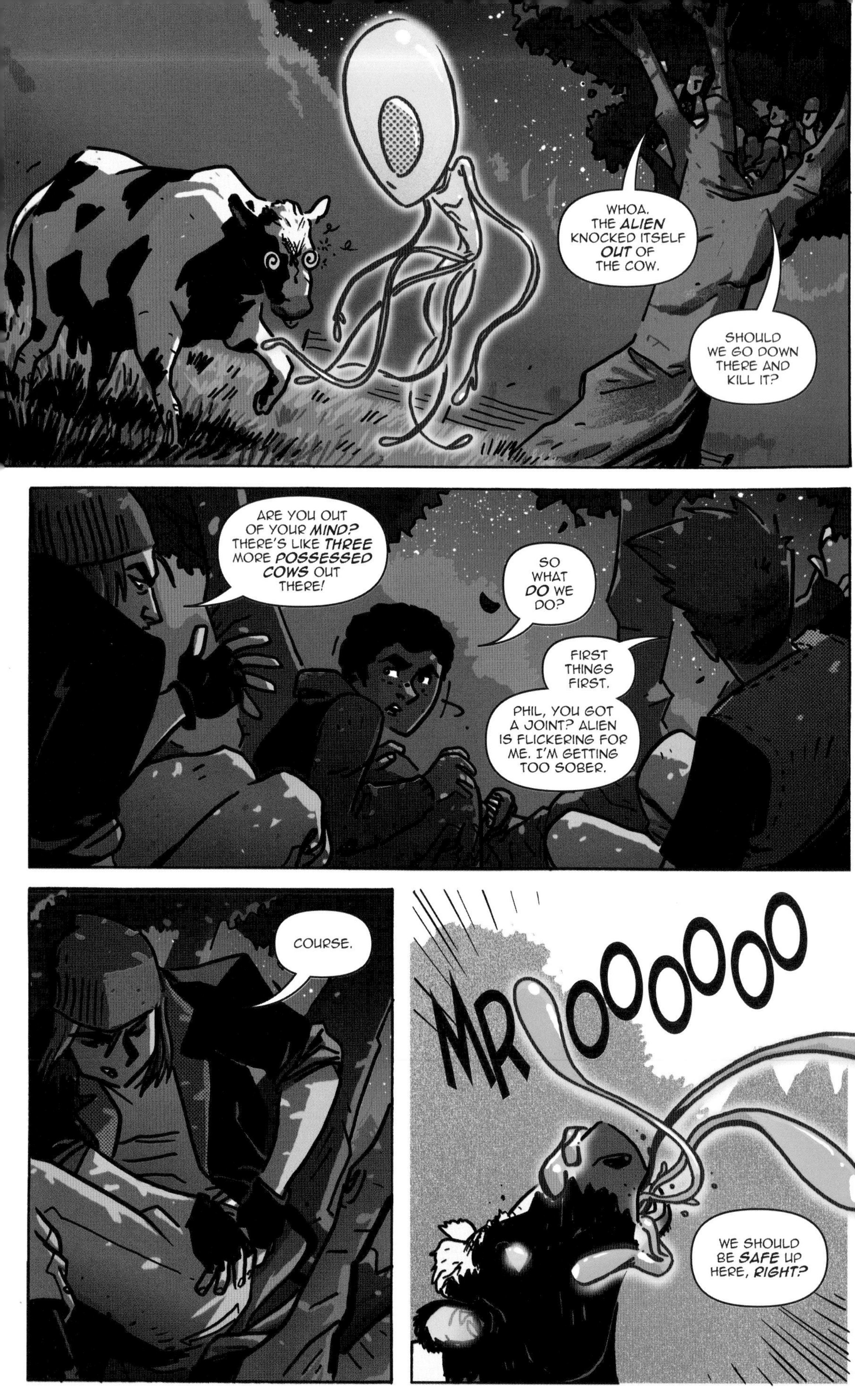
WHOA. THE ALIEN KNOCKED ITSELF OUT OF THE COW.
SHOULD WE GO DOWN THERE AND KILL IT?
ARE YOU OUT OF YOUR MIND? THERE'S LIKE THREE MORE POSSESSED COWS OUT THERE!
SO WHAT DO WE DO?
FIRST THINGS FIRST.
PHIL, YOU GOT A JOINT? ALIEN IS FLICKERING FOR ME. I'M GETTING TOO SOBER.
COURSE.
MROOOOOOO
WE SHOULD BE SAFE UP HERE, RIGHT?

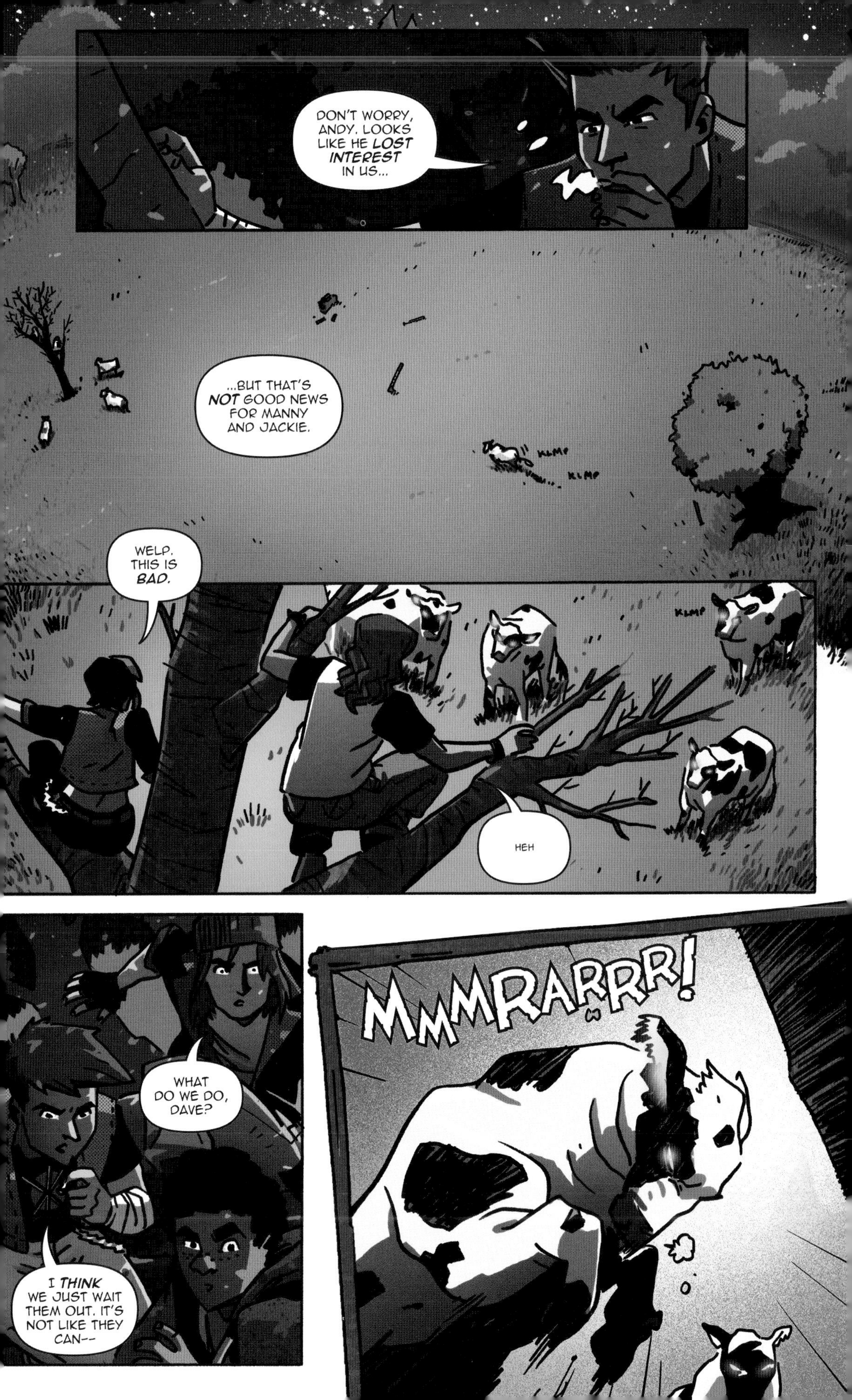
DON'T WORRY, ANDY. LOOKS LIKE HE LOST INTEREST IN US...
...BUT THAT'S NOT GOOD NEWS FOR MANNY AND JACKIE.
KLMP
KLMP
WELP. THIS IS BAD.
KLMP
HEH
WHAT DO WE DO, DAVE?
I THINK WE JUST WAIT THEM OUT. IT'S NOT LIKE THEY CAN--
MMMRARRR!

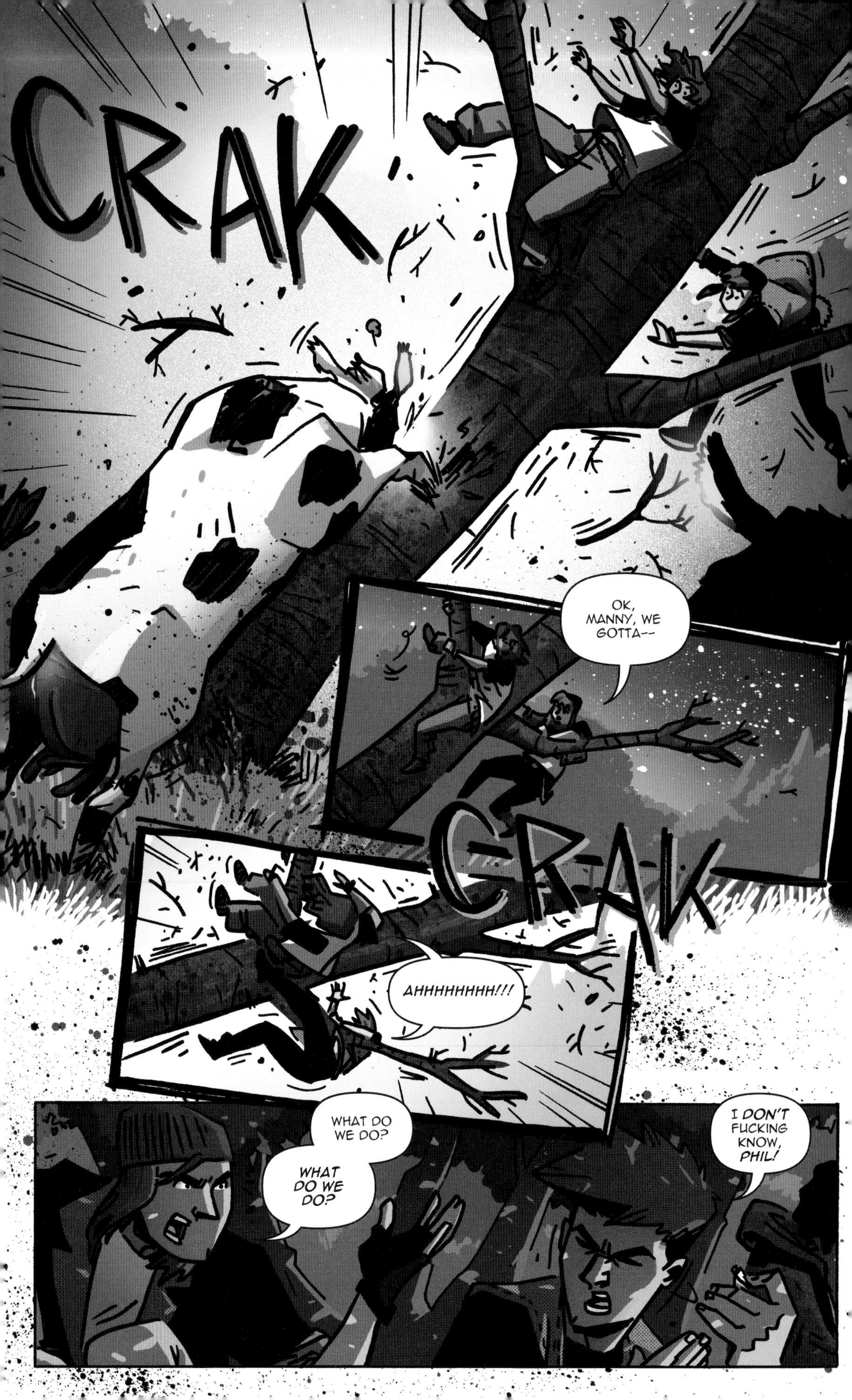
CRAK
OK, MANNY, WE GOTTA--
CRAK
AHHHHHHHHH!!!
WHAT DO WE DO?
WHAT DO WE DO?
I DON'T FUCKING KNOW, PHIL!

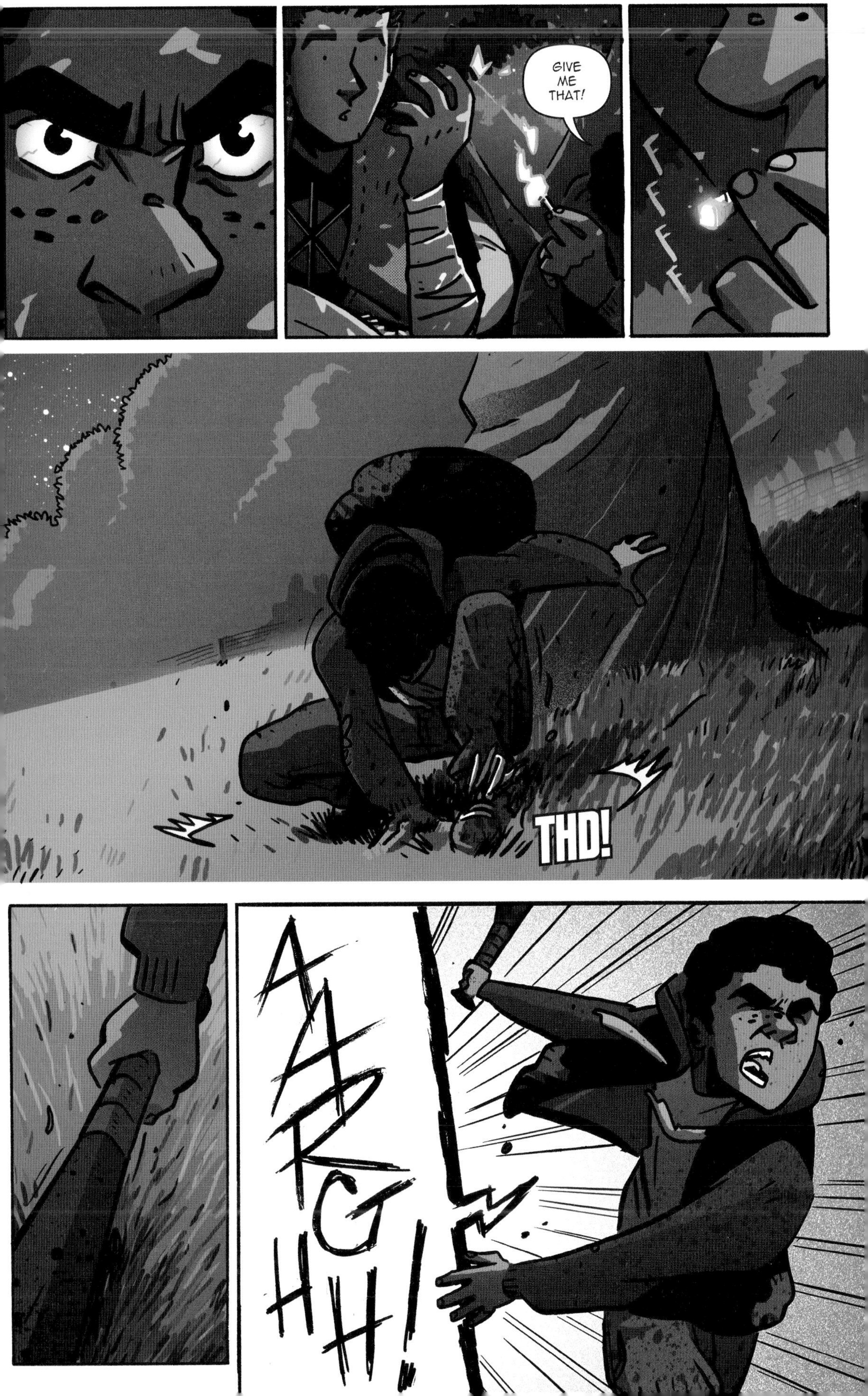
GIVE ME THAT!
FFFF
THD!
AARGHH!

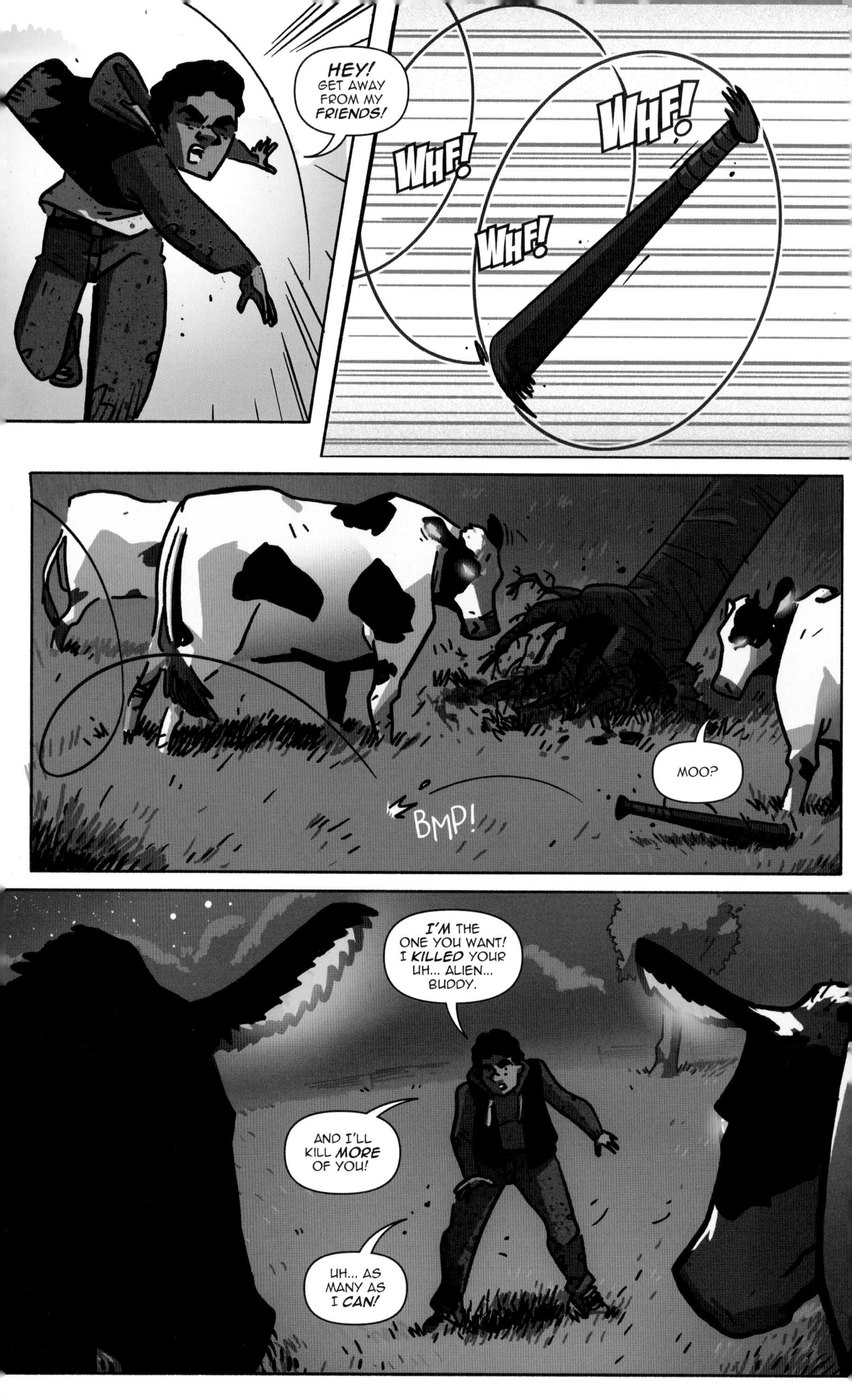
HEY! GET AWAY FROM MY FRIENDS!
WHF!
WHF!
WHF!
MOO?
BMP!
I'M THE ONE YOU WANT! I KILLED YOUR UH... ALIEN... BUDDY.
AND I'LL KILL MORE OF YOU!
UH... AS MANY AS I CAN!

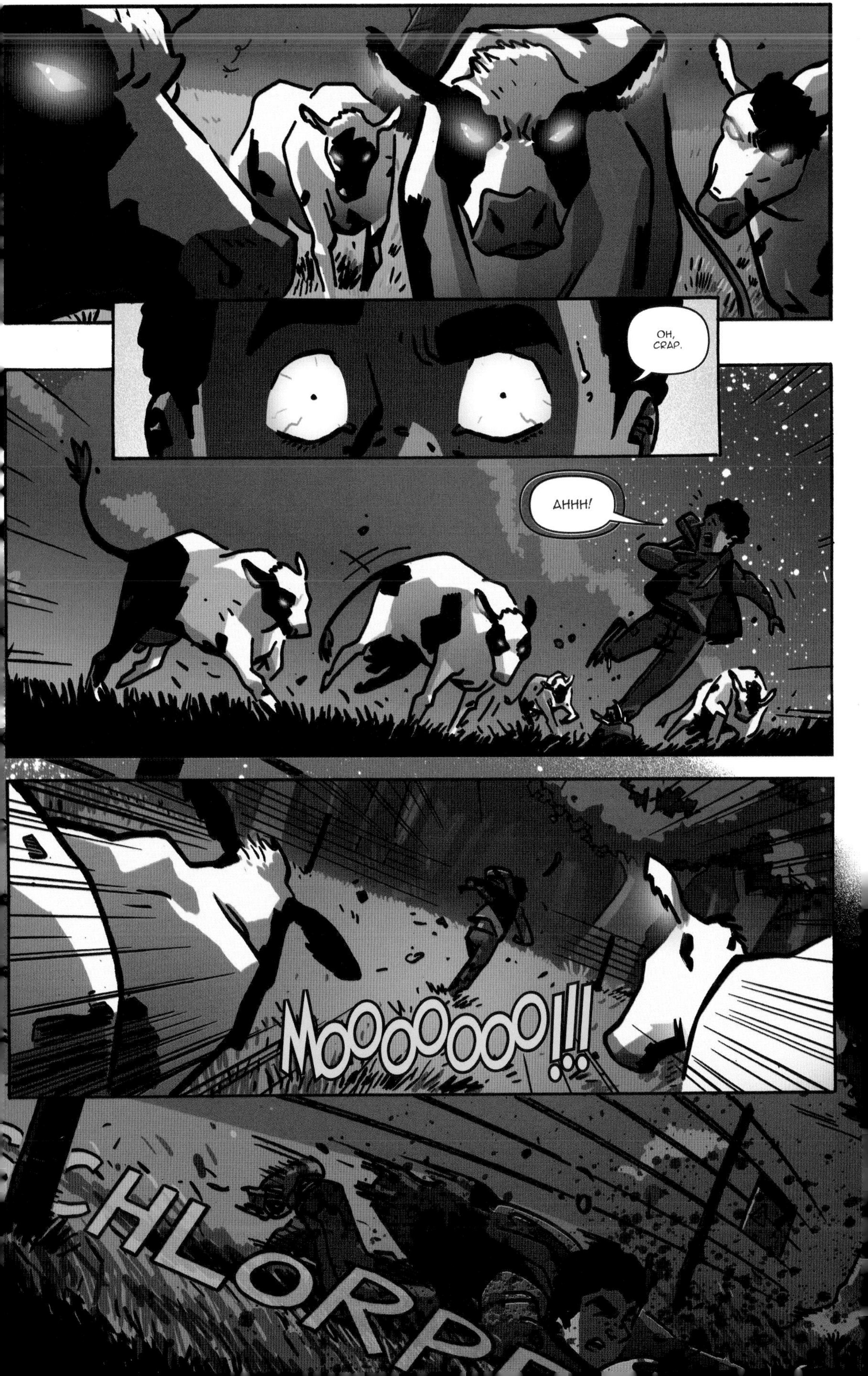
OH, CRAP.
AHHH!
MOOOOOOO!!!
SCHLORPP

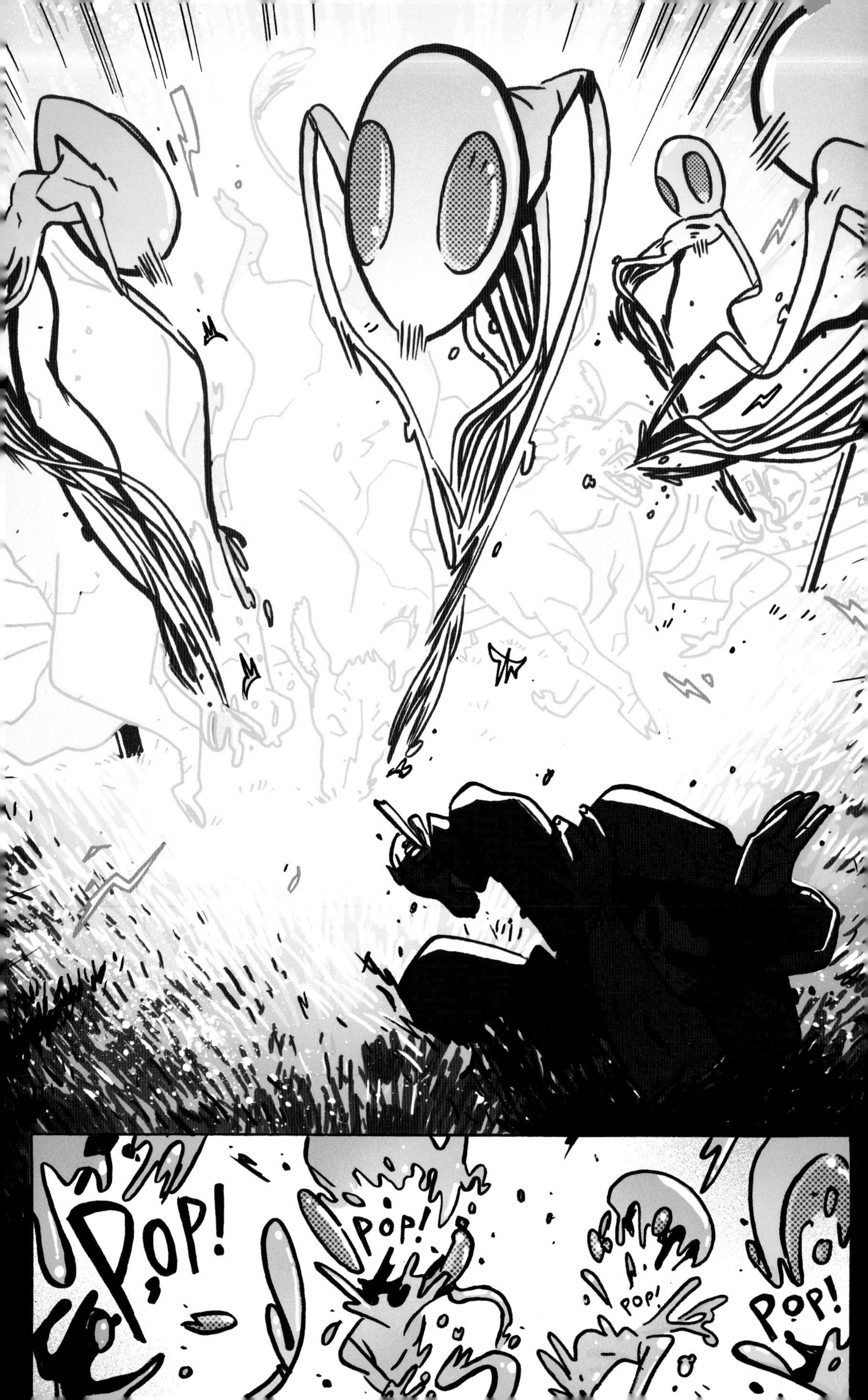
POP!
POP!
POP!
POP!

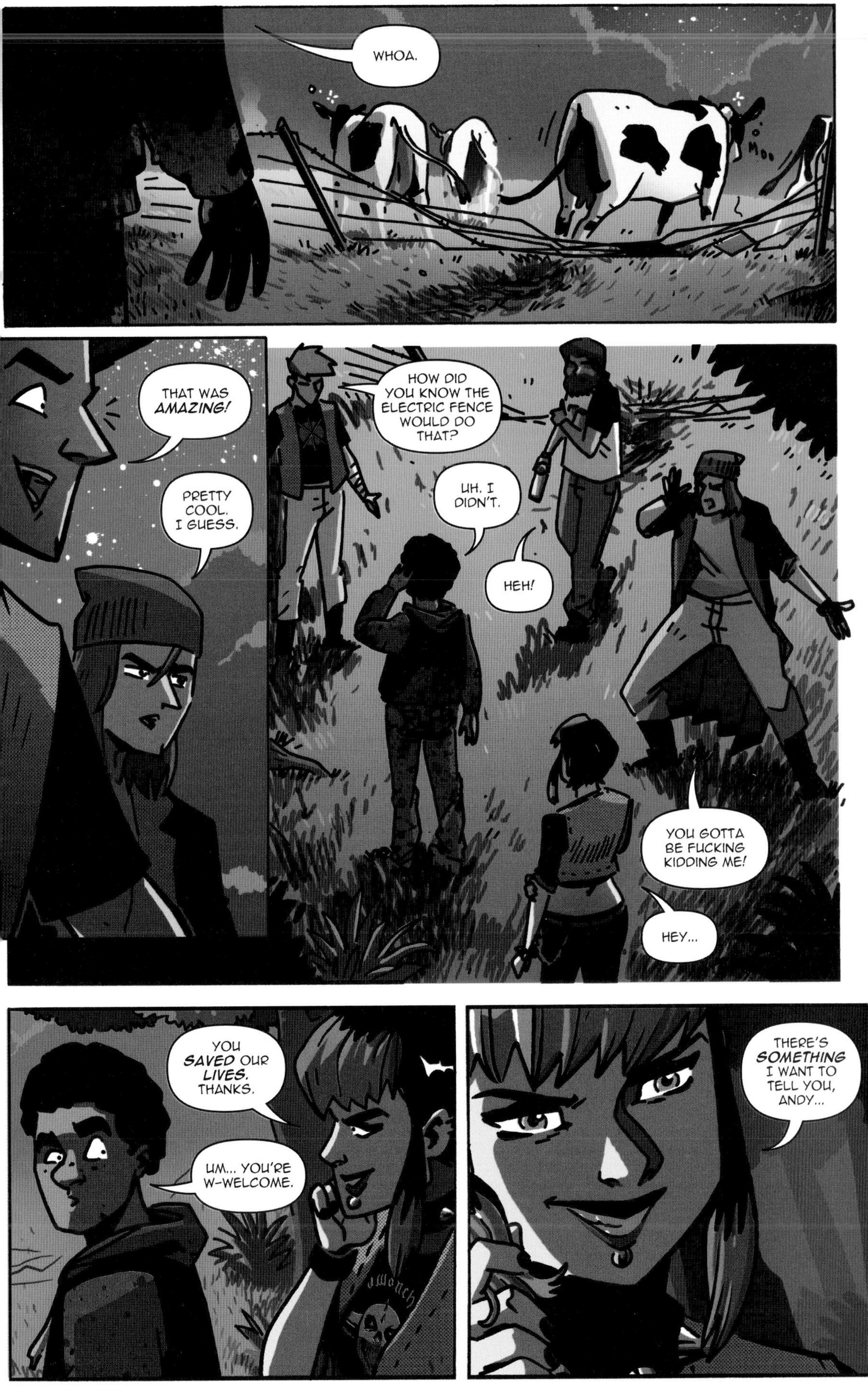
WHOA.
MOO
THAT WAS AMAZING!
PRETTY COOL. I GUESS.
HOW DID YOU KNOW THE ELECTRIC FENCE WOULD DO THAT?
UH. I DIDN'T.
HEH!
YOU GOTTA BE FUCKING KIDDING ME!
HEY...
YOU SAVED OUR LIVES. THANKS.
UM... YOU'RE W-WELCOME.
THERE'S SOMETHING I WANT TO TELL YOU, ANDY...

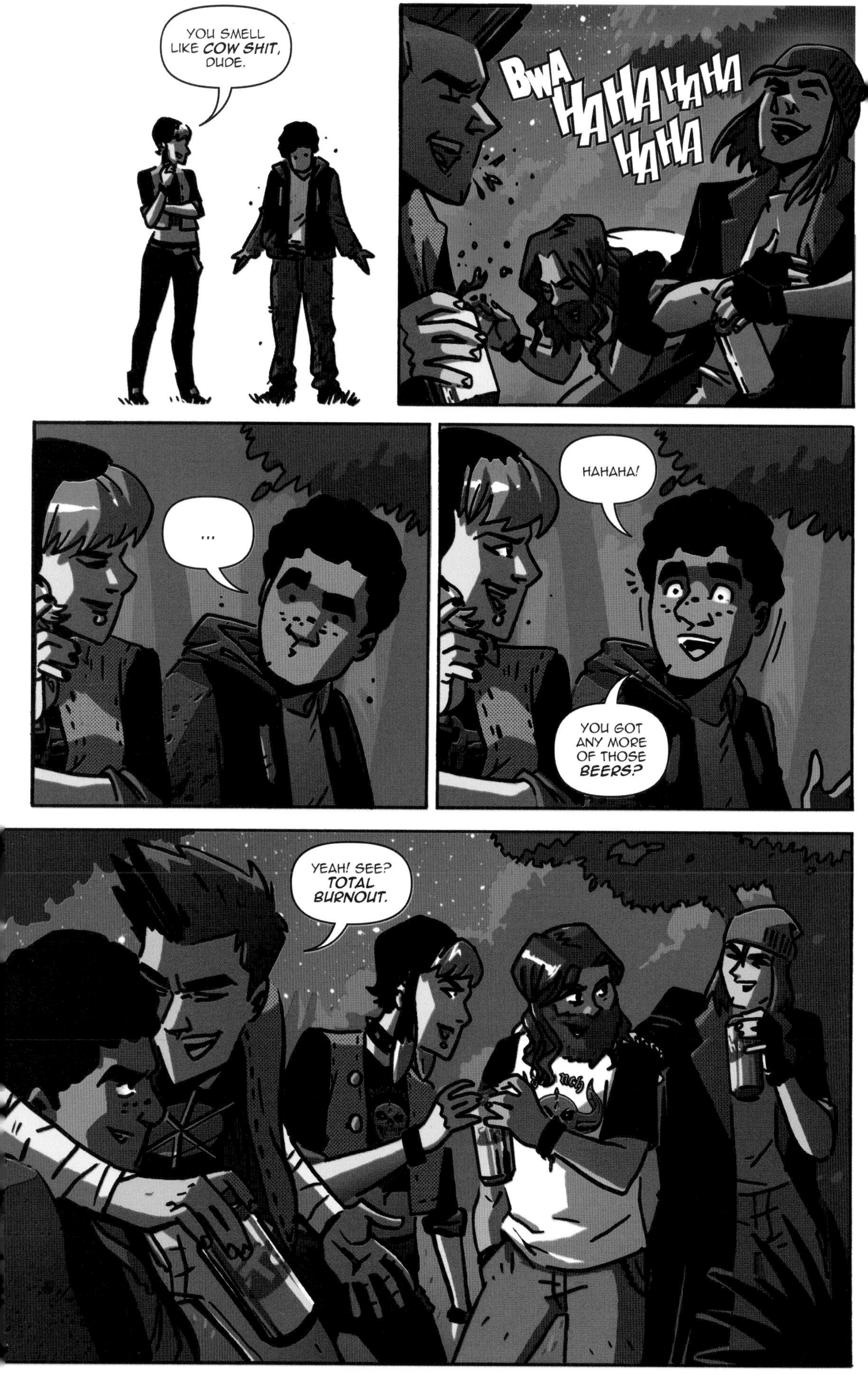
YOU SMELL LIKE COW SHIT, DUDE.
BWAHAHAHAHAHAHAHA
...
HAHAHA!
YOU GOT ANY MORE OF THOSE BEERS?
YEAH! SEE? TOTAL BURNOUT.

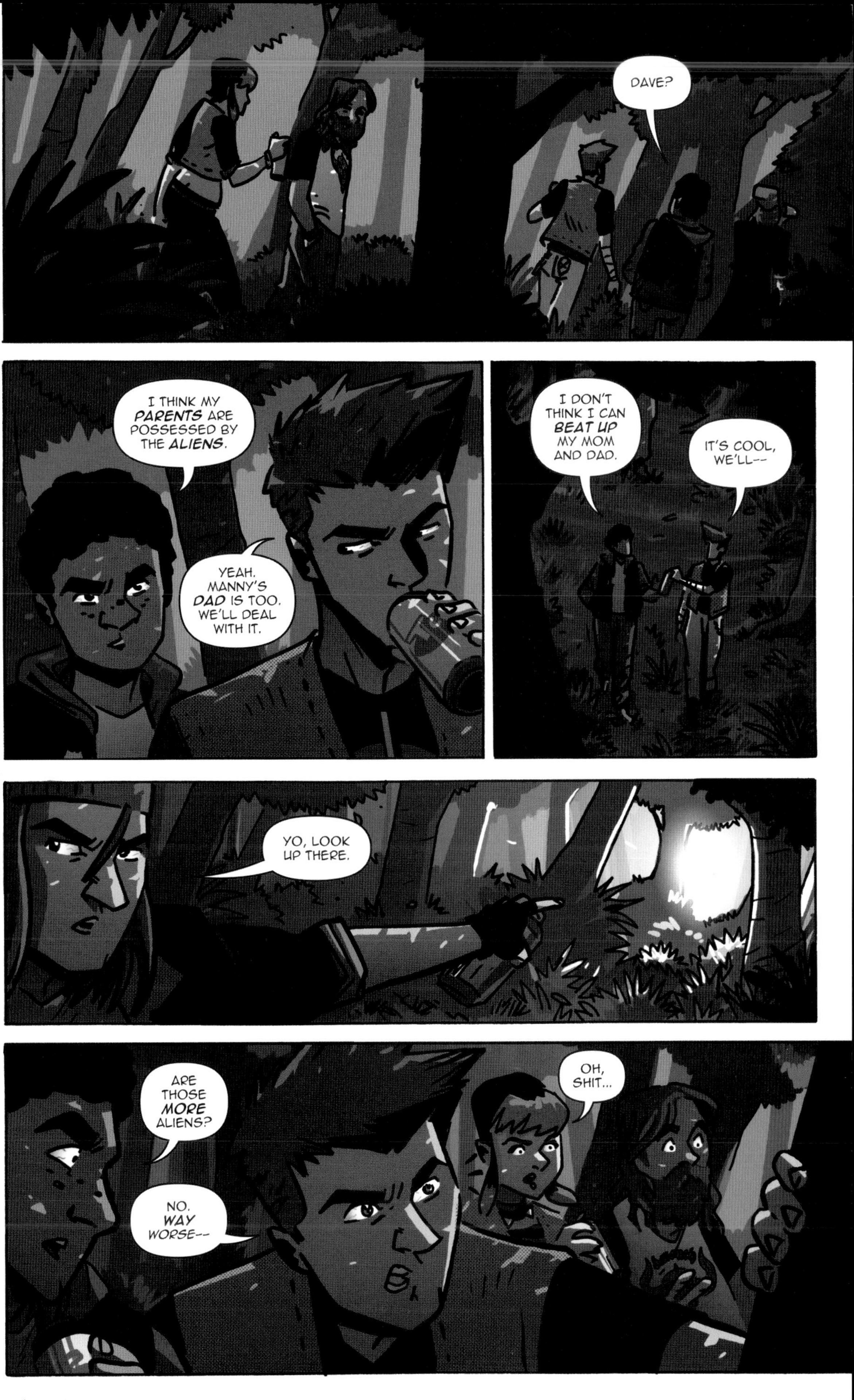
DAVE?
I THINK MY PARENTS ARE POSSESSED BY THE ALIENS.
YEAH. MANNY'S DAD IS TOO. WE'LL DEAL WITH IT.
I DON'T THINK I CAN BEAT UP MY MOM AND DAD.
IT'S COOL, WE'LL--
YO, LOOK UP THERE.
ARE THOSE MORE ALIENS?
NO. WAY WORSE--
OH, SHIT...

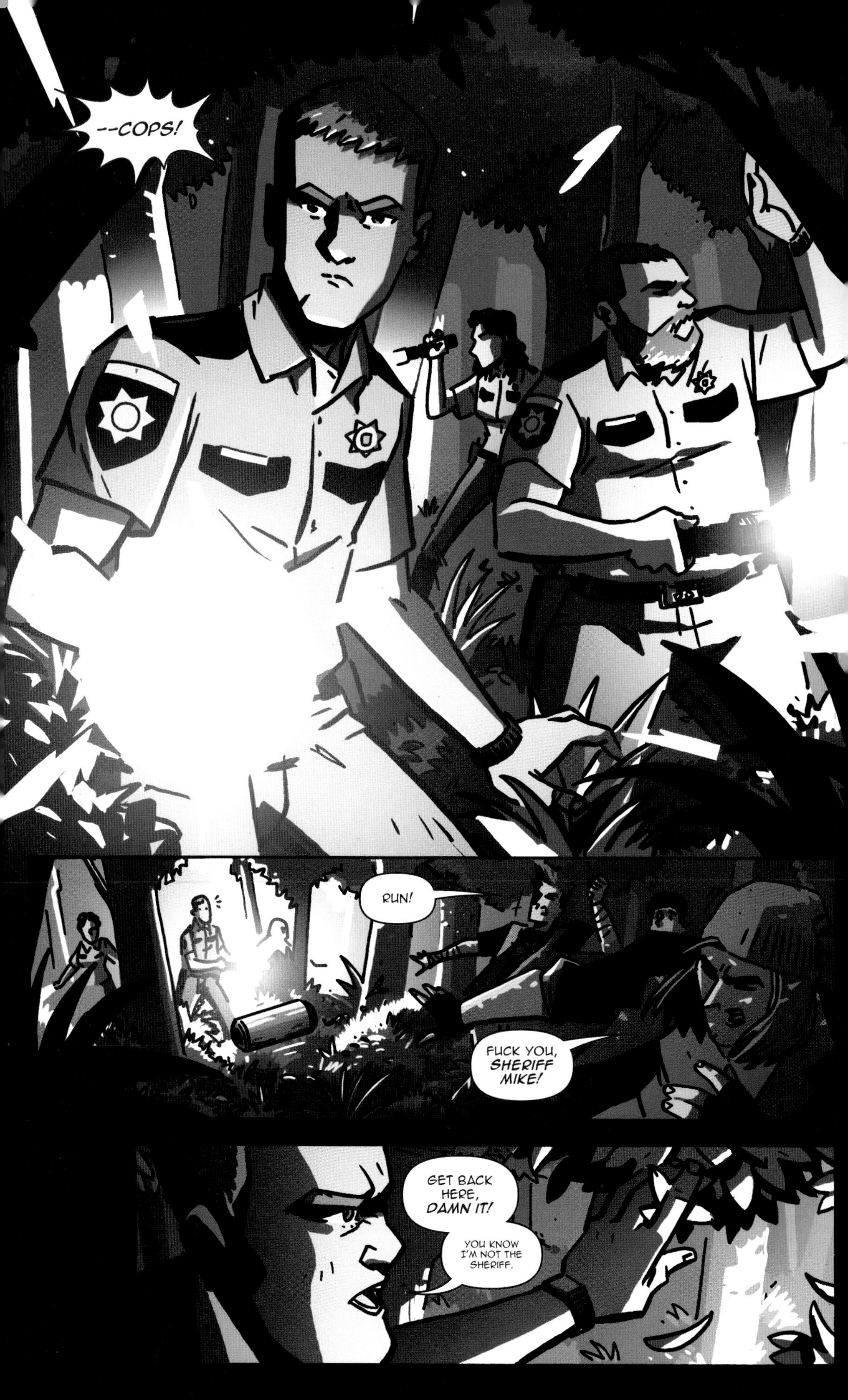
--COPS!
RUN!
FUCK YOU, SHERIFF MIKE!
GET BACK HERE, DAMN IT!
YOU KNOW I'M NOT THE SHERIFF.

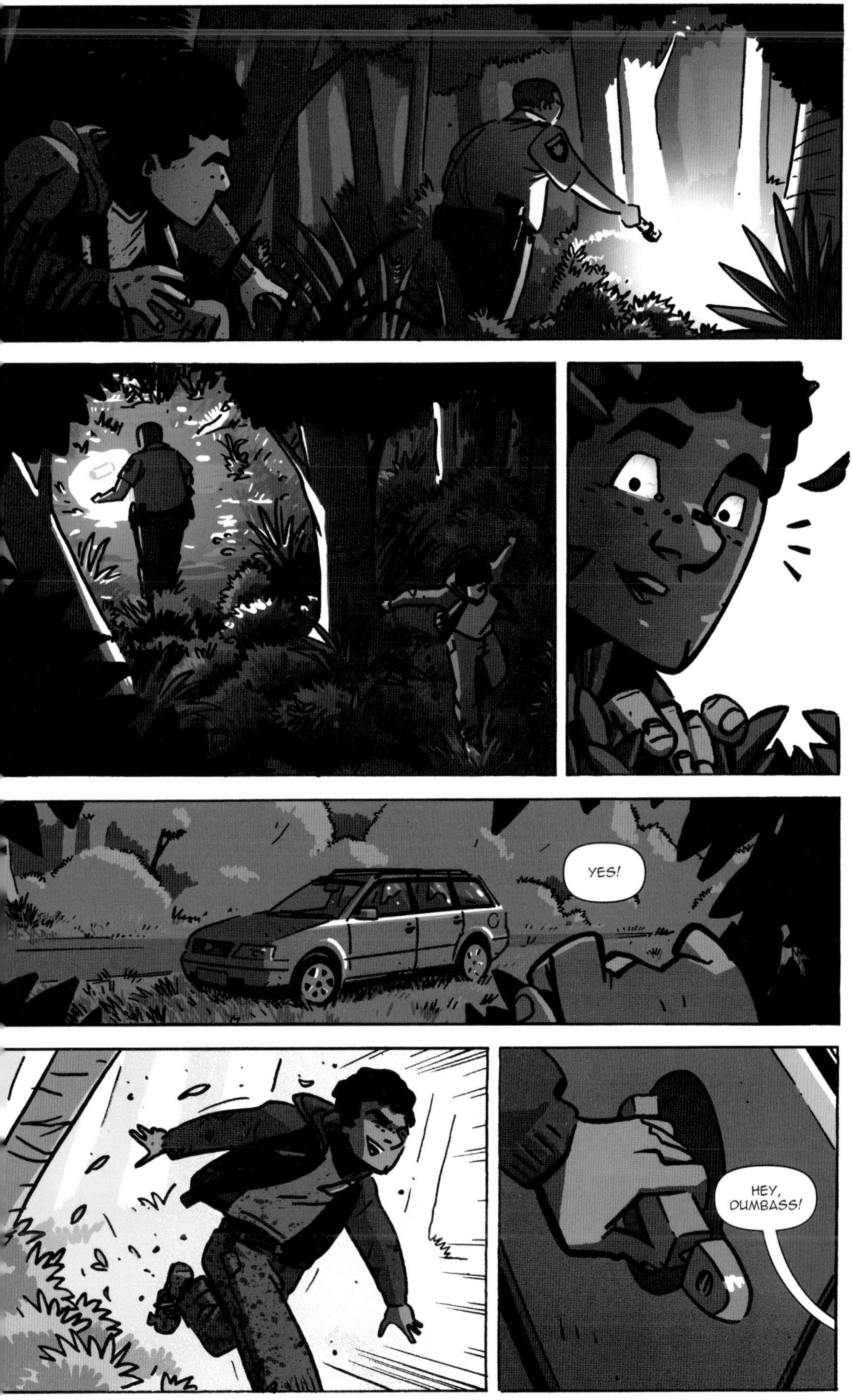
YES!
HEY, DUMBASS!

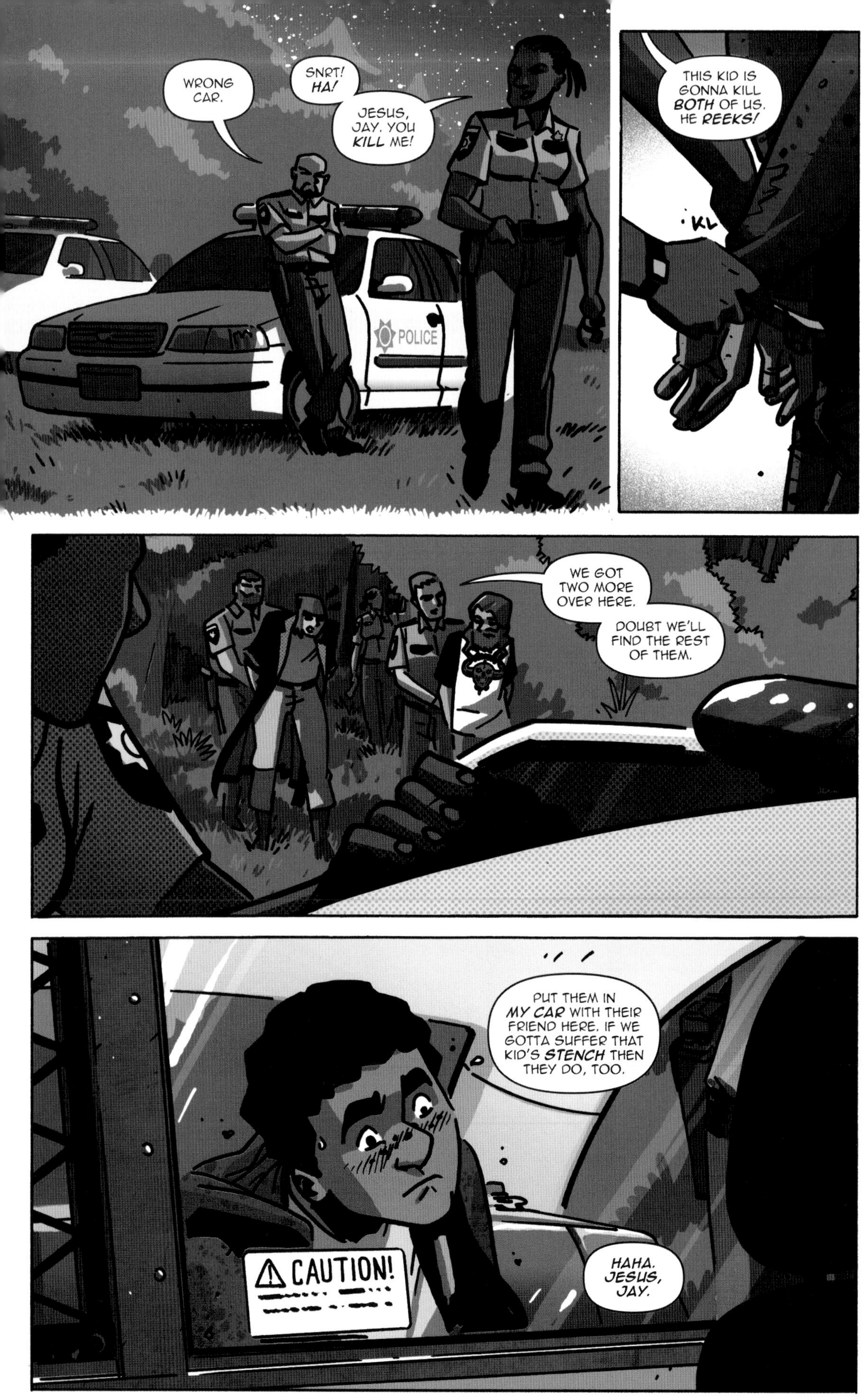
WRONG CAR.
SNRT! HA!
JESUS, JAY. YOU KILL ME!
THIS KID IS GONNA KILL BOTH OF US. HE REEKS!
KL
WE GOT TWO MORE OVER HERE.
DOUBT WE'LL FIND THE REST OF THEM.
PUT THEM IN MY CAR WITH THEIR FRIEND HERE. IF WE GOTTA SUFFER THAT KID'S STENCH THEN THEY DO, TOO.
HAHA. JESUS, JAY.
CAUTION!
POLICE

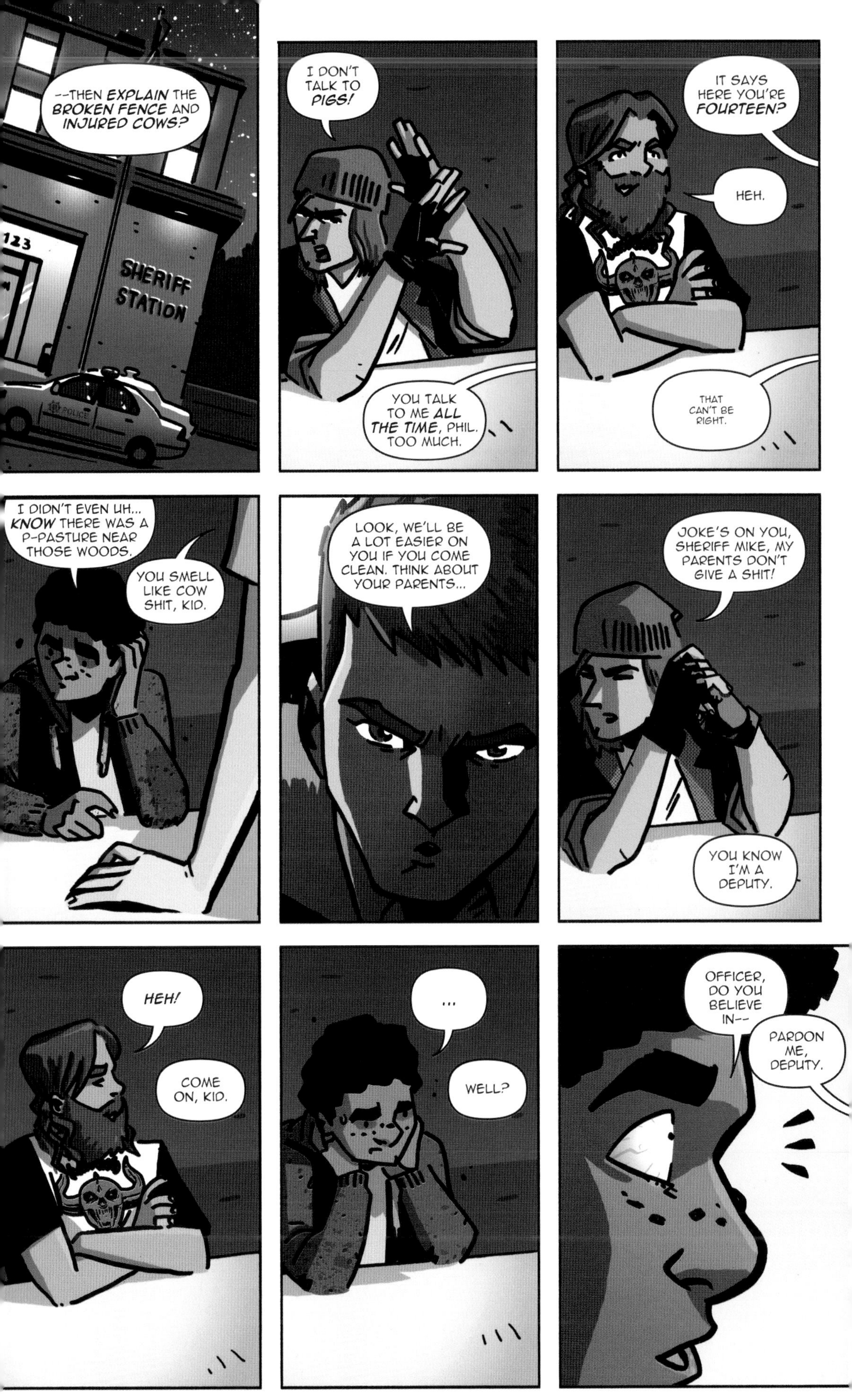
--THEN EXPLAIN THE BROKEN FENCE AND INJURED COWS?
123
SHERIFF STATION
POLICE
I DON'T TALK TO PIGS!
YOU TALK TO ME ALL THE TIME, PHIL. TOO MUCH.
IT SAYS HERE YOU'RE FOURTEEN?
HEH.
THAT CAN'T BE RIGHT.
I DIDN'T EVEN UH... KNOW THERE WAS A P-PASTURE NEAR THOSE WOODS.
YOU SMELL LIKE COW SHIT, KID.
LOOK, WE'LL BE A LOT EASIER ON YOU IF YOU COME CLEAN. THINK ABOUT YOUR PARENTS...
JOKE'S ON YOU, SHERIFF MIKE, MY PARENTS DON'T GIVE A SHIT!
YOU KNOW I'M A DEPUTY.
HEH!
COME ON, KID.
...
WELL?
OFFICER, DO YOU BELIEVE IN--
PARDON ME, DEPUTY.

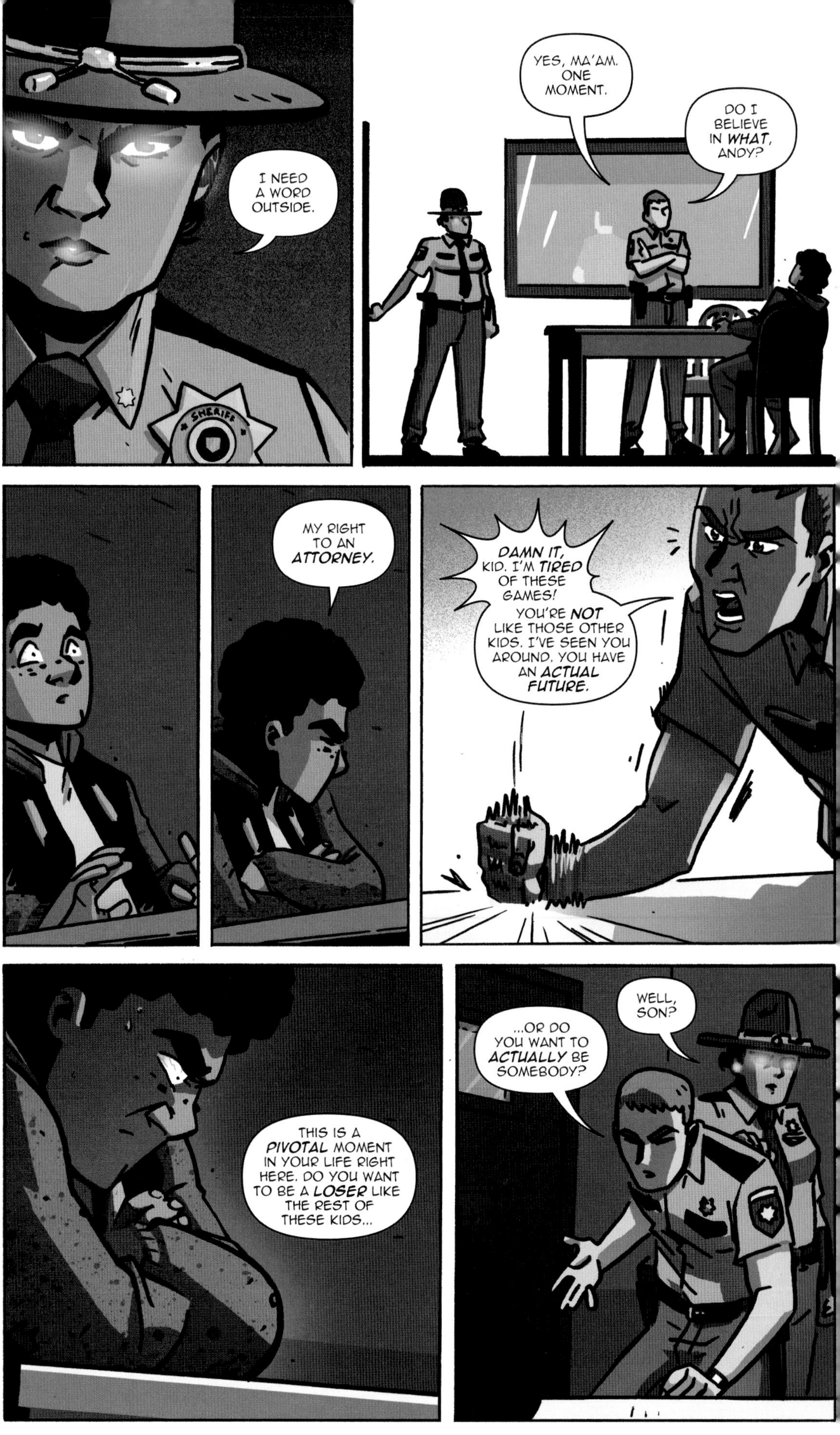
I NEED A WORD OUTSIDE.
YES, MA'AM. ONE MOMENT.
DO I BELIEVE IN *WHAT*, ANDY?
MY RIGHT TO AN *ATTORNEY*.
DAMN IT, KID. I'M *TIRED* OF THESE GAMES!
YOU'RE *NOT* LIKE THOSE OTHER KIDS. I'VE SEEN YOU AROUND. YOU HAVE AN *ACTUAL FUTURE*.
THIS IS A *PIVOTAL* MOMENT IN YOUR LIFE RIGHT HERE. DO YOU WANT TO BE A *LOSER* LIKE THE REST OF THESE KIDS...
...OR DO YOU WANT TO *ACTUALLY* BE SOMEBODY?
WELL, SON?

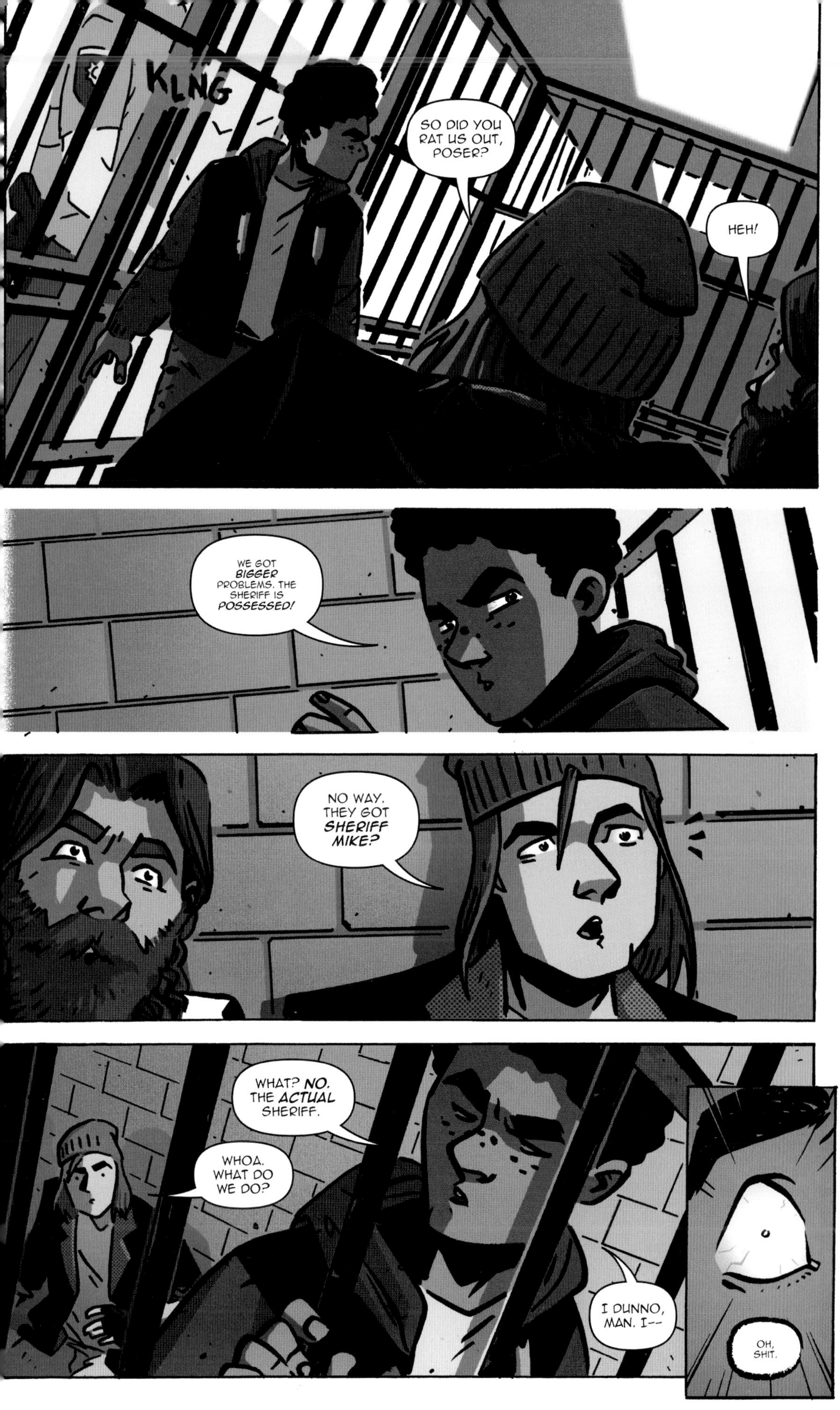
KLNG
SO DID YOU RAT US OUT, POSER?
HEH!
WE GOT BIGGER PROBLEMS. THE SHERIFF IS POSSESSED!
NO WAY. THEY GOT SHERIFF MIKE?
WHAT? NO. THE ACTUAL SHERIFF.
WHOA. WHAT DO WE DO?
I DUNNO, MAN. I--
OH, SHIT.

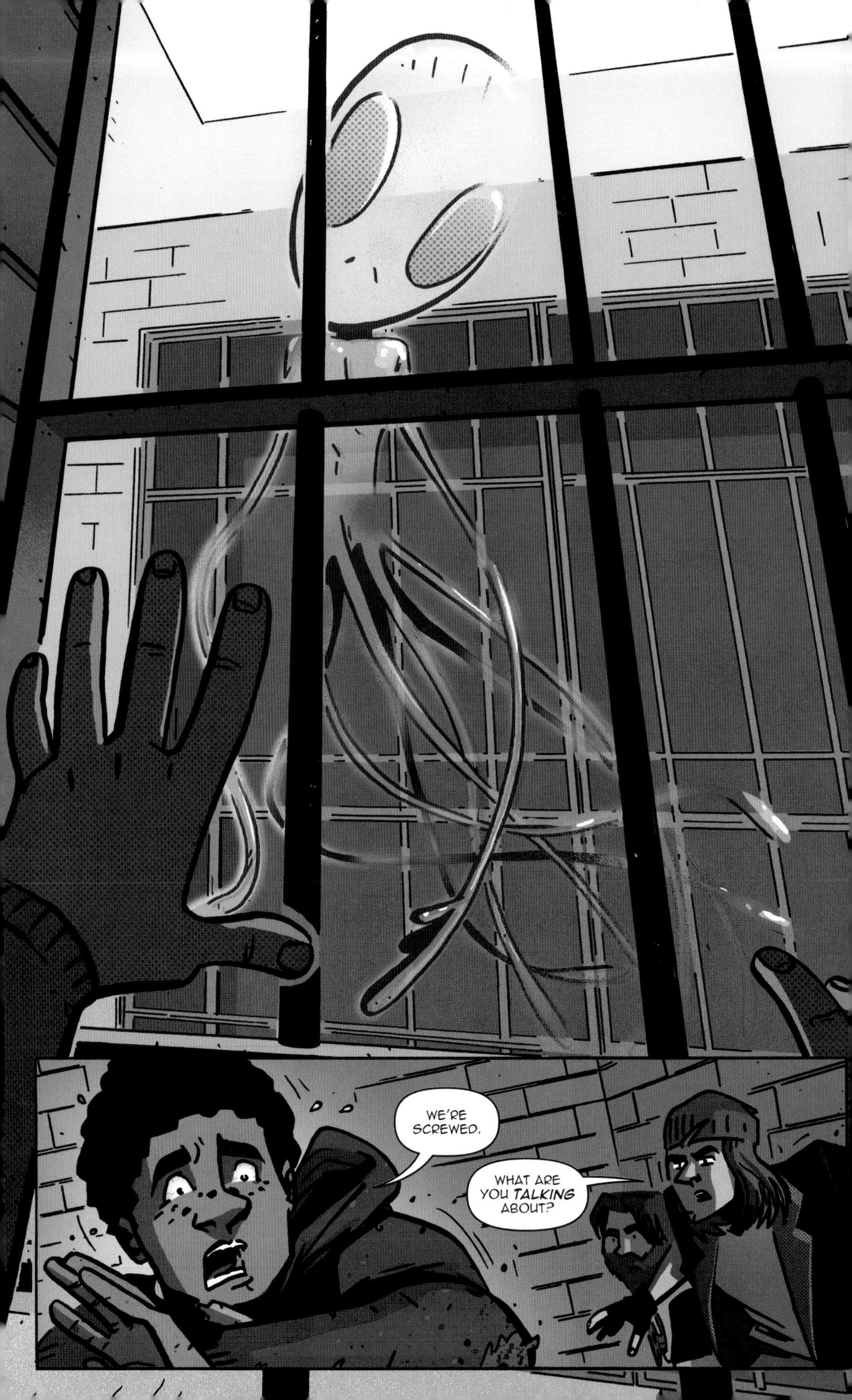
WE'RE SCREWED.
WHAT ARE YOU *TALKING* ABOUT?

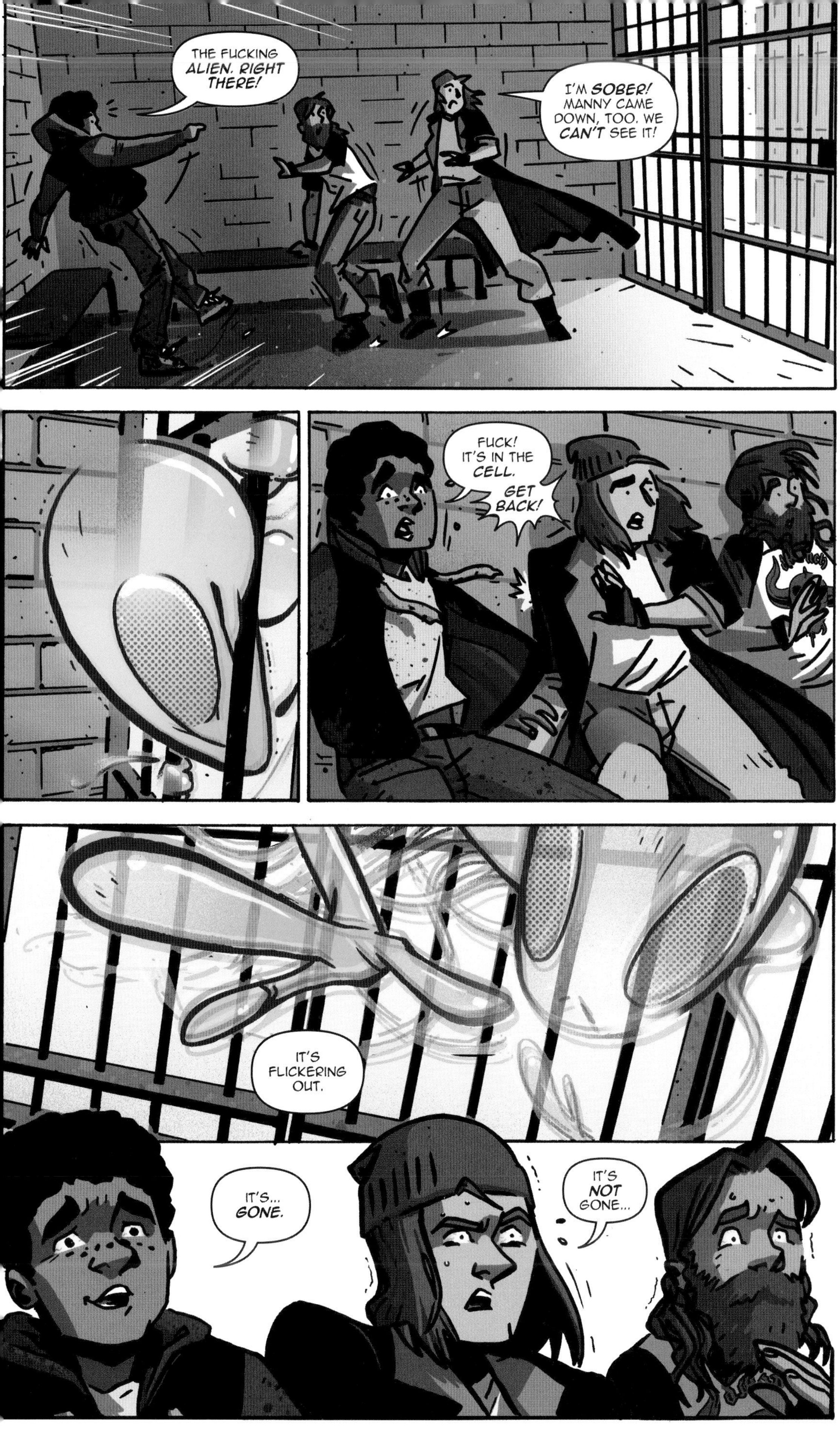
THE FUCKING ALIEN. RIGHT THERE!
I'M SOBER! MANNY CAME DOWN, TOO. WE CAN'T SEE IT!
FUCK! IT'S IN THE CELL.
GET BACK!
IT'S FLICKERING OUT.
IT'S... GONE.
IT'S NOT GONE...

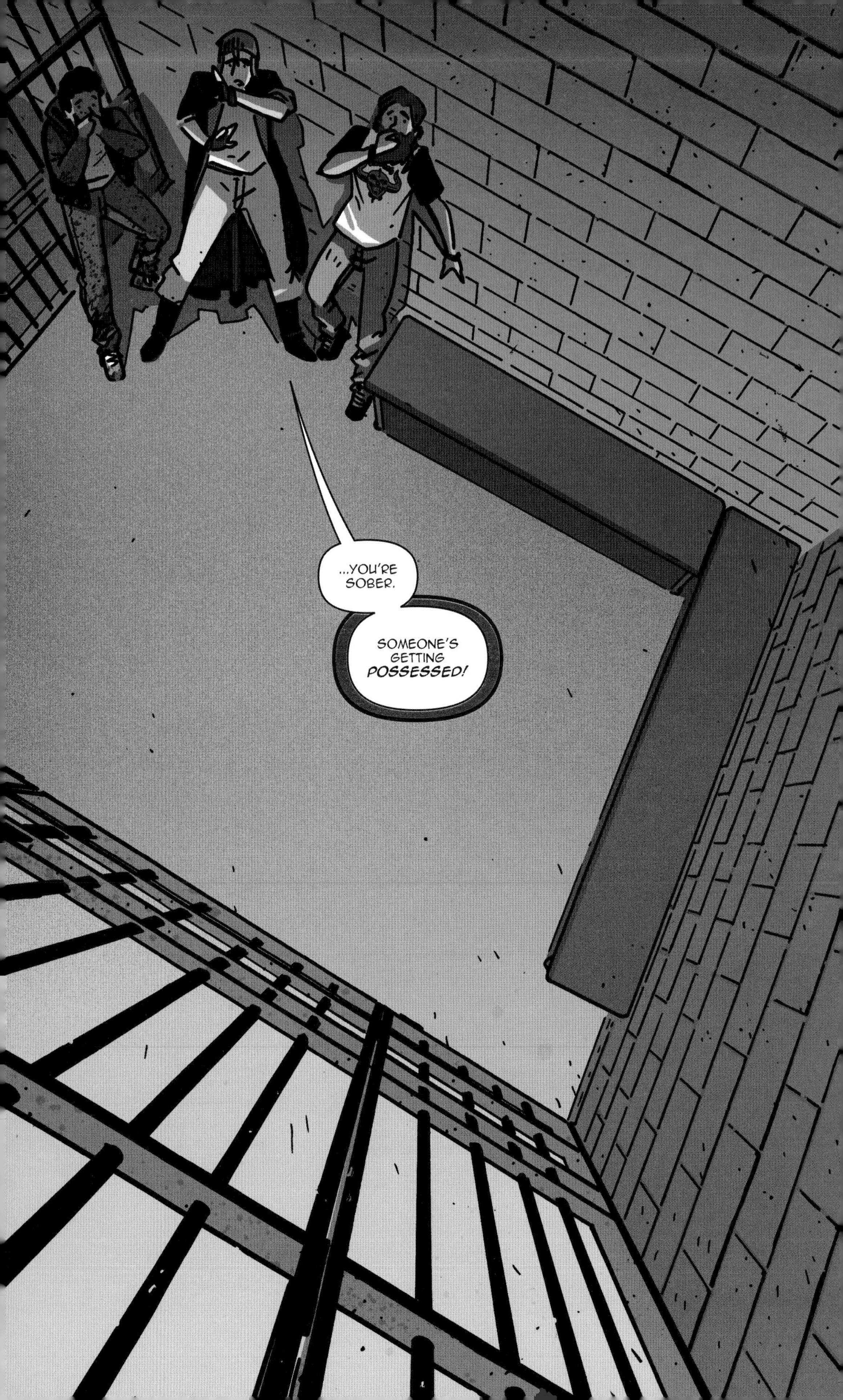
...YOU'RE SOBER.
SOMEONE'S GETTING *POSSESSED!*

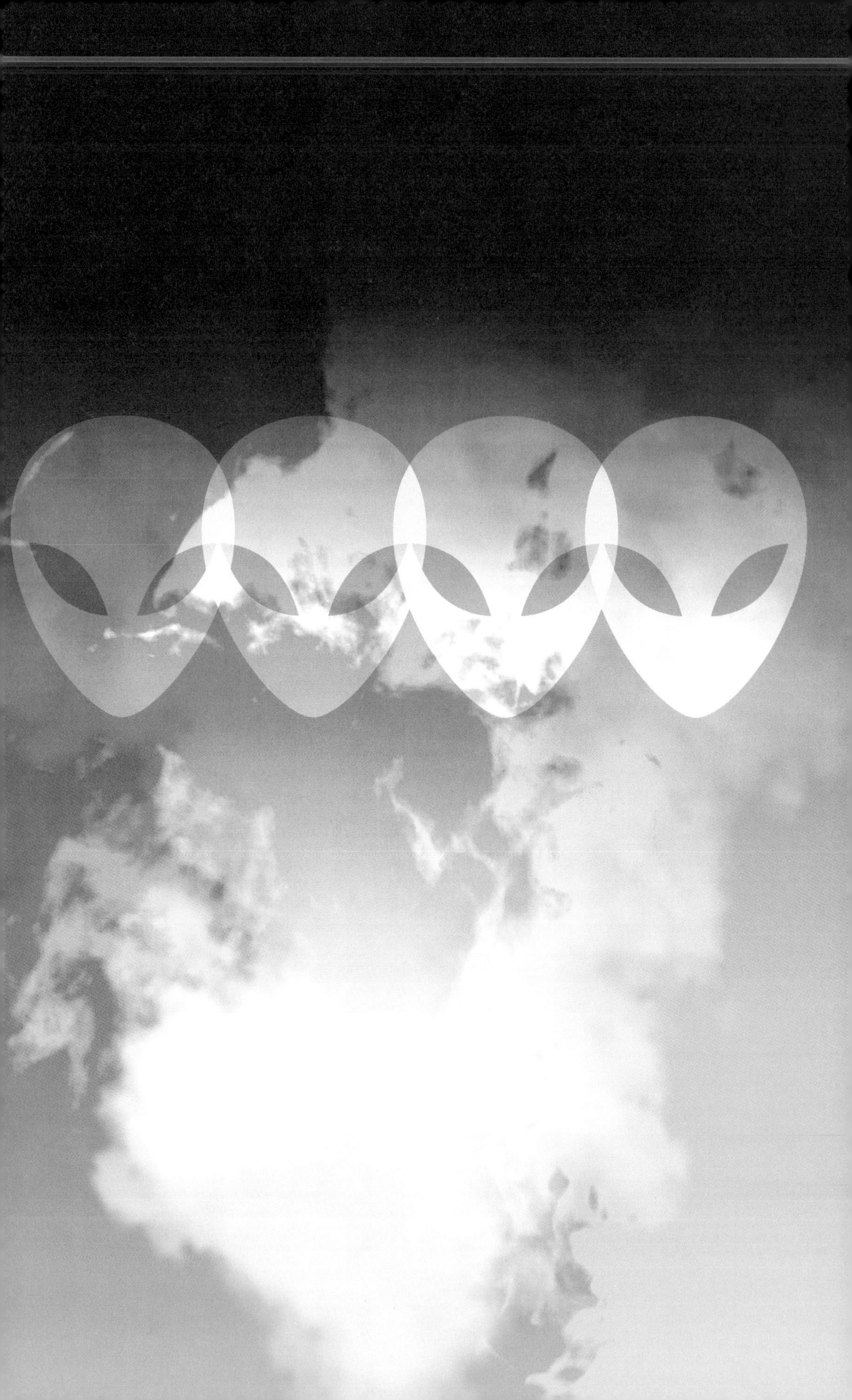

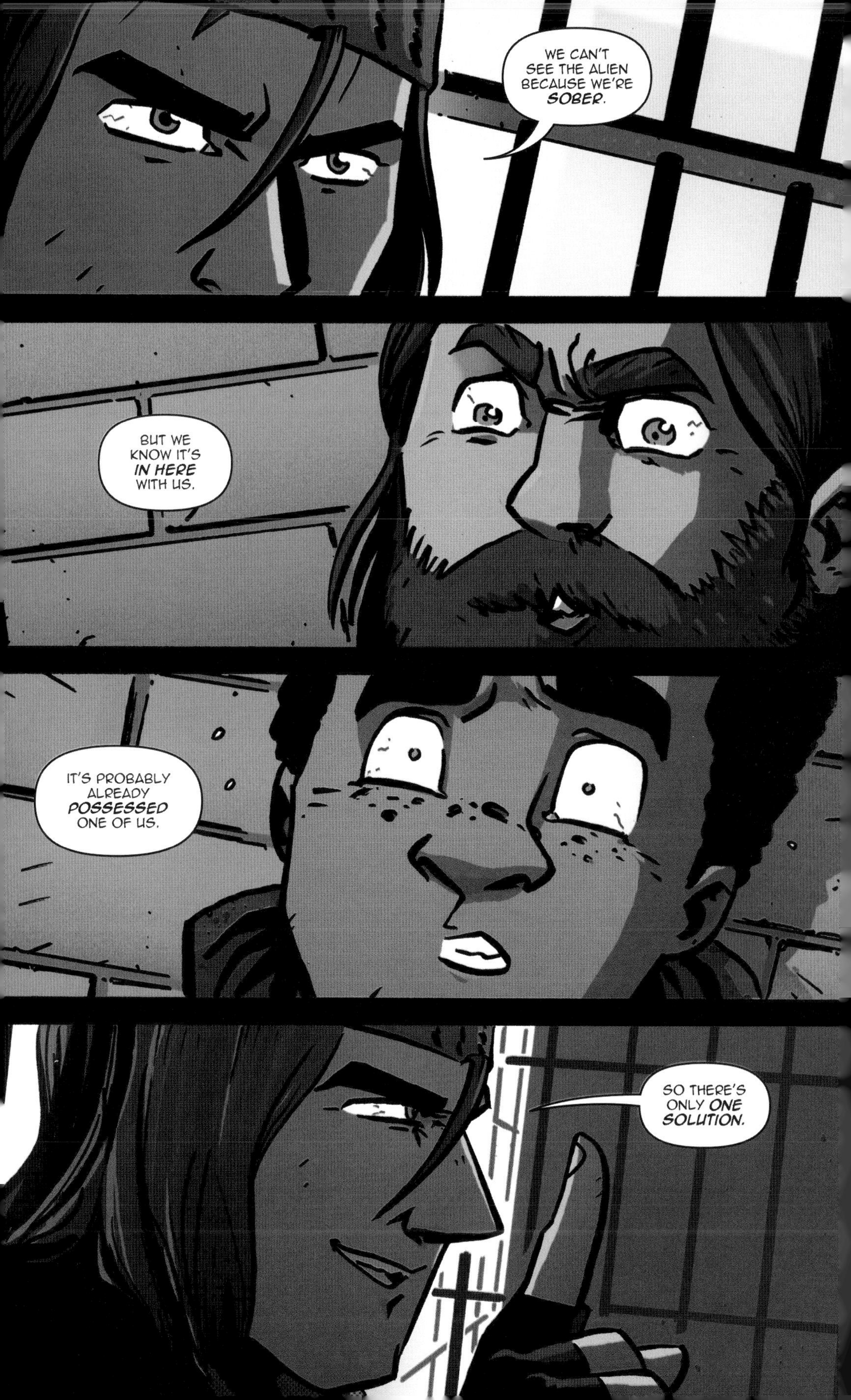
WE CAN'T SEE THE ALIEN BECAUSE WE'RE SOBER.
BUT WE KNOW IT'S IN HERE WITH US.
IT'S PROBABLY ALREADY POSSESSED ONE OF US.
SO THERE'S ONLY ONE SOLUTION.

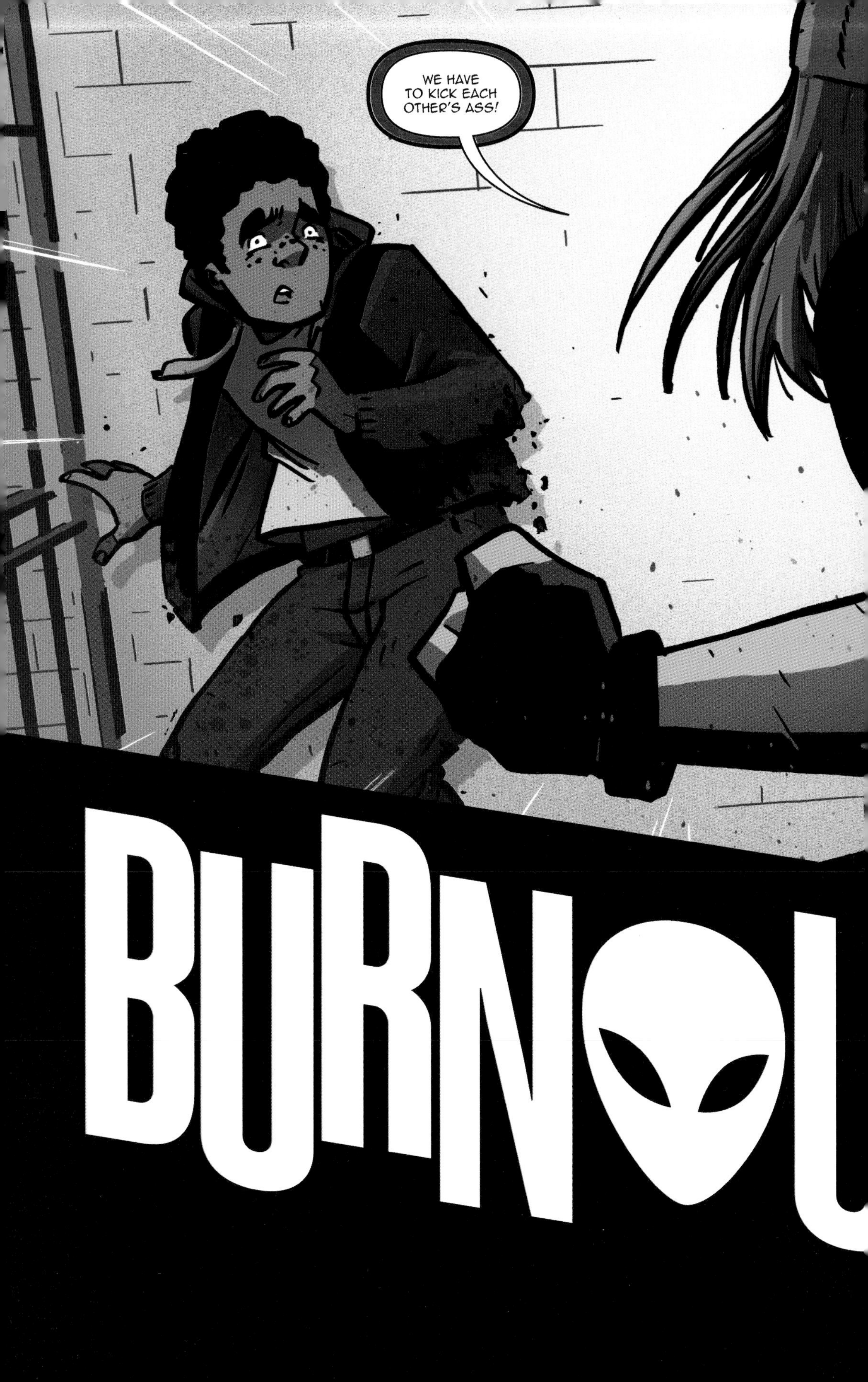
WE HAVE TO KICK EACH OTHER'S ASS!
BURNOU

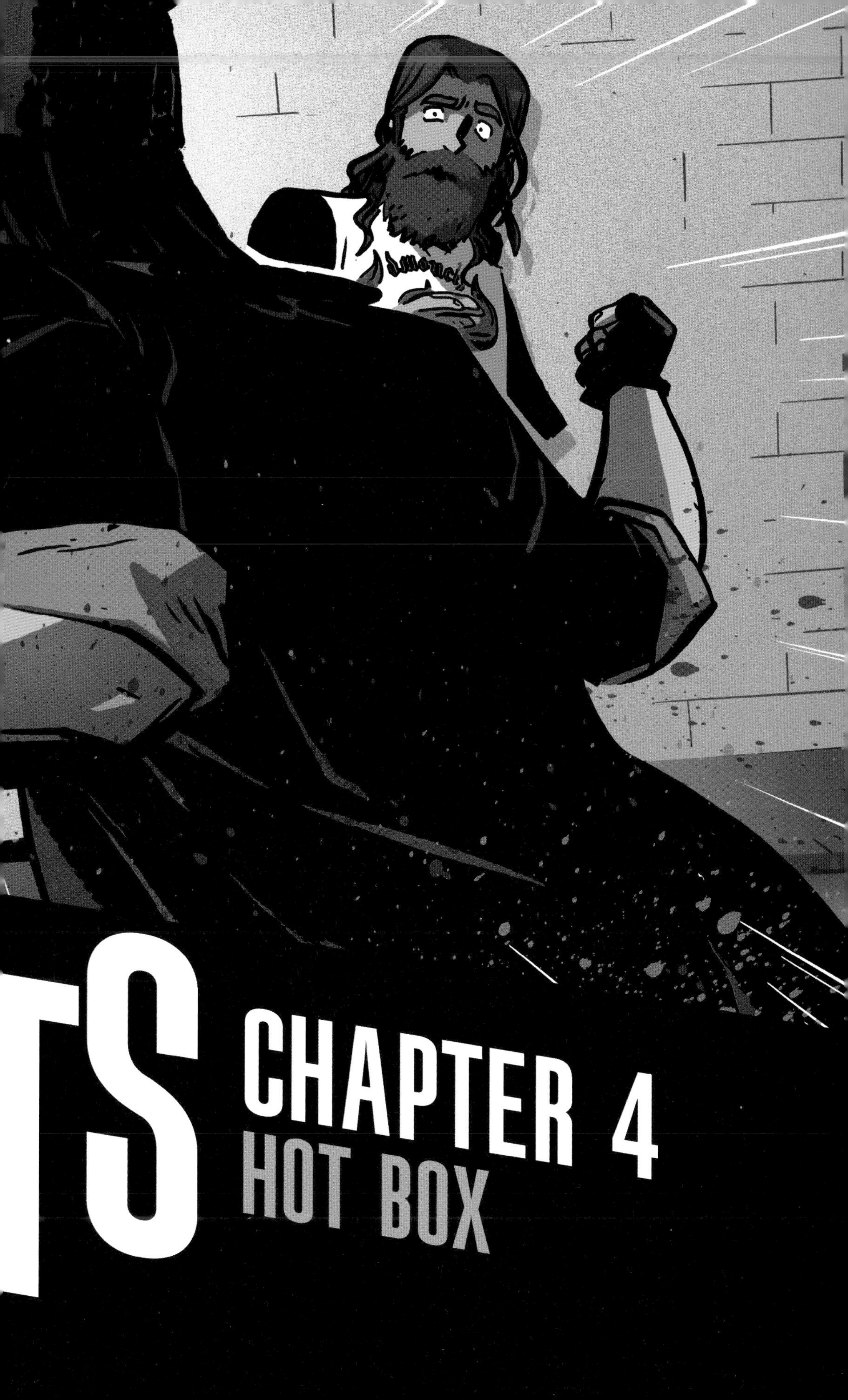
TS
CHAPTER 4
HOT BOX

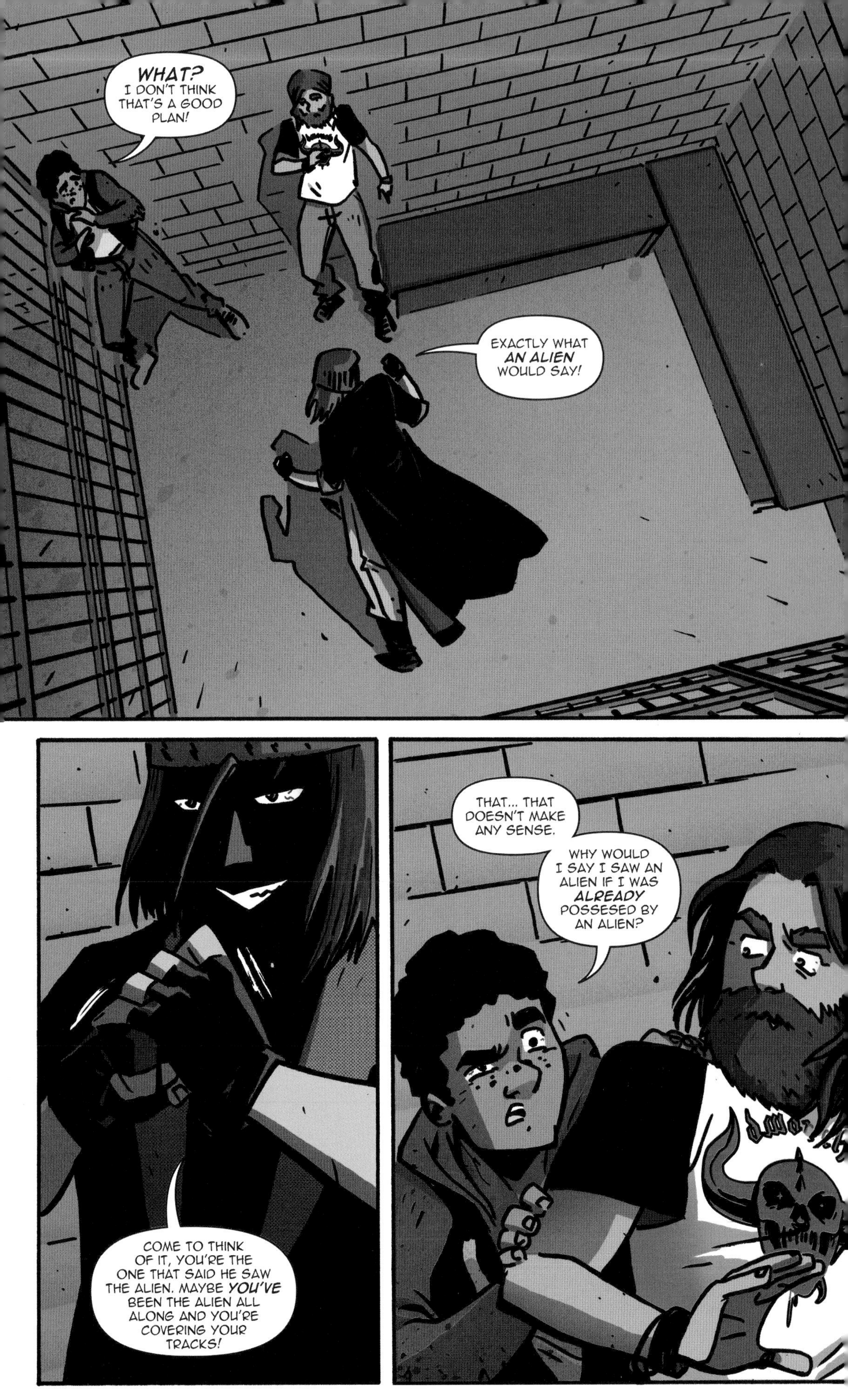
WHAT? I DON'T THINK THAT'S A GOOD PLAN!
EXACTLY WHAT AN ALIEN WOULD SAY!
COME TO THINK OF IT, YOU'RE THE ONE THAT SAID HE SAW THE ALIEN. MAYBE YOU'VE BEEN THE ALIEN ALL ALONG AND YOU'RE COVERING YOUR TRACKS!
THAT... THAT DOESN'T MAKE ANY SENSE.
WHY WOULD I SAY I SAW AN ALIEN IF I WAS ALREADY POSSESED BY AN ALIEN?

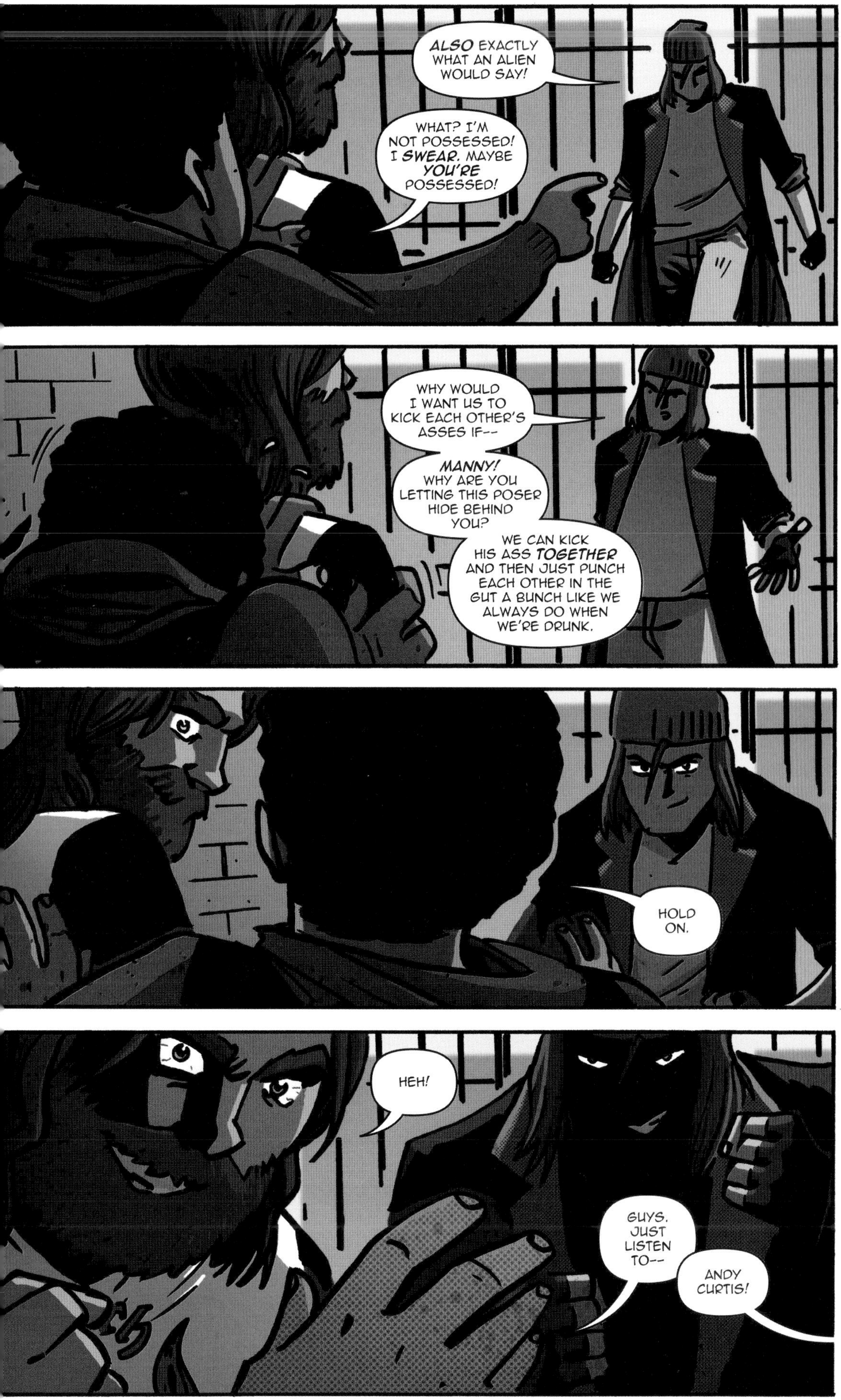
ALSO EXACTLY WHAT AN ALIEN WOULD SAY!
WHAT? I'M NOT POSSESSED! I SWEAR. MAYBE YOU'RE POSSESSED!
WHY WOULD I WANT US TO KICK EACH OTHER'S ASSES IF--
MANNY! WHY ARE YOU LETTING THIS POSER HIDE BEHIND YOU?
WE CAN KICK HIS ASS TOGETHER AND THEN JUST PUNCH EACH OTHER IN THE GUT A BUNCH LIKE WE ALWAYS DO WHEN WE'RE DRUNK.
HOLD ON.
HEH!
GUYS. JUST LISTEN TO--
ANDY CURTIS!

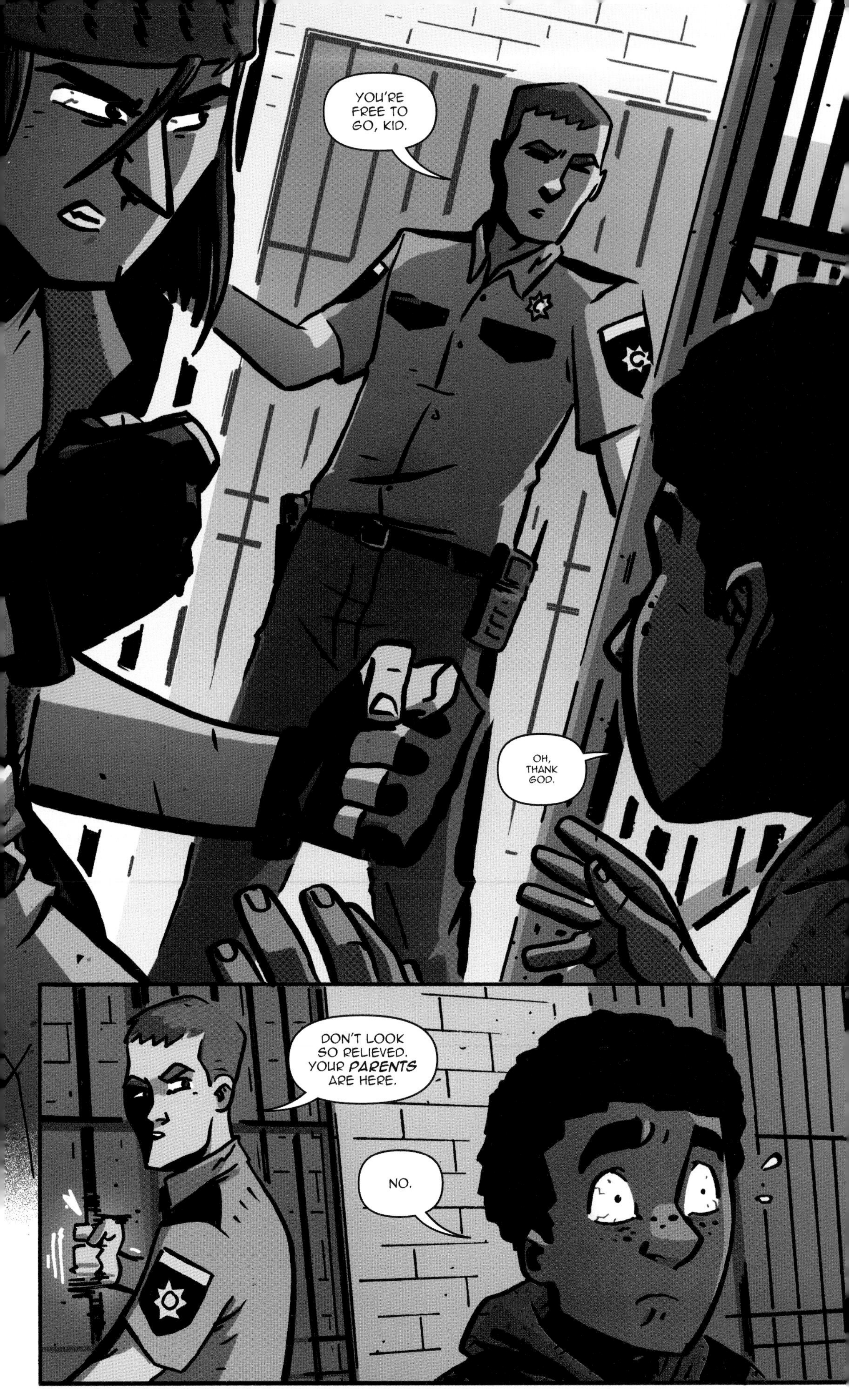
YOU'RE FREE TO GO, KID.
OH, THANK GOD.
DON'T LOOK SO RELIEVED. YOUR *PARENTS* ARE HERE.
NO.

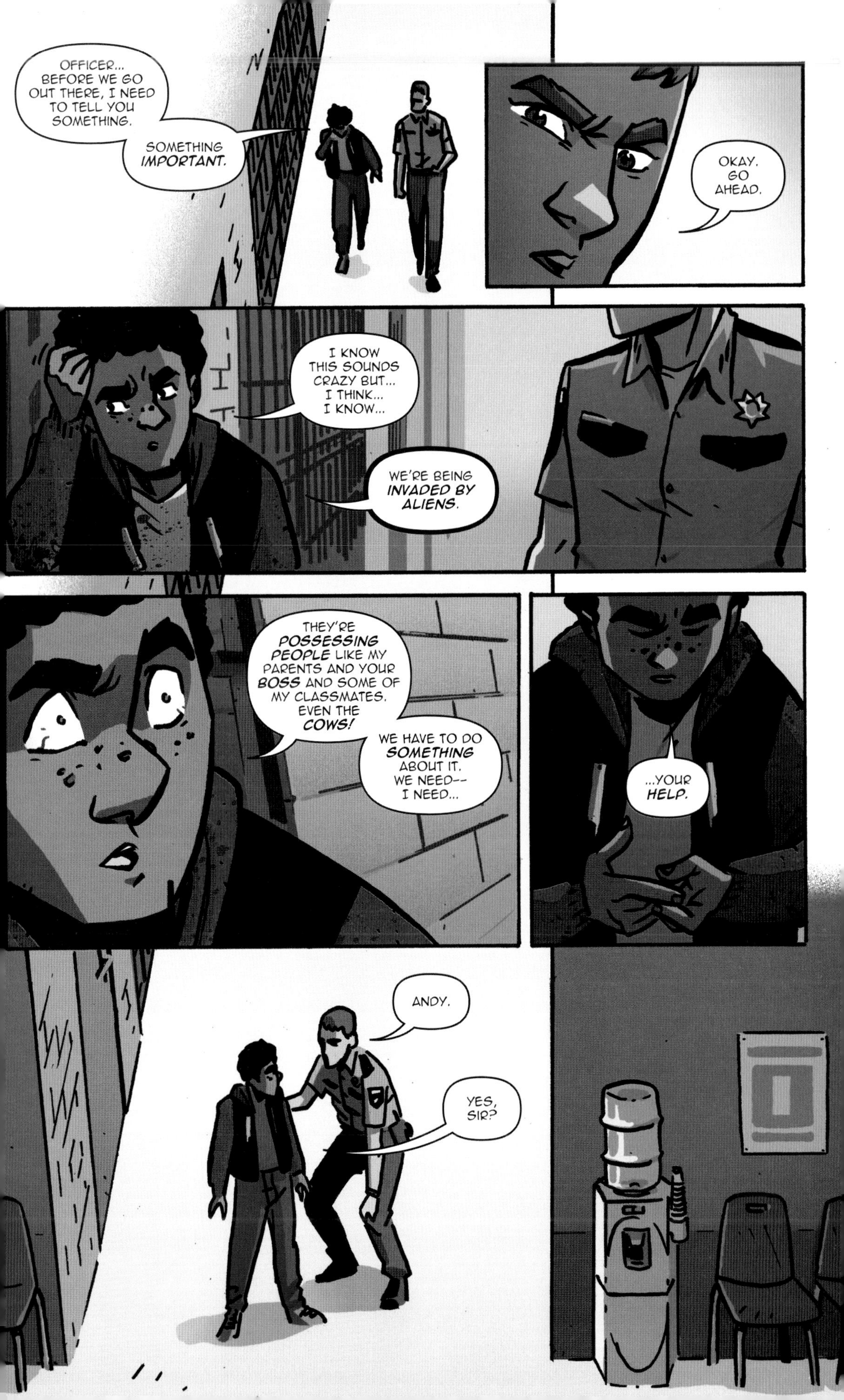
OFFICER... BEFORE WE GO OUT THERE, I NEED TO TELL YOU SOMETHING.
SOMETHING IMPORTANT.
OKAY. GO AHEAD.
I KNOW THIS SOUNDS CRAZY BUT... I THINK... I KNOW...
WE'RE BEING INVADED BY ALIENS.
THEY'RE POSSESSING PEOPLE LIKE MY PARENTS AND YOUR BOSS AND SOME OF MY CLASSMATES. EVEN THE COWS!
WE HAVE TO DO SOMETHING ABOUT IT. WE NEED-- I NEED...
...YOUR HELP.
ANDY.
YES, SIR?

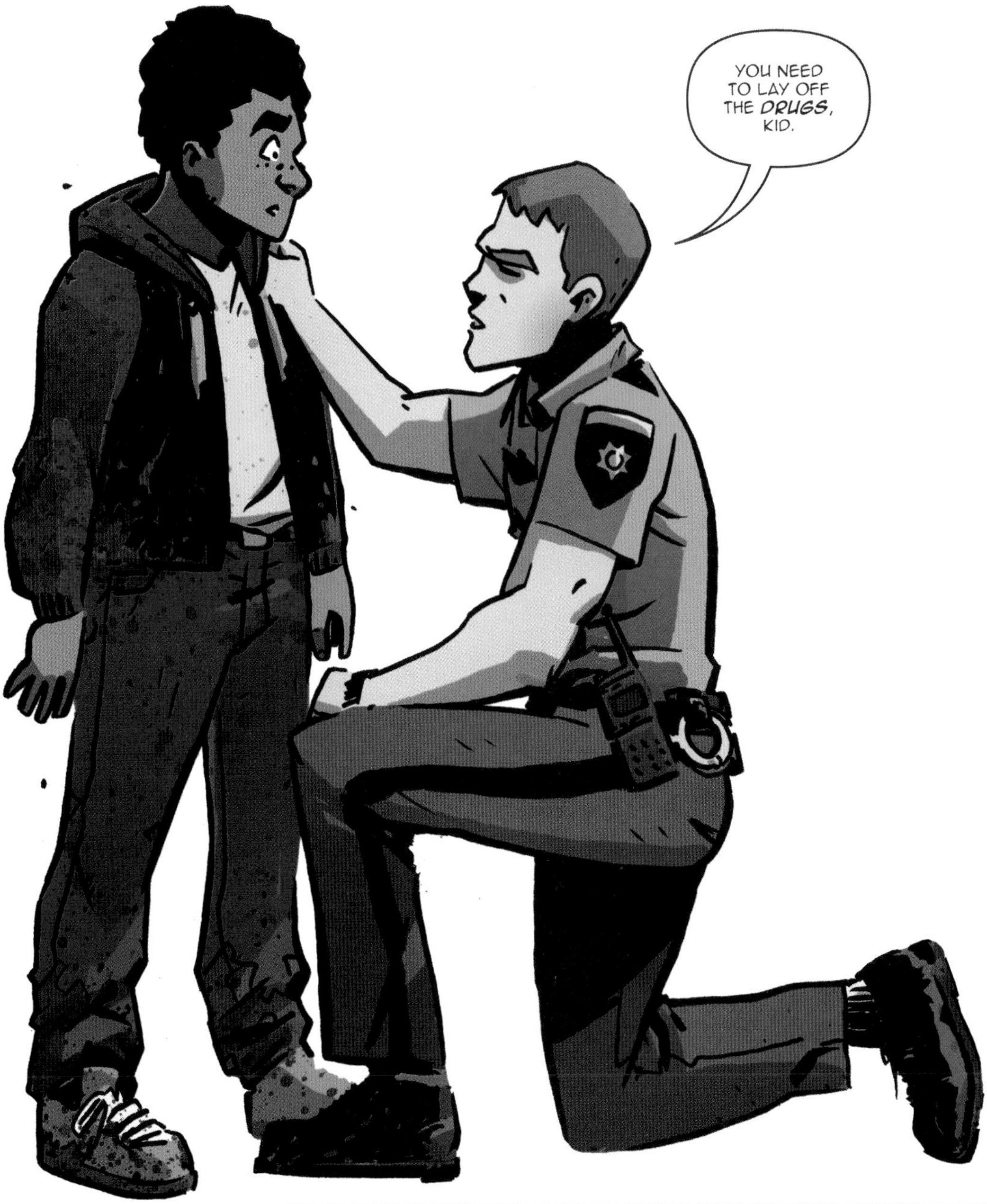
YOU NEED TO LAY OFF THE *DRUGS*, KID.

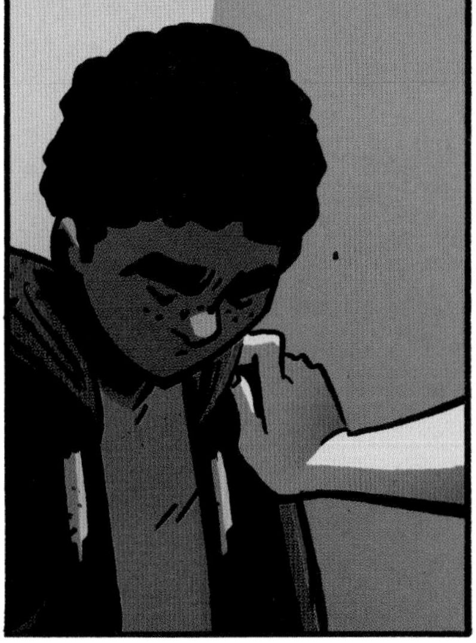

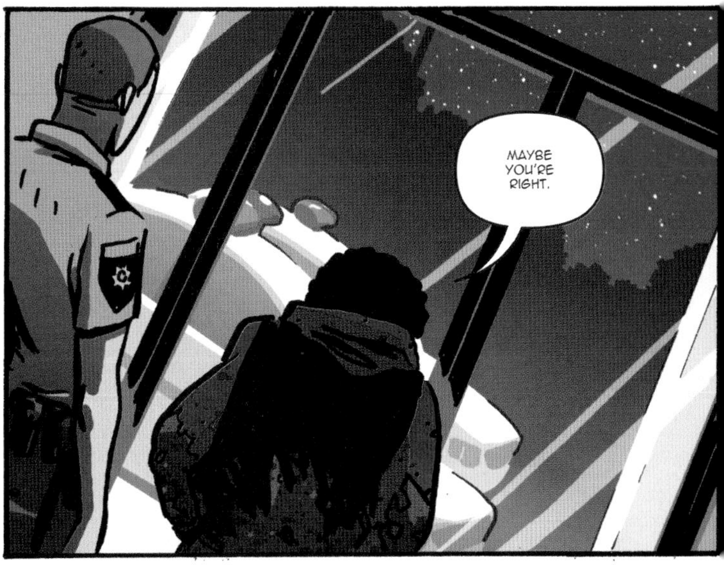
MAYBE YOU'RE RIGHT.

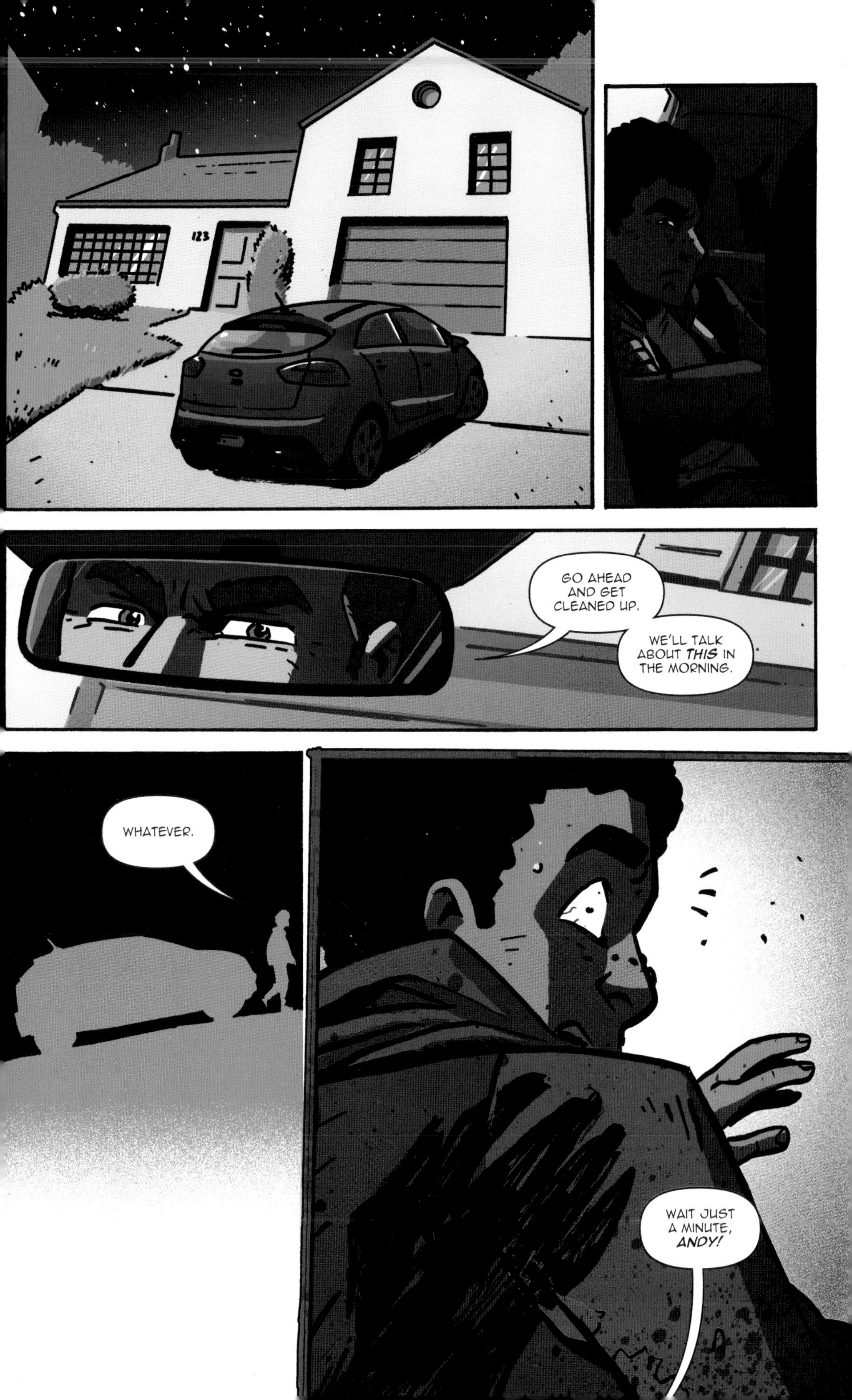
123
GO AHEAD AND GET CLEANED UP.
WE'LL TALK ABOUT THIS IN THE MORNING.
WHATEVER.
WAIT JUST A MINUTE, ANDY!

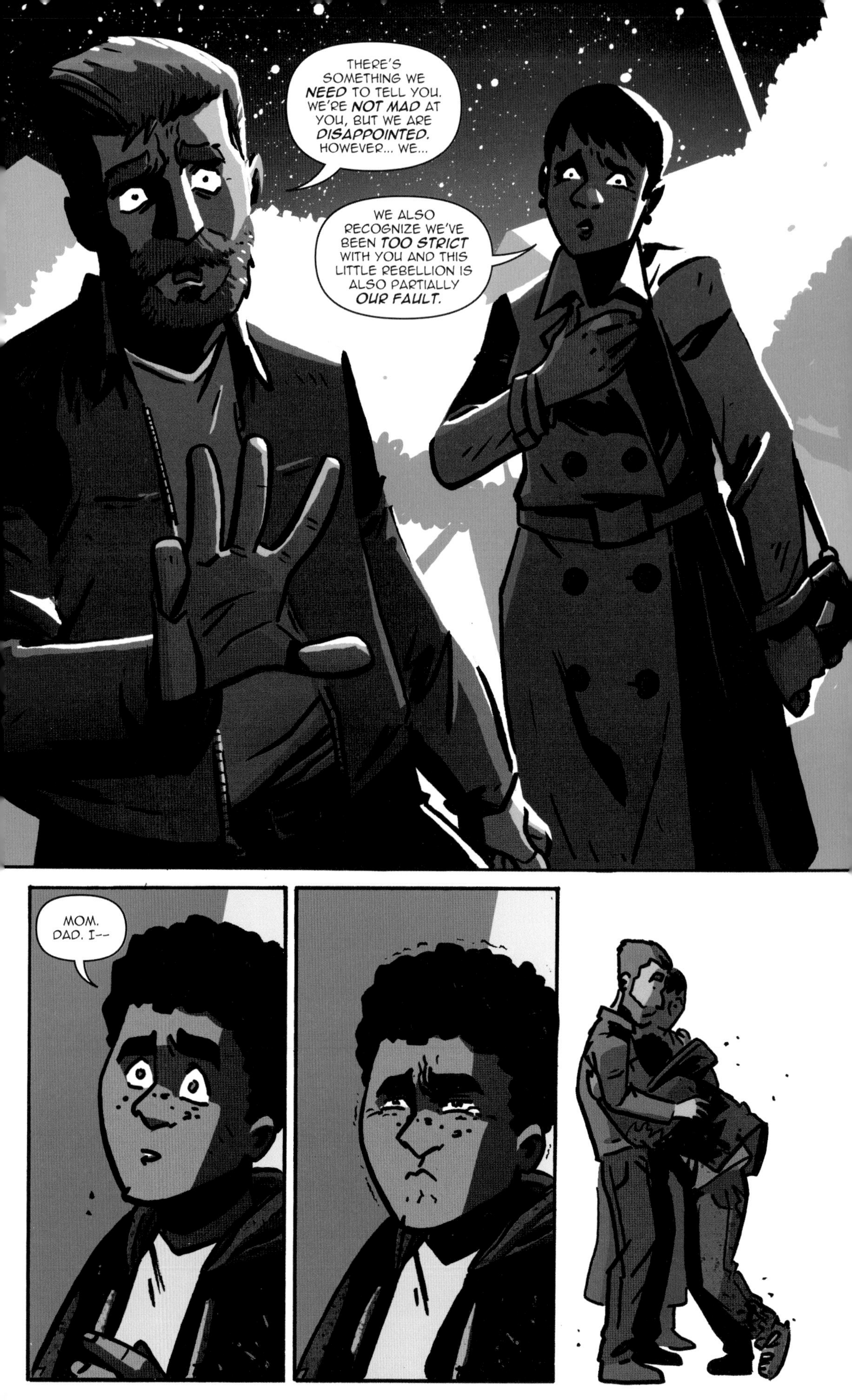
THERE'S SOMETHING WE NEED TO TELL YOU. WE'RE NOT MAD AT YOU, BUT WE ARE DISAPPOINTED. HOWEVER... WE...
WE ALSO RECOGNIZE WE'VE BEEN TOO STRICT WITH YOU AND THIS LITTLE REBELLION IS ALSO PARTIALLY OUR FAULT.
MOM. DAD. I--

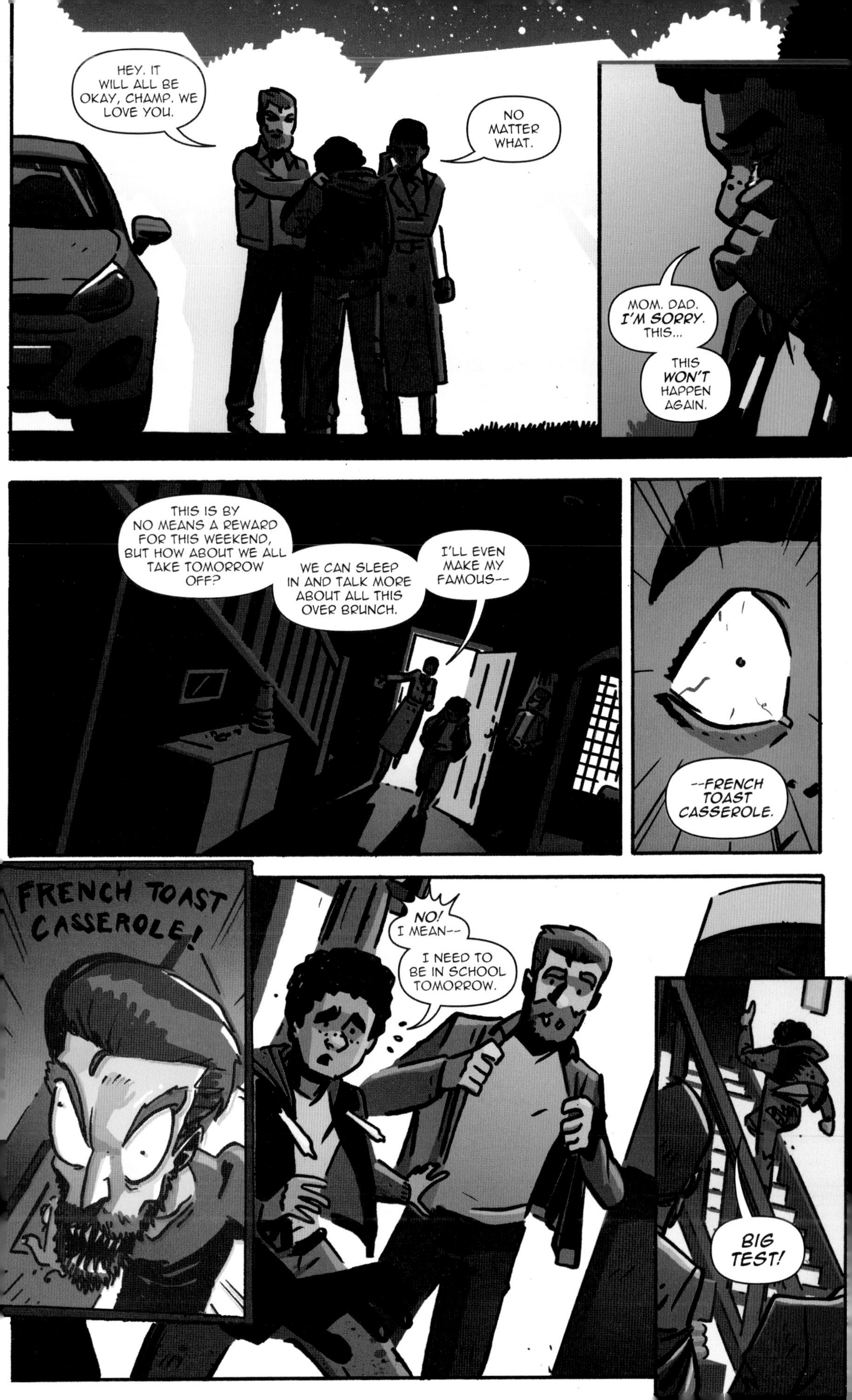
HEY. IT WILL ALL BE OKAY, CHAMP. WE LOVE YOU.
NO MATTER WHAT.
MOM. DAD. *I'M SORRY.* THIS...
THIS *WON'T* HAPPEN AGAIN.
THIS IS BY NO MEANS A REWARD FOR THIS WEEKEND, BUT HOW ABOUT WE ALL TAKE TOMORROW OFF?
WE CAN SLEEP IN AND TALK MORE ABOUT ALL THIS OVER BRUNCH.
I'LL EVEN MAKE MY FAMOUS--
--FRENCH TOAST CASSEROLE.
FRENCH TOAST CASSEROLE!
NO! I MEAN--
I NEED TO BE IN SCHOOL TOMORROW.
BIG TEST!

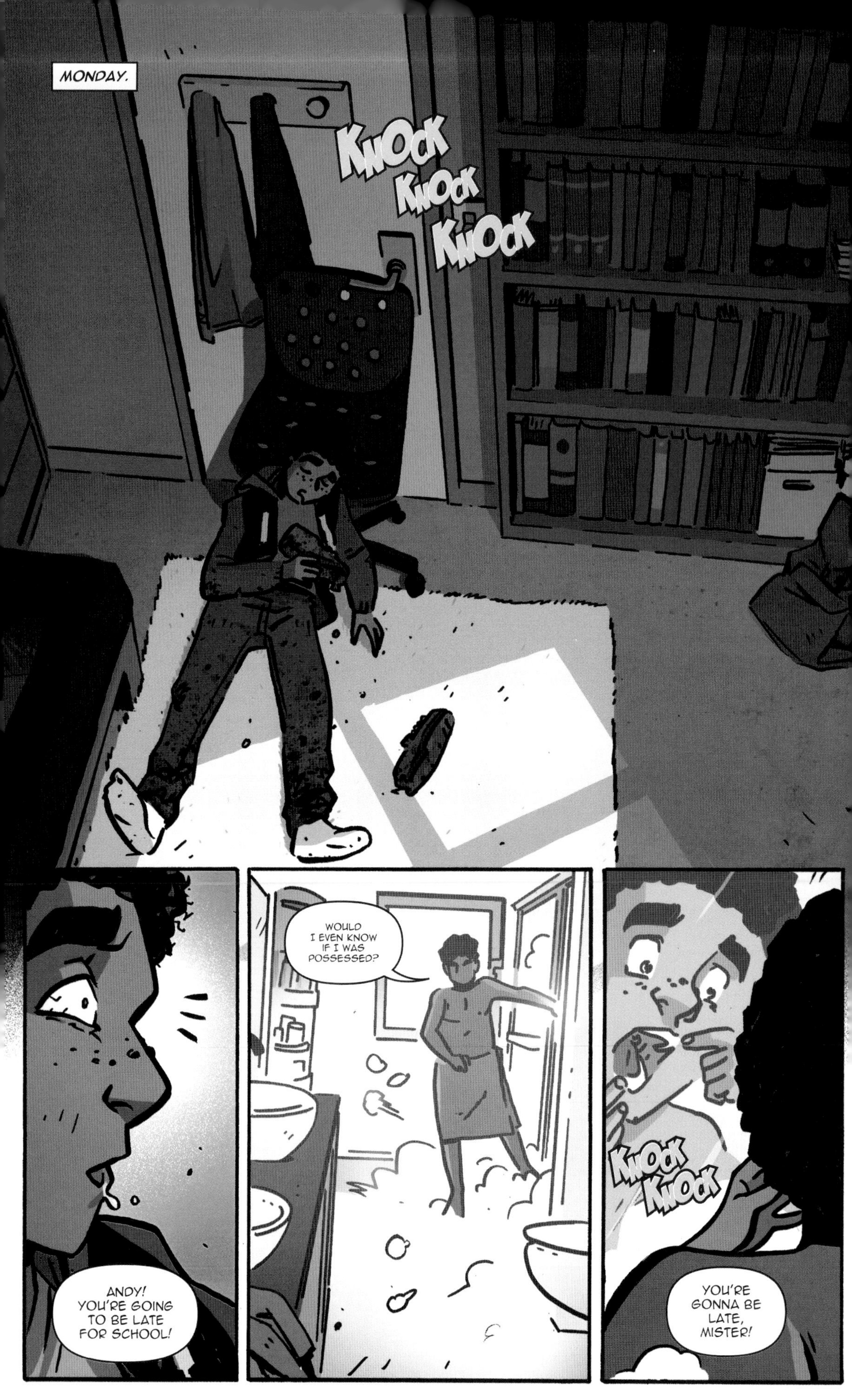
MONDAY.
KNOCK KNOCK KNOCK
ANDY! YOU'RE GOING TO BE LATE FOR SCHOOL!
WOULD I EVEN KNOW IF I WAS POSSESSED?
KNOCK KNOCK
YOU'RE GONNA BE LATE, MISTER!

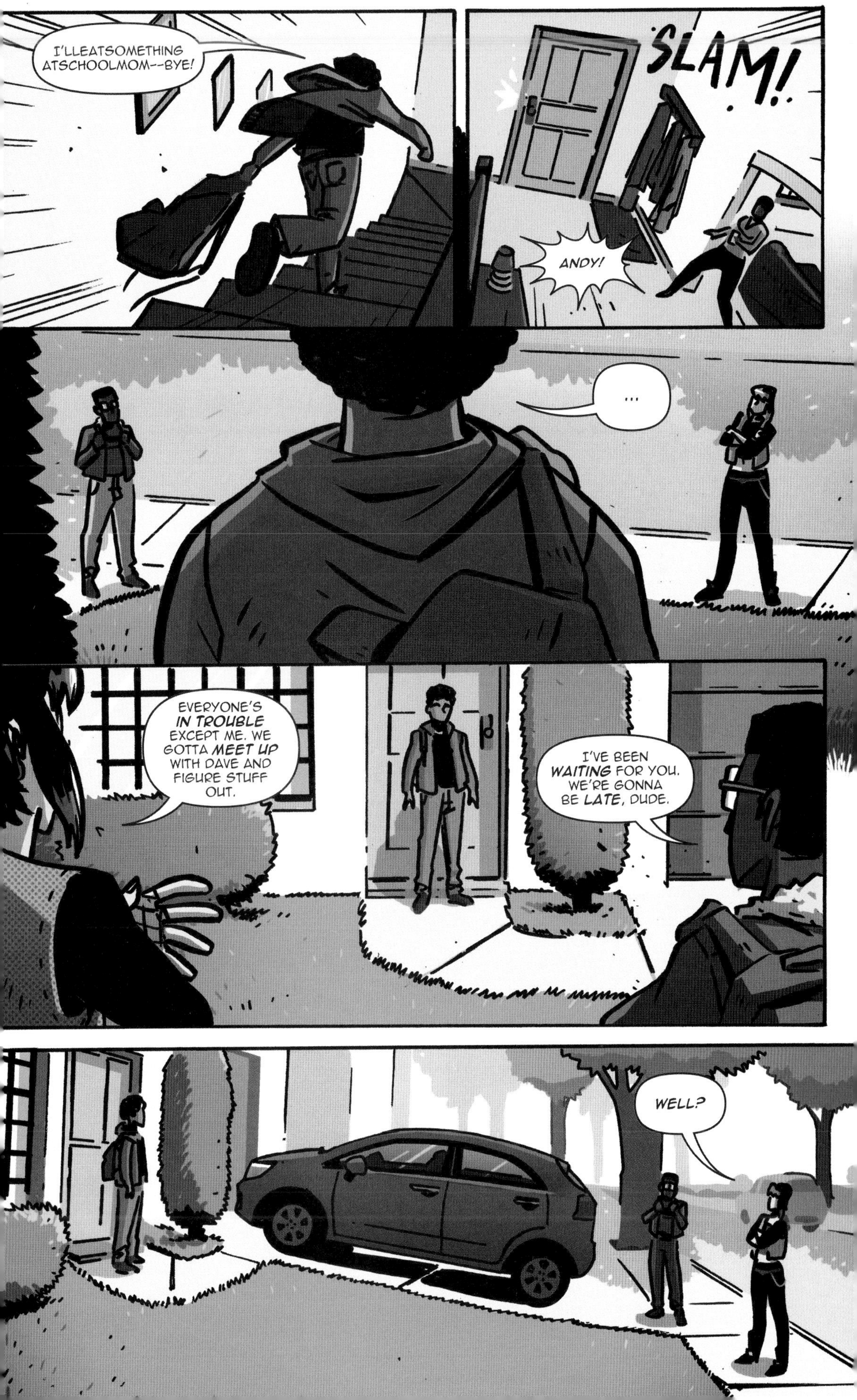
I'LLEATSOMETHING ATSCHOOLMOM--BYE!
SLAM!
ANDY!
...
EVERYONE'S IN TROUBLE EXCEPT ME. WE GOTTA MEET UP WITH DAVE AND FIGURE STUFF OUT.
I'VE BEEN WAITING FOR YOU. WE'RE GONNA BE LATE, DUDE.
WELL?

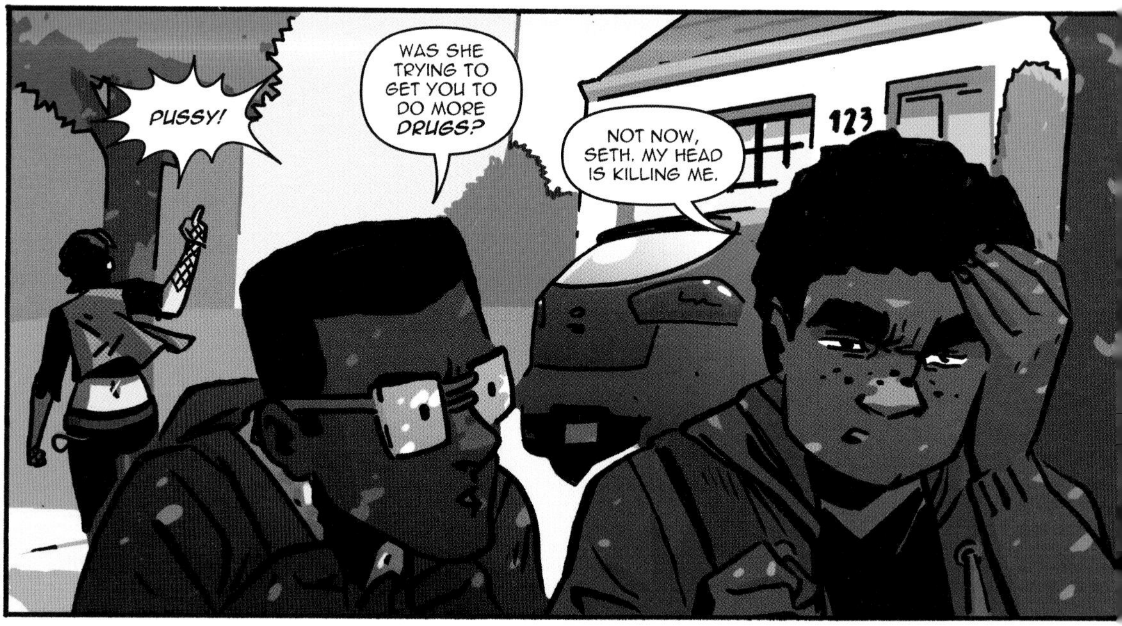
PUSSY!
WAS SHE TRYING TO GET YOU TO DO MORE DRUGS?
NOT NOW, SETH. MY HEAD IS KILLING ME.
123

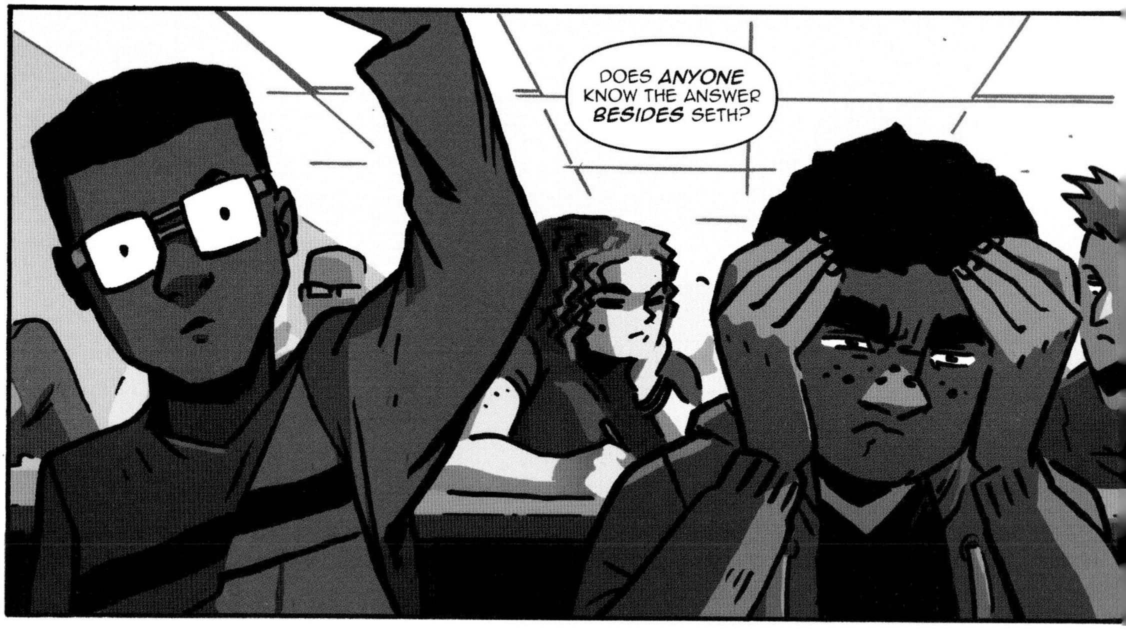
DOES ANYONE KNOW THE ANSWER BESIDES SETH?

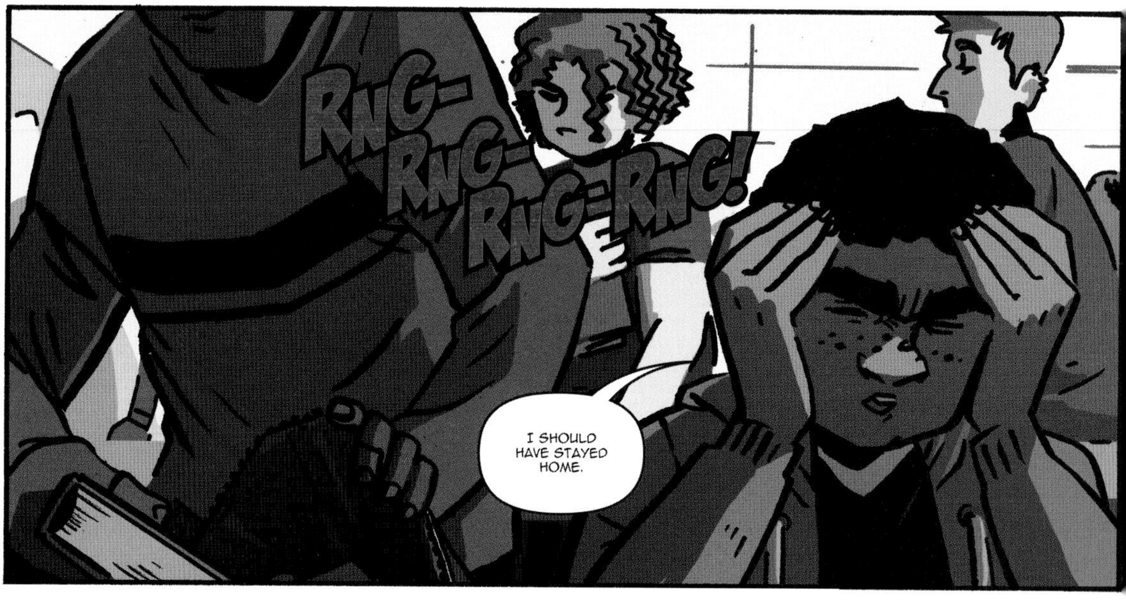
RNG-RNG-RNG-RNG!
I SHOULD HAVE STAYED HOME.

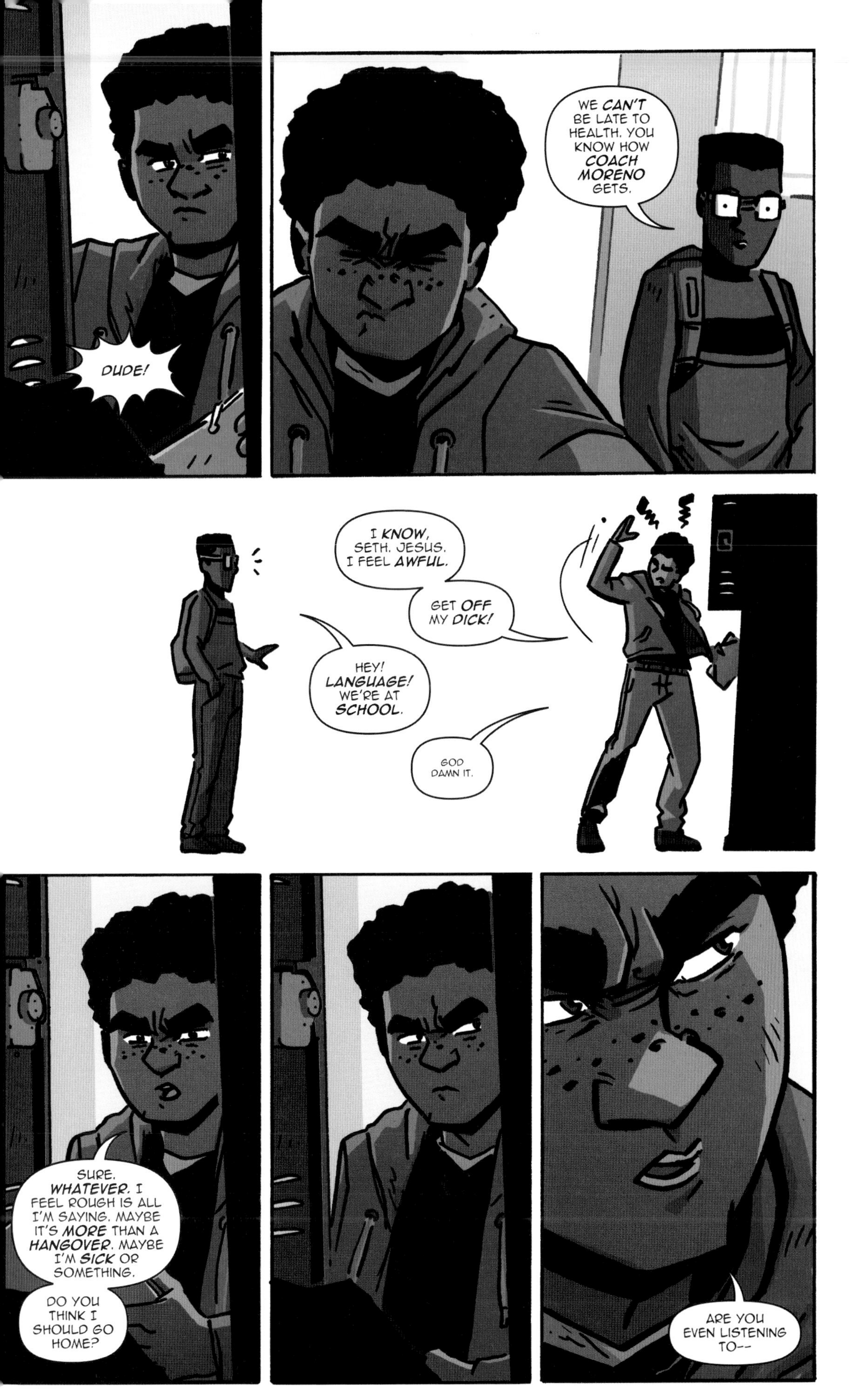
DUDE!
WE CAN'T BE LATE TO HEALTH. YOU KNOW HOW COACH MORENO GETS.
I KNOW, SETH. JESUS. I FEEL AWFUL.
GET OFF MY DICK!
HEY! LANGUAGE! WE'RE AT SCHOOL.
GOD DAMN IT.
SURE. WHATEVER. I FEEL ROUGH IS ALL I'M SAYING. MAYBE IT'S MORE THAN A HANGOVER. MAYBE I'M SICK OR SOMETHING.
DO YOU THINK I SHOULD GO HOME?
ARE YOU EVEN LISTENING TO--

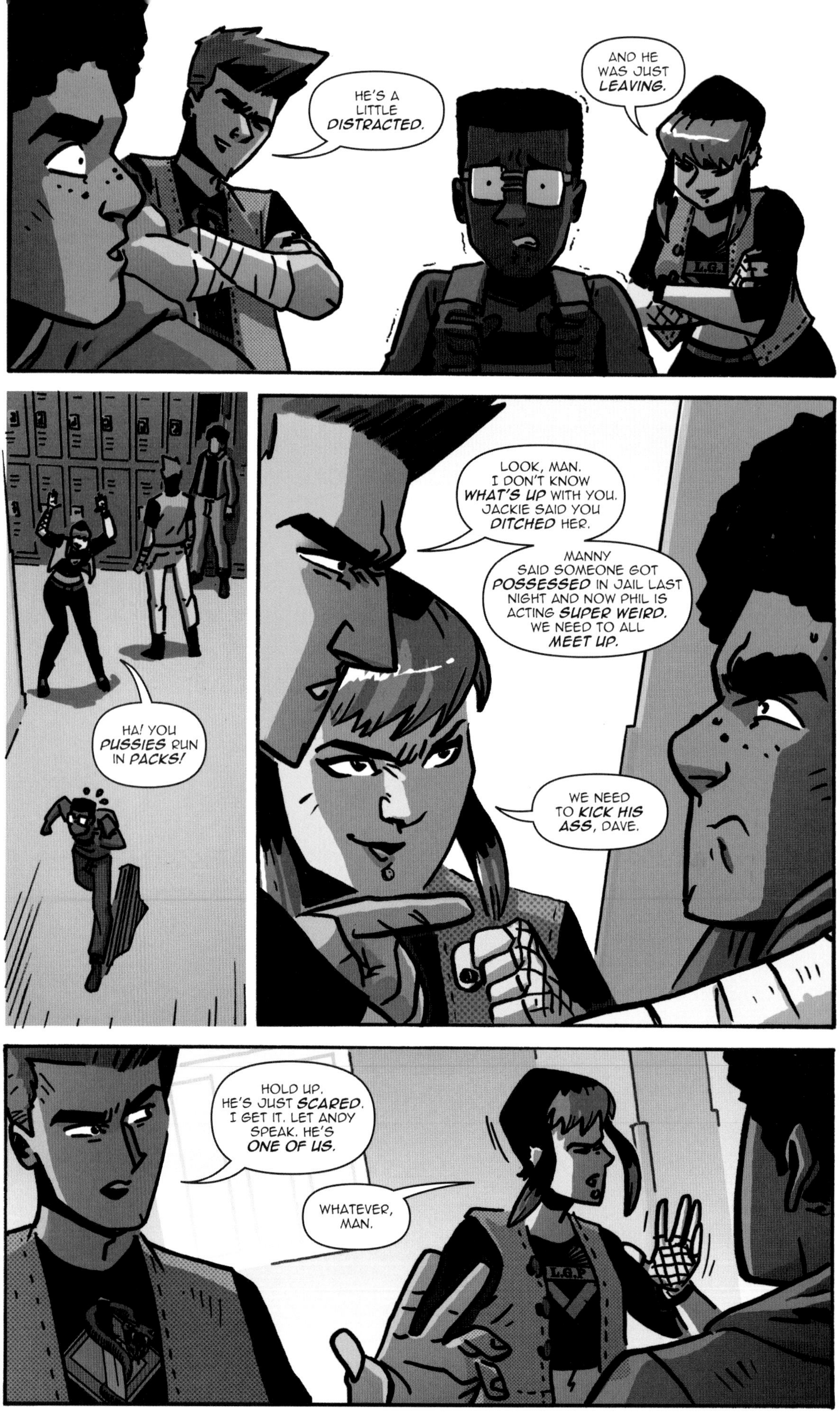
HE'S A LITTLE DISTRACTED.
AND HE WAS JUST LEAVING.
L.G.
HA! YOU PUSSIES RUN IN PACKS!
LOOK, MAN. I DON'T KNOW WHAT'S UP WITH YOU. JACKIE SAID YOU DITCHED HER.
MANNY SAID SOMEONE GOT POSSESSED IN JAIL LAST NIGHT AND NOW PHIL IS ACTING SUPER WEIRD. WE NEED TO ALL MEET UP.
WE NEED TO KICK HIS ASS, DAVE.
HOLD UP. HE'S JUST SCARED. I GET IT. LET ANDY SPEAK. HE'S ONE OF US.
WHATEVER, MAN.
L.G.P

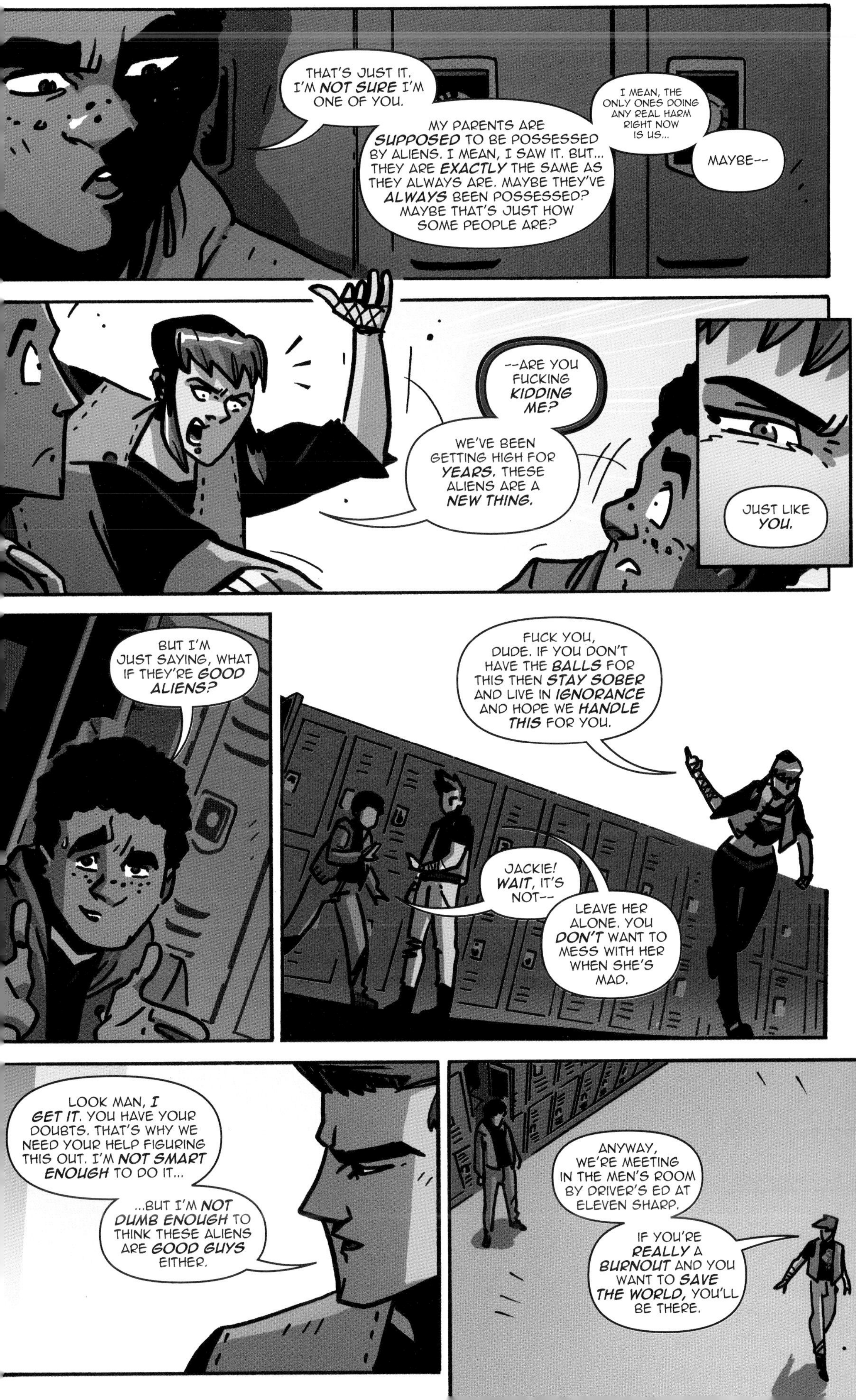
THAT'S JUST IT. I'M NOT SURE I'M ONE OF YOU.
MY PARENTS ARE SUPPOSED TO BE POSSESSED BY ALIENS. I MEAN, I SAW IT. BUT... THEY ARE EXACTLY THE SAME AS THEY ALWAYS ARE. MAYBE THEY'VE ALWAYS BEEN POSSESSED? MAYBE THAT'S JUST HOW SOME PEOPLE ARE?
I MEAN, THE ONLY ONES DOING ANY REAL HARM RIGHT NOW IS US...
MAYBE--
--ARE YOU FUCKING KIDDING ME?
WE'VE BEEN GETTING HIGH FOR YEARS. THESE ALIENS ARE A NEW THING.
JUST LIKE YOU.
BUT I'M JUST SAYING, WHAT IF THEY'RE GOOD ALIENS?
FUCK YOU, DUDE. IF YOU DON'T HAVE THE BALLS FOR THIS THEN STAY SOBER AND LIVE IN IGNORANCE AND HOPE WE HANDLE THIS FOR YOU.
JACKIE! WAIT, IT'S NOT--
LEAVE HER ALONE. YOU DON'T WANT TO MESS WITH HER WHEN SHE'S MAD.
LOOK MAN, I GET IT. YOU HAVE YOUR DOUBTS. THAT'S WHY WE NEED YOUR HELP FIGURING THIS OUT. I'M NOT SMART ENOUGH TO DO IT...
...BUT I'M NOT DUMB ENOUGH TO THINK THESE ALIENS ARE GOOD GUYS EITHER.
ANYWAY, WE'RE MEETING IN THE MEN'S ROOM BY DRIVER'S ED AT ELEVEN SHARP.
IF YOU'RE REALLY A BURNOUT AND YOU WANT TO SAVE THE WORLD, YOU'LL BE THERE.

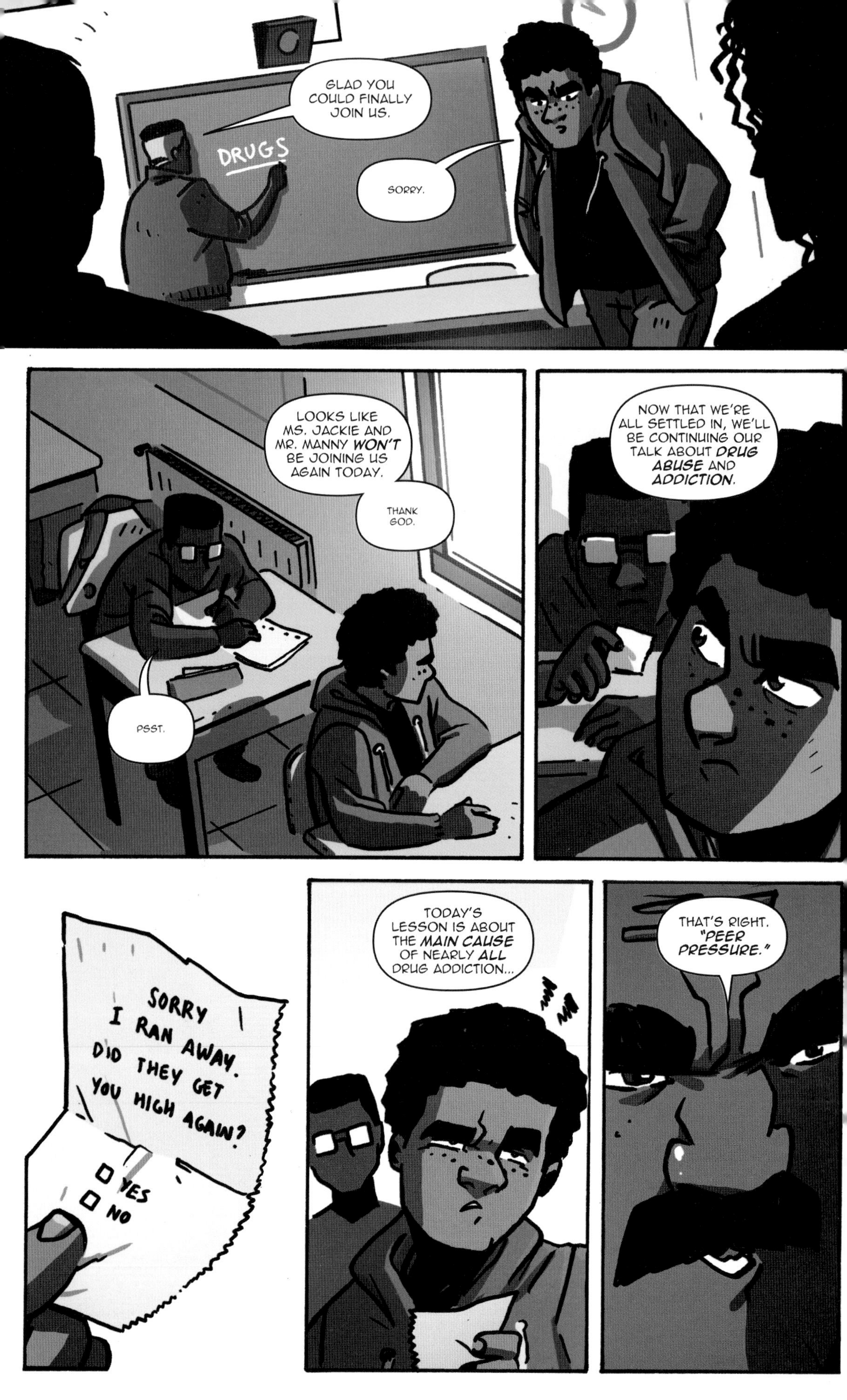
GLAD YOU COULD FINALLY JOIN US.
DRUGS
SORRY.
LOOKS LIKE MS. JACKIE AND MR. MANNY WON'T BE JOINING US AGAIN TODAY.
THANK GOD.
PSST.
NOW THAT WE'RE ALL SETTLED IN, WE'LL BE CONTINUING OUR TALK ABOUT DRUG ABUSE AND ADDICTION.
SORRY I RAN AWAY. DID THEY GET YOU HIGH AGAIN?
YES
NO
TODAY'S LESSON IS ABOUT THE MAIN CAUSE OF NEARLY ALL DRUG ADDICTION...
THAT'S RIGHT. "PEER PRESSURE."

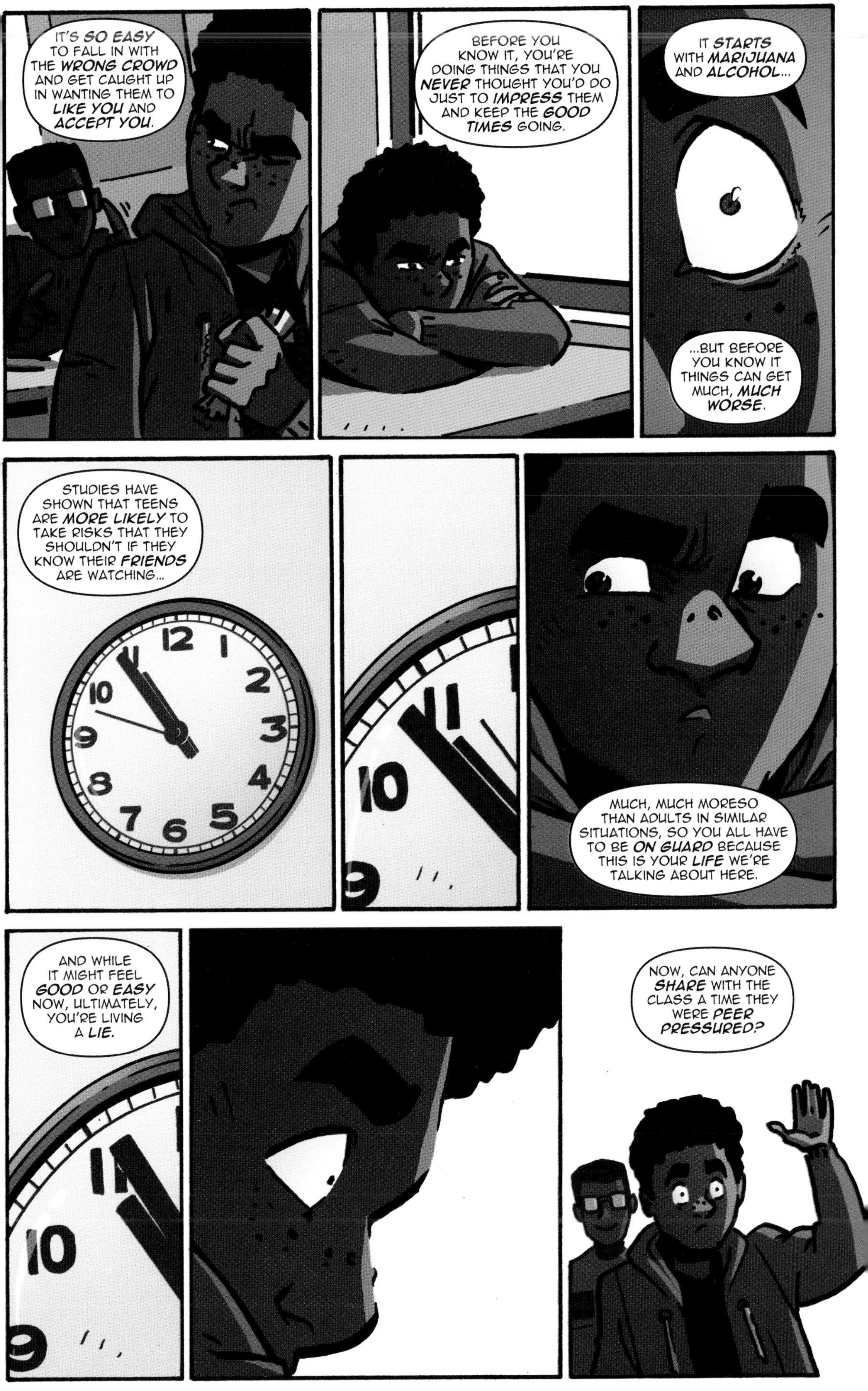
IT'S SO EASY TO FALL IN WITH THE WRONG CROWD AND GET CAUGHT UP IN WANTING THEM TO LIKE YOU AND ACCEPT YOU.
BEFORE YOU KNOW IT, YOU'RE DOING THINGS THAT YOU NEVER THOUGHT YOU'D DO JUST TO IMPRESS THEM AND KEEP THE GOOD TIMES GOING.
IT STARTS WITH MARIJUANA AND ALCOHOL...
...BUT BEFORE YOU KNOW IT THINGS CAN GET MUCH, MUCH WORSE.
STUDIES HAVE SHOWN THAT TEENS ARE MORE LIKELY TO TAKE RISKS THAT THEY SHOULDN'T IF THEY KNOW THEIR FRIENDS ARE WATCHING...
MUCH, MUCH MORESO THAN ADULTS IN SIMILAR SITUATIONS, SO YOU ALL HAVE TO BE ON GUARD BECAUSE THIS IS YOUR LIFE WE'RE TALKING ABOUT HERE.
AND WHILE IT MIGHT FEEL GOOD OR EASY NOW, ULTIMATELY, YOU'RE LIVING A LIE.
NOW, CAN ANYONE SHARE WITH THE CLASS A TIME THEY WERE PEER PRESSURED?

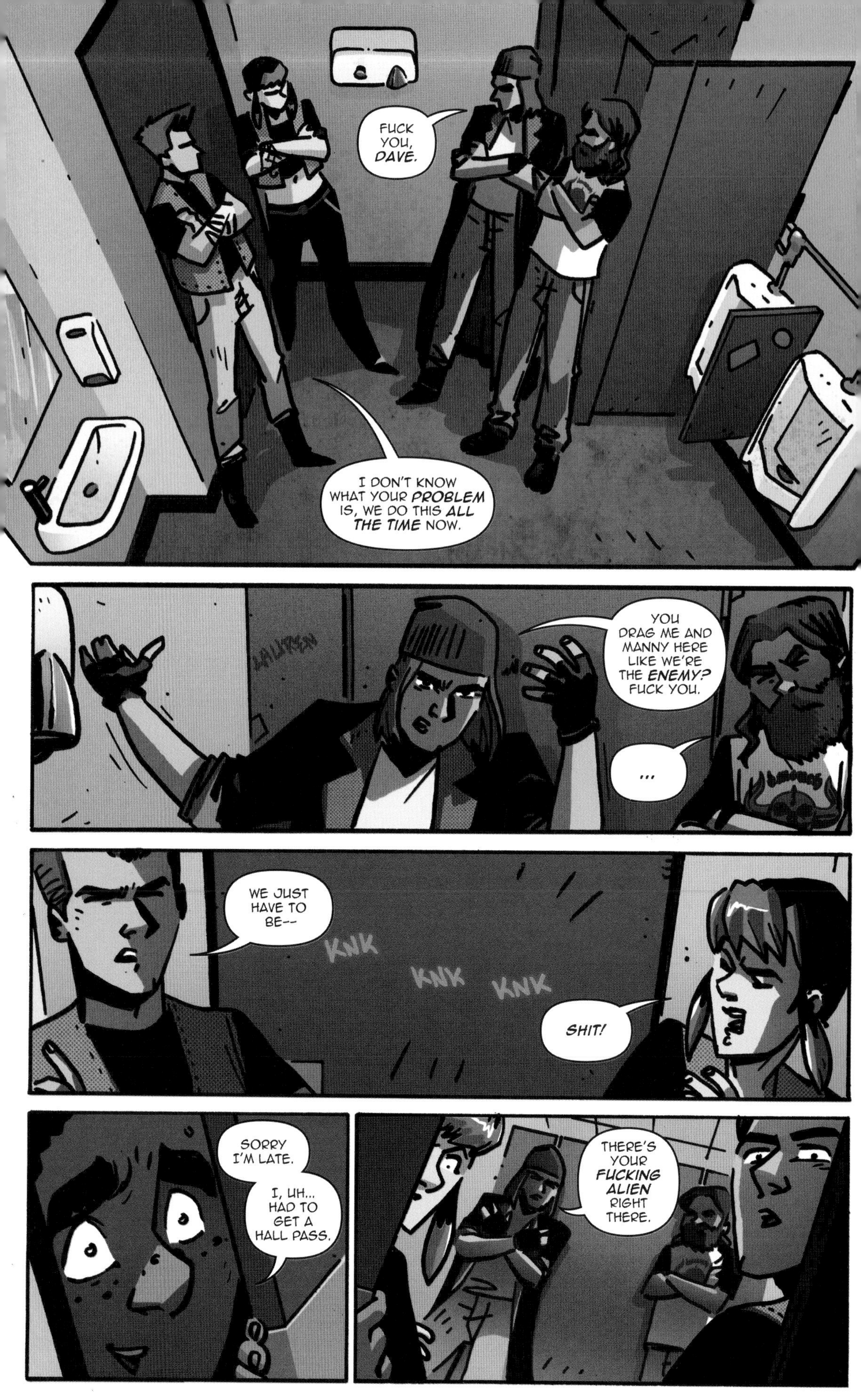
FUCK YOU, DAVE.
I DON'T KNOW WHAT YOUR PROBLEM IS, WE DO THIS ALL THE TIME NOW.
YOU DRAG ME AND MANNY HERE LIKE WE'RE THE ENEMY? FUCK YOU.
...
WE JUST HAVE TO BE--
KNK
KNK
KNK
SHIT!
SORRY I'M LATE.
I, UH... HAD TO GET A HALL PASS.
THERE'S YOUR FUCKING ALIEN RIGHT THERE.

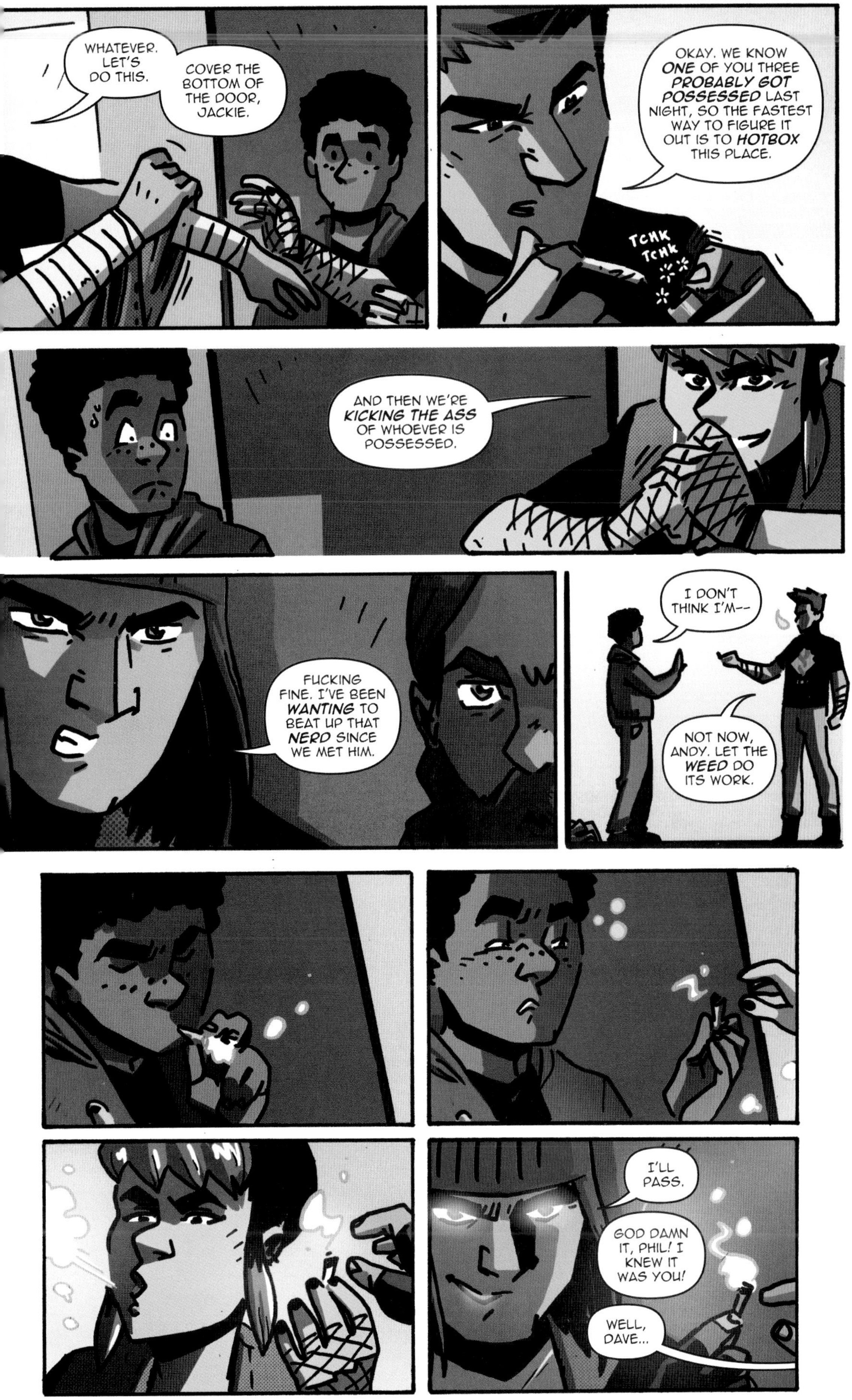
WHATEVER. LET'S DO THIS.
COVER THE BOTTOM OF THE DOOR, JACKIE.
OKAY. WE KNOW ONE OF YOU THREE PROBABLY GOT POSSESSED LAST NIGHT, SO THE FASTEST WAY TO FIGURE IT OUT IS TO HOTBOX THIS PLACE.
TCHK TCHK
AND THEN WE'RE KICKING THE ASS OF WHOEVER IS POSSESSED.
FUCKING FINE. I'VE BEEN WANTING TO BEAT UP THAT NERD SINCE WE MET HIM.
I DON'T THINK I'M--
NOT NOW, ANDY. LET THE WEED DO ITS WORK.
I'LL PASS.
GOD DAMN IT, PHIL! I KNEW IT WAS YOU!
WELL, DAVE...

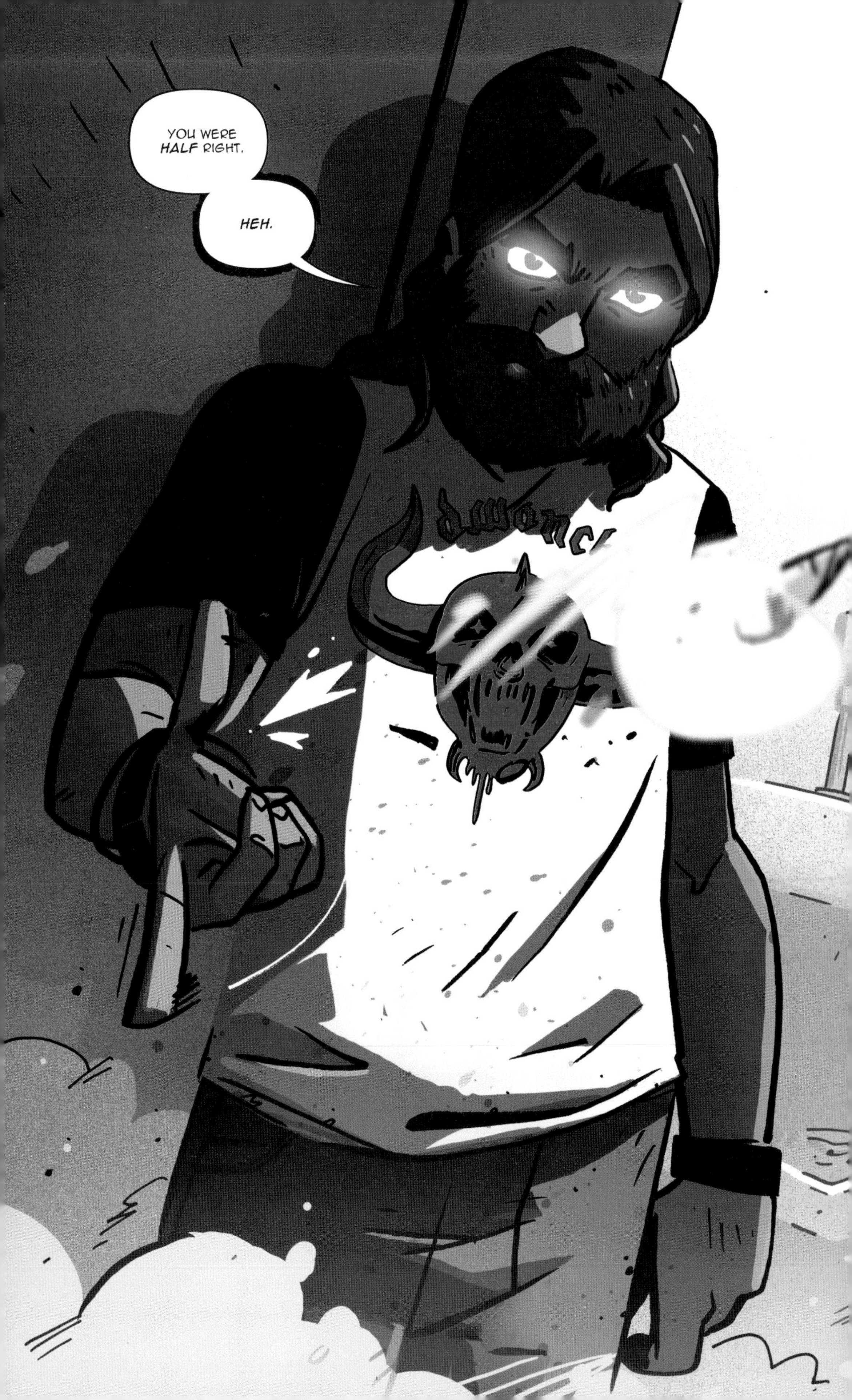
YOU WERE *HALF* RIGHT.
HEH.

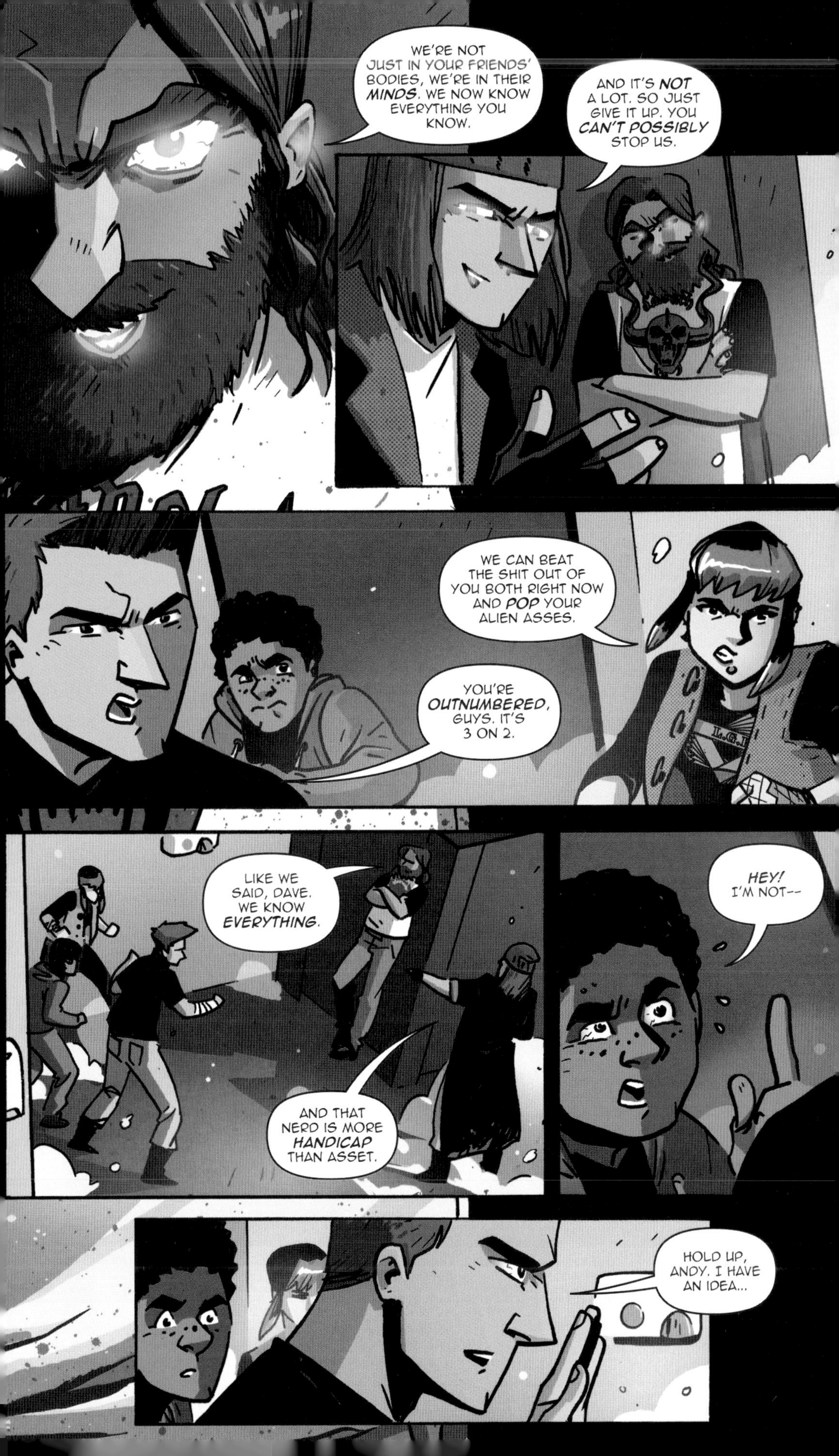
WE'RE NOT JUST IN YOUR FRIENDS' BODIES, WE'RE IN THEIR MINDS. WE NOW KNOW EVERYTHING YOU KNOW.
AND IT'S NOT A LOT. SO JUST GIVE IT UP. YOU CAN'T POSSIBLY STOP US.
WE CAN BEAT THE SHIT OUT OF YOU BOTH RIGHT NOW AND POP YOUR ALIEN ASSES.
YOU'RE OUTNUMBERED, GUYS. IT'S 3 ON 2.
LIKE WE SAID, DAVE. WE KNOW EVERYTHING.
AND THAT NERD IS MORE HANDICAP THAN ASSET.
HEY! I'M NOT--
HOLD UP, ANDY. I HAVE AN IDEA...

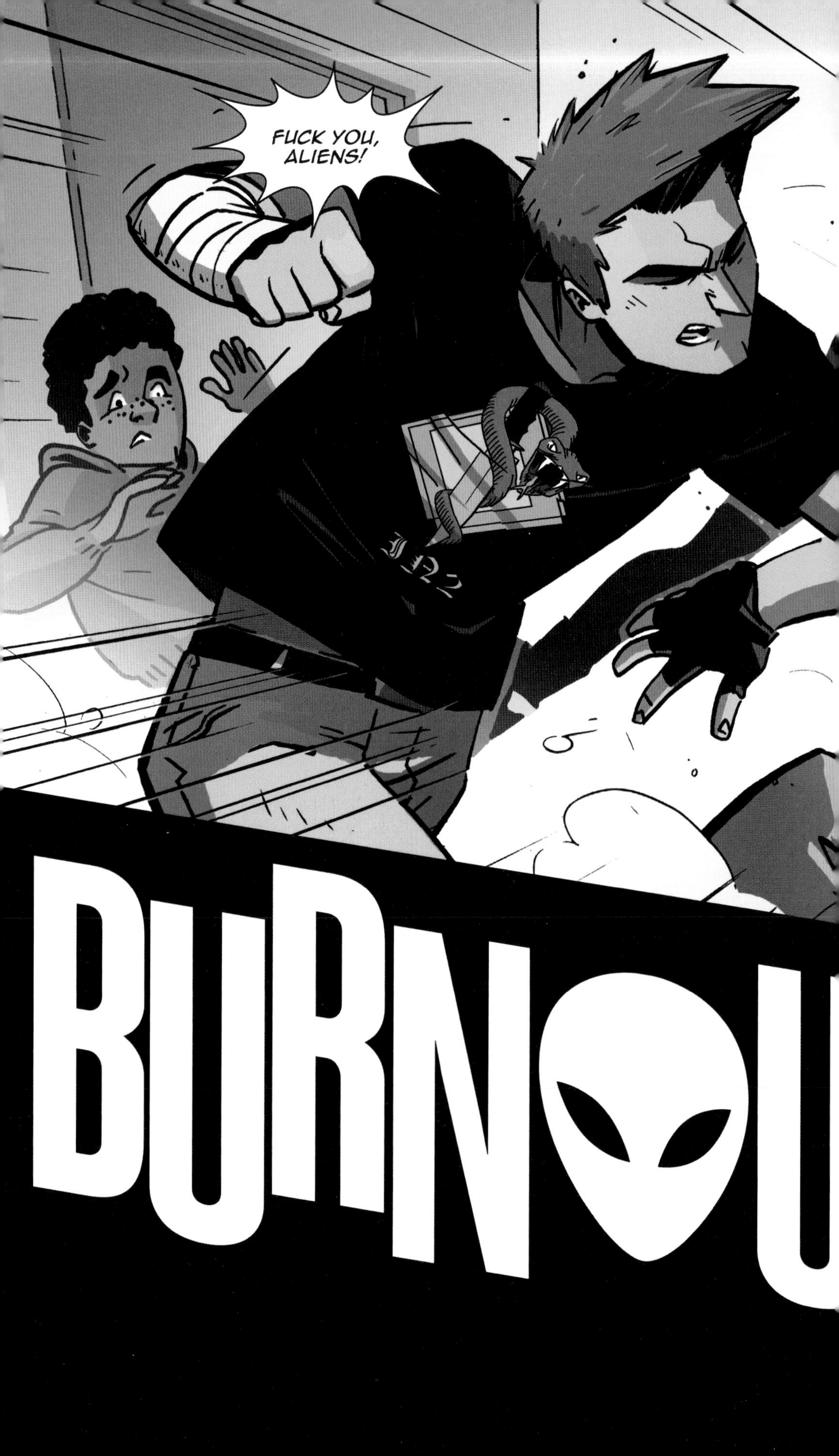
FUCK YOU, ALIENS!
BURNOU

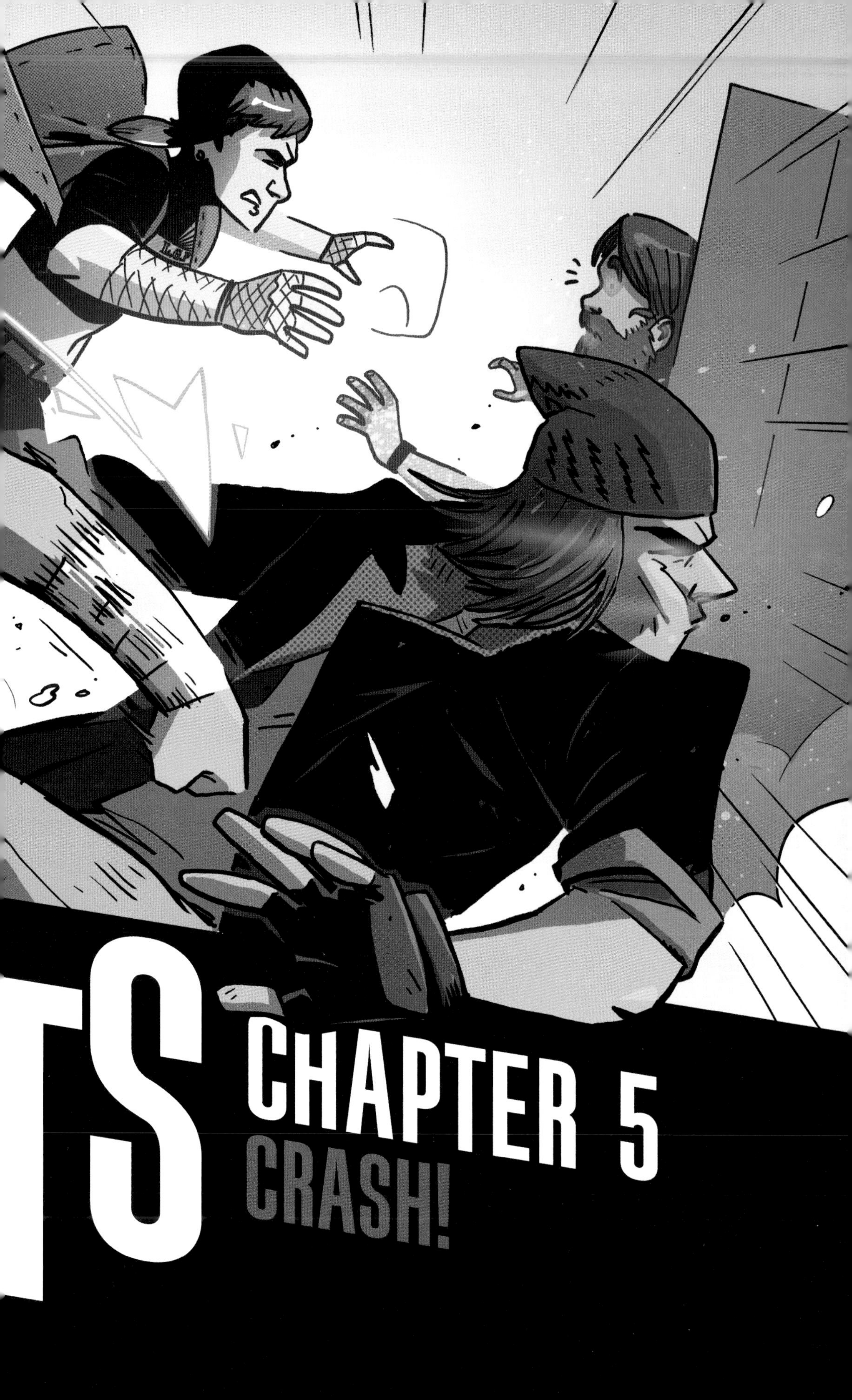

CHAPTER 5
CRASH!

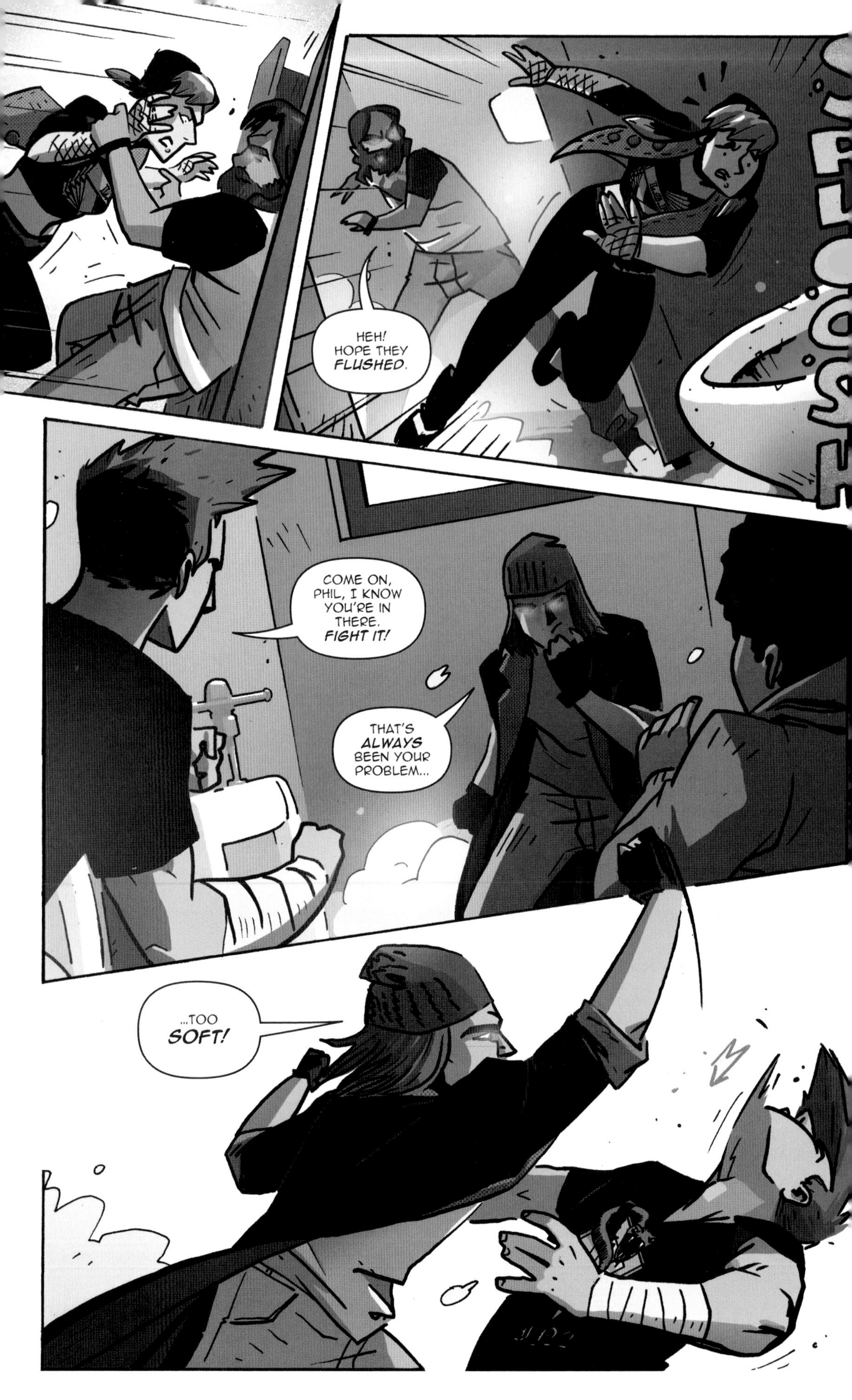
HEH! HOPE THEY *FLUSHED*.
COME ON, PHIL, I KNOW YOU'RE IN THERE. *FIGHT IT!*
THAT'S *ALWAYS* BEEN YOUR PROBLEM...
...TOO *SOFT!*

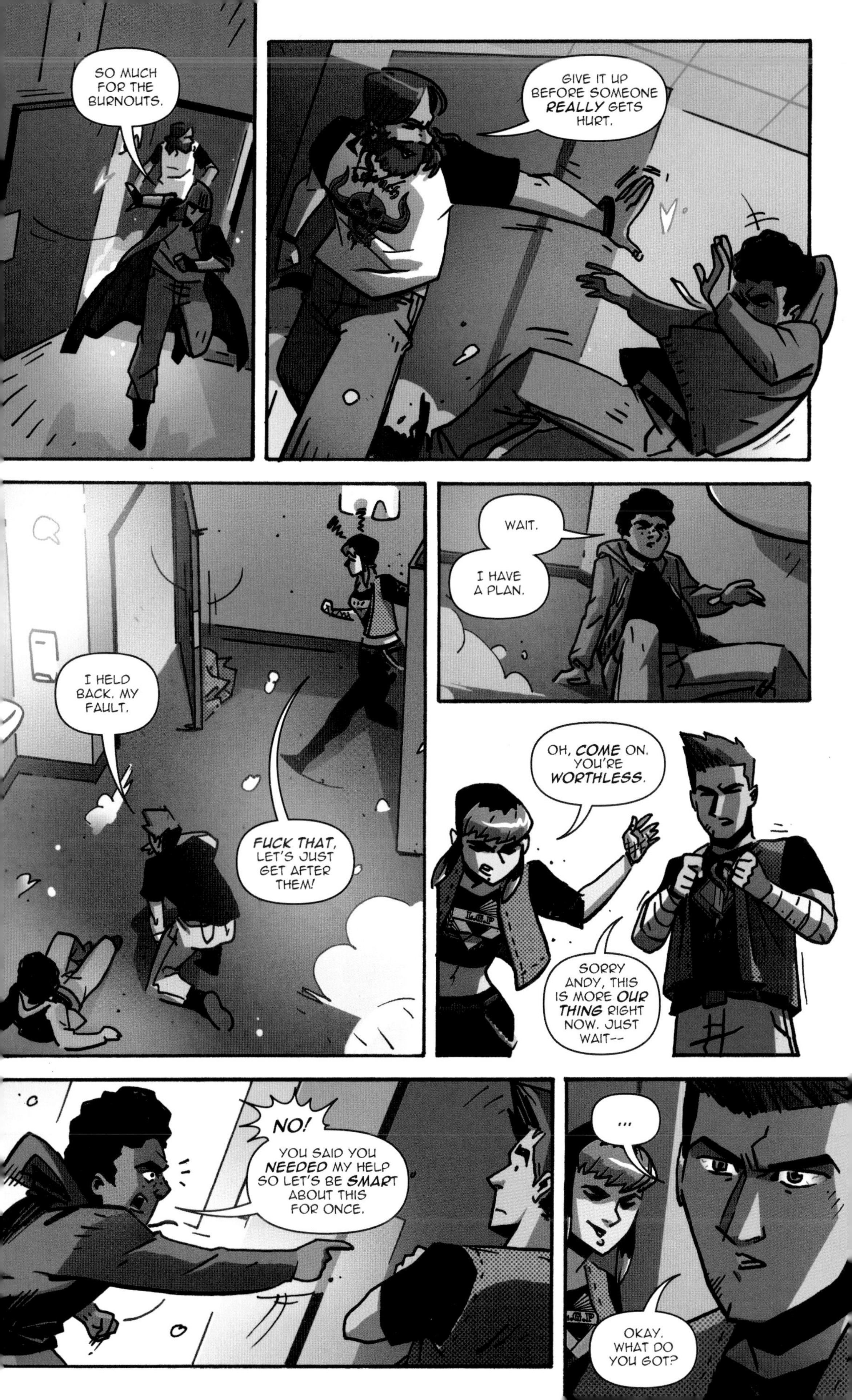
SO MUCH FOR THE BURNOUTS.
GIVE IT UP BEFORE SOMEONE REALLY GETS HURT.
I HELD BACK. MY FAULT.
FUCK THAT, LET'S JUST GET AFTER THEM!
WAIT.
I HAVE A PLAN.
OH, COME ON. YOU'RE WORTHLESS.
SORRY ANDY, THIS IS MORE OUR THING RIGHT NOW. JUST WAIT--
NO!
YOU SAID YOU NEEDED MY HELP SO LET'S BE SMART ABOUT THIS FOR ONCE.
...
OKAY. WHAT DO YOU GOT?

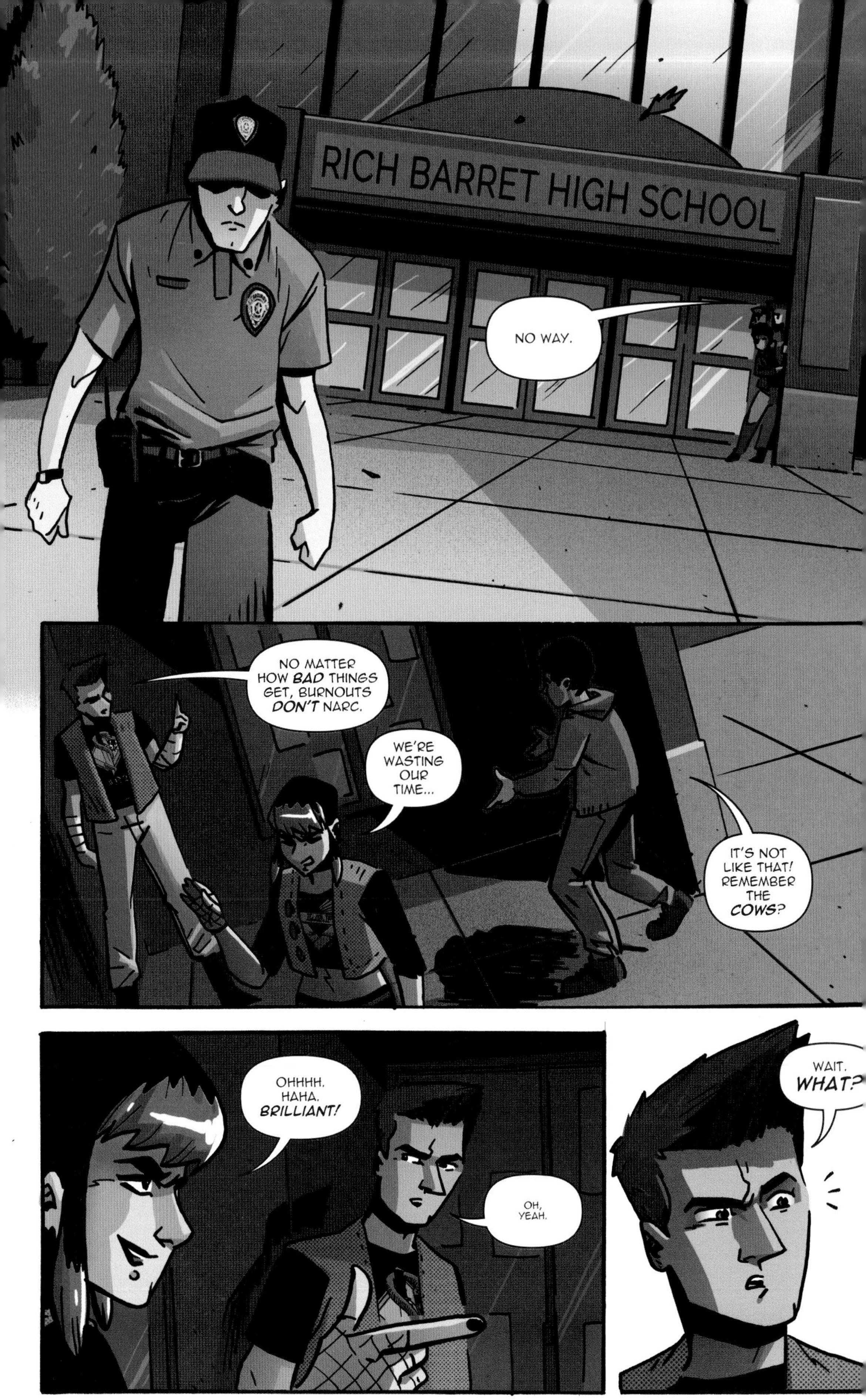
RICH BARRET HIGH SCHOOL
NO WAY.
NO MATTER HOW *BAD* THINGS GET, BURNOUTS *DON'T* NARC.
WE'RE WASTING OUR TIME...
IT'S NOT LIKE THAT! REMEMBER THE *COWS*?
OHHHH. HAHA. *BRILLIANT!*
OH, YEAH.
WAIT. *WHAT?*

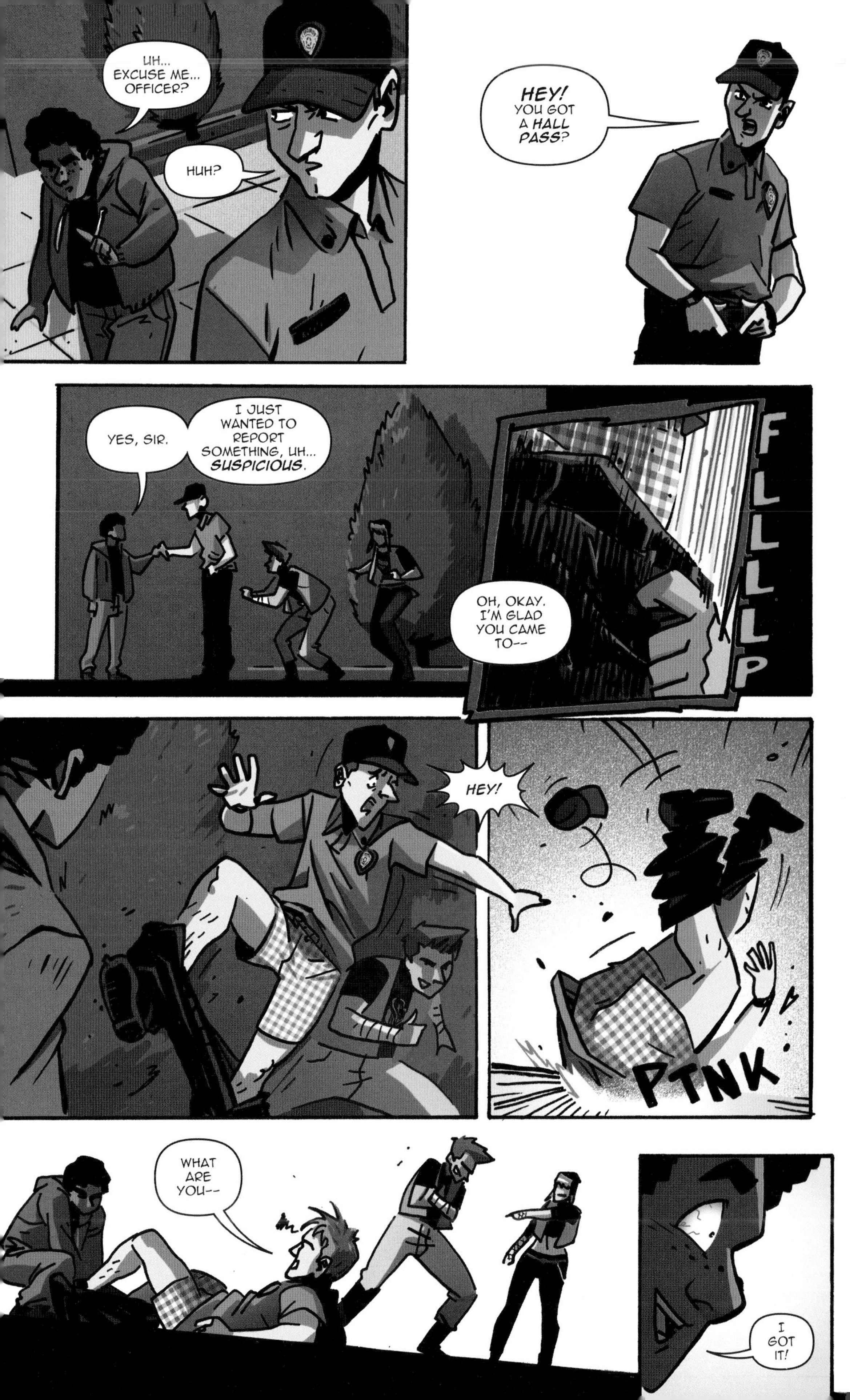
UH... EXCUSE ME... OFFICER?
HUH?
HEY! YOU GOT A HALL PASS?
YES, SIR.
I JUST WANTED TO REPORT SOMETHING, UH... SUSPICIOUS.
OH, OKAY. I'M GLAD YOU CAME TO--
FLLLLP
HEY!
PTNK
WHAT ARE YOU--
I GOT IT!

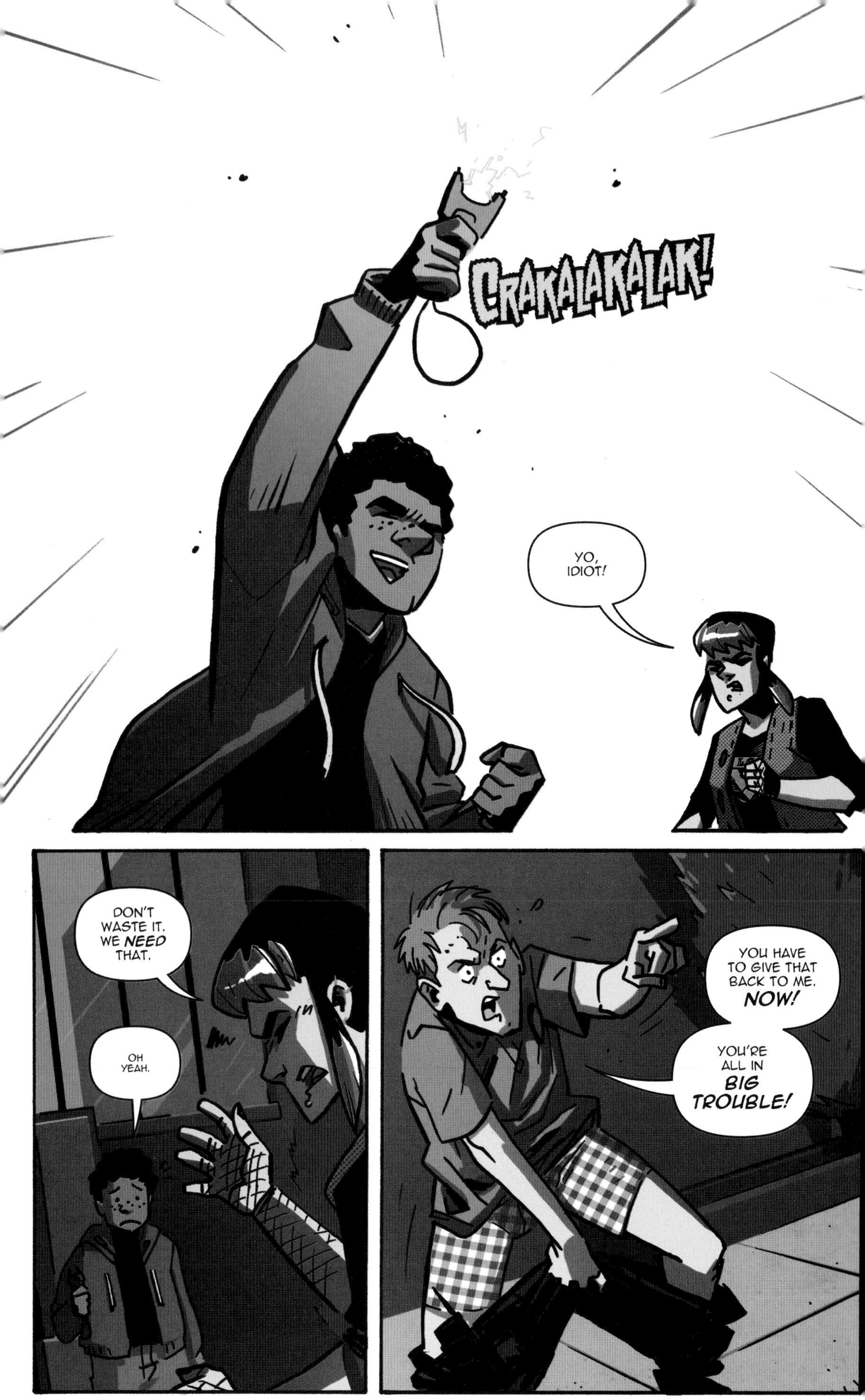
CRAKALAKALAK!
YO, IDIOT!
DON'T WASTE IT. WE *NEED* THAT.
OH YEAH.
YOU HAVE TO GIVE THAT BACK TO ME. *NOW!*
YOU'RE ALL IN *BIG TROUBLE!*

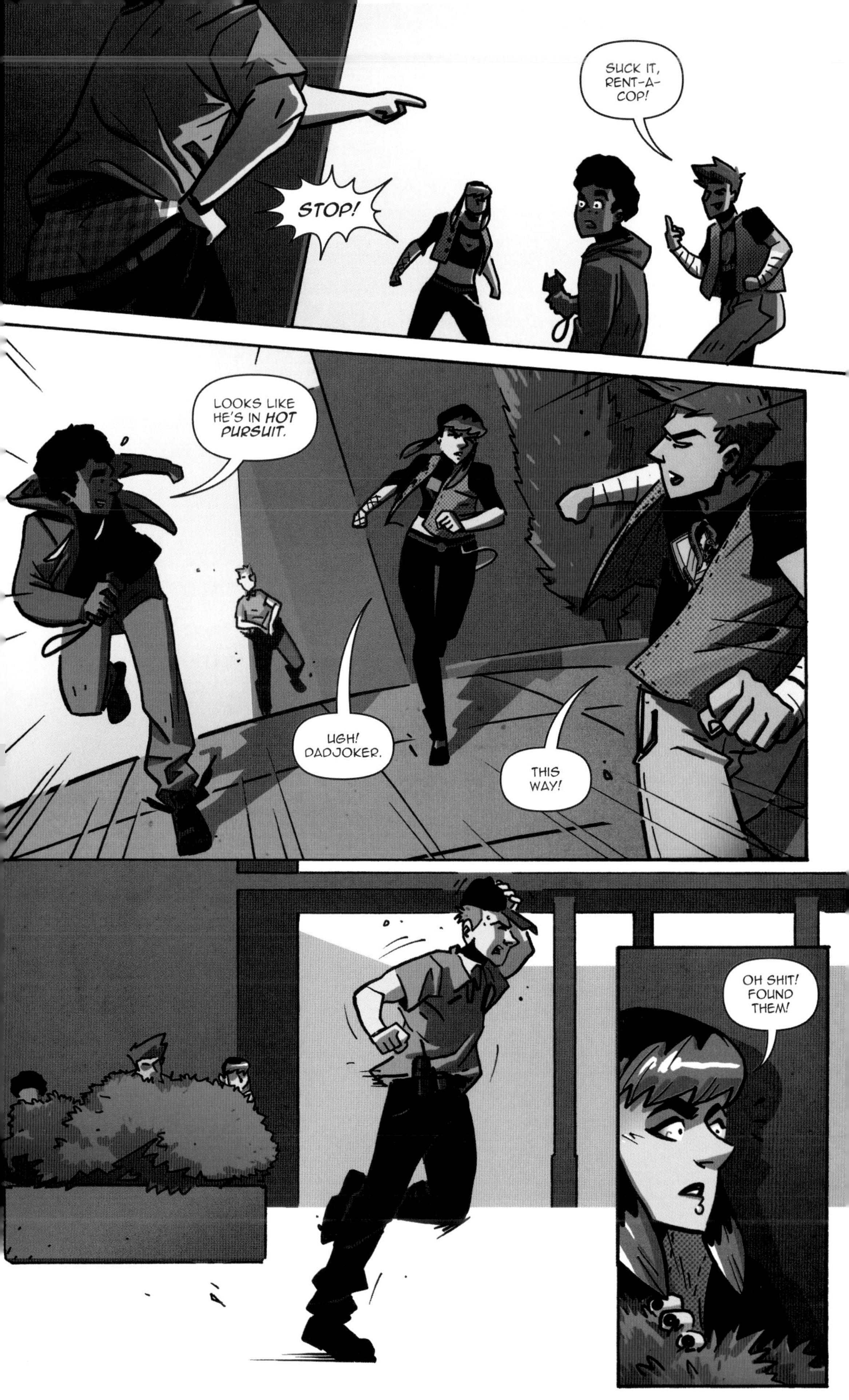
SUCK IT, RENT-A-COP!
STOP!
LOOKS LIKE HE'S IN HOT PURSUIT.
UGH! DADJOKER.
THIS WAY!
OH SHIT! FOUND THEM!

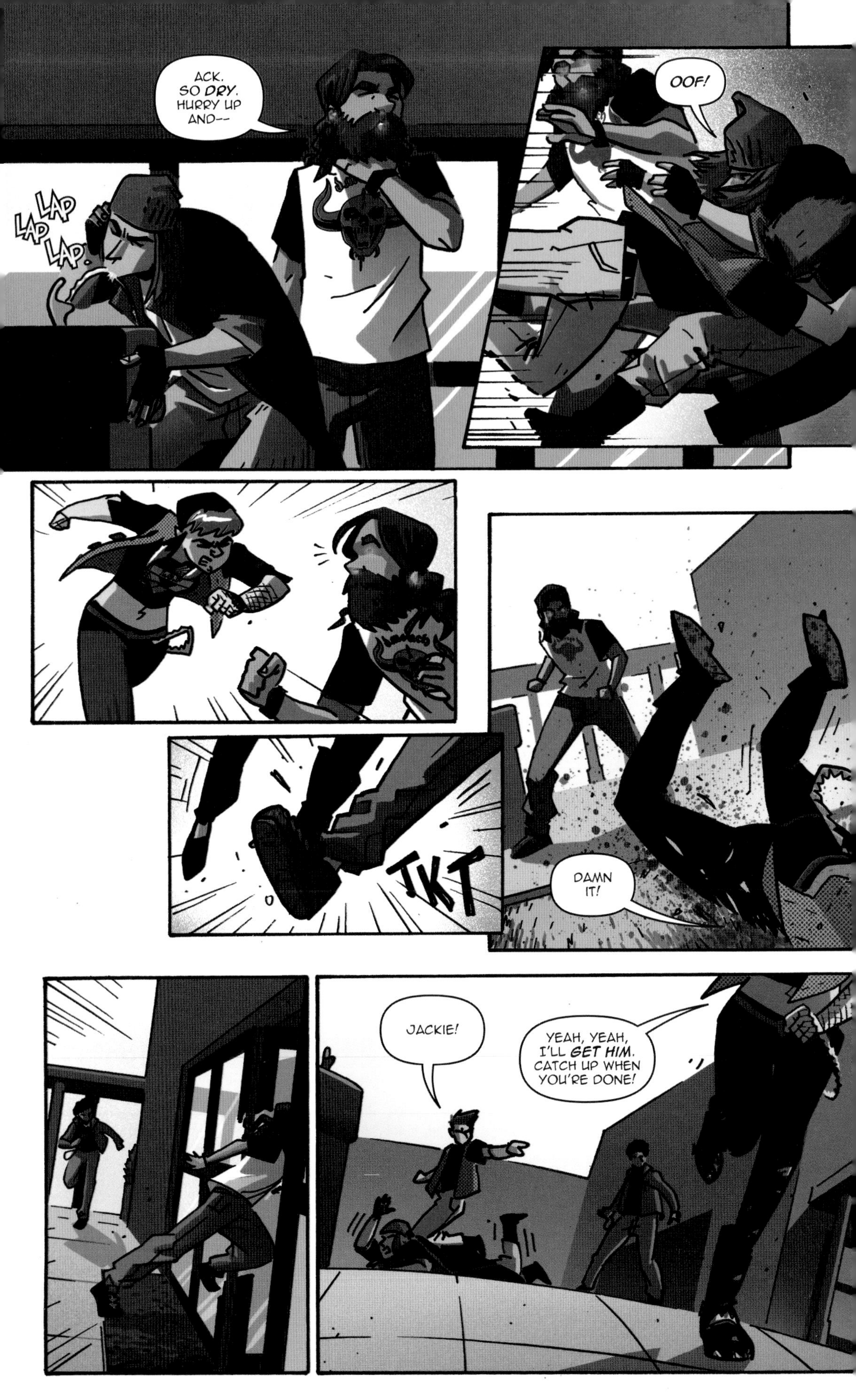
ACK. SO DRY. HURRY UP AND--
LAP LAP LAP
OOF!
TKT
DAMN IT!
JACKIE!
YEAH, YEAH, I'LL GET HIM. CATCH UP WHEN YOU'RE DONE!

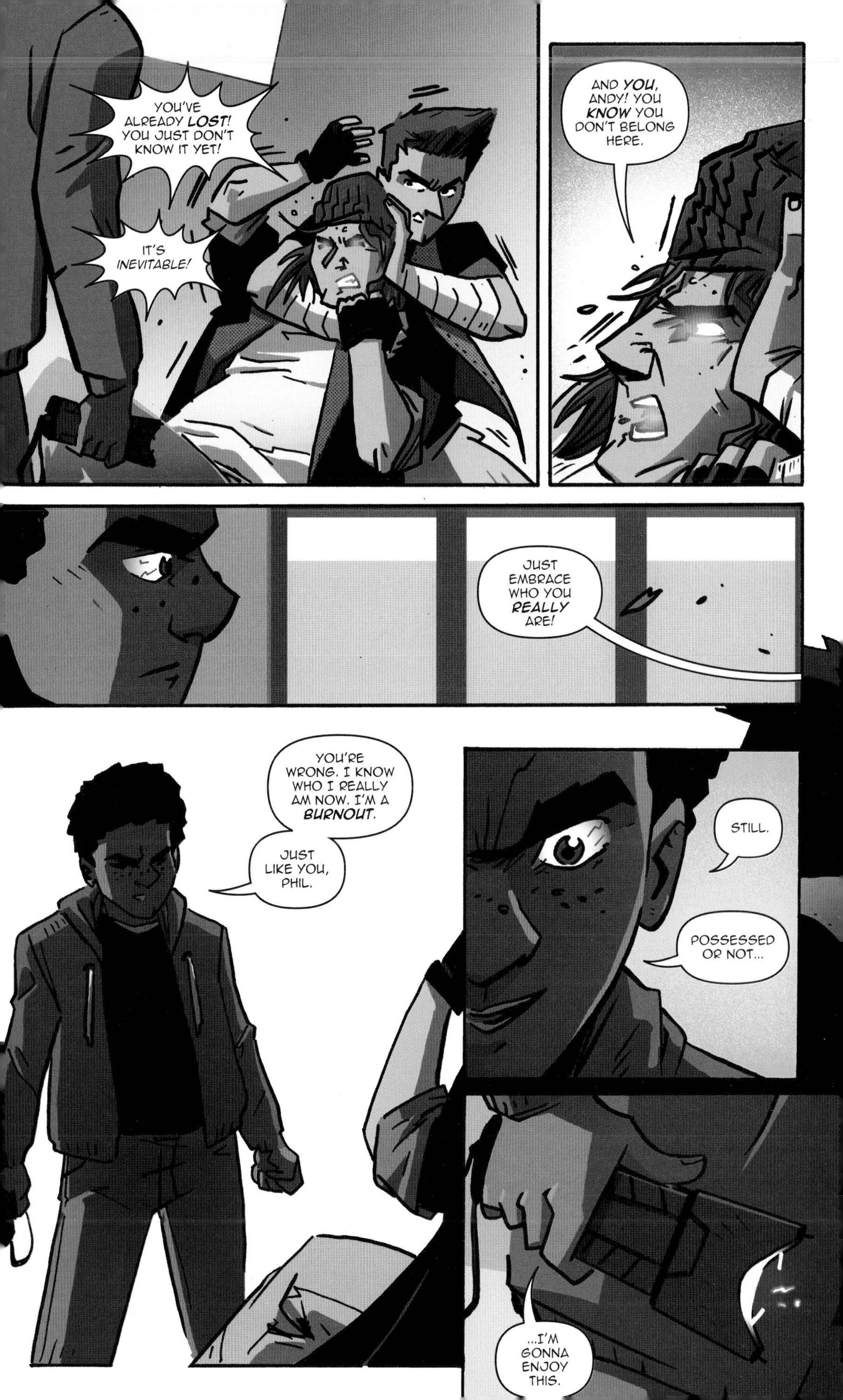

YOU'VE ALREADY LOST! YOU JUST DON'T KNOW IT YET!
IT'S INEVITABLE!
AND YOU, ANDY! YOU KNOW YOU DON'T BELONG HERE.
JUST EMBRACE WHO YOU REALLY ARE!
YOU'RE WRONG. I KNOW WHO I REALLY AM NOW. I'M A BURNOUT.
JUST LIKE YOU, PHIL.
STILL.
POSSESSED OR NOT...
...I'M GONNA ENJOY THIS.

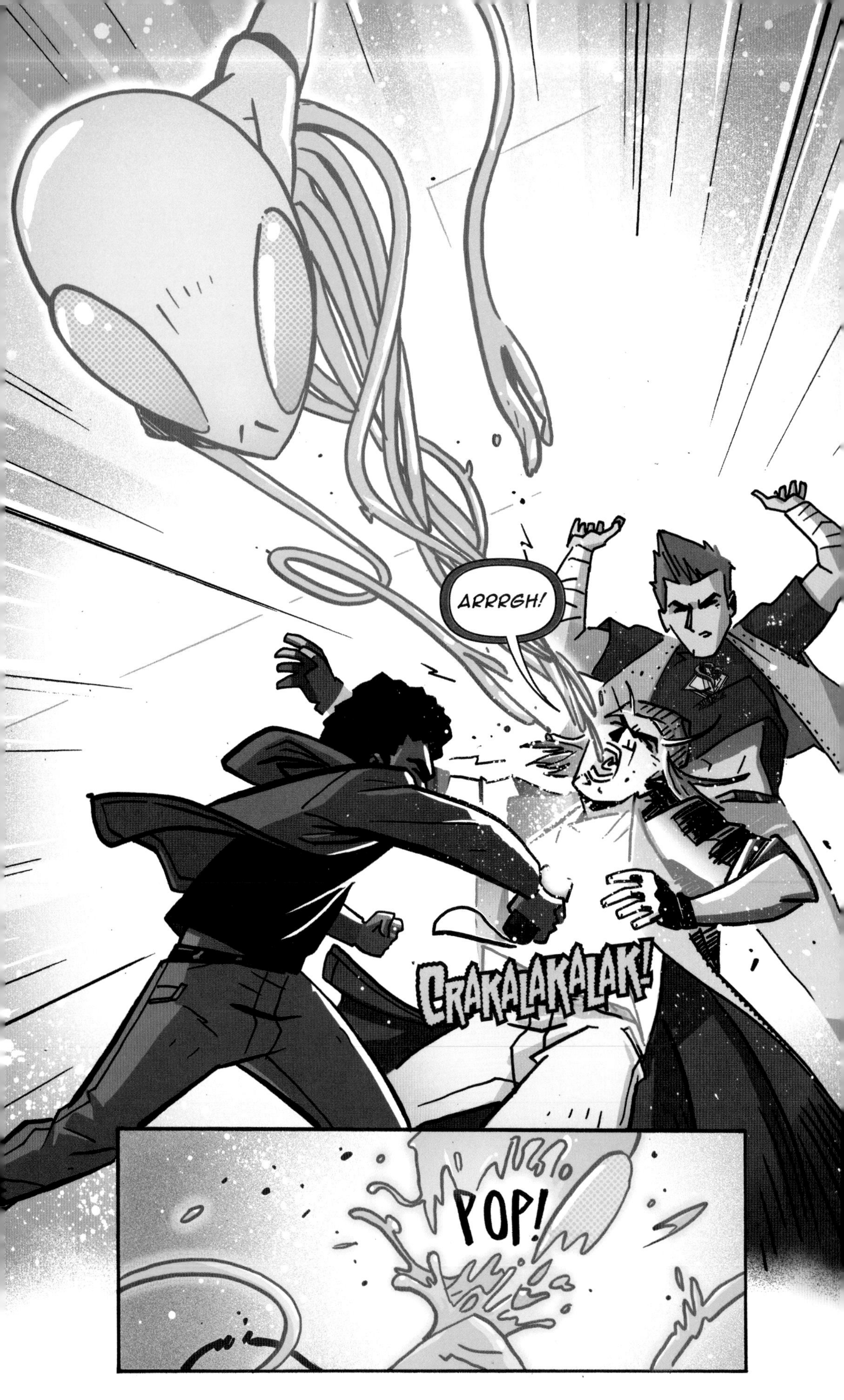
ARRRGH!
CRAKALAKALAK!
POP!

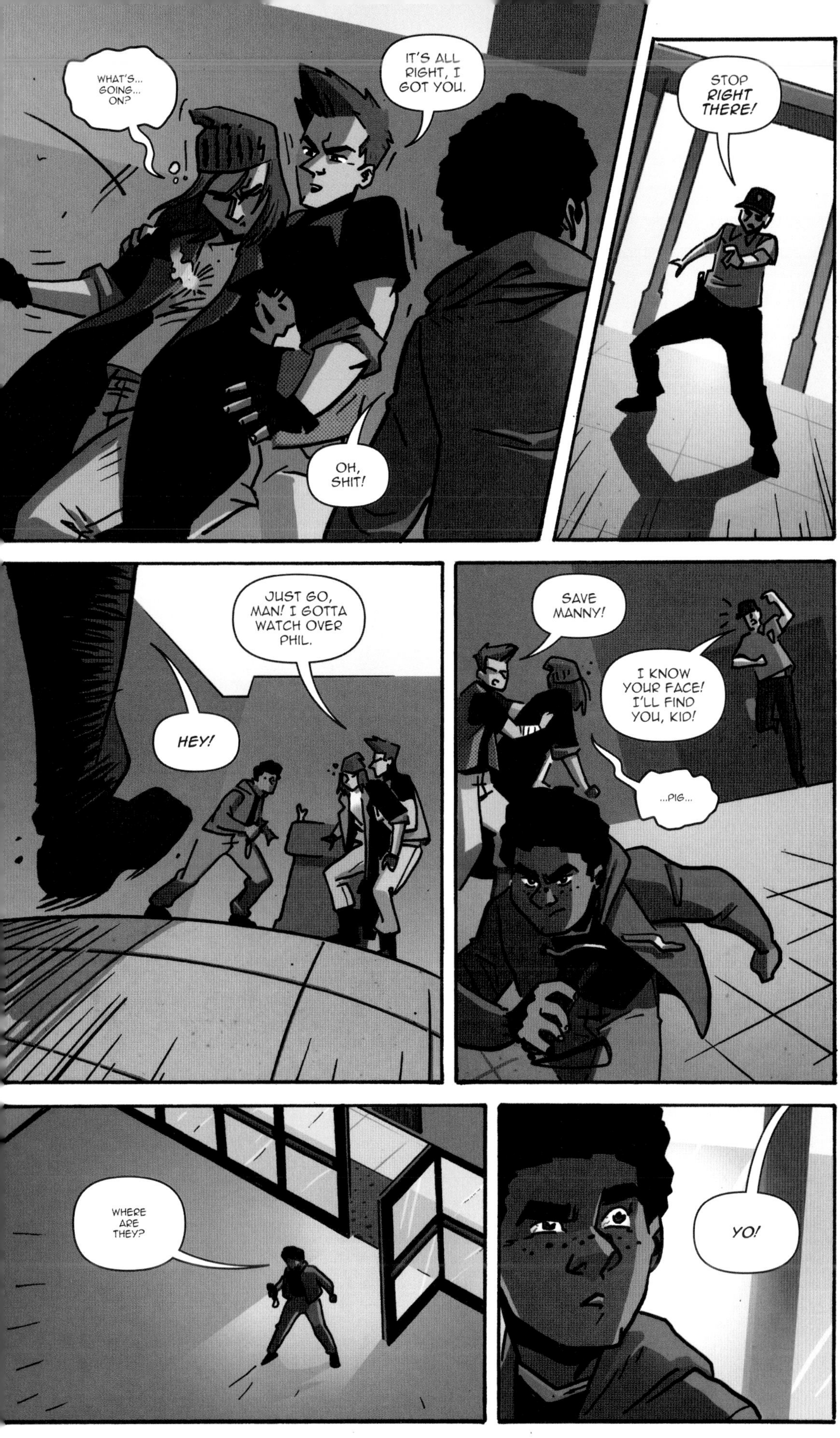
WHAT'S... GOING... ON?
IT'S ALL RIGHT, I GOT YOU.
OH, SHIT!
STOP RIGHT THERE!
HEY!
JUST GO, MAN! I GOTTA WATCH OVER PHIL.
SAVE MANNY!
I KNOW YOUR FACE! I'LL FIND YOU, KID!
...PIG...
WHERE ARE THEY?
YO!

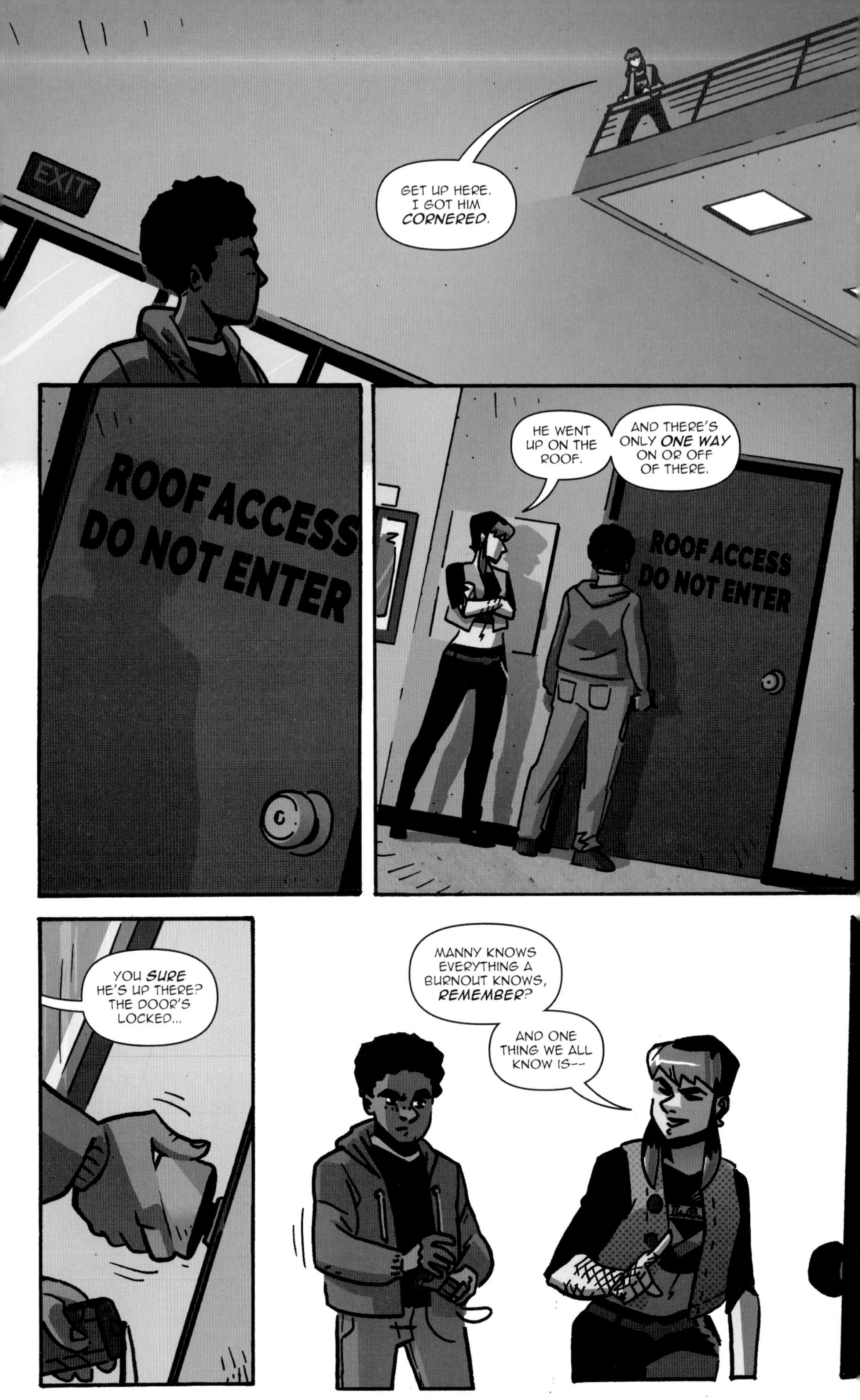
EXIT
GET UP HERE. I GOT HIM CORNERED.
ROOF ACCESS DO NOT ENTER
HE WENT UP ON THE ROOF.
AND THERE'S ONLY ONE WAY ON OR OFF OF THERE.
ROOF ACCESS DO NOT ENTER
YOU SURE HE'S UP THERE? THE DOOR'S LOCKED...
MANNY KNOWS EVERYTHING A BURNOUT KNOWS, REMEMBER?
AND ONE THING WE ALL KNOW IS--

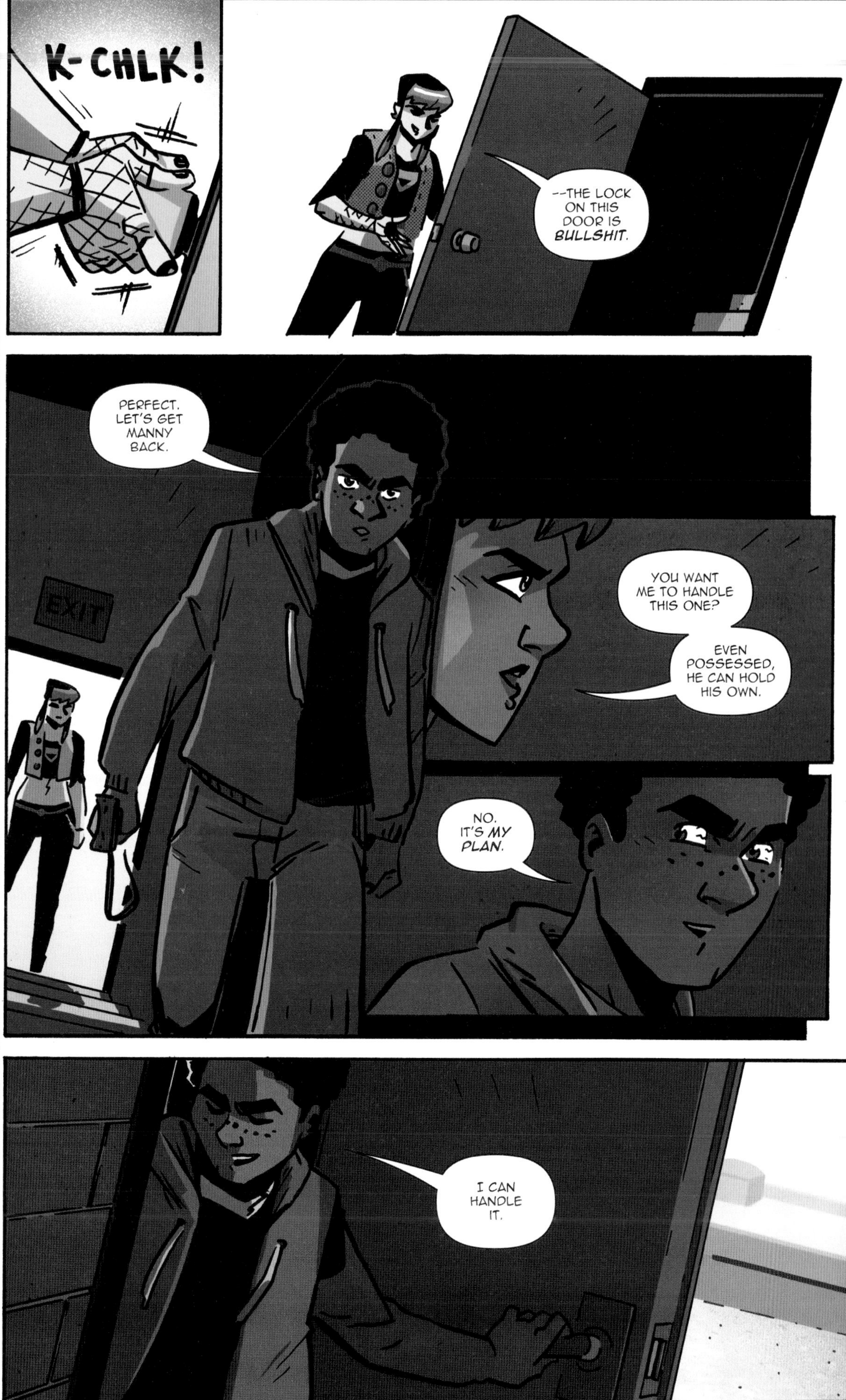
K-CHLK!
--THE LOCK ON THIS DOOR IS BULLSHIT.
PERFECT. LET'S GET MANNY BACK.
EXIT
YOU WANT ME TO HANDLE THIS ONE?
EVEN POSSESSED, HE CAN HOLD HIS OWN.
NO. IT'S MY PLAN.
I CAN HANDLE IT.

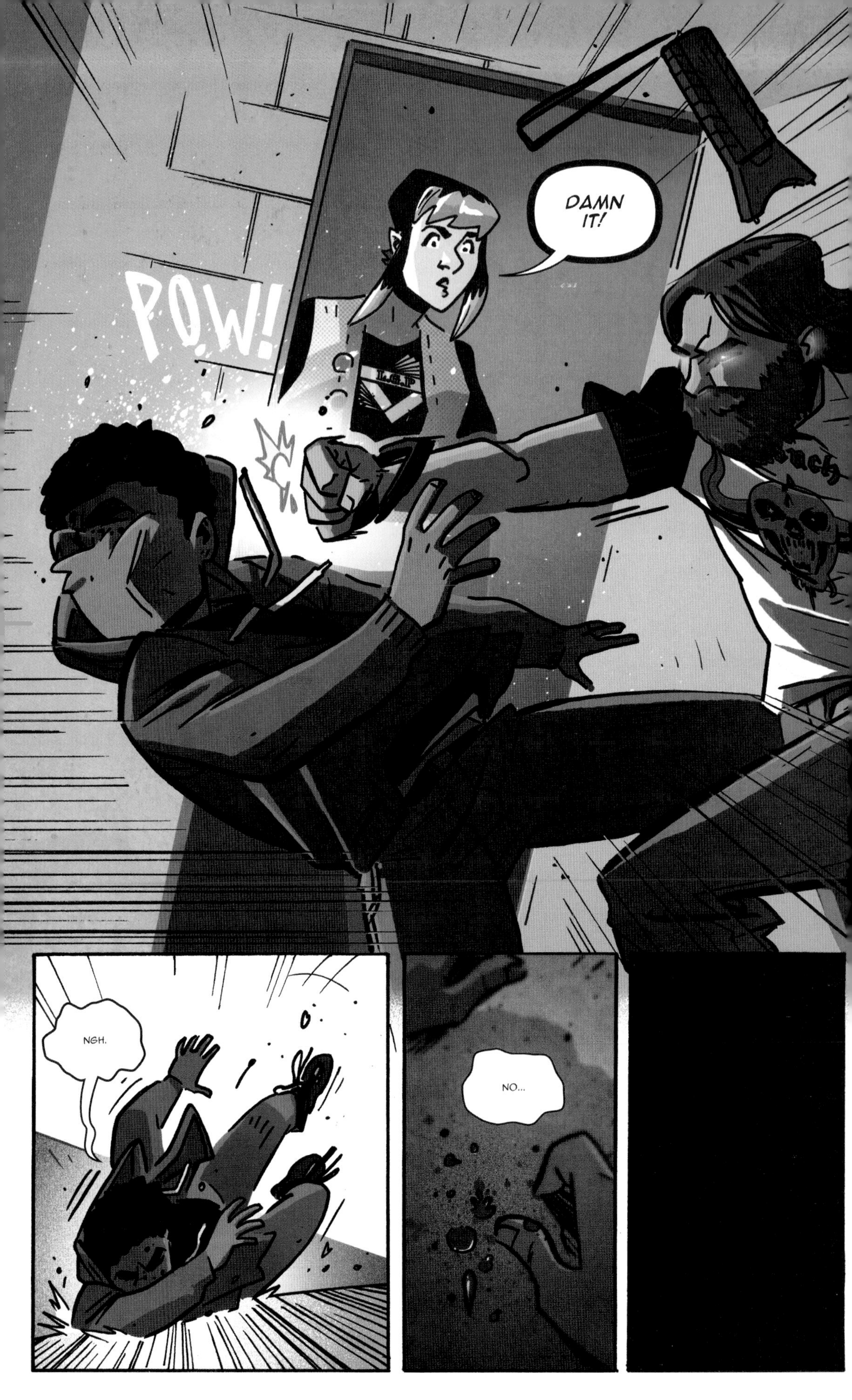
DAMN IT!
POW!
NGH.
NO...

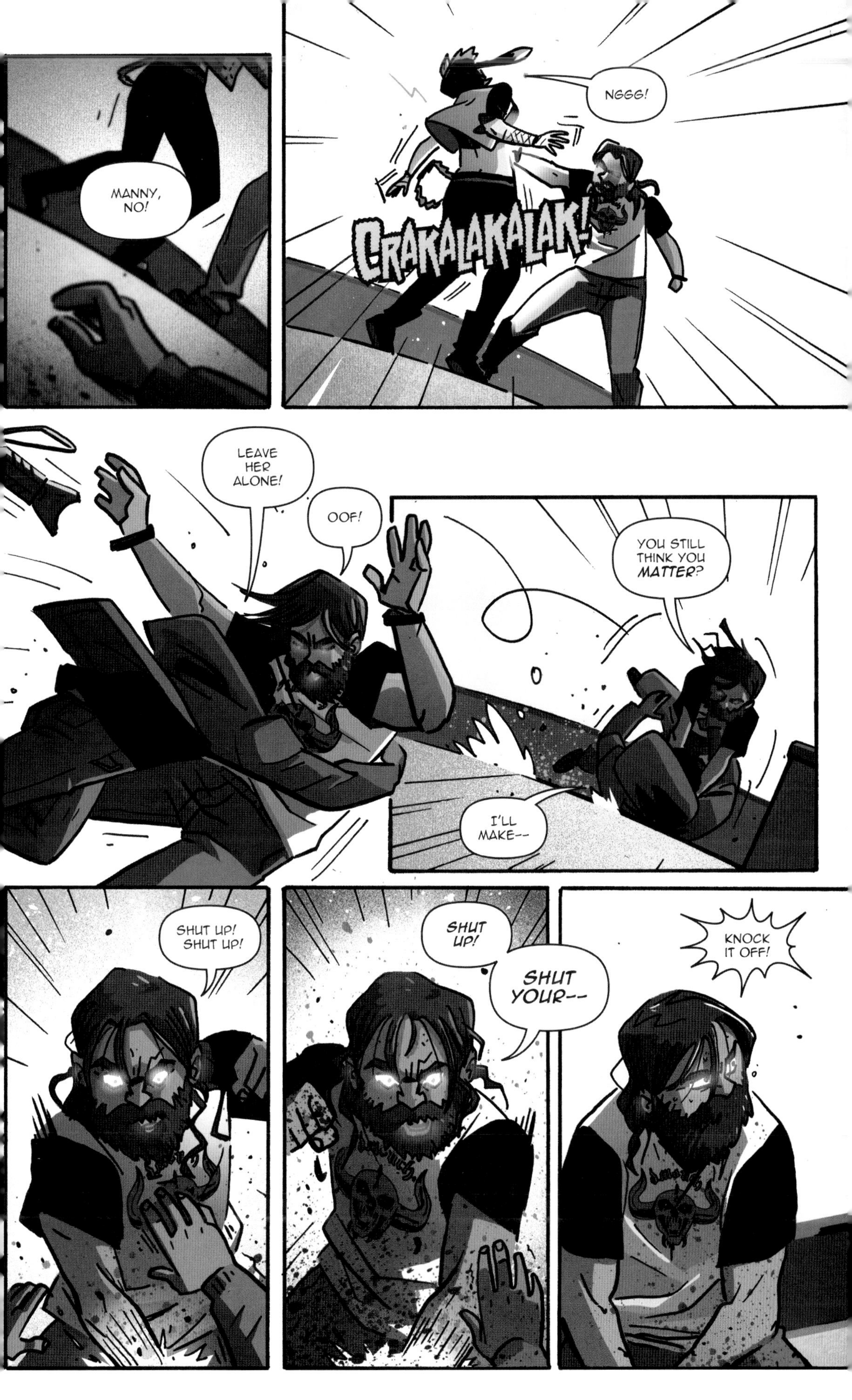
MANNY, NO!
NGGG!
CRAKALAKALAK!
LEAVE HER ALONE!
OOF!
YOU STILL THINK YOU MATTER?
I'LL MAKE--
SHUT UP! SHUT UP!
SHUT UP!
SHUT YOUR--
KNOCK IT OFF!

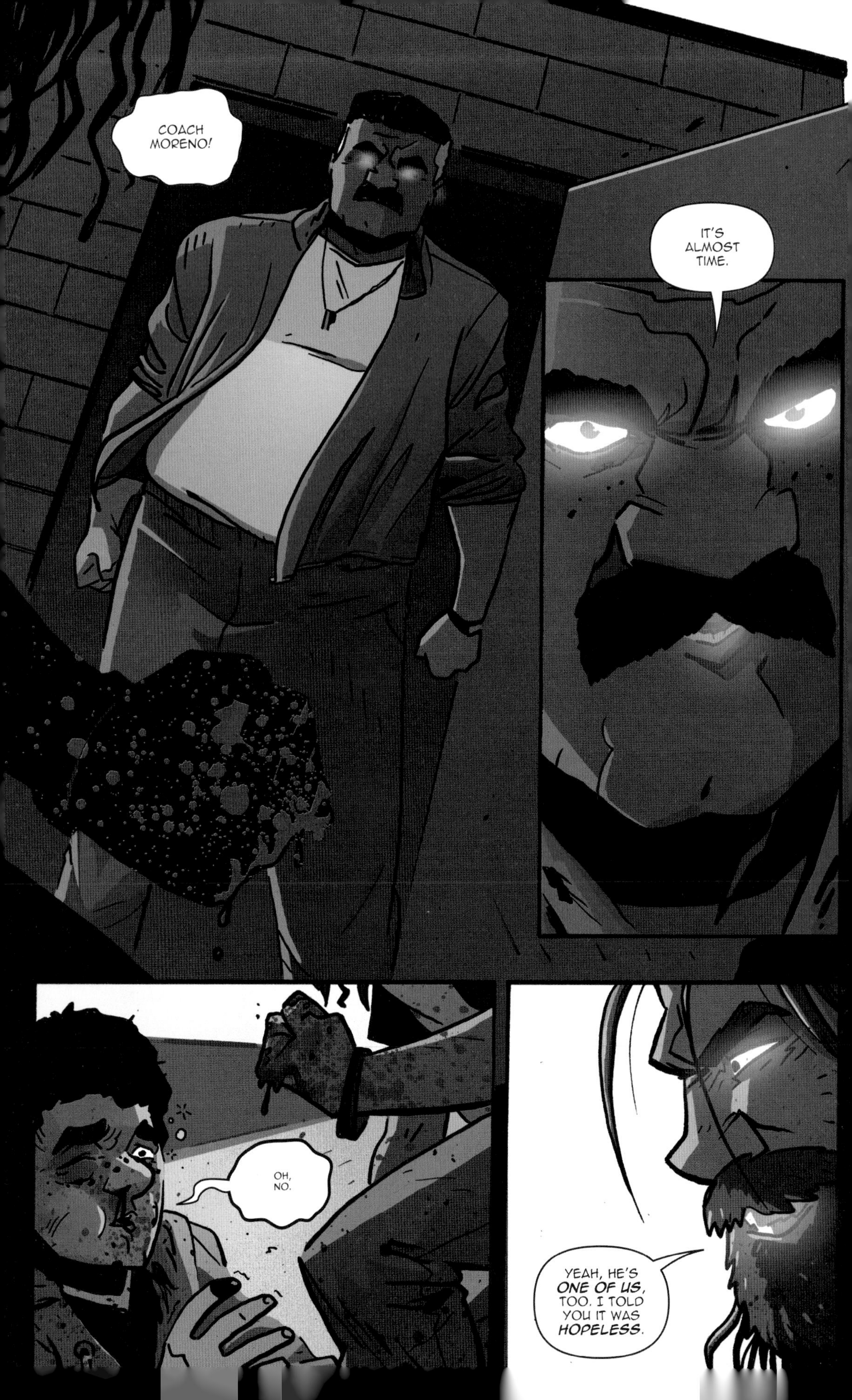
COACH MORENO!
IT'S ALMOST TIME.
OH, NO.
YEAH, HE'S ONE OF US, TOO. I TOLD YOU IT WAS HOPELESS.

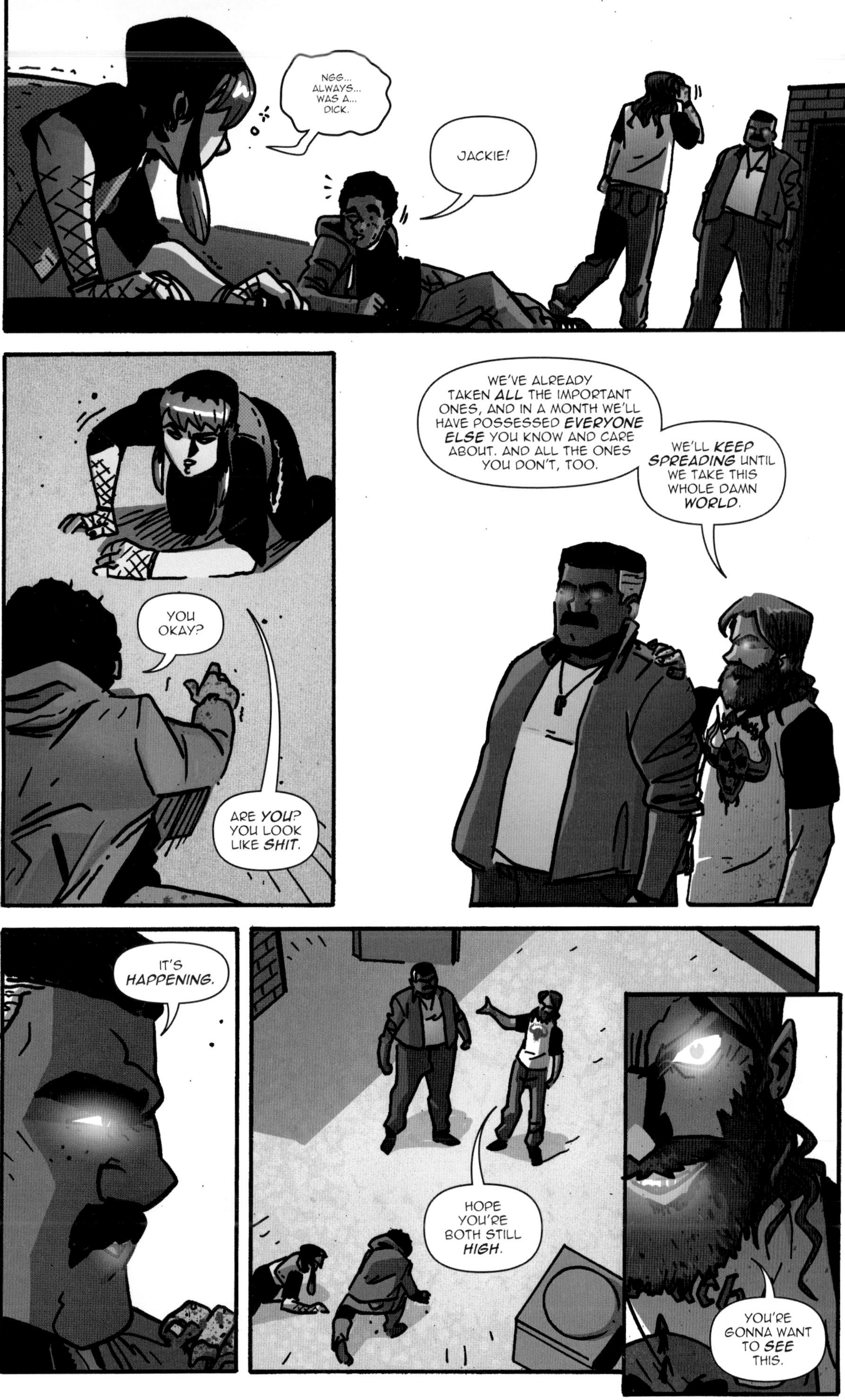
NGG... ALWAYS... WAS A... DICK.
JACKIE!
YOU OKAY?
ARE YOU? YOU LOOK LIKE SHIT.
WE'VE ALREADY TAKEN ALL THE IMPORTANT ONES, AND IN A MONTH WE'LL HAVE POSSESSED EVERYONE ELSE YOU KNOW AND CARE ABOUT. AND ALL THE ONES YOU DON'T, TOO.
WE'LL KEEP SPREADING UNTIL WE TAKE THIS WHOLE DAMN WORLD.
IT'S HAPPENING.
HOPE YOU'RE BOTH STILL HIGH.
YOU'RE GONNA WANT TO SEE THIS.

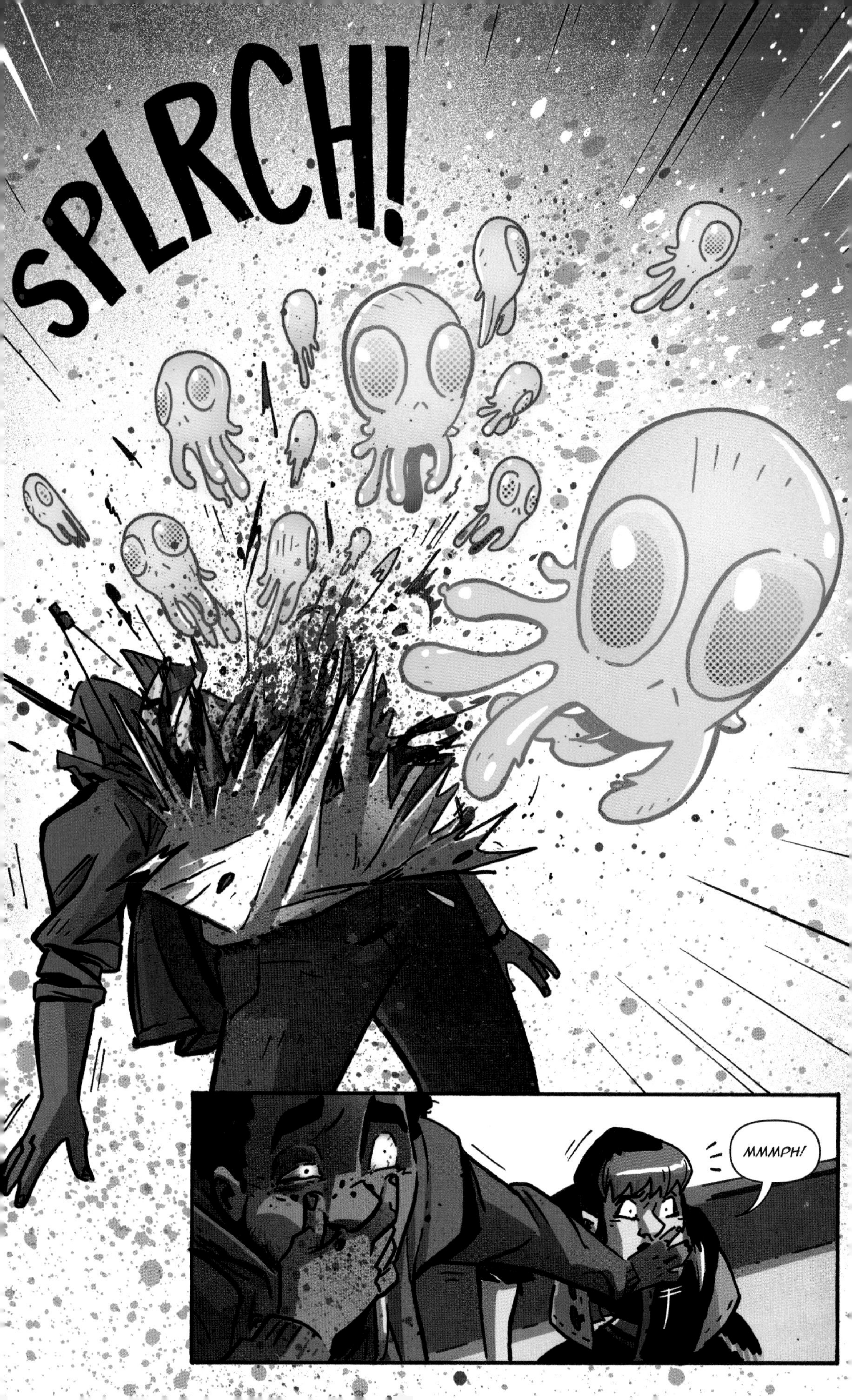
SPLRCH!
MMMPH!

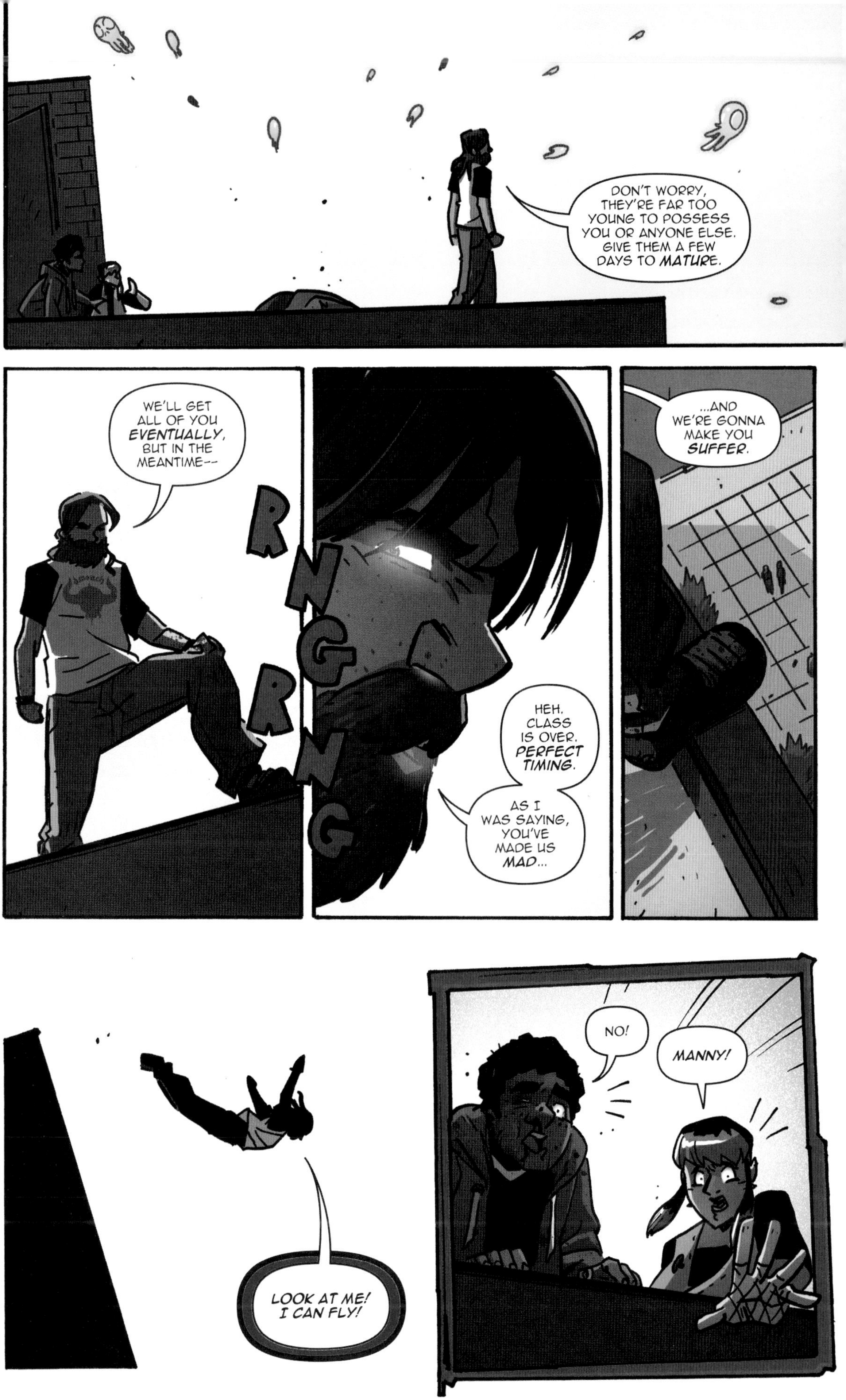
DON'T WORRY, THEY'RE FAR TOO YOUNG TO POSSESS YOU OR ANYONE ELSE. GIVE THEM A FEW DAYS TO MATURE.
WE'LL GET ALL OF YOU EVENTUALLY, BUT IN THE MEANTIME--
RNGRNG
HEH. CLASS IS OVER. PERFECT TIMING.
AS I WAS SAYING, YOU'VE MADE US MAD...
...AND WE'RE GONNA MAKE YOU SUFFER.
LOOK AT ME! I CAN FLY!
NO!
MANNY!

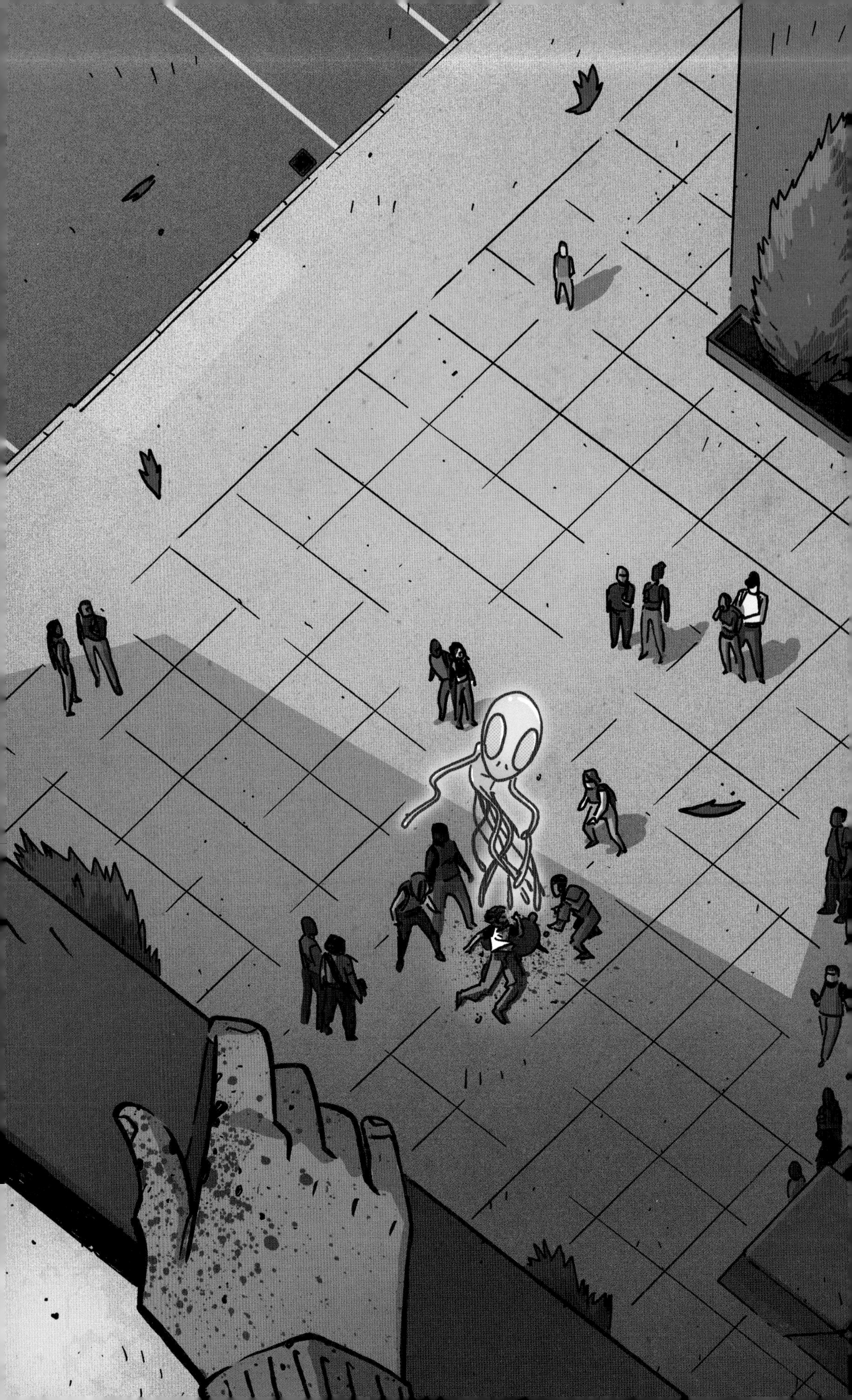

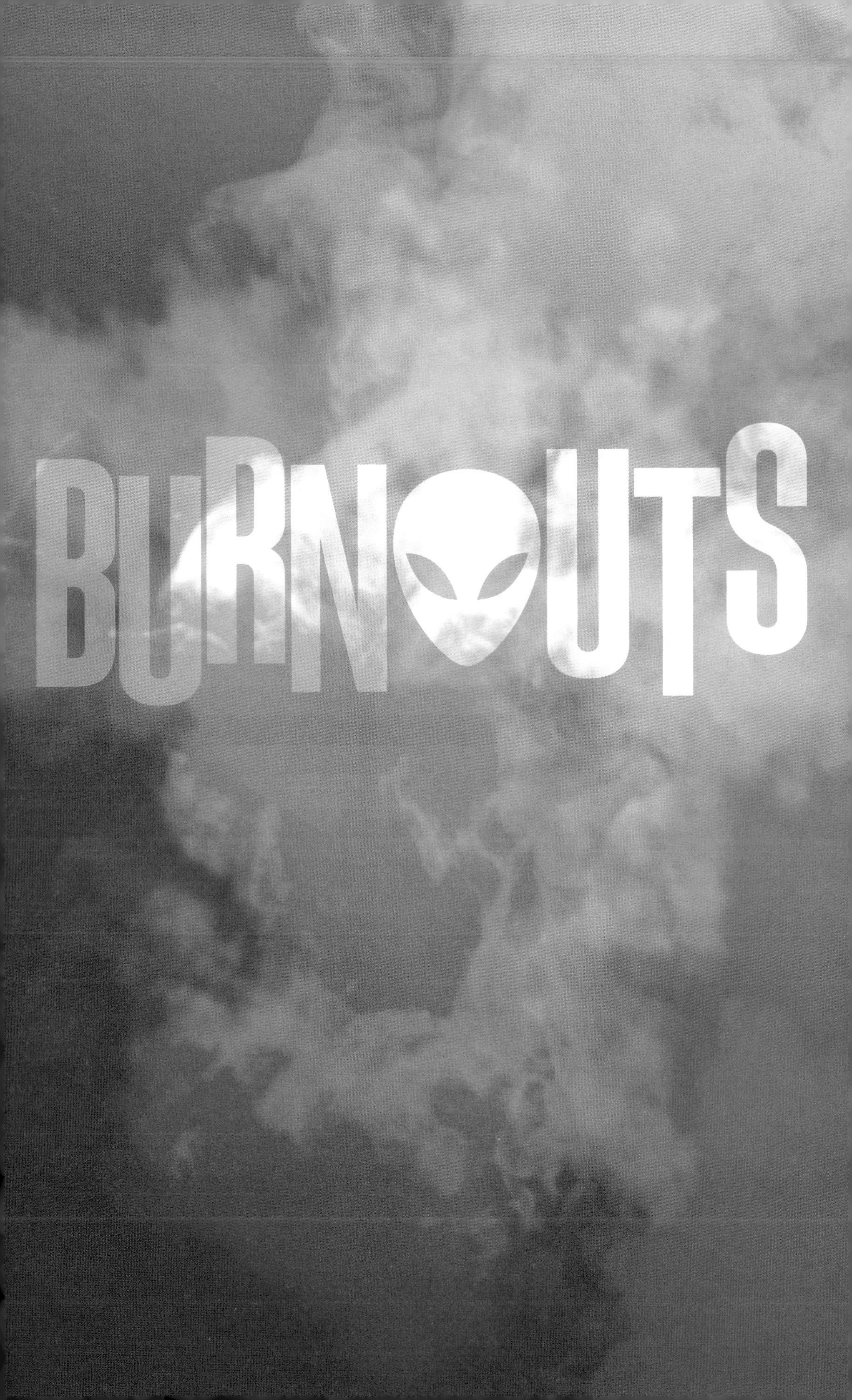
BURNOUTS

COVER
GALLERY

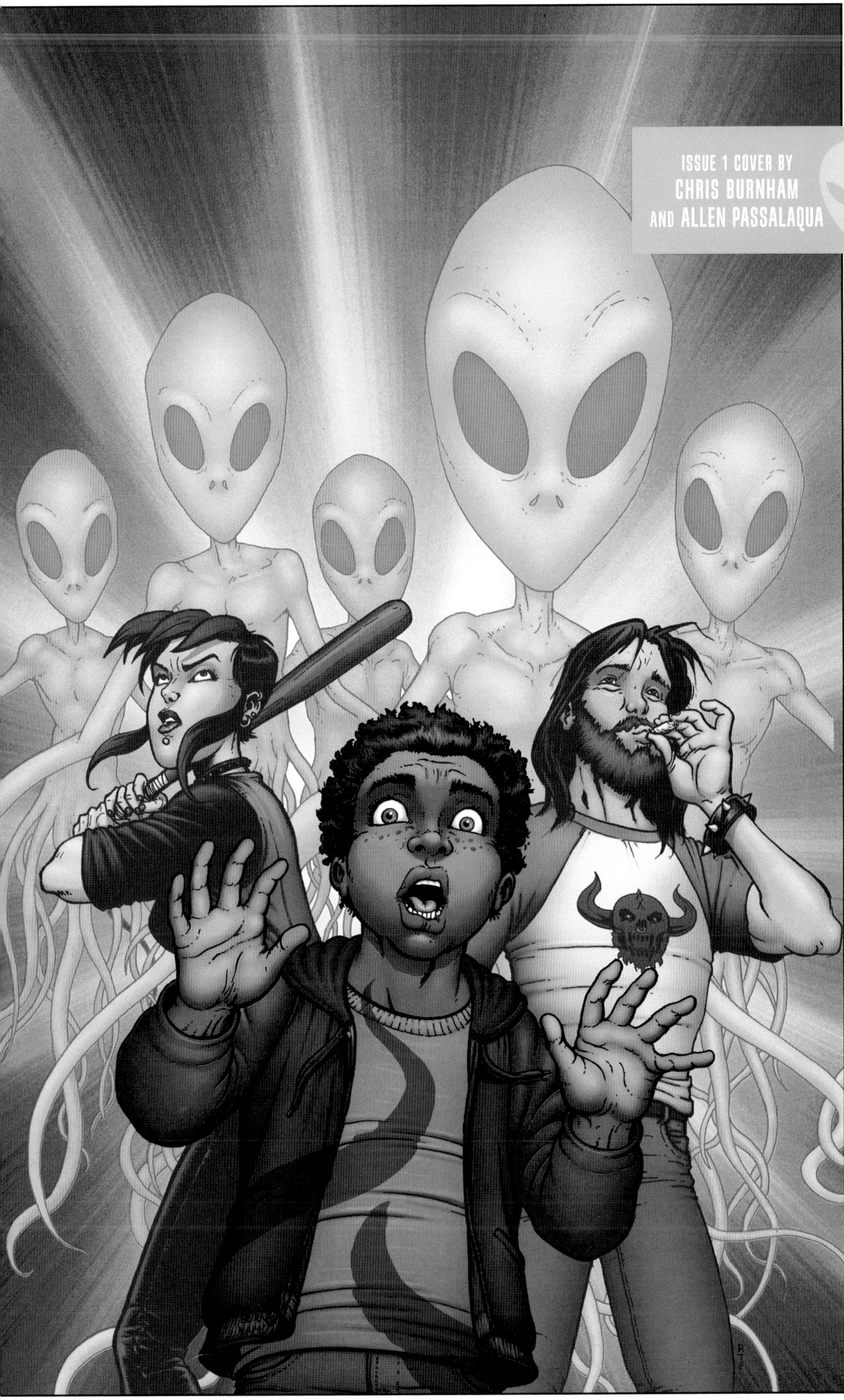

ISSUE 1 COVER BY
CHRIS BURNHAM
AND ALLEN PASSALAQUA

ISSUE 1 CBLDF
CENSORED VARIANT BY
GEOFFO

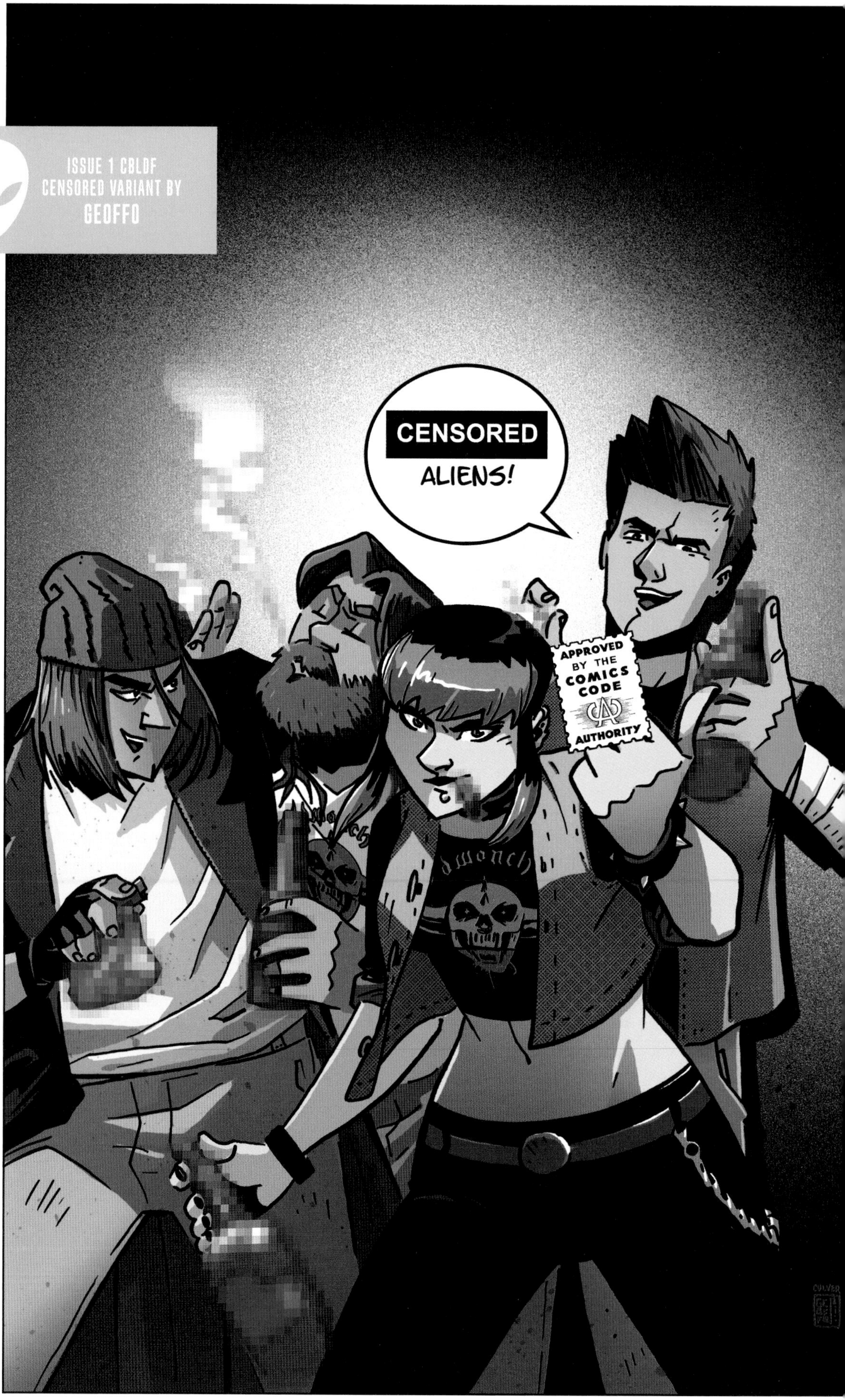
CENSORED
ALIENS!
APPROVED BY THE COMICS CODE AUTHORITY

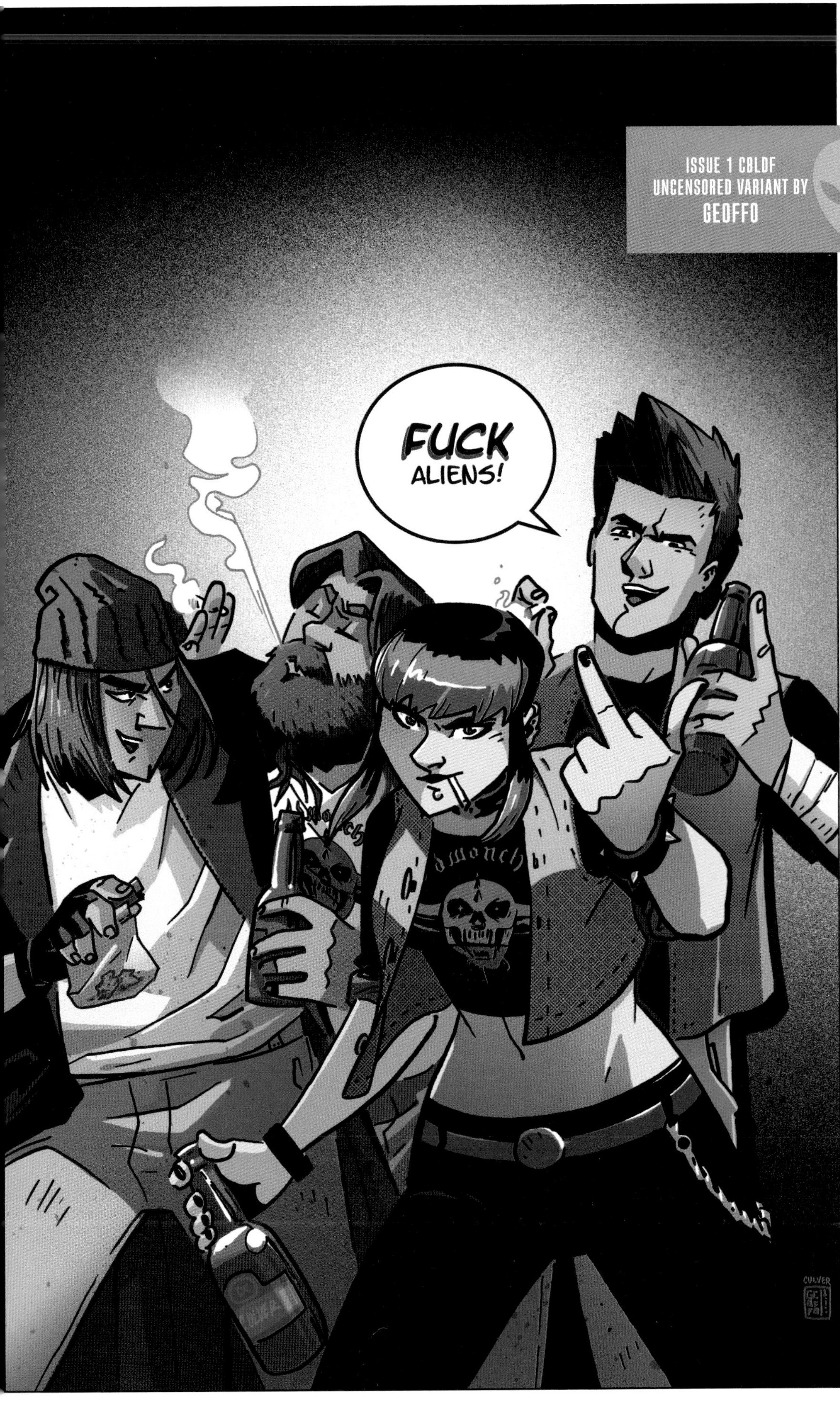

ISSUE 1 CBLDF
UNCENSORED VARIANT BY
GEOFFO

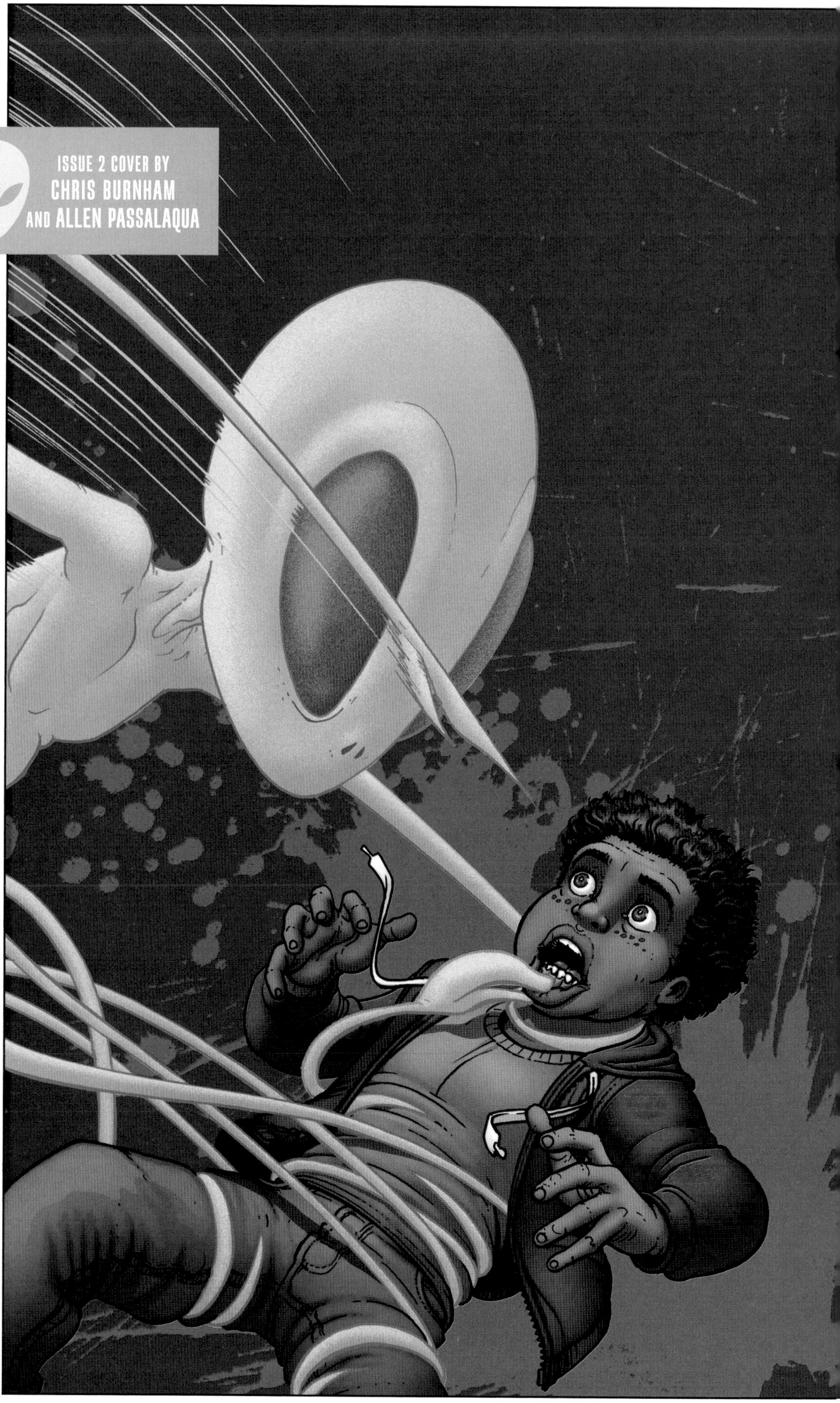

ISSUE 2 COVER BY
CHRIS BURNHAM
AND ALLEN PASSALAQUA

ISSUE 2 VARIANT BY
GEOFFO

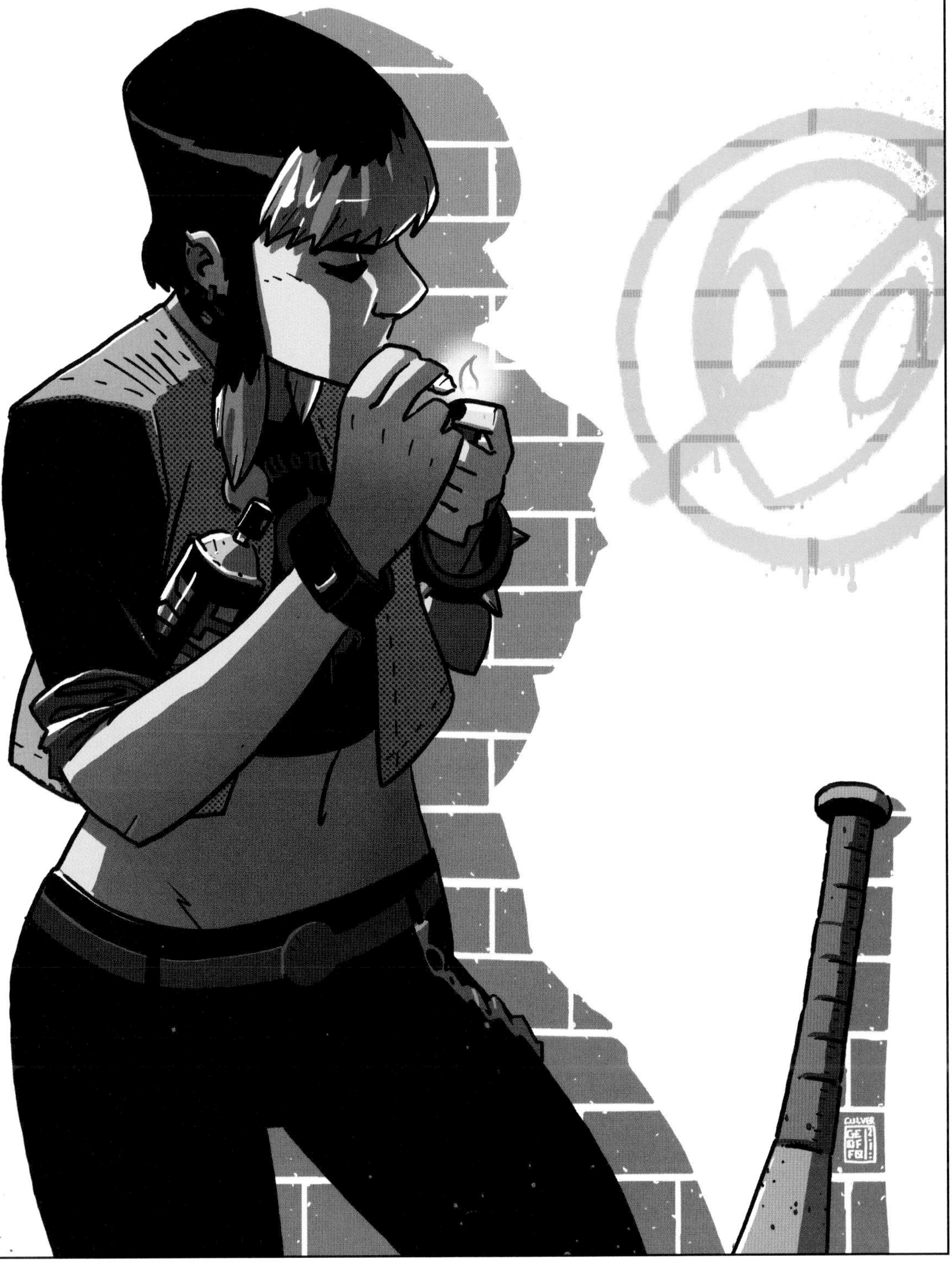

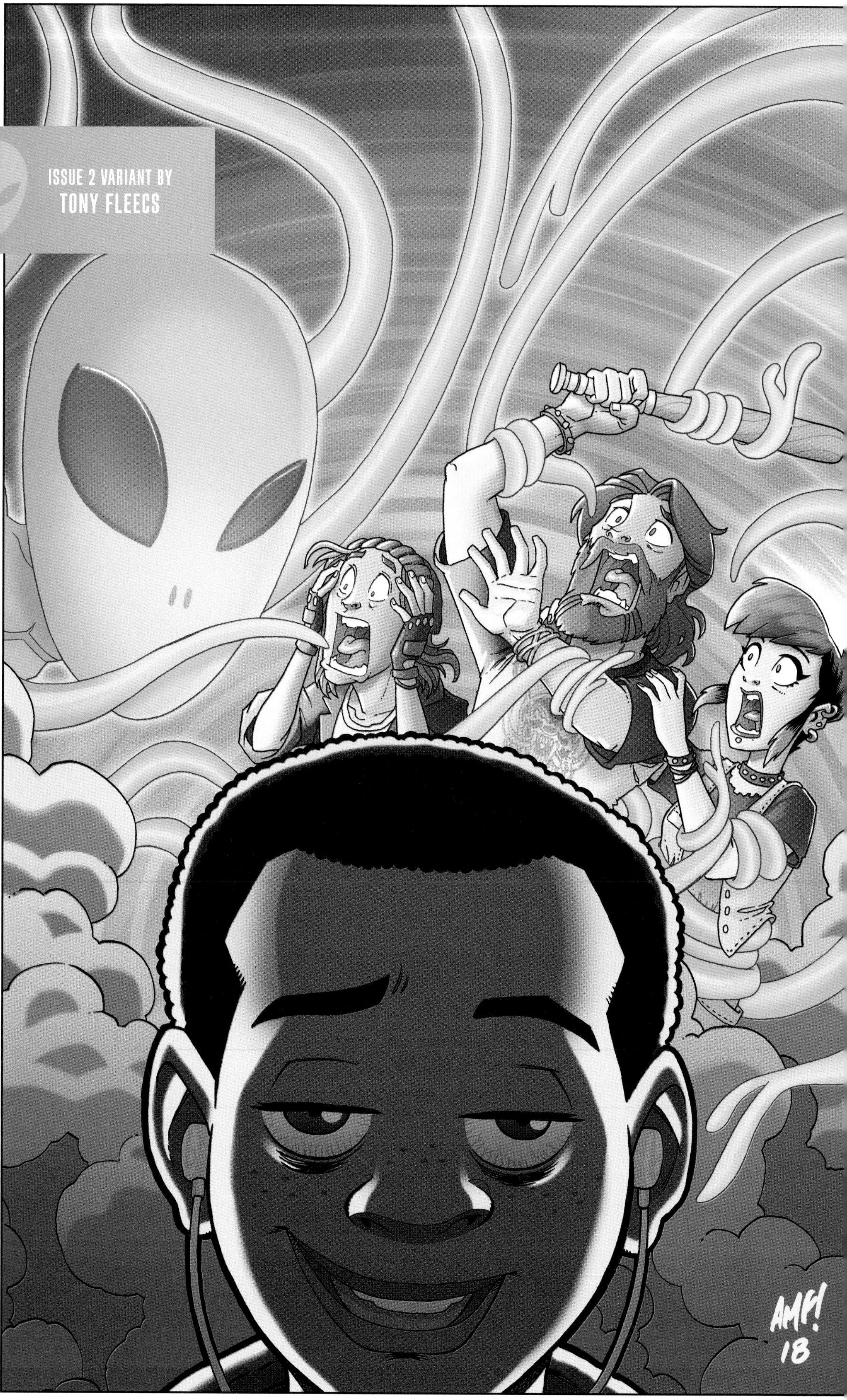
ISSUE 2 VARIANT BY
TONY FLEECS
AMP!
18

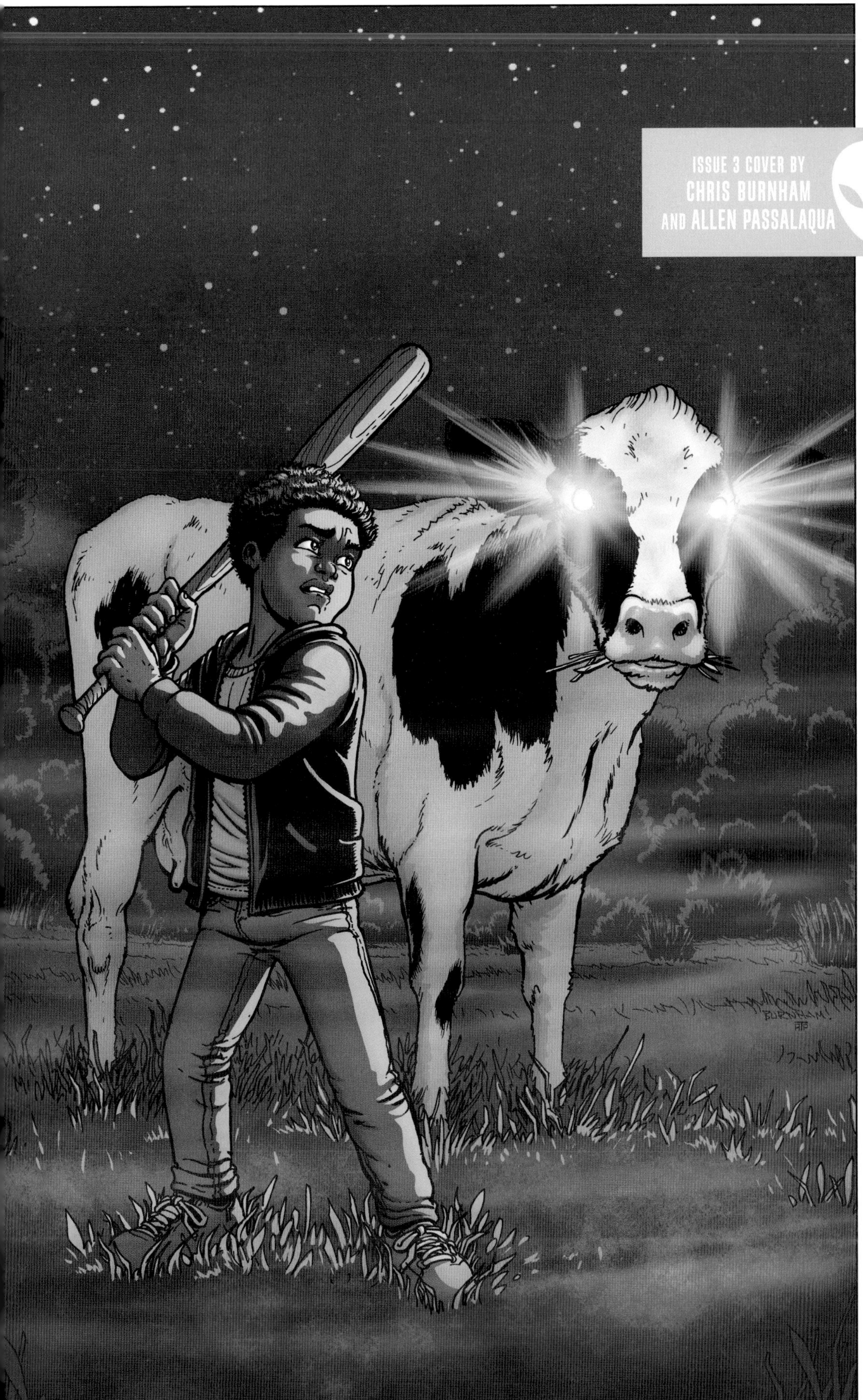

ISSUE 3 COVER BY
CHRIS BURNHAM
AND ALLEN PASSALAQUA

ISSUE 3 VARIANT BY
GEOFFO

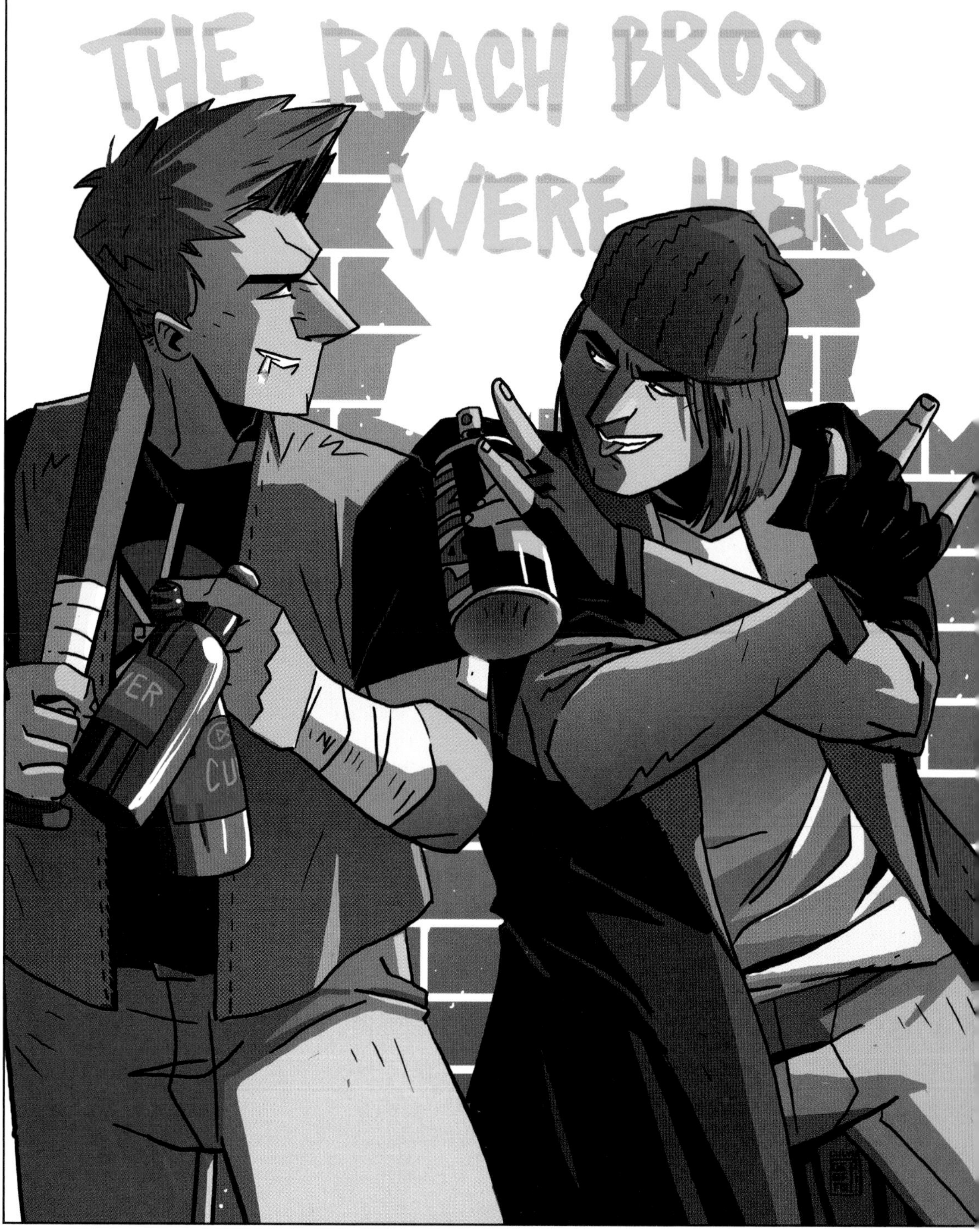
THE ROACH BROS
WERE HERE

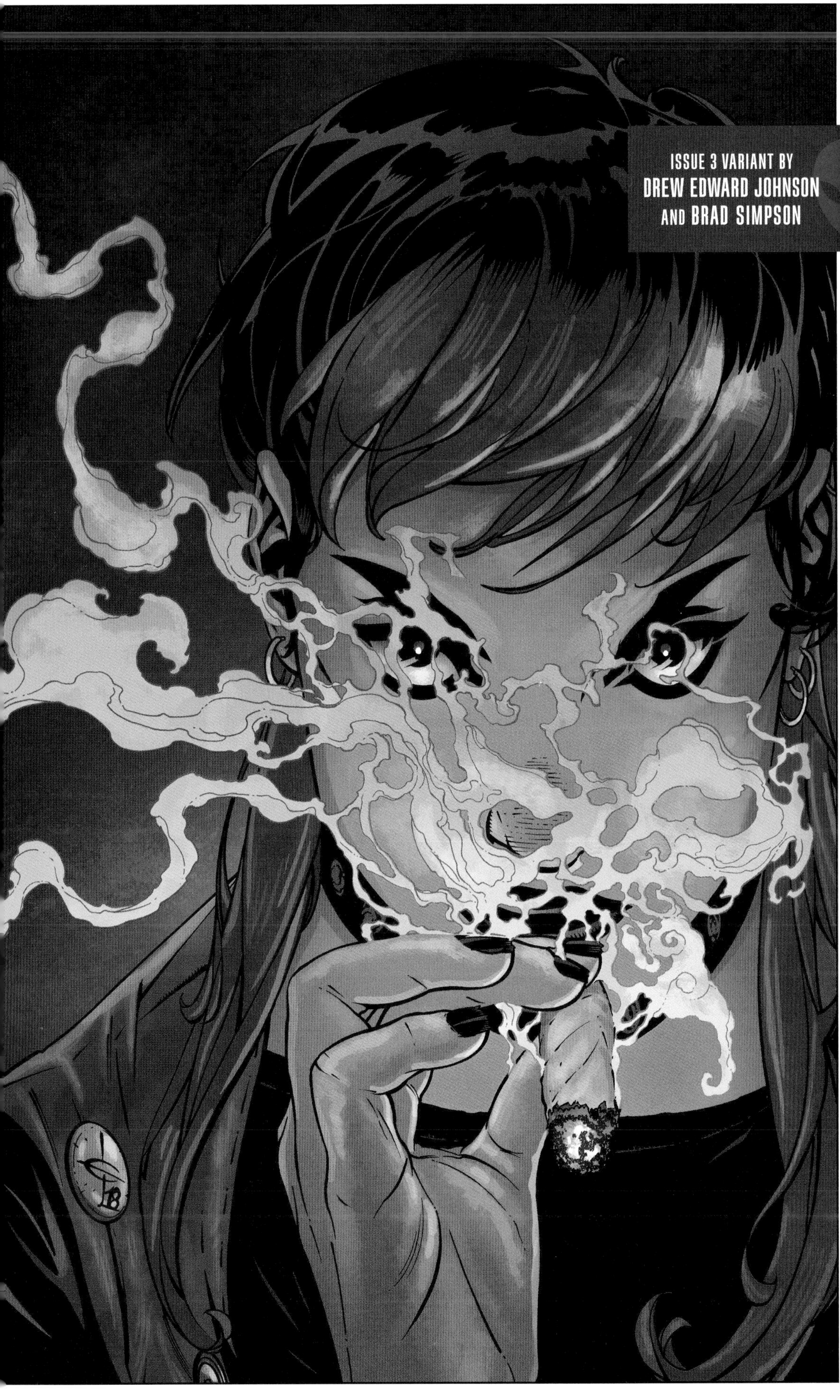

ISSUE 3 VARIANT BY
DREW EDWARD JOHNSON
AND BRAD SIMPSON

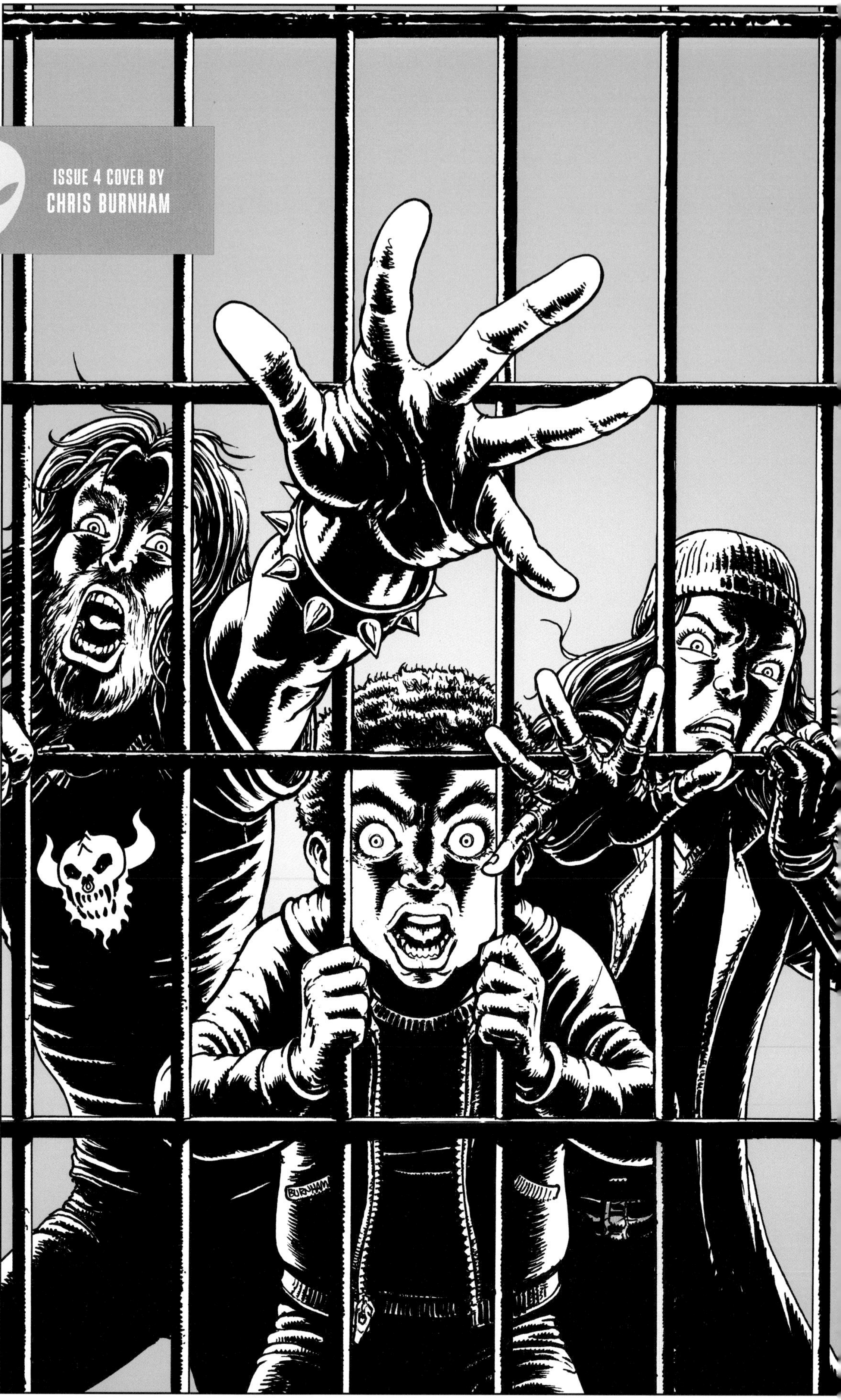
BURNHAM

ISSUE 4 COVER BY
CHRIS BURNHAM

ISSUE 4 VARIANT BY
GEOFFO

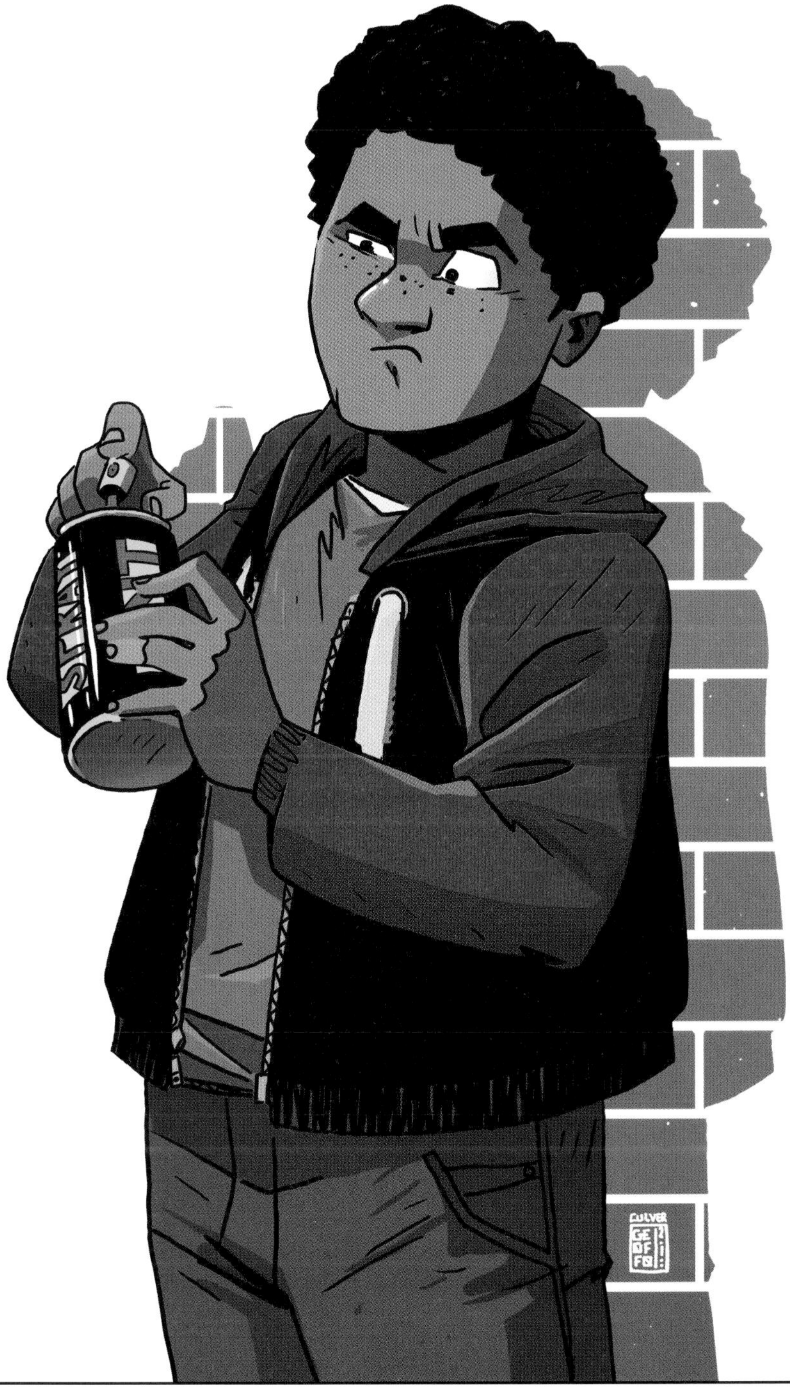

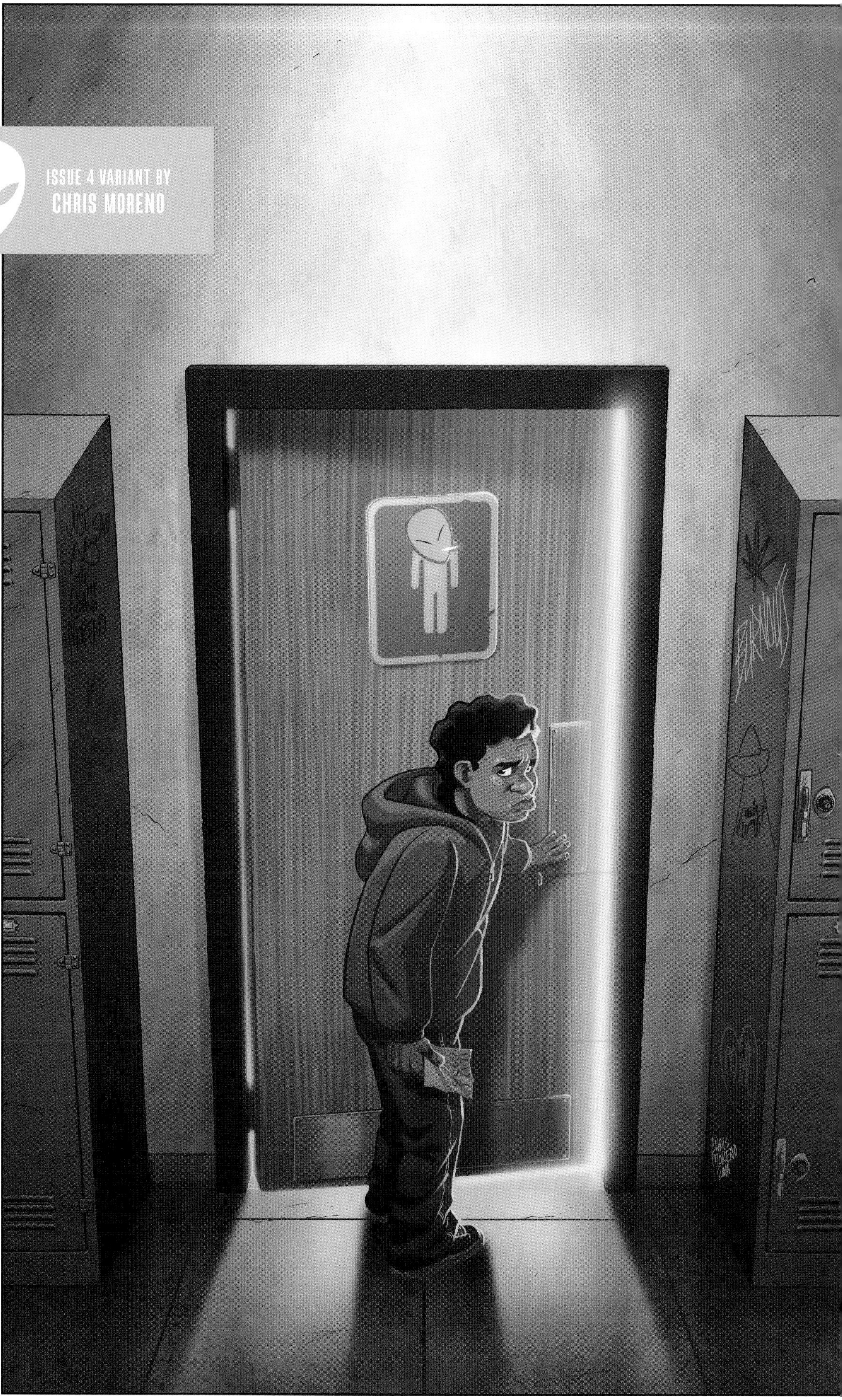

ISSUE 4 VARIANT BY
CHRIS MORENO

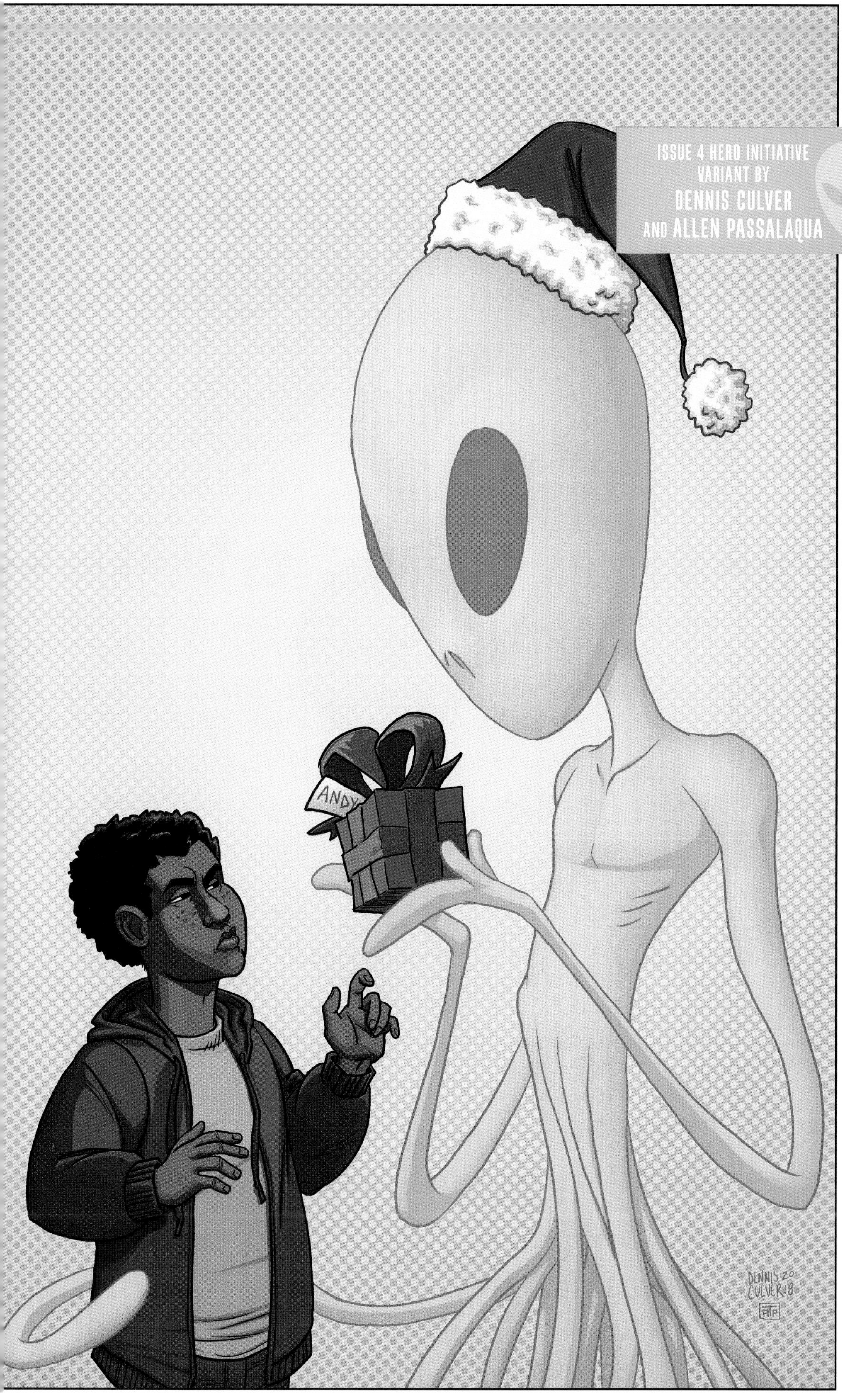
ANDY
DENNIS 20
CULVER 18
ATP

ISSUE 4 HERO INITIATIVE
VARIANT BY
DENNIS CULVER
AND ALLEN PASSALAQUA

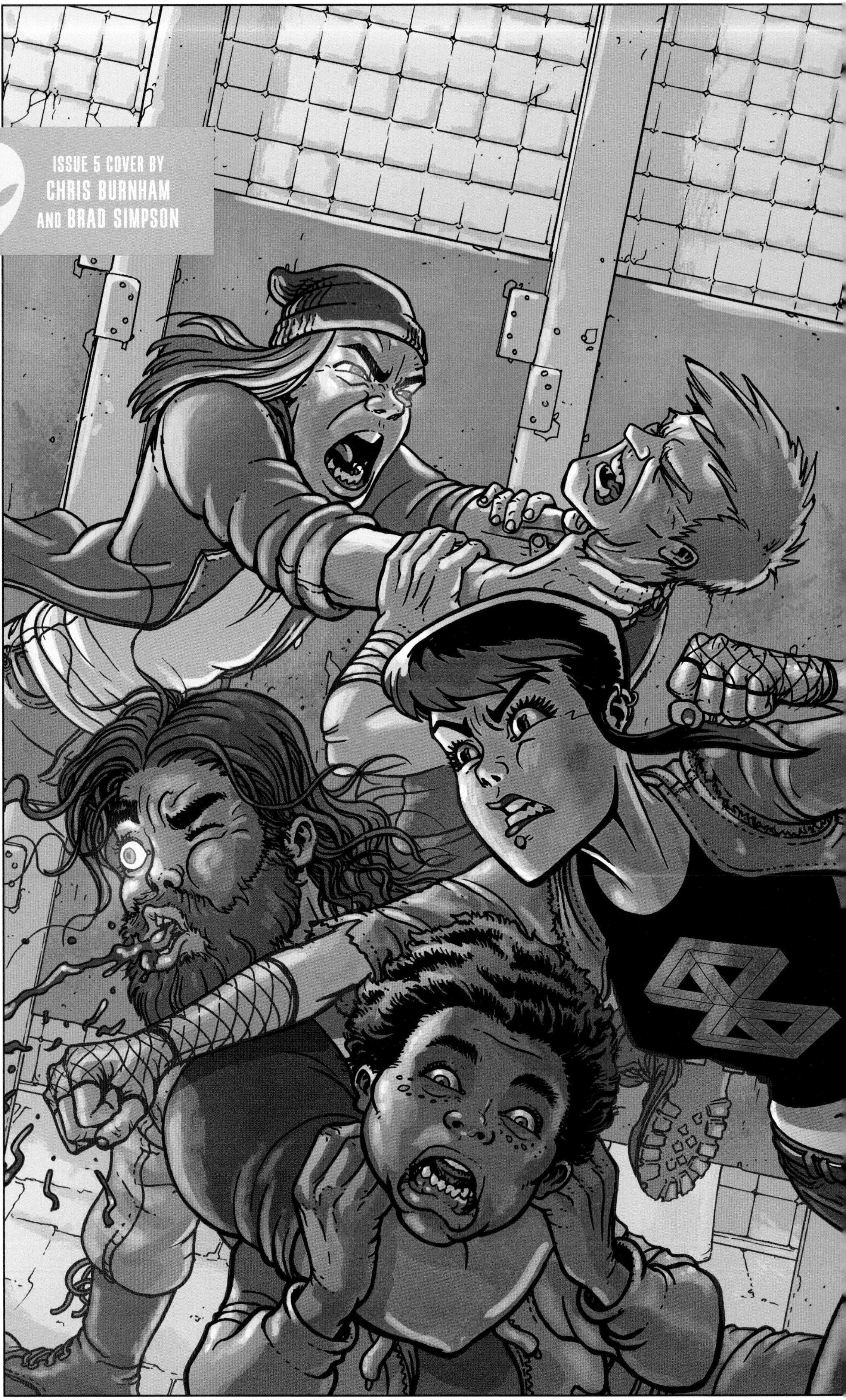

ISSUE 5 COVER BY
CHRIS BURNHAM
AND BRAD SIMPSON

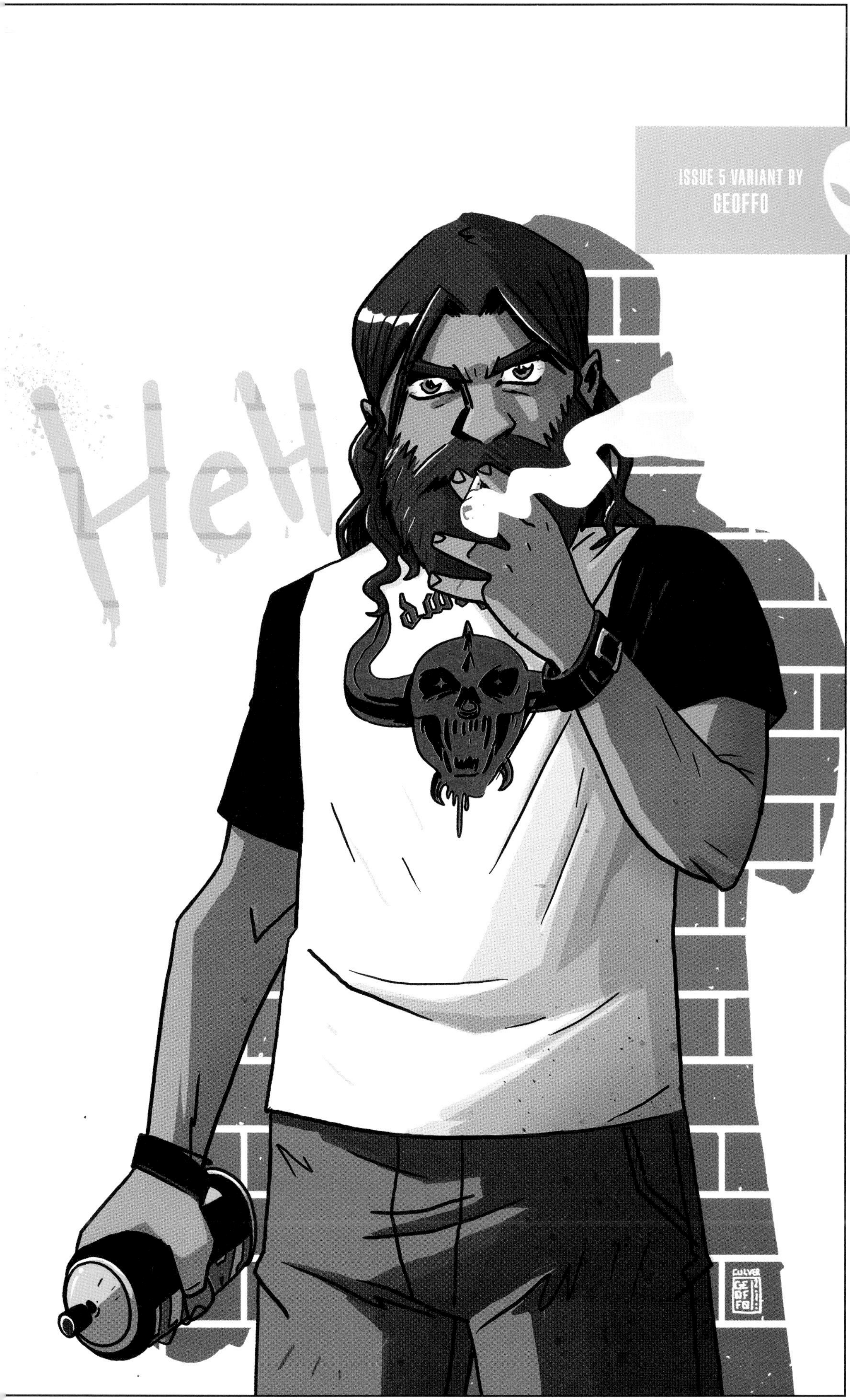

ISSUE 5 VARIANT BY
GEOFFO

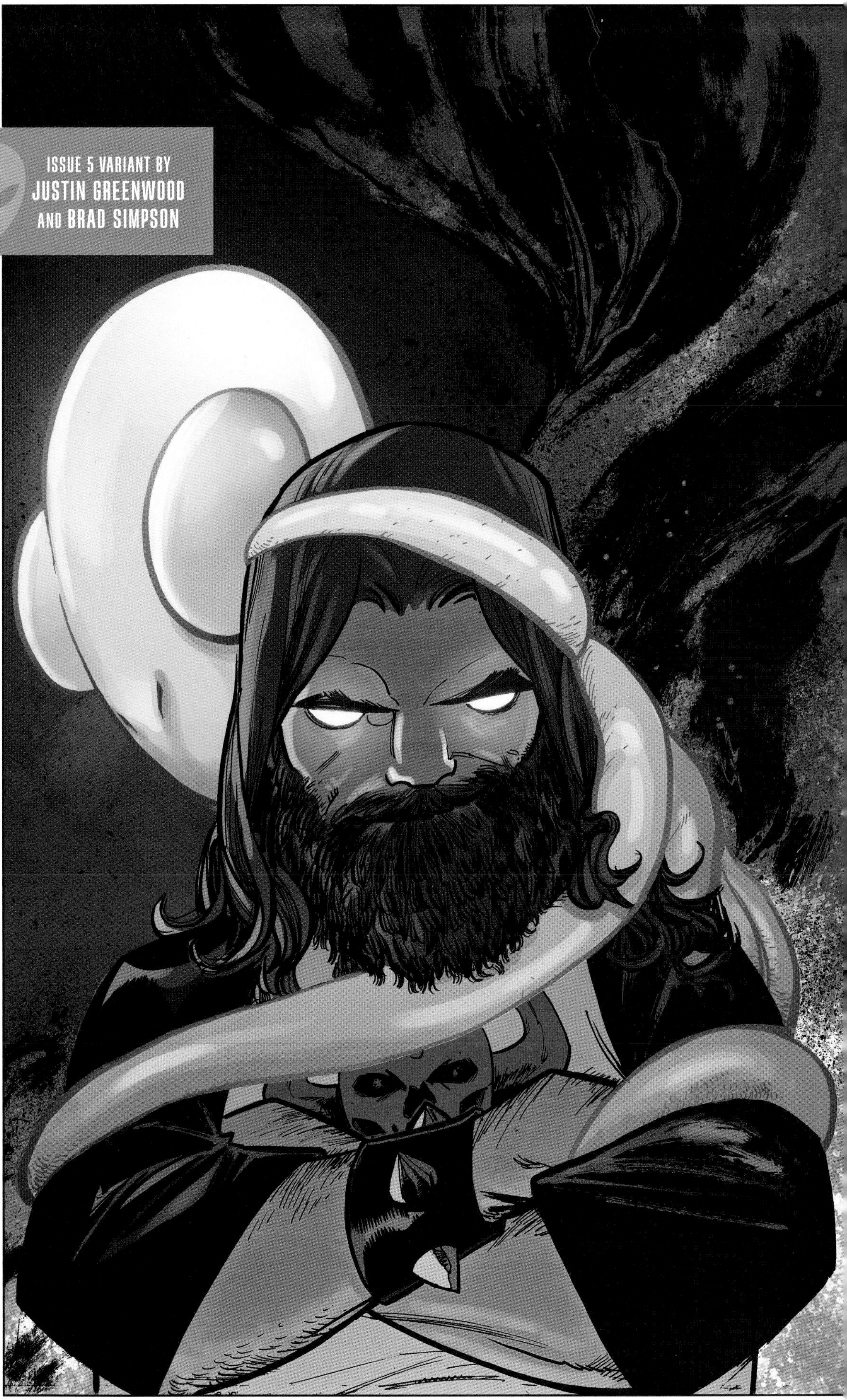

ISSUE 5 VARIANT BY
JUSTIN GREENWOOD
AND BRAD SIMPSON

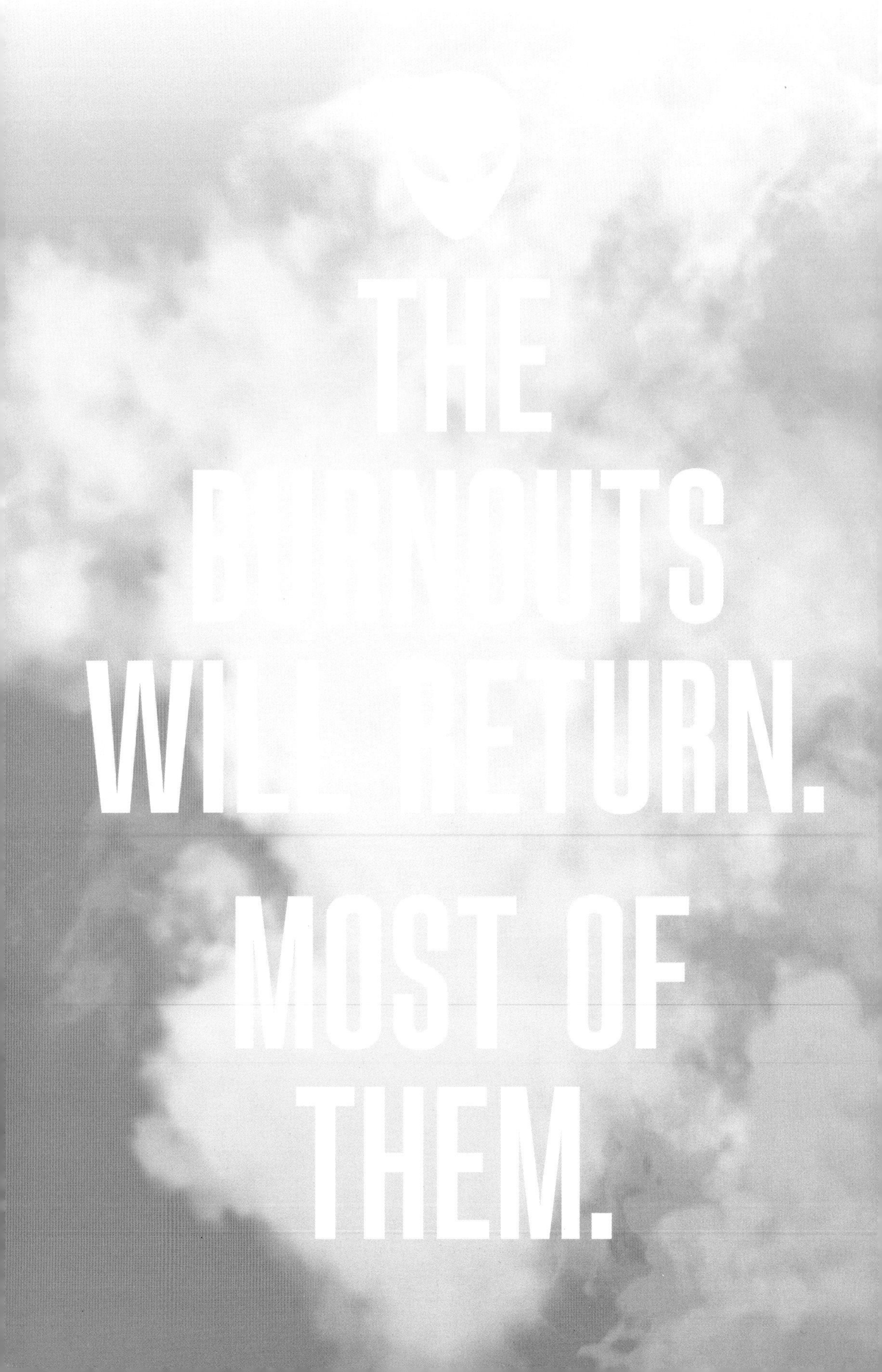
THE
BURNOUTS
WILL RETURN.
MOST OF
THEM.